The

City

of

Shadows

and

Nightmares

Book one of The City Series

Trigger Warnings

1. Death

2. Abuse of minor (in a flashback)

3. Violence

4. Strong language

5. Nudity

6. Pornographic content

7. Demons

DEDICATION

To those who ever wondered if the fairy tales their parents told them could come to life and give you the ride of your life.

Now spread those pages and immerse yourself into the fairytale of The City of Shadows and Nightmares like the good reader you are.

Prologue

Age Six

"Nyathera!" My mothers voice rings through the forest that separates the river and sector five where I live. I made my way to the river to look for rocks. With it being the middle of August, the riverbed is almost dry.

"Nyathera Marie Nighting! Get your butt back here!" My mother is the nicest of my two parents, she is stern but loving. Wiping my dirty hands on my pants, I stand. Looking around the forest a yellow ball of light catches my attention—popping out from behind a rock on the other side. It flitters up and to the right, taking off into the forest.

Ignoring my mother's call, I follow it. A vibration flows through me, static lining my bones as I watch the light float through the thick foliage. The dense earth covered in twigs and old leaves, crunching beneath my feet as I follow after the light.

Weaving through the forest and standing in the tree line I watch the ball of light stop, seeming to turn and look at me. Tilting my head, wondering what it could be.

It moves up and then down again before taking off towards the pit. A shiver runs down my spine, the pit is where all the dead are thrown. Mother always told us to stay away from it. The light stops above the endless abyss, floating there. A beautiful humming song fills my mind, and my body moves on its own. Forcing me towards the hole in the ground. Calmness and fear rip through my body as I have no control over what is happening.

"Nye! What are you doing?!" My brothers voice cuts through the haze. It is like a string is cut from my body and I stop within a few feet of the pit. The ball of light drops into it and disappears as Bartholomew reaches me and grabs my arm. "Nye! You know we can't be out here." He searches my eyes, and I wipe a tear from my cheek.

"The light." I point towards the pit.

"What light?"

I turn and look at the pit again.

Age ten

Bartholomew stands at the door when two men stand in the threshold. My mother cries in the corner [and my father pats my brother on the shoulder.

"Bartholomew Nighting?" The man missing an eye asks, his deep ringing in my skull like a death bell.

"That's me" Bartholomew answers, straightening his back.

"Today is collection day…"

Bartholomew grabs his bag and hugs our father. And then looks to our mother, "I will be okay mom." He says gently. My mother rushes to him, wrapping her arms around his neck, sobs wrack her body as she cries for her only son. I stay in my spot by the fireplace, not moving. My brother is leaving for the Mearin battle college. I don't know if I will ever see him again. A tear runs down my cheek as Bartholomew walks towards me, he squats in front of me and wipes the tear away with a smile, "Hey now," he whispers, "I will see you soon."

Sadness fills my chest with abnormal force as I wrap my arms around his neck, squeezing him tight. "What if I never see you again?" I whisper.

He runs his hand up and down my back, "I will be back before you know it." He kisses my cheek and stands. "Take care of mom and dad for me." He tousles my hair and walks out the door. Little did I know he would be walking out of our life for good.

Age Fifteen

The wind rips through the valley as me and the people who tend to the pit stand in the late autumn air. My parents' wrapped bodies lay on the ground next to it, lifeless and defeated. I tear my eyes away from them as I search the paths leading to where we stand.

"Miss Nighting, we have to start." An older gentleman says to me as I wipe away a tear.

"He will be here, please just a few more minutes." I beg. Bartholomew should be here. I sent four letters to him, beginning when my parents started to show symptoms of the sickness.

The other man standing by the pit sighs, "Miss Nighting, we are going to start."

I look around once more and lower my head, my chest cracking, "Okay, let's begin."

"We are gathered today to remember the lives of Bert and Natalia Nighting. Parents, siblings, children. Their lives have been cut short as the sickness that has swept across our lands has taken their lives too soon. Natalia and Bert are survived by their son Bartholomew Nighting and Nyathera Nighting."

I look away from the man speaking as I hear footsteps coming down the path. I know it is Bartholomew; he wouldn't miss this. When I turn, it is just a lonely sheep herder and my heart sinks. Anger sits deep in my chest as another tear slips down my cheek. How could anyone miss the funeral for their parents? How could he not want to be there for them? For me? We used to be close!

"We will begin the lowering of the bodies, if anyone wants to say anything, please step forward."

I take a step forward towards my parents, placing a hand on each of their wrapped bodies, "I am sorry I couldn't be more for you." Another tear escapes and I step away from them. The last time I will ever see them, the last time I won't be alone. Taking a deep breath in, I nod to the men.

One by one my parents bodies are thrown over the edge. The wraps flutter behind them as they fall into the endless darkness. My heart sinks lower and my stomach knots. Fear creeps up my spine as they disappear from view. The loss settles over my bones, and I drop to the earth, my life shattering to pieces. A scream tears through my body at the realization that they are really gone, and my brother isn't here. The realization that I am on my own, at the age of fifteen, I have to take care of myself.

My parents weren't the sweetest, but they were mine. I wasn't ready to be on my own, I wasn't ready to watch the only constants in my life disappear into oblivion.

I wasn't ready.

Chapter

I

Once upon a time, a group of children who loved to play, laugh, and explore lived in a quaint village nestled between towering mountains and dark woods. But there was one thing they often ignored: their parents' warnings about the mysterious The City of Shadows and Nightmares.

Present Day

******

"Fuck." My boots pound the dusty earth as we continue our climb. Sighing with heaving breaths I continue walking, thinking about the time my brother and I ran through the forest surrounding our village, he trained day and night to prepare for this, and enjoyed my bitching the entire time. Knowing that one day I would be here. I have walked this path a thousand times over the last two years, following in my brother's footsteps. The man that had saved Somania from an attack, gained fame, and now travels the continents helping other battle bases. They call him the all-savior, but even with all my training, I am *nothing* like him.

The beautifully carved front gates still stand in the same way they did when he approached them almost eleven years ago and haven't changed in over 500 years that the building has stood. The worn limestone is chipped and crumbling. They are beautiful, but the fear that the new trainees feel as they step through them is torturing and valid.

Xavier, a few steps ahead of me—breathing heavy with his own exertion—turns and rolls his eyes at me, "Come on, Nye. You've walked this a thousand times already."

Waving a hand, I dismiss him. Next month we will graduate and go on to separate bases. He'll stay here and help with the new trainees beside his father, and I'll go to Somania as a lieutenant. We have trained side by side for two years, originally hating each other, but slowly falling in love as the trials and tribulations of training brought us closer.

A huff of exhaustion leaves my lips, "Do you remember how this walk felt on the first day?" I look over at X, his beautiful copper hair reflecting the sunlight.

"I walked this many times before the day of collection. My father is the General?" He smiles through his hard breaths, his body leaning forward slightly as we get to a steeper part of the path.

Rolling my eyes, I gently slap his arm, "Yeah yeah, I know. But the feeling must have been different," sucking in a quick breath, "knowing that you were going to be training instead of visiting."

"It did, but I also didn't expect to be met with a fiery little beauty." His face stretches into a grin as he grabs my hand, stopping me.

Turning to face him, a smile stretches my face, "you Xavier Nortick, are still a presumptuous asshole."

"And you Nyathera Nighting, are still a pain in my ass." He kisses my lips quickly as I turn away and he slaps my ass.

A yelp escapes my lips, and I take off running towards those massive gates. Towards the entrance that made me into a soldier, into someone I never truly thought I.

could be. The gates that led me to Xavier—to my future.

Stopping in front of the gates, I place my hands on my knees, bending over and sucking in breaths, attempting to fill my lungs with much needed oxygen.

Xavier stops next to me putting his hands on his hips straightening his back and smiling at me, "Do you remember your first day?" He asks as he grabs my hand, and we walk through the front gates together.

"I do, and let me tell you, I did not think I would be here this long." We sit on the limestone bench off to the side of the gates, just behind the statues that line the hall. I turn to Xavier and smile, recounting the first year and a half I was here.

******

2 years ago

Every hard breath I take feels like my lungs have frozen over. The steep mountain, barren of any green, spreads across the land like a snake through the forest surrounding it. Tall peaks form in perfect points stretching skyward, lengthening the mountains of Mearin. The wind rips around me, stinging my cheeks, whistling through the dark caverns surrounding us. Walking towards the Mearin battle college, the snow crunches beneath my feet. The pack on my back weighs more than I do, and even with my legs screaming at me to sit down, I won't give up now. With each shaky step, I sigh and keep pushing forward. Sucking in shallow breaths, each one resulting in steamy clouds circling around me. I continue my uphill climb towards the building on the side of the mountain.

Slipping in the mud, my leg stretches in an unnatural way. With a snort I regain my balance and round the last corner. Stopping and staring at the front of the building with its intricate runes carved into the limestone. The large stone gates are open and anything but inviting.

Mearin has hosted training for the previous 300 years. Everyone who has walked through those gates during that time has either made it to battle or died trying.

From what I have heard, training is cutthroat. It is kill or be killed.

As beautiful as the building is, I know nothing is beautiful about this place. I am going to have to fight to stay alive and then possibly die in battle. A bead of sweat runs down my spine at the thought. All the men and women of collection day walking along side me.

The first soldiers made the battle college to house those injured during war, it grew every day for hundreds of years. Now, it houses the trainees. In the center of the front training yard lies 'the pit.' An endless black hole where all the dead are thrown so that the smell of decay doesn't rise from the ground and ruin our lands. It is also where their souls go to rest. We have never understood why or how, but we throw them in there per the request of the goddess of death, Therina—or so the book of Mearin says.

The Gods and Goddesses created Mearin thousands of years before the war began. Disappearing into the unknown when things got hard. The sector system was the choice of Brinton—the God of classes.

I belong to sector five, sectors one through four are farmers, and sectors five through ten are soldiers. For centuries men have been defending the continents, women were never brought into the battle. All that 'we need to ensure they stay home and have babies' bullshit. If a woman wanted to be a soldier, she had to go in front of a board of men, and they had to unanimously agree that she was fit to join. But about fifty years ago, they started bringing women to the training mat, teaching us how to defend ourselves and fight with bows, swords, and daggers.

They didn't give us a choice, and many in my sector were proud to fight. This year, I came of age for collection. The twenty-first birthday for every woman has been a secret for the last fifty years. Parents were too scared to send their daughters to battle, and the women wanted to fight, wanted to protect Mearin and the allied continents. Luckily enough, my parents are dead— I didn't have anyone to help protect me. I didn't even try to stay hidden on that dreaded day that they came for collection.

******

I took a deep breath in and swung open the wooden door. The loud knock and the two massive men standing in my doorway were a stark reminder of what day it was. My stance is much smaller than most in the soldier sector, standing at only five-five, I have had to fight for everything alone since I was fifteen—today was no different, but also knowing I will be fed and learn to protect myself better— I didn't fight being collected. I swung the door wide and stared into their eyes without hesitation.

"Miss Nighting?" The burly man missing one eye said.

"That's me."

They look down at me and share a quick glance of confusion, "Today is Collection Day. Which I am sure your parents have told you about…"

"My parents are dead," Bile rising in my stomach at the thought of it.

The other man clears his throat, "We have been instructed to collect all men and women who have come of the age of twenty-one. Do you understand that you do not have a choice as you were born in sector number five?"

I nod. I knew this was coming.

"Please take five minutes and pack your belongings."

I reach to the side and grab my bag, staggering with its weight, stepping out the door and into the cold.

"Let's go." The two large men look at each other as I squeeze by them, and we go to the holding bay.

******

I make my way down the corridor in step with everyone else when a tall blonde woman bumps into me.

"Oh, my gods, I am so sorry. Are you ok?" she asks, looking down at me.

I look at her, "Yeah, no worries."

Her long blonde hair and stunning blue eyes are the picture of perfection. She holds her hand out, "I'm Fallon." She smiles.

Placing mine in hers, "I'm Nyathera, but you can call me Nye."

She smiles and walks alongside me, "I can't believe we are here—who would've thought women would be more than incubators?" she says, her gaze fixed ahead.

"I don't know, I didn't even want to be here, but I also don't want to be birthing children—like—ever." I shrug the best I can, the straps of my bag biting into my shoulders. I rearrange the pack quickly.

She laughs, "You are kinda small to be a soldier, didn't your parents try to hide you?"

"My parents died when I was fifteen." I say with a straight face, ignoring the heartache. I grin at her, "Besides, it's the small ones you need to watch out for." I wink with a small chuckle.

"I'm so sorry." She says sweetly.

I shrug, "it is what it is." With a tight smile we continue walking towards the crowd of people. I stop at the back of the group, gathering my white hair on top of my head, fingers snagging in the wind-blown knots.

Fallon watches my movement and looks back down at my face. "Is that natural?"

Nodding I look at her, "I was born with one white stripe in jet-black hair, but the older I got, the lighter my hair got," I say, shrugging. "My parents used to say it's because a piece of my soul was sacrificed to the city of shadows and nightmares." I titter.

Fallon follows with her own chuckle. We move a little closer to everyone and wait for whatever comes next.

The gathering hall is packed with men and women ready to fight. Their voices echo off the walls. And the humidity from the bodies surrounding us makes me nauseous. At the front is a large wooden stage where all the generals and the trainers stand. I look at each one of them individually. The trainers are made up of men and women, all otherworldly in looks. The women look like goddesses, and the men look like they are carved of stone. All are beautiful in their own way. The man in the middle starts to speak, his voice carrying without a microphone. General

Nortick, a handsome older gentleman with an unnerving look in his eyes. He has led many to war and won with minimal losses every time.

"Welcome to the Mearin battle college. We are so glad you joined us as a unified front to protect our homes, continent, and the lives of millions. The sacrifice that you are making will be remembered from this day forward. Please say 'here' when your name is called." His voice is robotic—no emotion lies behind his eyes. A pure soldier, through and through. He clears his throat and starts reading off the names of those collected.

His voice seems to fade as he reads the list on and on. The exhaustion from my hike up the mountain and the six years of restless sleep on an old spring twin bed sweeps over my body—finally relaxing, I zone out on the vibrant color of each flag behind the stage. The five gods and goddesses depicted in each one.

"Here!" Fallon says beside me making my muscles jump with a sharp inhale.

He continues reading names one by one. "Nyathera Nighting." The room falls quiet, whispers spreading wall to wall. The energy shift is palpable.

"Here!" I shout, raising my hand.

Fallon slowly looks to me, a brow raised, "As in Bartholomew Nighting?"

My eyes meet hers, slowly lowering my hand, "Yes, but I don't really associate myself with him anymore."

Her eyes widen and she pulls them away glancing around the room, "that might be hard now that everyone knows who you are."

I follow her gaze around the room, realizing everyone is staring at me. "Well, shit," My heart hammers in my chest.

I have been a target by so many since my brother's savior facade. Anyone who upsets him or disagrees with him ends up dead.

This is going to be more challenging than I thought it would be. I knew I should've given a different name when those men came to my cabin.

General Nortick clears his throat, finishing the long list of names, "Everyone will see the healers to ensure you are healthy for battle training. You will be given three pairs of brown and three pairs of black leathers and placed into a house with a minimum of four other candidates. Each house will vote on a leader in the coming weeks. The leader will help form the houses into weapons and will help form an alliance between the other houses. Two years from now, you will be stationed at a new duty station and prepare to be sent to battle. Please do not ignore what you are taught here—it is meant to prepare you for what you will be fighting—enemies and companions."

He pauses and takes a deep breath, a solemn look crossing his face, "Good luck, trainees. And may the power of the Gods be on your side." He dips his chin to us and steps to the left to walk down the stairs.

The room immediately erupts into chaos. Eyes dart my way, and whispers skate across the gathering hall. I ignore the stares, the best I can at least. Everyone is moving around and speaking. A young man approaches us—his bright blue eyes perfectly contrast his raven-black hair.

"Hi! I'm Kenzo!" he says, looking at us, "are you really Bartholomew's sister?" He looks at me with hope in his eyes. "I was really hoping to meet him one day, I have been a huge fan of his for years now."

I roll my eyes, "Unfortunately, I am," I state blandly. "I don't think talking to me will get you the meet and greet you are hoping for" The happiness in his eyes dims a little with my words.

He straightens his back, "That's perfectly fine. I won't mention his name again." He pretends to zip his lips, "Are you ready for the next couple of years?" he asks.

I sigh with relief at not needing to explain how I can't introduce them, "I don't even want to be here." He looks at me with question in his gaze. "I have been alone since I was fifteen. I don't do well in large groups. Or small groups for that matter. It's going to be an adjustment." I pause for a breath, "plus being alone I have learned to protect myself, so it shouldn't be too hard."

He laughs, "How much combat training have you done? Riding training? Hand to hand?"

I roll my lip between my teeth in thought, "Well, I taught myself how to throw fairly accurately with daggers, and I am pretty decent with a bow, but I prefer not to hurt or kill anyone or anything."

He smiles, "well that is certainly a plus, with everything else, though, I'd be happy to help you!" he says with a bright smile. "Although, death at your hand is inevitable in this world."

Something in my chest cracks at the idea of taking a life. Even ones that are threatening our continent. They are following orders, and who knows what they have been told about us.

Fallon looks between us and clears her throat, "Hi, I'm Fallon." She sticks her hand in his face.

"Hello! I'm sorry! I wasn't trying to ignore you." He says.

"No, you were just trying to get on Nye's good side in hopes you could get in her brother's pants." She smirks.

He laughs, putting his hands up in defeat, "Okay, okay. You caught me."

We all laugh. It feels good not to be standing here alone. Laughing is something I haven't done in so long that I didn't realize I remembered how.

"*SILENCE!*" a loud voice booms over the crowd, everyone stops and look to the front. A beautiful dark-haired man stands on the stage, his gaze menacing as he watches everyone and waits for complete silence. He exudes confidence and power, his long black hair is tied perfectly in a knot at the base of his head, and his biceps flex as he crosses his arms over his broad.

"Who is that?" I whisper to Fallon. She shrugs and stares.

"My name is Beckham; I am a trainer here at Mearin battle college and will instruct house one. We are going to break you into houses. These houses will be your training buddies for the next two years, and the house that has the most points at the end of those two years can choose to go to the same duty station together." His arms drop to his sides as he begins pacing back and forth, "You will eat, sleep, and fight together. Be sure to get to know who is in your house." He stops at the right side of the stage. His facial expressions stretching, "you never know who you are standing next to."

My blood runs cold as they start pairing houses.

Names are read out by a nasally woman at the end of the stage. She gets through houses one and two and then the names for house three are read, "Nyathera Nighting, Fallon May, Kenzo Bonders, Dylan Waters, Abigail Winters, and Xavier Nortick."

We look at each other and shrug. "Well, the Gods knew we would be in the same house, so I guess that's why we found each other." Fallon smiles wide.

"Let's go," I grin, walking to the side of the room.

The stone walls create an arch where we meet up with a man who looks bored. His copper hair in perfect curls on top of his head and the freckles tracing his nose look like constellations.

He picks something invisible from his shirt and looks at us, his amber eyes bore into my soul, coaxing a gasp from my lips.

He smirks and his eyes glance to each of us, "Took you long enough. If you will be in my house, you must be on time and at your best at all times."

Chapter

2

But there was one thing they often ignored: their parents' warnings about the mysterious The City of Shadows and Nightmares.

Oh, how I truly despise egotistical men. I stare at him a moment, his gaze looking me up and down, fueling the annoyance in my bones. That fascination with how handsome he is fading away.

I cock my head, anger bubbling in my chest, "your house? Who made you the leader?"

"Seeing as how my father is the general, I made myself the leader." The unyielding confidence radiating off him in nauseating waves.

Xavier Nortick.

"I don't care who your father is—the leader is to be voted on, not just given," I let the venom in my chest spew into my words. I can already tell him, and I will *not* be getting along. That's too bad.

He steps towards me, "Just because you are a Nighting doesn't mean you will get your way or be *safe*. I would watch yourself little one." He flicks my nose, and I swat his hand away.

He takes a step forward, towering over me, staring down at me like I am nothing more than the shit on his boot. He has to have at *least* a foot on me.

I smile and poke him in the middle of the chest pushing, trying to ignore the definition under my finger. "Back. Up. Or I will show you just how unsafe it can be here."

I wear a wide smile as I cock my head to the side. "Either you follow the rules, or I will make sure the Nighting name is the *last* thing you are able to remember before your body is thrown in the pit with the other candidates that couldn't handle the training, *Nortick*." Saying his name with emphasis so he understands I know *exactly* who he is, and that I have no intentions on playing nice. "Names mean nothing here, but pure determination does. It just so happens I have been perfecting determination since I was fifteen. Daddy's name didn't protect me."

He backs away with his hands up and palms out, "Don't say I didn't warn you."

As much as I don't want to admit it, having the Nighting name has either put a target on me or has given me a leg up. Either way, I have to prove myself. No mess-ups. No backing down. No sign of fear. *Nothing.*

We get to our wing of the massive stone building and continue down the hallway, our boots echoing off the stone walls. The only light is in Xavier's hand at the front of the group. The smell of mildew wafts in the air, and you can hear the water from the mountains rushing behind the walls.

A chill runs down my spine as a slight breeze comes from the dark end of the hallway. I run my hand along the stones to keep myself walking straight. It is smooth and bumpy and feels cold under my fingers. Xavier turns as if making sure he isn't entering the house by himself. I reassure him with a nod—even though I'd like to hit him in the back of the head with a rock instead, I want to get out of this cold, humid tunnel. A couple of minutes later, we come to a large stone door. It is arched and covered in intricate golden runes. Xavier reaches forward and places his hand on the stone.

He jumps and looks at his finger. "It pricked my finger," he says with annoyance. The door opens, and he walks through. I start to move forward, and the door slams in front of me. Jumping back, I narrowly avoid a concussion.

"You have to offer it a drop of blood. It uses magic to ward off anyone who has not sacrificed. It's a way to keep everyone safe." Fallon says next to me.

I nod, taking in a deep breath and put my hand in the middle of the door. A slight pinch and hum later, and the door opens for me. I walk towards Xavier, who is still standing in the doorway. "You have to move so we can all fit." I roll my eyes at him.

"I was just making sure you guys didn't fuck up somehow." His tone dripping with annoyance.

"Right," is all I manage as I push past him, rolling my eyes, before the door moves again.

Fallon comes skipping in. "Woah." She says, turning in a circle, "It's lovely".

The house is made of wood, and arches create entrances to different rooms and hallways. The kitchen and living room look as if they were crafted as a homage to a cabin. There are five doors lining the hallway on the left, and three lining the hallway on the right. Tree branches were used to make a chandelier in the middle of the dining room that boasts a large dark table. It is gorgeous. Homey.

We all make it inside safely, and head in different directions to inspect our new home for the next two years. Fallon and I head towards the hallway with the three doors.

"The females can sleep on this side, and the males on that side. This way, there is no argument over who goes where." I look at Fallon and nod my head in agreement. "I think we should split up chores as well. With training, we will all be exhausted, so if we all pitch in, it'll make it easier." She states.

Xavier appears leaning on the corner at the end of the hall. One boot hooked over the ankle of the other, and he crosses his arms. His biceps bulge against his form-fitting shirt. And I admire his sharp jaw and straight nose. I roll my eyes, something so annoying and arrogant should not be so handsome.

"You girls should remember your place. Just because you are allowed to fight doesn't mean you've made your way out of the kitchen." He smiles at himself, so proud of being a prick.

I fully turn towards him and cross my arms, popping a hip out—the anger rolls through me like a freight train. It is men like him who want to keep women under their thumb, not to give us equality. "I am unsure what your daddy has told you, but women have been a very beneficial aspect of the war for the last fifty years. The number of civilians we have saved because a woman has created the battle plans is *astronomical*. Not to mention all the potions created by women that have helped so many men on the battlefield." I take a deep breath, watching his emotionless face, "So, before you say something stupid, try *really* hard to rub those last two brain cells together, and maybe come up with something less sexist." I step closer to him, "and before you even *try* to invalidate what I have to say, it is common knowledge amongst everyone in the sectors. So, not only do women give life, but we are also protecting it. I think what you meant to say was, 'Yes, Fallon, you're right." We are all equals, and we should split the chores,' Am I right?" I say with a cock of my head and a smile.

He looks me up and down, *still* smiling. He licks his lips and steps towards me, smooth—like a tiger readying to pounce. "You're really going to be a pain in my ass Nyathera." He continues his slow descent on me. I step back, being in his proximity makes my blood boil. My back hits the wall, and I splay my hands on it to ground myself, "I can think of a few ways to work off the energy wound up in that tight little body of yours. I was just winding you up, which I see worked. And I must say—" his voice drops a few octaves as he gets close and dips his head to my ear, "it did things to me. I like a woman with a fiery side. I might hate you, but I can still fuck you like I don't." He breathes on my ear, "And I have a feeling you would thank me."

His voice soaks into my skull like a drug. It is low and husky and dark. I shudder and squeeze my legs together before I step to the side and turn towards him— opening my mouth to say something and snapping it closed. He chuckles as he straightens his back, watching me scurry away from him.

"You, Xavier Nortick, are a presumptuous asshole." placing my hands on his chest I shove him back and stomp towards the room that hasn't been taken by Fallon or Abigail—before entering, I throw over my shoulder, "I will make sure to take my *fiery side* out on someone who doesn't make me want to commit murder."

I walk into my room and turn to close the door. Fallon and Abigail burst through before I get the chance. They both smile at me.

"Oh, my gods, that was hot, Nye," Abigail says. Her pretty brown hair cut right below her ears bobbing with her dramatic head movements. Her doe eyes bore into me as she smiles widely. With a huff I start unpacking.

"I have to agree with Abbi here; that was the hottest argument I have ever seen. I need a smoke after that, the way he spoke in your ear and devoured your body with his eyes," she fans herself, "gods damn," she giggles.

I turn and glare holding back the laughter. "Y'all are crazy. If he wasn't such an arrogant, spoiled, sexist *troll*, I would totally entertain him. There are plenty of men here for me to use my 'fiery side' with."

They stare at me for a breath, and we all start laughing—so hard, we are doubling over. My sides start to cramp, and I can't breathe. Wheezing, I manage, "Let's get out there and pick our chores for the week before the boys get the chance to take the easy ones." Still laughing, we head to the door.

I am turned talking to Fallon when I open the door and back right into something solid. I move my hands over it before looking at what it is. It is warm and solid and smells faintly of mint.

Clearing his throat, "Ummm, Nye." I jump at the sound of Xavier's voice.

"*Oh, my gods*, I am so sorry," I say, wiping my hands on my pants as hard as possible.

Looking appalled that I feel the need to wipe him away, he watches the movement, and I thoroughly prepare to fight with him again, but he smirks.

"Girl, all you had to do was ask for a feel," he says with that sideways smile that makes me want to throttle him.

I huff at him, "You are disgusting, Xavier."

He smiles, again, "It won't be long, Nighting, and you'll be begging for it." He says with a wink.

Storming past him, Fallon and Abbi are on my heels, "What the fuck is wrong with that man?!"

"I don't know, girl, but he is going to get you. I saw the way your face reddened. He will win." Abbi says, picking at her nails, fighting a smile.

"He will not win, not with me," I say before grabbing some beef from the refrigerator, slapping it onto the cutting board.

"Whatever you say, Nye. But, you don't have to love each other to take some of the stress out on one another." Fallon taps her finger on her temple. "Plus, we will go to battle in a couple of years. Who knows when we will see someone so attractive next, let alone get to roll in the hay with them." She says blandly.

I continue chopping the hunk of meat in front of me as the guys come out. One by one, they sit at the barstools across from us. Xavier grabs an apple and leans over the island, smirking at me as he takes a bite.

"Don't say a damn word, X. I am cooking because I don't want to do the dishes," I smirk.

He cocks a brow, "X, huh?"

"I don't like your name, so I figured I'd give you a name that doesn't sound like a disease." I wave the knife in my hand around. "Ease your pain of being here a little more." He takes a bite of his apple and looks down with a smirk. I follow his gaze, and he's staring at my tits. The zipper of my black outfit has tugged too low in the last few hours, exposing my cleavage to everyone.

I look up at him through my lashes, "are you fuckin serious?" I growl so only he can hear.

"Absolutely," he licks his lips, "What man doesn't admire such a beautiful rack."

Dylan chuckles at the end of the island. I throw him a menacing glare. He looks away, coughing, and covers his mouth. Xavier glances over to Dylan and chuckles.

Xavier's eyes meet mine again, "you're what? A C cup?"

My mouth drops open, "I am not discussing this with you, are you kidding me?!" I can feel my cheeks blazing as his eyes darken the longer he stares. I zip my top to my chin dramatically. "If you think for one minute I will be the one wetting your dick while we are here, you are sadly mistaken," I whisper to him. "I might wet my blade with your blood if you keep up your sexist shit."

I wash my hands quickly in the sink that sits on the island. I dry them and walk towards him, running my hand across his back as I walk by, pausing with over his shoulder, I move closer to him, making sure my lips brush the shell of his ear. "I am a fantastic lay, X. But I don't like scum." His cheeks redden to a beautiful rogue, and he turns to meet my gaze partially.

His eyes twinkle, and his full lips turn up at the corners before taking a bite of his apple, "We will see, Nighting, we will see." He shifts and adjusts himself before getting up and walking to the table to set it.

I look over at Fallon, who is mixing the salad with aggression, excitement flashing in her eyes as she stares at us. Holding up one finger, "Don't," before she can even open her mouth. She smiles and continues what she is doing.

Abigail hides behind the refrigerator door and sticks her tongue in her cheek, "I would before someone else does," she chuckles quietly. I slap her arm and throw the meat in the pan as I walk around her.

I catch myself glancing at Xavier now and then. He sits on the couch, his legs spread, talking to the other guys. I find myself wondering what it would be like to kneel in front of him. I shake my head to throw that image out of my thoughts, and quick. Occasionally, he leans forward and rests his elbows on his knees. His amber eyes dance, and his broad chest shakes with his laughter. The tattoo crawling up his left arm is intricate, and I want to see more.

Fallon comes up behind me and whispers in my ear, "No one would judge you. He's hot, Nye." I shake my head and move away from her.

"That is never happening. He's not even my type." I whisper back.

"He doesn't have to be your type, types change."

"Mine don't." I stare off thinking of the love I lost. Fallon pats my shoulder and walks to the table. I grab the meat and follow her.

Chapter

3

The village elders spoke of a place far beyond the woods, hidden in the fog, where shadows danced, and nightmares roamed free.

We all sit down at the table and start to pass food around, filling our plates. Kenzo clears his throat, "do we care if I say a prayer to the Gods?" he asks.

We all look at each other and scramble to stop our actions. Everyone lays down their silverware.

"My family raised me to be a provider." Interesting for him. Providers spread the word of the Gods. The old rules wouldn't exactly accept him for who he is.

We all acknowledge it. Standing, I put my hands in front of me and tilt my head back. Kenzo starts his prayer, and I can feel someone staring at me. I open one eye and look around; Xavier is across the table, his eyes boring into my soul, looking me up and down like I am dessert. I close my eyes and tilt my head back again. Whoever decided that this is how we should show respect to our Gods…had some weird kinks for sure. I don't like my throat exposed to anyone, especially people I barely know. Kenzo finishes his prayer, and we all sit back down. Passing the food around the table, everyone digs in. I take a bite of the meat and suppress a moan. I didn't realize how hungry I was.

Fallon leans in close, "X is watching you." She teases, circling her finger in my face. I roll my eyes and keep eating.

At the end of dinner, when everyone finishes up, I start clearing the table. Dylan comes over and grabs the plates from my hand, pushing up against me as he does.

"We've got this, Nye, you cooked. Go sit down with the other girls." I look over and Fallon and Abbi have already been sent to the living room. I look back at Dylan; he is a good-looking guy. Brown buzz cut, baby blue eyes, a pointed nose, and stubble on his jaw. Any woman would be lucky.

"Okay," I state quietly as his eyes bore into me. "Thank you." He smiles, and his teeth are insanely white. I linger there for a moment, admiring his features.

"You can go now, beautiful". He winks.

I scramble and blush. "Thanks again, Dylan." I turn and head into the living room and sit on the couch.

I can see Xavier looking at me and glaring at Dylan. I smile and wave at Dylan. Noticing the anger that dances across Xavier's face. I look at Dylan and smile and he returns one as well. Laughing to myself I jump into the conversation with Fallon and Abbi about our first day of classes come Monday. We get to start with hand-to-hand, which makes me nauseous to think about. That gives us a three days to get to know each other so we are in tune with one another before then. I drag a pillow onto my lap and get comfortable in the corner of the oversized couch. The guys finish cleaning up and come into the living room.

"Let's watch a movie!" Kenzo says. Everyone agrees, and Dylan turns on the television.

"What are we watching?" I ask.

"Astronauts," Dylan blurts.

Abbi glares at him, "No! We are watching a rom-com." They go back and forth for a few moments. Kenzo chimes in about gorillas, and Fallon agrees with Dylan.

"What about something that incorporates everything everyone wants to watch?" I say. "A rom com about astronauts and gorillas?"

Everyone looks at me and laughs, but we are sifting through, looking for one. We find something fairly quickly. Who would've known there would be a movie like that? I smile, and they turn it on. Xavier plops down beside me, and I roll my eyes at him. He slings an arm on the back of the couch behind my shoulders.

I look for an escape, but everyone has settled into the couches already, so I look at him, "One move, and I will rip your balls off with my bare hands."

He smiles at me, "At least you would have to touch them beforehand." He winks, and I huff.

"Whatever." I shake my head, and he smirks before focusing on the fire screen.

I get about halfway through before my eyes start threatening to shut. I try my best to stay awake, but sleep wins, and I am pulled into darkness. I feel strong arms wrapping around my back and under my legs, and then I am weightless. My head lulls onto a muscled shoulder, and I slowly open my eyes. I look up and see copper hair.

Startling as Xavier comes into view, "Shhh…I am just taking you to your room; you fell asleep on the couch."

"I am able to walk." I retort.

"I know" he says, looking down at me and smiling quickly. "I'm not doing anything besides taking you to your room. Relax, little one."

I am tired. And he does smell good. "Fine." I huff.

He opens the door with ease and walks me over to my bed. He lays me down, the bed dips on either side of me, bringing him closer. He hovers over me for a breath. Shaking his head he pushes to his feet. He grabs my ankle.

"What the fuck are you doing?" I ask as he starts unlacing my boot.

"Being a gentleman. But I can be a troll if you'd like." He smiles.

I stare at him, so he heard me? Good. He doesn't deserve me to feel anything but hatred towards him.

"I can do that, thanks." I pull my foot out of his grasp, and he steps back, puts his hands in his pockets, and turns on his heel.

Calling over his shoulder, "That's the last time I will be gentlemanly to you, Nyathera. Should've taken it while you could!"

"Fuck you, Xavier." I spit back.

"Only if you ask nicely." He laughs and walks away. I roll my eyes and get up to lock my door. I lean against it for a moment and take deep breaths, centering myself. I need to find a way to get through this.

Chapter

4

It was said that children who disobeyed their parents or refused to listen to their advice would find themselves lost in this eerie city, at the bottom of the pit never to return.

THe small twin-size bed squeaks as I move. The walls are sandstone, and the floor is covered in planked flooring. The sun shines like light through sea glass. Stretching, I sit up and groan. I swing my legs over the edge of the bed and jump down. Barefoot, I make my way to the kitchen to get some much-needed caffeine.

I get to the kitchen, and it's empty. The only sound is the water rushing behind the walls. A sense of serenity washes over me. Well as serene as it can get in such a shitty situation. I start the espresso machine, lay my head on my arms on the countertop, and stretch my hips backward, lengthening my spine.

I hear a whistle come from behind me. "Damn, Nye," Dylan says, coming up from behind me.

I stand up straight and spin around, looking at him. He smiles and runs his hand over his head. He quickly scans his eyes over me and heads towards the fridge.

"I am delighted in the fact that, that" he gestures to my body with one finger, "is the first thing I see in the morning." He smiles around the refrigerator door at me. He is in nothing but shorts and sleepy eyes.

Gods, I roam my eyes over his perfect skin, admiring his biceps and the contours of his back muscles. Just as I can feel myself drooling, I turn towards the espresso machine, and Kenzo comes strolling in, in…nothing but shorts. And Gods have it, here comes X in low-slung sweats. His chest is vast, and his abs go on for days. The sweats don't even hide that beautiful v leading below the waistband. He has a sleepy smile on his face when he sees me and rubs the back of his neck. What did I do to deserve such luck? I turn around and lean my hip against the countertop, watching the men move around in the kitchen in all their half-dressed glory.

Surrounded by men who look like they are carved from the same limestone as the building surrounding us. Abs and biceps and muscular legs.

Xavier dips his head quickly when he walks by me, "You're staring, Nye."

I shake my head. "I am just zoning out. It's early, and I slept horribly with nightmares of a troll standing over my bed." I stick my tongue out at him.

Xavier watches my movements, "Mhmm." Is all he says before opening the cabinet over my head, pinning me to the counter as he grabs a cup from it.

He lowers his hand slowly, still pressed against me, and smirks. I have to hold my breath, so I don't gasp at the feel of his hard body against mine. I have a direct view of his chest and slowly look lower and back up to his face. All I would have to do is stick my tongue out, *Get your head out of the gutter, Nyathera!* I suck in a quick breath when our eyes meet. His eyes flash with amusement and a darkness lies deep behind them. A heat creeps up my chest and dusts my cheeks the longer he holds my gaze. His lips turn at the corners as he notices what he's doing to me. He backs up and grabs the cup of coffee before heading back to his room.

"Hey! That's my *espresso!*" I say as he walks away.

He turns his head and looks at me for a moment, and I see the trace of a smile on his lips as he looks at me over the rim of the cup, taking a sip. Shoving a hand into the pocket of his sweats, he turns away once more. The movement makes his muscles stretch and twitch and I am practically drooling. I watch him walk all the way back to the hallway, staring at his tattoo made up of skulls and runes and his ass—*man, if he wasn't such a dick*. I let out a long breath and both Kenzo and Dylan laugh.

"Oh, man…" Kenzo says.

"You can cut that tension with a knife" Dylan adds.

I glare at them both. They look me up and down again and I remember I am in nothing but a tiny tank top and shorts. I remake my coffee and grab a banana before I basically run back to my room.

Maybe Fallon is right. It won't be long before we will go off to battle—we don't know how often we will get to fuck someone. But I *can't* give into X. Dylan, though, is a snack in and of himself. I shake my head and continue to my room.

Theres a knock at my door about fifteen minutes later. "Come in!" I yell, not thinking about who could be knocking.

Fallon peaks through the door. "Hey! I just wanted to say good morning. I am going to go work out. Do you want to join me?"

I smile at her. "Is anyone else going?"

"Everyone except X," she says with a knowing smile.

"I have to shower first, but I will be there!" I say back.

"Great!" She shuts my door.

Exhaling, I finish my coffee in one long pull and head to the attached bathroom. Sun comes through slits in the ceiling, and the shower takes up one wall.

Everyone gets an attached bathroom, but they all look different. Abigail's looks like it is straight from a rainforest, and Fallon's looks like it belongs in the desert.

Mine looks like it was crafted from the night sky. Dark blues and blacks with accents of glittering stones that look like stars. It is gorgeous.

I turn on the water and let it warm up. Undressing I stumble and hit just above my eyebrow on the countertop.

"Fuck!" I yell.

Touching my forehead I wince at the already protruding bump. Looking up into the mirror the red mark is turning purple. Fuck, I am already beating myself up. I sigh and strip off the tank top and step into the water. It cascades down my body, warming my muscles.

"What happened?!" A deep voice echoes around me, bouncing off the stone walls.

My head snaps towards the voice and see Xavier stands there with outstretched arms and wide eyes, staring at me.

"What the fuck?!" my voice shrill, and I try covering as much as I can.

"I heard something crash and someone yell." He says, covering his eyes, "I'm sorry! I wasn't expecting you to be...." He pauses, "naked and wet." He peeks through his fingers and turns his head to try and look around the shower wall. "I was making sure you were ok." His lips twitch, trying to hide a small smile.

I sigh. "I'm fine. Now leave."

"Are you sure you don't want someone to join you?" he waggles his eyebrows.

"Fuck off, Xavier!" I yell.

He laughs and walks out. Lingering in the door for a second too long. I throw my loofa at him, and he closes the door just in time. I can't help but smile when the loofa sloshes off the door. I am overly hot now, not just from the water, but because a man just saw me naked, a man I absolutely loathe…right? It's been so long since a man has taken me…in any sense. The last was a dirty man who I slept with for food back in my sector.

Shaking my head as excitement from Xavier seeing me pools low in my belly, and I decide then that I will talk to Dylan. I have to work off some of this pent-up energy. Because, apparently, if I don't fuck someone, I am going to lose my sanity.

I throw on some black leggings and a black sports bra, lace up my sneakers and braid my hair into two braided rows. Checking myself in the mirror one last time, I head out to the living room. My head down looking at my watch, I collide with something solid. Looking up, I sigh when

Xavier stands there staring down at me. His hand on my waist, and a grin on his face. How the fuck do I keep running into him—literally. I am all too aware of his hand on me. The size of it takes up the entirety of my side. He rubs his thumb along the exposed skin and I almost purr at the thought of what his hands would feel like all over me.

"Careful little one, you don't want another bruise on your pretty little face." He says, tracing his thumb across my brow bone.

My body shudders at his touch but I push him away. "Go find someone else to torture. I don't have the time or the patience for it. And I have half the mind to go tell the professors that you are harassing me."

He chuckles at that, "You think they will do anything about that, Nye? They said everything here is to prepare you for battle. In the real world, you will hear much worse than what I say to you." He pokes my forehead, "Just because your last name is Nighting doesn't mean you will get your way with everyone. You have to earn that title, and with your size," his eyes roam up and down my body. "I'll be surprised if you make it to graduation day." he says with a snarl.

My mouth drops, and I close it, "you really are an asshole. Do you know that Xavier? I cannot wait to show you that I am more than capable of living up to these fake standards people have laid out for me based on my brother's actions." My breaths heavy, annoyance coursing through my veins, "He isn't some saint, and he isn't a hero." I stomp away from him, no longer wanting to work out.

Chapter

5

One day, a curious little girl named Nyathera decided she didn't need to listen. "I'm not afraid of any shadows!" she declared as she and her friends giggled and ran deeper into the woods, ignoring the fading calls of their parents.

Monday morning, we head to the fighting arena. Wall-to-wall mats line each side, and all the houses are lined up along the outside of the space, waiting for instructions. The noise is deafening, with over 200 trainees this year. I stand by Fallon and Dylan, wringing my hands together.

"You'll be okay, Nye. This is to teach us, not kill us." Fallon says reassuringly.

"Although, many trainees are killed on the mats each year," Dylan adds. I look at him with wide eyes. My breathing erratic.

"Hey, remember what I said. I'll help you in hand to hand. We have your back." Kenzo says as he snakes up beside me.

I smile warily at him. "Thanks, you guys. It means a lot to me that you are willing to risk your lives to help me save mine." Breathing deep, I push the panic deep inside—no one needs to see my weakness.

"I'll spar with you first. That way we can see where you are and work off that to better your fighting style." Kenzo leans into my side and wraps an arm around my shoulders.

The nauseating sounds of sparring to my right catches my attention. My gaze flicks over to the mat where a man from house two and a woman are duking it out. They aren't holding back as the man slams a fist into her mouth.

A tooth flies to the ground, blood sprays across the mat, and I cringe. The look of pure brutality lingers in her eyes as she raises her gaze in his direction, and in the blink of an eye she has him pinned to the ground. Throwing fists and kicks in his direction, tearing at his eyes, his howls of agony tear through the area, bouncing off the walls and landing straight into my gut. Dropping to the ground she places a boot on his chest, spitting blood on the mat beside him. I turn away, burying my face into Kenzo's side.

Rubbing my arm, he looks down to me, "It won't be like that, Nye, I promise."

I nod and look back to him, "Where is Abigail and Xavier?" I haven't seen Xavier since our last argument. I'm not complaining, but it's been weird.

Kenzo and Dylan share a look. Fallon puts her hand on my shoulder. "They went off to the back locker rooms together; we think we can deduce what they are doing," she says gently.

"I wish he took me back with him instead" Kenzo adds with a sheepish grin.

I chuckle, "we know you do Kenzo," I pat his arm. He smiles at me.

I shouldn't feel the anger I do when I look to the entrance and see them walking over together. I let that anger bubble. "Kenzo," I say, "I am going to spar with Xavier first."

"Are you—"

Putting a hand up, I cut him off, "Yes."

Kenzo studies me for a second, "alright, Nye."

They reach the mat, and everyone is quiet. Xavier looks at Kenzo and Dylan and smiles, "What's up, guys?" He asks. No one says anything to him. "Okay. What's with the silent treatment?"

"You know good and well what is with the silent treatment, X," Fallon says with malice. I grab her hand to calm down the anger I feel showing in her eyes.

Xavier looks at Fallon and then at me. "Are you two synched or something?" Fallon leaps, but Kenzo catches her.

"I need your help," Kenzo says to Fallon. She looks at me, question in her beautiful blue eyes.

"I'm ok," I whisper. She nods and heads with Kenzo.

"What the fuck is that about." Xavier throws his hand towards Fallon. I stare and turn from him, heading towards where Dylan is standing.

I reach Dylan and stand with my shoulder against his arm. "How are you feeling Nye?" he asks quietly.

"I'm okay. I just have so much anger built up over the last six years that I am ready to explode." He wraps an arm around my shoulders, his arm warm and comforting.

"It will all work out, Nye. We are all here to work with each other and help one another—whether Xavier wants to be a part of that or not is up to him." He looks down at me, "But, you have me, Kenzo, and Fallon. We are right here with you. It is an honor to help you protect yourself." He smiles sweetly at me, and I return it.

"Thank you," I mouth to him.

"Everyone will pair up on the mats in front of your house. Male and female, male and male, and female and female will fight today. There is no use of weapons and tapping out can save your life. There are no rules about whether you will make it off these mats today." Professor Mary says. She is a large, muscular woman, with black hair and green eyes.

"I wouldn't want to be caught in the woods with her alone. She's daunting." I say to Fallon, who has come up beside me.

"She is the best of the best. Everyone who has trained with her has survived attack after attack. I trust her with my life," she looks away from Professor Mary to me, "but she is scary," she giggles.

Xavier steps towards us all, "I'll pair up with Abigail." reaching for her.

"We already paired up. Fortunately for us, you're paired with Nyathera." Fallon says to him. I smirk at him.

"I'm sorry, what?" He asks her. "You already chose? She is so inadequate; are we finally in agreement that she needs to be taught a lesson?"

"No, we just have more confidence in her than you do," Kenzo says, looking down his nose at him. "I'll pair up with Abbi." He says.

"Okay!" Abbi says with a smile and a little hop. I roll my eyes. Xavier decides we need to take the mat first. He smirks as he stands in front of me, getting into a fighting stance. My stomach clenches, and my heart races.

"You should've picked someone else, little one. I plan to make this hurt." His smile turning reptilian, "You think you'll coast through because your brother is the all savior. Guess what, princess…"

He doesn't have a chance to finish what he is saying before I charge towards him and grab the back of his neck. Using my feet I climb around him with ease. The release of adrenaline has me shaking and feeling confident. I wrap my arms around his neck and squeeze. Not tight enough to kill him but enough to cut his breathing short.

"I am not coasting by." I bite the words into his ear. "I will fight daily to prove that I am better than my con artist of a brother." I grip my elbow with the opposite hand to tighten the chokehold I have him in, "He is nothing but a piece of shit. He didn't save all those people."

He struggles in my grip.

Being small has its advantages. "His friend Matthew did. The man I was in love with was brutally killed, and my brother took the glory of Matt's heroic actions."

He gets a hold of the fabric around my shoulders and throws me over his head. My back hits the mat, and the wind is struck from my lungs. Stars shine in the corner of my eyes, and I try to scramble to my feet. Before I can get to my knees, Xavier pushes his body over mine, pinning my legs with his and my arms above my head in one hand, his other moving to my waist. His nose barely touches mine, and I am all too aware of where our bodies are touching.

I struggle under his hold, twisting my wrists trying to break his grip.

"Your brother let my sister die so he could save all those people." He digs his fingers into my hip flexor sending shocks of pain down my leg. I growl at him. "And since he didn't save anyone, I believe that calls for a blood-for-blood sacrifice." He spits out. I had no idea he had a sister or that she died because of my brother's actions.

"I didn't know…" is all I get out. He puts his forearm against my throat, still holding both wrists in one hand.

"I will not be defeated by a small, insignificant bitch, Nyathera. Especially one that shares a bloodline with that monster." He pushes harder.

The corners of my vision starts going black and the sounds around me are muffling. This is it. This is how I join my parents on the other side.

They didn't care if I was around or not when they were alive—they wouldn't care when I am dead with them. The thought surges anger through my veins.

I buck my hips, trying to free myself. He is strong, and I have to use all my strength to pull my leg from under his. With all that I have left, I bring up one shaking knee into Xavier's groin. He instinctively grabs himself and gets on his knees. Instead of taking him down, I stand in front of him, wrapping his hair in my fist, tugging his head back so he has to look me in the face. My breathing is erratic, and my head is swimming. He peers up at me with hatred in his gaze. Sweat beads on his brow and I half smile at the exertion he had to put into fighting a 'small insignificant bitch'.

Lowering my nose an inch from his, I spit, "I may be small, and you might think I am insignificant, but I am a survivor, a fighter, and I will be a soldier." I tighten my grip, taking a deep breath as his nose crinkles. "Regardless of who wants me dead or alive. Do you really think I care about who believes me, and who doesn't? I know my capabilities and what I bring to the table."

He smiles and my blood boils.

"Do not think for a second that because I share the same genetics as my brother that I am the same as him, your sister's death is a tragedy, but yours would be much more tragic if at the hands of the weak sister to the all-savior." I cock my head, "Either work with me or stay out of my way, Xavier. It's the little ones you need to watch out for."

He looks at me, the hatred in his eyes burns bright. He opens his mouth to say something, and before he is able to spill vile words, I punch him with full force. Bone on bone, skin splitting, and a searing pain sprawls over my hand, as my knuckles make contact with his teeth. I hiss at the impact and shake my hand, noticing the split that crosses my knuckles. Fuck, that hurt but was so insanely satisfying. I grin a little.

He looks up and smiles, his blood and my blood coating his white teeth. "You, Nyathera, will be the death of me." His words laced with something I can't read. "We can call a truce, but one fuck up, one betrayal, and your life will end in my hands." I throw his head to the side, letting go of his hair.

I reach a hand towards him, and he takes it. His grip tightens with bruising force as he jerks me to the side, throwing me to the ground. I groan with the impact. He stands up, looks down on me like I am nothing but a bug.

He squats, whispering, "I would watch yourself Nighting. There are a lot of people who want to take you out."

He walks away. I lay there for a moment. What the hell just happened? I force myself to stand up, my bones groaning at the movement and notice everyone is staring at me. Whispering flutters throughout the arena. I fix my shirt and walk back over to Fallon.

"I have no idea whether I should be upset or fanning myself. The tension between the two of you is so thick it can be cut with a sword." I roll my eyes at her and walk away. I don't need to keep hearing it. I won't be fucking him, and I won't be letting him kill me. There has to be a middle ground that we, as adults, can meet on.

Chapter

6

As they ventured further, the trees grew thicker, and the light began to fade, swallowed by the encroaching darkness.

I get back to the house before anyone else. The weight of everything I said and everything that X said to me is pushing hard on my chest. I need a good cry or a good fucking. Maybe both. I walk into my room and sit on the chair at my desk. Staring at my hand where it is split from the force I put behind that punch. The dried blood cracking along the edges, pulling on the wound painfully. I pull out some healer's balm from the desk drawer, the slimy substance shining in the light, and rub it on the wound. It soothes the pain a little, and the edges slowly start to piece themselves together.

I watch the fibers of my skin slowly slide into place like a patchwork blanket. Putting my face in my hands, I let Xavier's words fall over me. Insignificant. Small. He isn't wrong. I have been both of those things since the day I was born, coming into this world too small to even cry. The tears well in my eyes, and before I know it, they are falling down my cheeks. Each one dropping onto the papers sitting in front of me. Each holding an emotion that has been suppressed for the last twenty-one years of my life.

My shoulders heave with a sob. It has been so long since I cried, like, *really* cried. I let everything out in those salty tears—every word that has been said to me, about me, every word I have said about myself, and everything my brother did.

Missing Matthew, my parents' death, being forced to be a soldier when I didn't even want to be alive.

I let everything wash over me and consume me like wildfire. The room spins, and I sob. I move to my bed and continue to let the tears fall. All the adrenaline leaving my body, all the anger and sadness no longer taking up house in my soul. The tears slow and replacing them is a hole. My crying stops, and exhaustion washes over me. I eventually fall asleep.

When I wake up, I hear whispers outside my door. Only one voice—Xavier. What the hell could he want? Ignoring him, I throw the covers over my head. A soft knock echoes through my room.

"What do you want?" I say.

"Can we talk?" He replies from the other side.

"Go away, Xavier. There is nothing for us to talk about." The hole in my chest grows with each word that leaves my mouth. Emptiness spans across my internal being.

"Please." He pleads.

I am silent for a breath. I inhale deeply and exhale. "Fine," I huff.

He is opening the door and entering before I can even shift to sit up in bed. "Nye." He says, looking at me. His gaze almost caring.

"What do you want, X?" I stare at him.

"You've been crying." He states.

"Women are allowed to cry." I bite.

"Is it because of me?" He asks without emotion.

My eyes roll so hard I swear I saw the Goddess of death, "What. Do. You. Want?" I enunciate.

"I wanted to check on you. Everyone else said to leave you alone, and I agreed until I heard you sobbing. I know how it feels to be empty, Nye."

I stand from my bed, my body shaking with the adrenaline dump and the anger that courses through my veins. "You don't know anything about me, Xavier. Nothing. So, stop pretending you care. You're giving me whiplash with this back-and-forth shit." I throw my arms to the sides, "One minute, you're flirting with me, and the next, you are so full of venom that I don't feel like I can survive your words. Either tell me what you want or get the *fuck* out of my room." I say, stepping towards him.

He stands still, just looking at me. He raises his hand like he is going to touch my arm. And then he drops it. I snort, "You really can't just say what is on your mind, can you?" I laugh, "Let's clear all of this up, real quick, huh? *Your* father is the general; if anything, *you* will get preferential treatment. My brother doesn't affect me in any way. It wasn't my actions that caused your sister's death. I am *not* my brother, X. So instead of fighting, we need to be united. I am not that bad of a person, and I think deep… deep… *deep* down, you may be halfway decent as well."

He stares at me for a second, and a grin spreads across his face. "I could be very deep." He says with a smirk. As much as I hate the man, I smile and slap his arm.

"Get out, Xavier," I say with ambivalence. He turns his back and walks to the door; before he walks out, he looks over his shoulder.

"I still hate you and your brother, Nye. I just won't try to kill you… yet"

I smirk, and he walks out. Maybe we can find a common ground, that ground being we absolutely loathe one another. Nonetheless, it is a common ground. We have to survive the two years together. Nothing more. I shake my head and climb into bed.

Chapter

7

When I walk into the kitchen the next morning, Dylan is talking to Abigail, and she smiles when she sees me. Sighing, I force a smile back.

She comes over to me, "Oh my gods Nye. That sparing between you and X yesterday was the second hottest thing I have ever seen in my entire life. The hatred, the sexual tension. The way you punched him in the mouth, and he smiled like a psychopath." She looks off into the distance. "Oh! Are you okay? I heard you crying last night, and I know that sometimes people need to be left alone to cry, but I also wanted to console you. Xavier wouldn't let any of us go in there, though. Something about 'it'll make her tougher,' blah blah blah."

I hold up my hand. "Abbi, stop." She blushes, gods she likes to ramble. "I am fine. I did need a good cry and to be alone. But I have to ask you something."

She nods, "okay."

I step closer to her, "Where were you and Xavier yesterday before sparring?" She looks at me wide eyed.

"Ummm…" she says looking around.

"Did you fuck him?"

She looks at me and starts laughing. "Nye, I am married to a woman." She laughs some more.

"But, you said you would—you know—" and I make the gesture she did the other day in the kitchen.

"Oh! No, silly, I meant you should before anyone else can. Not that I personally would!" She puts her hand on her heart, and she keeps giggling. "I was having a breakdown, and X came to talk to me. I really miss my wife. She is part of the farming sectors, so we didn't see each other much before I was collected." She looks to the floor and back to me, "Xavier is a good man, Nye. I would give him a chance."

Guilt immediately fills my chest. "I am so sorry for assuming, Abbi." I wring my hands together in embarrassment, "I don't even know why I am asking. It shouldn't matter."

She smiles. "It's okay. I see why you'd think that, but I also think there is more between you two than you want to believe. Hatred can turn into love quickly, Nye."

I snort, "Not in this case."

"Whatever you say, girl." She looks over my shoulder, "Anyways, I'll talk to you later." I watch her walk off and meet up with Fallon. Shaking my head I dig through the refrigerator for a snack.

One year ago

Day by day and month by month, we continue our training. Weekends are filled with annoying flirting with Xavier or lying in bed with Fallon and Dylan watching movies and gossiping. Fallon and I head to the gym every morning to lift and work on our cardio because, let's be honest, my cardio needs work. Dylan trains me nightly in hand-to-hand combat. Kenzo has been studying to be transferred to the provider's wing, and he is *fantastic* at it. It is where he belongs. And Abbi, Gods bless her. Her wife has been struggling with her health, so she has spent most of her time on calls. Dylan has become my safe place, my home—if Fallon isn't available, he is there for me. He keeps me grounded.

We have been assigned courses to learn about the war, what needs to be done mentally, and kinesiology to ensure we understand how our body works and natural ways to heal it. We are also in potion classes and have had a few trainees poison themselves trying to learn new ways to heal or kill.

It is monotonous work.

It has built friendships.

It has built families and lovers.

It has created *enemies*.

Another Saturday rolls around and I go to Fallon's room. Knocking softly, I wait for her to answer. When she doesn't answer I knock again, "Fallon! Are you ready to hit the gym?" I call through the heavy door. I wait, again, for her to answer.

"She isn't here, she went out with a woman from house two last night and didn't come home." Dylan's lazy voice sounds behind me.

"Oh." I suck in a breath when I turn toward him. His sleep pants are slung low on his hips, framing the deep V that travels below the waistband. I let my eyes roam up his abdomen, and I count the abs. My heart rate increases as I examine his strong chest and shoulders. Continuing my ascent up his body, I catch a smile on his full lips. I swallow hard.

"Like what you see, Nye?" His smile widens.

I choke on a laugh, "sorry." I dip my head and start to scurry to my room.

"I'll go to the gym with you." Dylan calls down the hall.

I pause at my door. Taking a deep breath, I lift my eyes back to him, "are you sure? Usually, you go to the common area with Kenzo and Xavier on Saturday mornings."

His smile lights up the hallway, "Kenzo is studying, and Xavier went to meet with his father. I am all yours."

Something in my stomach flips at the sound of his voice. I look over his body again, "you might want to change." I say, darting my tongue out to moisten my dry lips. His eyes track the movement.

"It'll only take me a moment." He says before rushing to his room and closing the door. He appears a second later in black shorts that fall at mid-thigh, tightening across his muscular legs. He must have forgotten his shirt because, Gods bless me, his deep muscles are on full display again.

I snap my gaze to his face and smile. "Ready?" I ask quickly.

He chuckles. "Let's go, peony." He starts towards the door, not waiting for me to catch up.

"Peony?" I scrunch my nose.

"Peonies are my favorite flowers, and you just so happen to be my favorite person." He smiles widely.

My heart melts. This handsome man, who has become one of my *very best* friends, has a soft spot.

I give him a tight smile, "Then peony it is."

We walk down the dark hallway that leads to the gathering hall. The gym is outside in the courtyard. Voices echo through the building. Dylan slings his arm over my shoulders, his birch and coal scent going straight to my head. "So, what are we doing today? Cardio?" He side eyes me with a grin.

"Nope. Today is leg day." I reply with a smirk.

His face falls, "leg day?" The huskiness of his voice catching me off guard.

"Is that okay?" I ask gently.

He smirks, "Of course, but only if you're ready to get your ass kicked." He smiles at me before sprinting through the large stone doors at the mouth of the courtyard.

"Hey!" I yell and take off after him, laughing as I go.

He rounds the large wall in the middle of the courtyard. It is made of stone with iron ladders along it. We use it to train climbing the ladders of the wall surrounding Mearin. I get to the other side, and he isn't there. Running to the other side I don't see him. I stop, putting my hands on my hips trying to catch my breath.

"Hey peony, what took you so long?"

I look up and Dylan is standing on the wall smiling down at me. The sun framing his form, he looks ethereal. I shake my head at him and grab a hold of the first iron wrung. Climbing up the fifty foot wall, huffing and puffing as I reach the top, I really hate cardio in any form, well, most forms.

Dylan holds out his hand and helps me balance myself on the flat surface of the top. I look out over Mearin, the limestone stretching on for miles, faintly in the distance the giant wall surrounding us stands five times as high as the one we are on now. I look down and the world begins to spin. The ground below looks like it is coming up to meet me as I stumble. Dylan's strong arms are there in an instant, pulling me into his embrace.

He smiles at me, "Don't look down, Nye. It will trick your brain into thinking you are falling."

"No shit." I grind out.

He chuckles and starts down the ladder, "You coming peony?"

I roll my eyes and climb down with him, not looking at the ground below. Once my feet hit the earth, I sigh with relief. Dylan slings an arm over my shoulders again and I wrap my arm around his waist, patting his chest. We walk to the gym equipment along the far wall. The sun is high in the sky and spring is in full swing. I walk over to the squat rack and add weight to each side. Dylan points at each one, adding the weight in his head.

"200 pounds? There's no way." He laughs.

I shoot him a glare and position myself below the bar, adjusting my stance and pushing up. I easily knock out eight reps before racking the bar again. I laugh at the look on Dylan's face. "Close your mouth big guy, the flies are out." I wink at him and gesture for him to take his turn.

He smirks and adds two more forty-fives to each side and positions himself below the bar. He gets in five reps before racking it. I smile at him and position myself below the bar.

"There's no way, Nye, don't hurt yourself." His voice laced with worry and entertainment.

That fuels my ambition. I get in position and lift the bar. The metal bites into my shoulders and my legs strain with the weight. Fallon and I have been working on strength for six months, I am considerably stronger than I was when we started, I've got this. I push through my thighs and bring the weight back up. Squatting down again, my legs tremble. I grit my teeth and push, halting halfway up. Without hesitation Dylan is behind me, hands on my hips encouraging me to push the weight the rest of the way. I rack the weight and grab my water bottle.

"That was impressive, Nye." Dylan says, holding his hand up for a high five.

I smack his hand in defeat, "I could have gotten it." I huff out. He rolls his eyes.

"I'm sure you could have." He grins.

We finish our workouts and walk back to the house, both of us drenched in sweat and burnt out. I put my hand on Dylan's arm and squeeze, "Thank you for coming with me today." He smiles and places a kiss to the top of my head.

"Any day, Nye." He smiles at me. He holds his hand out and I twist our pinkies together, flip our hands so they are palms together, and then flip our fingertips to the ground and place our knuckles against one another's, and finally interlace our pinkies again and kiss our fists. A silly handshake we came up with one evening while waiting on Fallon to start the movie.

I smile widely at him as he walks to his room. I open the door to my room. The light is trailing through the large slits in the ceiling, casting shadows across the floor. The bed in the middle has fresh linens laying on it, meaning Abigail did the laundry today. The wood floor creaks below my feet as I walk to the bathroom. Turning on the water I get undressed and step into the shower. The water cascades down my sore muscles and I groan at the release.

I think about the next few months as I wash my hair. The next step is learning to ride. Six months in, and they are just now allowing us to do so; they wanted us to create those bonds in order to kick ass on the machines. There is no telling what tomorrow will bring, but we are ready, I think.

I step out of the shower and towel off. Running a brush through my hair, I hear a knock on the door. Swinging it wide, Fallon is standing in the doorway with a grin on her face. "I heard you worked out with Dylan today."

"Yes, I did." I cross my arms over the towel around my breasts. "You weren't home."

Her smile widens and she heads to my bed, flopping down she lays on the pillows. "I saw Hayden last night. She took me dancing at one of the house parties, and then we walked the wall until sunrise." She sighs and smiles, "it was perfect Nye."

I flop down next to her and smile at her, "I am glad you had a good night Fallon, next time please tell me you're not going to be home, so I am not caught in the hall with a half-naked Dylan."

She laughs and turns on her side, propping her head up on her hand. "Did you like it?" she waggles her eyebrows.

"Like what?"

"Seeing Dylan half naked. All the girls are constantly talking about how hot he is." She rolls her eyes but continues smiling at me.

I stare at her for a moment before giggling, "he is definitely a great guy, with a *great* body. And he has an amazing heart." I roll to meet her gaze, "but no, there is no potential there besides him being one of my best friends."

"You never know, Nye." She kisses my cheek and jumps up, "get dressed. It is movie night!" her high-pitched sing songy voice floating around the room, and just like that she disappears out of my room. I roll onto my back and stare at the ceiling. With so much going on I never thought about Dylan as more than friends. He is attractive, caring, smart, but is it worth ruining a friendship? I huff and get dressed, opting for my flannel pj bottoms and a tank top. Just as I finish getting dressed, Fallon and Dylan rush through my door.

"Let's get tonight started!" Dylan yells before jumping onto my bed and dragging me into his arms. I laugh as Fallon comes up behind me and nuzzles her nose in my hair.

"I love you guys." I smile at each of them.

"We love you too, Nye." Dylan says, sweeping a loose hair out of my face, "More than you will ever know." I smile wide.

Fallon wraps her arms around me tight, "I love you too, girl!" I look at each of them again, a true family I never thought I'd experience. Happiness washes over me as we get comfortable before starting our movie night.

Chapter

8

Suddenly, they stumbled upon the pit where a mysterious shadowed ladder laid. "Let's use it!" Nyathera exclaimed, her curiosity overpowering her sense of caution.

After the third movie Dylan and Fallon leave. Fallon kisses my cheek and skips to her room. Dylan lingers in the doorway, leaning against the doorframe. I admire him for a moment before smiling, "thank you for today." He reaches his hand out and places his palm on my cheek. Without a thought I lean into it.

"I will do anything with you Nyathera, you mean more to me than you will ever know." He drops his hand and walks down the hall, leaving me standing there, frozen in place. My heart thrums in my ears. Tomorrow will be a long day as we complete our weapons and riding certifications. I take a deep breath in and let it out slow, closing my door. Heading back to my bed I climb in and nuzzle into my pillows, falling asleep quickly.

I wake up and change into my brown leathers. Throwing my hair on top of my head, I shove my feet into my boots, lacing them up and leave my room. Fallon is coming out at the same time that I am. "How are you feeling today?" she asks me gently.

"I'm okay." I smile at her.

She smiles back. "Good because we need you in tip-top shape for today. I heard that the houses are competing but also competing in pairs."

I look at her confusedly, "I thought these weren't important?"

"They aren't per se, but these certifications will put you at your level for the entire year. We have to do the best we can." I nod and round the corner.

I turn around when she opens the refrigerator and notice Xavier entering the living room. "Good morning Nye." He says.

I smile, "Good morning."

He strides toward me, "Are you ready for today? We can bench you if you aren't up for it."

I look him dead in the eyes. "You're kidding, right? Because what the actual fuck, X" he smiles. I punch his arm, and he bumps my chin.

"I'll see you there," he winks and throws me a sideways smile.

My knees grow weak, and my hatred for him dies just a little. A *very* minute amount. Quite possibly unseen by the naked eye. But it does shrink. I catch up to Dylan and Fallon. They smile at me.

"Good morning beautiful" Dylan says.

"Good morning, are you ready for today?" I ask, wrapping a hand around his elbow.

"I was born ready." He stands up straighter, flexing a large bicep.

I laugh as we walk out of the house. Winding through the hallway, the mildew invading my senses, I try to mentally prepare myself for today. Who knows what will happen in the riding arena. Nothing we have done so far has been easy, my eyes are constantly blurry from studying and staying up far too late. If I can master a revival potion, I can definitely master riding—I think.

We exit the hallway, and the college is filled with laughter and people walking towards the training arena. Instead of having one house train at a time, they instruct all houses to show up and watch. The fire screen on the ceiling is where they will broadcast replays of our rides today. I remember in the *one* letter that Bartholomew sent to us, he described the riding arena. Stating it was his favorite training and that one day it would me mine as well. I grew up watching everyone riding around the sectors, saw a few crashes as well. I was infatuated with the idea of controlling one of those vehicles one day. As I got older and lost more and more people from our sector who were the same age as me, I developed a fear of them.

Now, here I am getting ready to get on one of the machines that could end my life.

Chapter

9

The ladder took them deeper and deeper into the pit, until they stumbled upon a shadowed gate.

We walk into the outdoor arena—the large area is consumed by a dome of glass, with the bright blue sky beyond it. As I step through the double doors to the arena, dirt blows around me shooting specks flittering into the air. The smell is strong, of earth and exhaust. Weapons are lined up on one side, hanging on a pegboard wall and the other side is lined with four-wheelers and dirt bikes, all different colors and sizes.

"Each team will be partnered up, one will drive, and the other will have to shoot, stab, or behead the dummy. We will start with House One and move on through the others. Please be prepared." Professor Mantel finishes what he is saying and leaves us to talk amongst ourselves as they prepare.

"What are you choosing, Nye?" Fallon asks me. I look at the choices. Daggers, swords, and bows.

I look at her and shrug, "What are you choosing?"

"I have always used a sword. Not good with daggers, and hand me a bow and immediately duck because I can't shoot straight to save my own life." She laughs, and I smile.

"I will either take the bow or the daggers."

Xavier and Kenzo turn towards me, "Women never use those—they usually use a sword because it is easier for them to wield one over many weapons."

I cock my head, "So?" I scrunch my nose at the audacity of suggesting women can't.

They smile and shake their heads before turning away.

"Ignore them, Nye; they're just mad because women have been showing them up," Abbi bumps my arm with hers. I laugh and turn away.

We wait and wait for an hour as professors prepare their trainers to keep score, and houses one and two finish. It is our turn to be paired and finish this certification. "Abigail and Dylan, Fallon and Kenzo, Xavier and Nyathera. You will be partners. Choose your vehicle and weapons wisely." Professor Mantel turns and walks away but nods at me first. I scrunch my nose and turn away. Xavier appears beside me.

"You know we will work well together, just try not to kill me." He slaps my back, causing me to stumble forward, and walks towards the vehicles.

"Which are you choosing?" I ask him. Xavier is a master rider. He has ridden around the sectors since he was little. I remember watching him and thinking it was so cool. Now? I can't stand it.

"I am better with a dirt bike, but if you can hold on better with those little legs on a four-wheeler, I can deal." He looks at me.

"Which has a better turn radius and can handle better for partner drills?" He smiles, his eyes lighting up as I ask about something he enjoys. All men are the same. Ask them about a vehicle, sports, or their dick, and they can talk for hours.

"I'll be right back." He disappears for a few minutes. I hear the rumbling of a motor and turn as a black dirt bike is heading straight towards me. I see my reflection in the driver' s visor *moments before* they stop directly in front of me. Dust flies into my face and I slap my hands on the front rim over the tire. The helmet is unbuckled, and Xavier is sitting there with a beaming smile on his face.

"What the fuck Xavier?! You could've killed me!" I yell, my body shaking.

"But I didn't," he winks, and he tosses me a helmet, almost knocking me out.

I switch weight on my feet from left to right, "you're right, you didn't." I put a hand on my hip, "you probably should have if you were smart" I wink and laugh.

Walking towards him I inspect the dirt bike, "Ummm, where do I sit?" He smiles and slides forward as far as he can, leaving very minimal space, even for me. He pats the leather seat right behind him.

"You can squeeze in right here, right against me." His smile has grown predatory.

I twist my mouth in disgust. "There isn't one with a bigger seat?"

He laughs. "Get on Nighting. Do you want to win or not?"

With a huff, I put the helmet on, the smell of sweat and dirt from previous riders literally shoves up my nose. Struggling to do up the buckle, Xavier appears before me and uses his finger to tip my head back—I swallow hard at the movement. His fingers brush my throat slightly as he does up the buckle for me and a chill runs through my body.

He holds the chin of the helmet and brings my head back to a normal position without letting go, "trust me, as much as I love to hate you, at least for now, I've got you, Nye." He shrugs his shoulders, "Plus, I want to win. And my father wouldn't appreciate me letting a pretty little thing like you die."

I swallow, nod, and watch him throw his left leg over the dirt bike. With a kick and a twist of his hand, it rumbles to life.

He reaches a hand towards me, and I take it. "We can practice just riding and pretend shooting before we grab your bow," he says, "or your daggers."

I nod again. I have never been on one of these. I tremble in time with the motor. The power of these machines always made my insides twist. I try to swing my left leg over and fail. Xavier grip tightens on my hand, and

I look towards him, with a sigh I lift my leg and try again, stumbling backwards. Xavier's hand tightens in mine, and he keeps me upright.

Xavier reaches around and flips down a metal peg. "You'll use these to get on and for your feet while riding."

"Okay. Please don't crash. I would like to make it to graduation, X." He nods, smiling and flipping the visor of his helmet down. I finally get on, feeling the eyes of everyone in the arena on me, and put my hands on my thighs.

"You have to hold on!" Xavier says over the engine. I grab his shoulders, and I can feel him laugh. "Lower," he says. I move my hands to his biceps, feeling the expanse of his muscles, "Now come on Nye, wrap those scrawny arms around my waist and hold on!"

I run my hands down his back to his waist and slowly wrap them around, cringing the entire time. I feel him shudder beneath his leathers. With a little bit of amusement at what my touch does to him, I splay my hands over his abdomen—feeling every muscle move below my fingertips. I instantly feel my core tighten at the thought of how he looked shirtless, he takes a deep breath in, and we take off.

Instinctually tightening my arms around him as I jolt backwards from the takeoff, holding on for dear life. The vibration of the bike reverberates through my entire body. I feel every muscle under his leathers pinch and move as he takes us through the trails.

"Try to stand up!" he yells.

I shake my head, "I can't. I'll fall!" the panic rising in my throat is a stark reminder of the speed at which we are travelling.

"Trust me!" he yells back.

Trust him? The man who said if I die it will be by his hands?

I roll my eyes and wait for a heartbeat before taking a deep breath. I have to do this. I have to prove myself. I am *not* my brother, and I will be better. I slowly unwrap my arms. Squeezing my legs around the bike, my thighs screaming at me, and try to stand. The butterflies in my stomach take off as I stumble sideways, and Xavier catches me just before I fall off completely.

Chapter

10

The gate swung open with a creak, revealing the City of Shadows and Nightmares.

My entire body starts shaking. I can't breathe. The world starts spinning. The bike slows and then comes to a stop. Before I realize what is happening, Xavier is off the bike and ripping me off with him. The dirt starts to wave around my feet as if it were trying to break free from under the soles of my boots. I wait for the scolding, but he quickly undoes my helmet and tears it off my head. Putting both hands on the sides of my face, he says something. But I am so busy dying that I have no idea what he is saying.

He keeps saying something, but my chest is constricting, and I can't see straight.

Inhale, exhale.

Inhale, exhale.

Over and over again.

The nausea starts to show its ugly head as my stomach clenches, and my mouth waters. I don't even realize what is happening before Xavier is pushing his lips to mine. At first, I just stand there, but my body slowly melts into his. His lips move expertly over mine, and his hands roam from my cheeks to my waist, where he pulls me against him. His body hard against me. I sigh as I wrap my arms around him. He tastes like mint and salt. Everything slows down, and the world stops spinning.

I notice my breathing has calmed down, and my core turns to molten lava. I want more, no, I *need* more. I feel it through my entire body—the warmth, the precision, the need. But then, I'm shoving him away, coming to my senses.

"What the fuck, Xavier!" I scream, shoving both hands on his chest. His *extremely* strong chest.

He smiles, and my mind starts spinning again. "You were having a panic attack and weren't listening to me. I did the next best thing I could think of since I was raised not to slap a lady." He is out of breath and smiling ear to ear. He shifts on his feet and reaches for me.

I shake my head at him, "So you kiss me?!" I start pacing in front of him. "*How* do you think that was the only other option?!" my voice pitchy as I yell. "Don't you think you could've, I don't know, waited for it to pass?! I mean, there are other options, X!"

He rushes towards me, licking his lips, ready to take on the task again. Before I can say anything, he grabs my waist and slams his lips to mine. This time harder and more vigorous. My body sinks into his as soon as our mouths collide. His warm body against me, melting together.

His tongue prods at my lips as he pulls me closer, tilting his head to deepen the kiss. I let him in on instinct alone. My body betrays my mind. His tongue is soft, moving over mine as they intertwine in what can only be described as the creation and destruction of the universe. Gods, this is hot.

His hands hand on my shoulders as he jerks me back to arm's length, "Shut up and get on that bike. We have a certification to complete and a competition to win."

My eyes grow wide, and I shove him again, ready to let him have the full force of my annoyance from what he does to me.

He puts a finger to my lips, "Shhh…yell at me later."

And then he slams my helmet on my head again. I stare at him for a moment, collecting my senses, and stomp on his foot. *Bastard.* He laughs and gets back on the dirt bike. I do up the helmet easily this time and get on the back of the bike. My mind swirls with what just happened and the way my body reacted. Did he enjoy it? I don't even want to know, because it will *never* happen again.

"All of house three to the center ring." The announcement rings around the arena.

We take off, and I hold on tight. Laying the side of my helmet against his back to block the wind. We stop suddenly in front of the weapons. I think for a minute and grab four daggers, a quiver, three arrows, and a bow. "Aren't you only supposed to take one?" Xavier asks.

"They never said anything about one. Just that we had to choose." I smirk at him.

Xavier nods with a grin, biting his lip as he stares at me. I jump back on the bike, winding my hands around his front and enjoying the shiver he lets out as I do.

"House three, are you ready?" Professor Mantel asks.

We all look at each other—Kenzo and Fallon on a four-wheeler and Dylan and Abigail on another dirt bike. Fallon shoots me a thumbs-up with a massive smile before shoving her helmet on. I confidently flip my visor down because at least for now, Xavier has me. We all nod to Professor Mantel. "If you all have the best time for collective team time, you win a day at the lake. Individual partner times will be calculated, and the best three teams will be taken to the forest lakes for the entire weekend. On your mark. Get set. GO!"

Xavier accelerates at the speed of light. My body flying backwards as he does, gripping his leathers I bring my front to his back. Dirt and stones whip by as he maneuvers over the path. Dust explodes around us in a red and tan cloud. He starts up a hill, and the view at the top is breathtaking.

The mountains have barely any snow left on top of them, and the forest surrounding them is dark green. The lake is a beautiful blue in the morning sunlight. I can't take my eyes off it as we go down the hill and head up another with a bend in it. X taps my leg and points to our right. A dummy pops up from behind a stone.

"Now, Nye!" he yells.

I slowly unlatch my fingers and move my hands around to his back and up to his shoulder. Tightening my thighs and sinking my feet into the pegs, I stand slowly. My stomach muscles quiver at the strain I am putting on them. I calm my breathing one deep breath at a time. I slip slightly, and my hands land on Xavier's shoulders before I stand up again. *You've got this, Nyathera. You are strong and fierce.*

I feel a hand slither up between my legs and a warm arm wrap around my thigh. I glance down and notice Xavier has a firm grip on my leg. I tap his hand in appreciation. I let out a deep breath and calm my racing heart. He nods without looking up at me. Tightening my core as we turn towards the dummy. Leaning slightly, I grab a dagger and propel it towards the target. It lands straight into the dummy's head.

"Yes!!!" Xavier yells.

I smile and try to move back to my seat, but his grip tightens as I see the next dummy appear around the bend. "I am going to lean into your turn. Do you promise not to kill me?" I yell over the dirt bike.

"I've got you, Nye!" he says.

He rubs small circles on the side of my thigh where his thumb sits. I know it is meant to be comforting, but it has other parts of my body reacting. My breathing starts to speed up, but not with panic. I shove any feeling of arousal deep down. *Head. Out. Of. Gutter*. I remind myself. Not the time.

I shake my head slightly and start leaning. His grip gets tighter again, and he starts turning the dirt bike. I grab the bow and fumble to knock an arrow. Once I get the arrow on the bow, I lean further so I can see the dummy just around the stone wall, lining it up and taking a deep breath—I pull the arrow back and let it go. The arrow sinks deep into the chest, right where the heart would be. I throw my arms up and Xavier is laughing as he heads for the final turn.

Two dummies pop out simultaneously, arrows flying through the air towards us. I manage to dodge them as Xavier holds onto my leg even tighter. The dirt bike bobbing side to side as Xavier tries to keep us upright. My breath hitches, and my heart explodes. Why the fuck would arrows be shot at us in a training exercise? Xavier steadies the bike quickly, and I grab two daggers and throw them in opposite directions, hitting each square in the chest. Xavier and I laugh as he rounds the corner to the finish line.

All the houses watch as we come around—my leg still firmly held over his shoulder. He slows and helps me move my foot back to the peg. Everyone is silent as Professor Mantel brings up the replay of our 'kills'. Everyone gasps, claps, and hoots and hollers as soon as the last replay is on the fire screen.

"That was extremely impressive, you two." Professor Mantel says. The look of disgust on his face.

I hold my breath waiting for him to continue. Xavier instinctually holds my knee as we wait. I look down at his arm and butterflies erupt in my core. Looking back up, I catch a large guy from house one staring. Anger in his eyes.

"That was also the fastest time, coming in at less than four minutes to complete the course. And you have taken out every threat." Professor Mantels words are spoken quickly, his eyes dart to Xavier and back to everyone else.

Everyone claps in the stands, except that guy. Something is eerily familiar about him. Xavier jumps off the dirt bike and takes off his helmet. His smile is full of beautiful white teeth and excitement. He holds out his hand and helps me down, my feet hit the dirt and I look up at Xavier. His slow wide smile has my cheeks darkening. The sound of a dirt biked engine snaps my attention back to reality. Dylan and Abbi come around the final corner, each with an arm held high.

Chapter

I I

The streets were paved with dark cobblestones, and the air was thick with an unsettling silence. As the children stepped inside, they felt a chill run down their spines.

I take off my helmet and make my way towards them. Fallon and Kenzo round the corner just as I get to Abigail. Her large brown eyes swimming with excitement. Dylan takes off his helmet and I am met with a massive grin that tells me he enjoyed himself. Fallon hops over to us, smiling and squealing and Kenzo almost mimics her with his own excitement.

"With a total time of ten minutes and thirty-five seconds, house three is in the lead!" Professor Mantel says.

Fallon and Abbi hug me, and we jump up and down. "Oh, my gods! Nye, that was awesome! I saw it all from behind, and that ass of yours" She moves her eyes over my shoulder and meets my gaze again, "is exquisite in those leathers" she smiles, and I hug her again, laughing with excitement.

"You did great," Xavier says with a small smile and taps my shoulder.

"You as well. Thank you." I smile widely, seeing him in a different light. Maybe he isn't as bad as I thought he was. Maybe Abbi is right, he isn't such a bad guy.

"Anytime, little one," he says, bumping my chin with his finger, "you're stronger than you think."

He walks off, and I watch him head towards Dylan and Kenzo. I smile at the ground and notice Fallon and Abbi staring. "What?"

"Nothing," they say in unison. The smile on their faces tells me it is definitely not nothing.

We wait for the other houses to finish. A few hours later we are all waiting for the results. "Coming in, in third place is house two! No chores for a week!" They all whoop and laugh. Professor Mantel continues, "Second place is…House one! No chores for a week, and a special meal of each of your choosing!"

They all high five and holler, except for grumpy. Who is *definitely* staring at me. He isn't even hiding it. His face is lowered and death flashes through his large eyes. Eyes I have seen before but can't recall where.

I jump as Professor Mantel speaks again. "The winners for the collective house prize is…." He pauses looking around, building suspense in all of us. I hold Fallon's hand. "…House three with a time of only ten minutes and thirty-five seconds!"

We all jump up and down. I hug everyone and then stand in front of Xavier—I stick out my hand, tingles running down my spine. "Good job partner." I smile. My stomach flips as nerves wrack my body.

He looks at my hand and then throws his arms around me, "right back at you little one." His deep voice vibrates trough his chest, where my head lies. He pushes me back, gripping my shoulders. He has the hint of a smile on his face. He clears his throat and lets go.

Professor Mantel speaks, "The winners for the partner competition, with not only the fastest time but the most dummies and the most advanced skills goes to…Xavier Nortick and Nyathera Nighting!"

I look at X and we stare at each other for a long moment.

"You two have won a weekend away in the forest lakes along with everyone else on your team." We break our staring contest and look at Professor Mantel, "You all had the best partner times as well as the best House time."

I smile at everyone. "We did it!"

Xavier stops me as soon as everything dies down and we collect our weapons and take care of the vehicles. "We need to talk" I look at him in confusion. "Please" he says.

I nod my head, studying his face. His eyes hold something that looks like guilt or anger, maybe both. I continue walking and notice he hasn't left my side. He keeps looking around like he is watching for something.

"Can I help you with something?" I ask.

He looks at me before quickly looking around. "I will tell you later, for right now let me hang around, protect you." I look around and can feel the panic rising.

"Protect me from what?!" I all but yell.

He clasps his hand over my mouth, "*Shh*! I will tell you later." He bites out—anger in his voice. I nod in agreement, and he drops his hand.

"I don't need a guard dog." I bite out with just as much attitude.

He looks at me and shakes his head. "You do. You will. And you will deal with it. There are people who want your head Nyathera."

I open my mouth to say something just as Professor Mantel comes around the corner. Xavier puts his hand on my lower back and pushes me towards a boulder, hiding us.

"You were supposed to take her out!" he whispers to someone else.

A male voice replies, "They were too fast. She has skills that I wasn't aware of, and I will need someone to help me."

"You said you were capable of handling it alone, I will find someone to assist you, but I want her taken out by the end of the month or your mother dies." His footsteps retreat, and the other male sighs.

His boots tap against the stone as he rounds the boulder. Moments before he sees us, Xavier shoves me against the boulder and kisses me hard. Xavier is kissing me for the third time today as if his life depends on it. He pushes my head back with his, and it feels like he is trying to break through my skull. I try to push him away as I catch a small glimpse of the guy from house one.

He's staring at Xavier and clears his throat. Xavier turns but pushes me behind him and into the crack between the boulder and the stone wall of the corridor.

"Who do you have back there, Xavier?" the guy says.

"No one of your concern, Micheal Malik." X bites.

Malik...that is a familiar name. I think about it and remember Matthews's last name. Malik is Matthew's last name! Micheal is Matthew's little brother. The eyes! He has Matthew's eyes. I try to push my way out, to apologize to Micheal, but Xavier leans harder.

"Have you seen Nyathera?" Micheal asks. "I want to congratulate her on the win today."

Xavier stares at Micheal, "No. I don't keep tabs on her." His voice picking up a tone of anger, "Just like everyone else, I am using the little bitch to survive." My stomach turns and fury bubbles in my chest.

"The way your hand rested on her knee while Professor Mantel spoke, I would say you do. Or you don't want people to know you do." He steps towards Xavier, who doesn't say a word. "I advise you let me carry out my plans, Nortick."

I watch Xavier's shoulders widen as he stands taller. Micheal puts his hands up, palms out, and steps back before spinning on his heels and walking away. "I'll find her, Xavier, and when I do, I'll make sure she knows how you feel about her." Micheal's laughter fills the corridor. Once Micheal's boots are barely a whisper, Xavier steps forward. I stare at him.

He puts a hand on my shoulder and sighs. "I told you that we would speak later, and we will. But right now, I have to go see my father." He turns to walk away, and I grab his hand.

"What the fuck was that about?" He smiles and turns, but I don't let go. "Xavier! Tell me now! You're using me for what?!"

He sighs, pinching the bridge of his nose, "I am not using you, he wants you dead, like I said before. Now I need to speak with my father about something, you will stay with the others."

Anger fills my being and all I want to do is punch him in his smug face, instead I ask, "Can you please walk me to where Fallon and the others are waiting? I don't want to walk alone."

I search his eyes and plead for him to say yes. He nods and starts walking forward. I follow him, not saying a word. But I keep looking over my shoulder.

Professor Mantel is plotting to have me killed. Xavier knew about it. Matthew's brother is supposed to take me out. Professor Mantel is threatening Micheal's— *Matthew's*, mother. And I am just, what? What does any of this have to do with me? I sigh and continue following Xavier to where the others are.

Chapter

12

The shadows whispered secrets, swirling around them, beckoning them to explore. But as they wandered, they soon realized they were not alone.

We catch up to Fallon, Dylan, and Abigail. Xavier walks over to Dylan and puts his hand on his arm, whispering something in his ear. Dylan nods and glances my way. Xavier walks back to me with Dylan at his side, "I am going to speak with my dad. Do not leave Dylan's side."

I scrunch my nose at him, "Are you telling me what to do still?"

"You need to stay by Dylan at all times until I am back. I have to talk to my dad. We have stuff to figure out. So, I, we, can keep you safe."

My hands fist and relax, I start to protest, and Dylan interrupts me, "We can go back to the house and watch a movie or something, Nye. It won't be bad, I promise."

The way he looks at me is terrifying. The pity in his eyes makes me uneasy and I don't have any way to change my situation, because I am pretty sure the only place I am safe is with them.

For the millionth time today, I sigh, "Okay…"

"You're just going to let them control you like that?" Fallon crosses her arms and stares at me. Her blonde hair falling around her face from the wind. She is the epitome of beauty.

"I don't exactly know what's going on, Fallon. We will discuss it as soon as we return to the house." She looks at me disapprovingly.

"We are going to a party." Abigail says, "Maybe you can come with us."

I look at Xavier, "only if Dylan goes with you."

I look at Dylan and pout, "Please, let's go dance, Dylan."

He sighs and rolls his eyes, "I'm not dancing."

I clap, "Yes, you are a big guy."

We all laugh, except Xavier. He grabs my elbow and pulls me to the side. "Please be careful—if anyone is going to kill you, it is going to be me." He leans down and kisses my cheek.

I pull away from him and stare, "Why did you do that?"

He smiles heartbreakingly, "So you know I won't let someone else hurt you."

"How reassuring, X" I roll my eyes and walk away. What an asshole.

If I am going to die, I am going to enjoy my time while I can. I never let fear stop me before, and there is no sense in doing so now. I wrap my arm around Fallon's, and we walk to the house.

"What is going on, Nye?" she whispers.

"I will tell you when we are getting ready, and I am sure X and Dylan are overexaggerating. It is just another day of being Nyathera Nighting." I throw her a smirk.

"I'm not sure about that. If the man who loathes you is trying to protect you, then it is definitely something crazy." Her eyes look at me with worry.

"Seriously, Fallon, don't make me keep it from you. I will be fine, I promise." She nods, and we continue to the house.

Once we get there, we head to our rooms to get ready, "Hey Nye, I don't want to know what's happening. I can't stop worrying once I start, so I will support you however I can." I nod at her and open my door.

Before I can shut it, a large hand wraps around the door frame. "I am coming in, Nye," Dylan says through the door.

"Are you kidding me? I am just getting dressed in a warded house." He walks through the door and looks straight into my soul.

"I promised not to take my eyes off you. I intend to keep that promise." The look on his face says he won't budge on this.

"I have to get changed."

He waves a hand at me, walks to the corner where he props a boot on the wall, and crosses his arms over his chest. I blow a stray hair out of my face.

Alright, we do this the hard way then. I stand in the middle of the room with my back to him, unzipping my top. I start to let it fall when a solid warm hand falls on my shoulder.

Dylan frowns, "Go in the bathroom and change." He folds his arms and stalks back to the corner.

I look through my clothing, realizing I didn't bring anything for dancing. Didn't really think it would be a necessity, but here we are. "Dylan, can you grab me one of your Mearin shirts?"

He stares at me with confusion dancing across his face, "Why?"

"I don't have anything to wear, and I figured I could borrow something long enough to at least cover my ass." I lift a brow at him.

He looks down my body briefly, "Stay here."

He walks to the door and stops before exiting. "You know I only want what is best for you, Nye. We haven't been here long, and already there is trouble. I am honored to be able to protect you." He looks down and walks out.

My heart skips a beat as guilt rises in my chest. I am giving him a hard time, when all he is doing is following orders. Trying to ensure that I make it to graduation day. Xavier is doing it because he sees me as weak, but Dylan, Dylan is doing it because he is a loyal friend and a soldier through and through.

I stand in front of the floor-length mirror and examine myself, turning ever so slightly to see my back— the scars that crawl across my shoulder blades are a brutal reminder of why I have to keep myself safe. I shake my head just as Dylan comes back through the door.

I throw my jacket back over my shoulders and turn to him. He smiles gently and hands me his shirt. "I didn't have a clean one, but I found the one that doesn't stink." I laugh at the embarrassment on his cheeks.

"Well, it doesn't smell as gods awful as the others," he blushes.

"Oh, how *gentlemanly* of you." I say smirking. He laughs and runs a hand over his head.

"I'm sorry this is how things are right now Nye. But they will get better, and we must keep you safe in the meantime."

I nod, "I know Dylan. And if someone has to babysit me, I am glad it is you."

He steps closer and takes my left hand. "I know. And I am not trying to make you feel like you are weak or can't protect yourself. My job isn't to dull your shine. It is to help you shine brighter. Your strength will only grow if you allow someone to help you."

I suck in a breath, "you're right."

He drops my hand with a little smile, "Get dressed. You have a night of fun with the girls."

He steps back and turns to go to his corner, "with all my friends…you included."

He throws a smile over his shoulder and props himself on the wall again. "I'm an honorary girl tonight."

I laugh at that and hurry to the bathroom and undress. I throw the shirt over my head, and it smells like birchwood, clean and masculine. The shirt swallows my body, so I tie the back with an elastic, so it is a little more form-fitting. I go into my closet and throw on one of the brown leather jackets that we use for training and a little lip stain. I mess my hair up a bit and head out to see if Dylan needs to get ready. When I return to my room, he is entirely in his browns and ready to go. "How did you change so quickly?"

He laughs, "When a woman takes an hour to get ready, it's fairly easy to be ready when she emerges." He smiles at me. "Are you ready to go?" He looks me up and down. "You look good."

I look down at the shirt that hits mid-thigh, I laugh at him, "Thanks, Dylan". Let's go make bad decisions!" I shimmy my hips biting my bottom lip, he starts to say something, "safely." I finish before he can reprimand me.

He nods and smiles, looping an arm over my shoulders, "You are going to be a joy to babysit." I glare up at him, and that grants me a full-blown laugh from him, "I am kidding!" he squeezes me gently. "You're babysitting me." He winks.

I laugh and slap his chest playfully, "alright big guy, let's go have fun."

Chapter

13

Dark figures loomed in the corners of their vision—creepy, shadowy creatures with glowing eyes that watched their every move.

We grab Fallon and Abbigail and head to the house party. "I am so ready to find a man or woman or both and get in their pants," Fallon says, examining herself in the little mirror she pulled from her purse.

"I just need to dance and forget about what is going on back home" Abigail has the saddest look on her face. I grab her hand and squeeze, giving her a reassuring smile. Dylan walks behind us like a stalker, and my heart feels light, knowing he is willing to risk his life for mine. And *not* because he has a hidden agenda.

I grab Fallon's elbow and jerk her to the side. She looks at me with disgust and I show her that she almost stepped in one of the potholes.

"Wow, thanks, Nye." She says. "I would have broken an ankle." She giggles.

"We are all here to protect each other, remember?" I grin at her.

She looks back at the hole, "right." She smiles and looks back at Dylan. I turn and look as well as we keep walking. He nods and doesn't say anything.

"Why did X have him follow us?" Abbi whines.

"I will tell you guys when I know more. Fallon doesn't want to know, but if something sketchy is going on, I want to tell you both. But I need all the information before I do so." I give her a fake smile.

I don't want to bring anyone down with me. None of them deserve it. It is her turn to grab my hand and squeeze. I smile at her the best I can. We continue walking, and every now and then, I glance back at Dylan. He has a stone-cold look on his face every time a man walks by us. I shoot him a smile and then see the building come into view.

We make it to the front entrance and the smell of alcohol and sweat meets my nose. People are filing through the door like a snake, and the bass is thrumming through my body. Step by little step we make it inside and head up the stairs.

"Let's find a spot on the balcony!" Fallon yells over the music, I nod.

Turning to make sure Dylan is still following us. He gives me a little nod and a smirk, I reach back and grab his hand, dragging him with us. His thumb rubbing reassuring circles on the back of my hand. Once we find a spot I survey the party down below. The music isn't as loud up here, and it's a little less cramped.

I tap Fallon on the arm, "there are trainers here.!"

She smiles, "It's the trainers house, Nye! They throw a party yearly to welcome the trainees and weed out those who can't handle pressure."

"Pressure? From what?" I ask.

As if on que, a beautiful brunette with cherry red lips holds a tray containing different drugs. I look it over and then look at Dylan, he shakes his head, and I pass.

"That" says Fallon. I make an 'oh' gesture with my mouth and start to sway my hips.

We go to the bottom floor to dance on the dance floor. I grab Dylan after my fifth shot of…something. "Come on big guy! Dance with me!"

He looks at me, "I can't you know I have a job to do!"

"Do it while dancing!" I shout back. Eagerness and happiness lace through my body. "*Pleeeeeease* Dylan." I pout.

He shakes his head and rolls his eyes, "fine, you win." I slap on a massive smile and grab his hands. Dragging him to the dance floor I let the alcohol wash over my senses. My body feels at ease and carefree. I dance along to the music, turning to grind against Dylan. His broad hands spread on my hips as he sways with me. Reaching my hands up I snake them around his neck and lull my head to the side. I let out laughter as we continue to dance to the upbeat music.

A man steps up next to us and I drag my head to face him. "Can I cut in?" he asks Dylan.

Dylan puts himself between me and the man. He's the trainer from the first day. His long black hair frames his face, and the lights make him look ethereal.

My body hums, seeing him stand there; I push around Dylan and grab the mystery trainer's hand. "I'm Nyathera!" I lazily yell over the music.

The lights have grown brighter, and my body is humming like white noise.

He spins me, "I'm Beckham." He replies with a smile.

Dylan tries to cut in, "I am fine big guy! Go find Fallon and Abbi."

"I can't leave you." Worry etches across his brow.

I gesture with my hand to Beckham, "he's a trainer. He isn't going to let anything happen to me!" All my common sense thrown out the window at the sight of a handsome man and a body full of liquor.

Dylan glares at me, "Xavier isn't going to like this." And he strides off.

"Is Xavier your boyfriend?" Beckham asks in my ear. His breath dancing across my cheek.

I laugh, "Gods no. We're like lava and ice. We can't stand each other."

"Ahhh…that's good to know." I can feel his mouth next to my ear and the smile on his lips. He grabs something as the waitress walks by and holds it to my mouth.

"Oh, no! I don't partake." I say, holding my hand over my mouth.

He gets a little pushier, "This will only relax you." He says with a smile. I look at him and then the candy in his hand. "Trust me." His words travel along the space between us and soak into my skull.

"Okay," I say, opening my mouth. He sticks the candy on my tongue, and I slowly drag it back into my mouth.

He smiles and we continue dancing. The room spins and the lights fly by me. I feel like I am floating. My heart is racing, and the sweat is beading on the back of my neck. Beckham pulls me close, pushing my hair over my shoulder, and kisses my neck. I lose my footing, and he catches me.

"We should get you out of here." He says with a grin.

Everything in my body says I shouldn't. Panic rolls in my chest, and I try to scream as he grabs me and guides me towards the door. "The savior will be so happy to see you." he whispers in my ear. My eyes widen as fear grips my chest, stealing the air from my lung. He grips my arm, pinching the skin beneath his fingers. My arms are too heavy to swing at him, and nausea is rolling in my stomach. When we reach the door a blur appears, and Beckham's arms release me with a brutal force.

In the distance, I can hear someone, Fallon, "Nye. Are you ok?"

My head is swimming with fear, and I can't pinpoint where the noises are coming from.

"Nye! Answer me, please." I see Fallon's face in the cloud of bright lights.

Before The world fades to black, strong arms wrap around my back and under my legs. My feet leave the ground, and I am weightless. My head drops back, and the world fades to nothingness.

Chapter

14

The Nightmares, they realized, were real!

******

My eyes flutter open to a dark room illuminated only by a candle sitting on a desk in the corner. Hushed voices sound like they are miles away. Echoing off the inside of my skull. "She could've been killed, Dylan!"

"But she wasn't."

"That's not the point! Someone drugged her with some sort of magic!" I can hear the anger in Xavier's voice.

"I know! And I feel horrible. She insisted she would be safe with him. I'm sorry!"

I croak. My throat is dry and my voice hoarse. "Can you shut up, please? My head is pounding."

Xavier rushes to my side, "are you okay? Did he hurt you? Besides drugging you, I mean."

I shake my head and try to sit up. My limbs still feel heavy, and they drag along the sheets. Xavier sits me up and moves the pillows behind my back, so I am leaning against the headboard.

"Where am I?" I ask. The room is all black with accents of emerald greens.

"You're in my room. You've been out for three days. We told the trainers you had the flu and weren't able to make it to classes." I look at him and his face comes into view.

I look towards the door and Dylan is standing there with his hands in his pockets. I give him a weak smile, "Hey big guy."

He gives me a little smile in return, and I can't help but see the guilt all over his face.

"This was my fault, X. I sent Dylan away because I thought I was safe."

Xavier looks over his shoulder at Dylan and then back to me, "I know. But you could've died. Or worse."

"Since when do you care if I live or die?" I ask him, seeping into my chest.

"Remember, I told you the only one who gets to kill you is me, little one." He taps his curled forefinger to my chin. "Get some rest. We are right here. You'll be safe."

I grin and nod, "Okay."

I slink down on the bed and roll to my side; Xavier has laid next to me and I bury my nose in his side. He jumps a little but doesn't move. He is so warm, and a slight electrical buzz shoots through my body. Before I know it the world fades away again.

The room is dark except for a small flickering candle on the nightstand. Dylan is sitting in a chair next to the bed; his head in his elbow, sleeping peacefully. The candlelight dances on his strong features, and I smile and run my hand over his buzzed hair. It is surprisingly soft. He startles, sitting up.

He smiles widely, "Let me get everyone," as he starts to move.

I grab his hand, and he stops abruptly, looking at me with confusion.

"I don't blame you, Dylan. It was my own stupidity that got me into this mess. And it was *you* that saved me." I smile at him; he stares at me.

"I was given a job; it was my duty to ensure you were safe, and I left you alone with someone you didn't know."

I squeeze his hand a little, "Now we know that I can't be left unsupervised."

He grins, "I guess you really do need a babysitter, huh?"

"And a guard dog," I add.

I smile and pat the bed next to me. "Everyone is sleeping. We can talk to them in the morning. You look like you need some sleep."

He hesitates, and I beg, "Please. For me. Rest."

He nods and lays down on his back, he puts his hands behind his head, and I lay my head on his chest. He inhales sharply, and he slowly moves an arm down and wraps it around my shoulders. I lift myself to my elbow and kiss his cheek, "thank you." I whisper.

He stiffens and watches me lay my head back down. "You know that I had to drag Xavier from your bedside and force him to go sleep in my room."

I look up at him, "you did?"

"Yeah, I have never seen someone worry so much. You have been in and out of sleep for over five days now. We have all been worried." He takes a deep breath, "X brought in some healers who work for his dad, and they have never seen anything like it. X has been in here everyday checking on you, washing your face, doting over everything to ensure you are clean, healthy, and survive. I don't think he hates you as much as he lets on, Nye." I am dumbfounded.

"Five days?"

He nods his head. "Xavier hasn't left your side without being dragged away."

I look up at him, "I guess we are all becoming friends."

I smile at him and nestle into his chest. He lets out a hum. I relish in his heat against my cool skin. And listen to his breathing. Slowly, it evens out, and his breaths become deeper. When I know he is asleep I lean over and blow out the candle, cuddling back into the hollow of his shoulder, inhaling his scent and let myself lull back into sleep.

Chapter

15

These creatures thrived on fear and mischief and began to creep closer, their laughter echoing in the air. "Come play with us!" one of the Nightmares taunted, its voice like a cold breeze. "We'll show you the city's wonders if you promise to stay forever!"

When I wake up, Dylan is gone. My body screams in protest when I pull back the blankets. Every muscle in my body feels like the fibers are being separated individually. The invasion of the cold is shocking, and my breath hitches. I grab one of the million blankets piled on top of me and wrap it around my shoulders. I stand, and the room spins. Taking a deep breath in, I center myself, and the room slowly comes into sight. I roll my neck and shoulders and pad across the stone floor to the door. It is eerily quiet in the house. No talking, no laughter, no bickering.

I make my way to the end of the hall and hear a guitar…and the most beautiful voice I have ever heard follows. A man is somewhere in the house singing about heartache and roses and the guitar is keeping perfect tune with it. I wander through the house until I come to a door, one I haven't noticed before. Opening it, a cold rush of air blows my hair back, taking the breath from my chest. The voice gets louder. I walk through the twists and turns of the cave, shivering with every cold step, and finally see an opening. It's the mouth of a cave overlooking the mountains.

The light is blinding, and the wind is ripping through it. My legs are wobbly and my body aches as I stand in the opening. Once my eyes adjust, Xavier comes into view, one leg dangling off the side of the cliff and the other bent, holding the guitar. Slow melodies are played intricately, as his fingers easily move over the strings. I stay quiet, slowing my breathing so he doesn't notice me. I walk toward him, looking for the person who was singing. And then he opens his mouth. The melancholy lyrics drifting to my ears and sinking into my soul. Every word is like a soft kiss to my brain and a lightning bolt to my heart. Tears fill my eyes, and butterflies erupt in my stomach. He continues singing, and I think the veil of hatred that I have held in my chest lifts a little more. My mind and body is drawn to his song like a moth to a flame.

I watch his fingers work over the chords with breathtaking precision and he closes his eyes with the words that cut deep. The sun bounces off his strong features, creating a halo around him. I listen until the end of the song. He lays the guitar next to him and stares out over the mountain range. I admire the contour of his nose and the freckles that trace over it. His jaw is strong and a muscle ticks in it as he looks to the sky. His red hair has become a mess on his head, and the bags under his eyes are as dark blue as the ocean itself. I slowly walk towards him, and he turns to stand.

"What the hell are you doing here?" he says, jumping.

"Wow, no 'hi how are you feeling?" Annoyance, the main emotion I feel when I am around Xavier Nortick.

"It is too cold out here for you. We need to get you inside."

"I'm fine, Xavier. I promise." I say. He studies me for a moment, a crease forming in his brow. "You're amazing," I blurt, rushing to change the subject. "At playing and singing…I mean." He smirks and then his face turns to stone.

"You have been sleeping for almost nine days, Nye." My heart sinks. Bile rises in the back of my throat, and the earth spins on its axis a little too quickly.

He looks me up and down, "You look sickly."

I gawk at him, "Seriously?"

He shakes his head and lets out a beautiful laugh. "I didn't mean it like that, Nye. Let's get you back inside."

He slings his guitar over his shoulder and walks towards me. "How are you feeling?" he asks with odd concern lacing his voice.

I stare up at him not knowing how to feel about the question coming from *his* mouth. The look in his eyes tells me he isn't being malicious but that he genuinely cares about how I am feeling.

"I'm ok. I swear." His shoulders relax, and he nods. He starts to walk, and I wrap my hand around his elbow before he gets too far.

He stops, turning to look at me, "do you need help?"

I nod at him. He wraps his arm over my shoulders and around my waist. I wrap my hand around his waist and lay my head on his side. We walk back to the house in silence. Once we walk through that door, I half expect everyone to be standing there. But the house is quiet; not a soul remains in this house besides Xavier and me.

"Where is everyone?" I ask, looking up from the couch where he instructed me to sit.

"They are on the weekend that we won."

"Why aren't you with them? You know a healer would have come and stayed with me." He walks back from the kitchen with a cup of water and hands it to me.

"I don't trust anyone with your safety besides me…"

"And Dylan," I interrupt.

"And Dylan," he nods. "So, I told my father I came down with something as well, and no one questioned it when the general said his son was sick."

I can't help but stare. For a man who hates my entire being and is a sexist pig, he really is beautiful. Inside and out. One of the most beautiful men I have ever seen. We stare at each other for a moment. I feel my cheeks blazing as he looks over my entire face. He breaks eye contact first and opens the blanket that I have wrapped around me, and I try to close the blanket to shield myself from the cold and from the burning of his eyes on me.

"I am just seeing if there are any marks. We had to smuggle special magic in to fix you."

I gasp, "What kind of magic?" He shrugs.

He looks over my body, and the way he caresses my hands and sides, looking for any damage, has me gasping for an entirely different reason. He smiles up at me quickly. My stomach doing somersaults. "You look fine. Just some dark bags under your eyes and that mark traveling up your neck. The healers said it was normal after that type of magic."

"What mark?" I ask slowly.

"You didn't see it? Did you not look in the mirror?"

Rolling my lip in my teeth, I shake my head. I get to my feet and run to my bathroom; there on my neck is a deep red mark traveling in mesmerizing swirls. It resembles a vine of thorns, and lilies. The deep red contrasting my pale skin. Starting under my left ear and traveling down under my shirt; I lift my shirt over my head and notice it goes all the way down my abdomen, wrapping around me like an embrace. I run my fingers over it when I hear a soft knock on the door, and Xavier peaks around it. I am standing in nothing but a bra and underwear. His eyes widen when he sees the mark. My skin heats at the way his eyes roam over my body. "I…I didn't know it was that big, and I didn't know that the magic would do that. I was just desperate because you weren't waking up."

I meet his gaze in the mirror, "It's okay, X."

"It is?" he says.

"Well, no, but you saved my life. I have never had anyone save me before." His throat bobs, and he walks forward.

He reaches a hand towards me slowly and drops it to his side. I just nod at him holding his gaze in the reflection. He slowly reaches up and brushes my hair to the side. He runs a finger along the mark, starting at the base of my ear and following its path down my neck, between my breasts, and across my torso. He looks back at my reflection in the mirror.

"It's…beautiful, Nye." He says breathlessly.

I giggle, "It is horrid."

He shakes his head, "Not on you, it's not."

My eyes widen and I just stare at his reflection. He clears his throat and looks away. Walking to the large tub in the corner, he turns the water on. I watch him as he adjusts it to what I assume is a satisfactory temperature. He throws some salts and bubbles in the water. He walks back to me, gesturing to the tub, "Take a bath, Nye. The salts will help with the pinching in your muscles, and you need a cleaning." He smiles.

I walk towards the tub, and he starts for the door. "Stay," I say. Stopping him abruptly.

"What?" His voice a whisper.

"Please. Stay with me. I don't want to be alone."

He inhales and coughs. "Are you sure?"

"Yes, the water will be deep enough that you won't see anything, and even if you did, it isn't like you haven't before." I smirk, remembering the way he gawked at me when he busted into my bathroom. I chuckle at the face he makes. Full of something I can't quite read mixed with amusement.

"Okay." He says and turns around towards the door. I undress and slink into the water. The warmth rushes over me like another blanket. I moan at the release of my muscles and the smell of lavender. Xavier clears his throat.

"I'm in," I say.

He turns around, and his cheeks are red. He takes a step forward and then a step back. I pat the stone on the side of the tub.

"I won't bite," I say with a smile.

He hums and turns the lights off so only the white candles light the room and walks over, perching on the side of the tub.

He grabs the loofa and some soap. "Lean forward." He says.

I do as I am told, and he washes my back ever so gently. He moves my hair to the side and washes around my neck.

"What are these marks on your back?" he asks, tracing a finger over the long, deep scars.

"A reminder of where I stand in this world." I say slowly. Pushing the memory deep. The images flash through my mind of that horrid day. Sadness sits heavy in my chest for the young girl who had to endure such horrors. He nods and doesn't say another word. Which I am grateful for.

I look over my shoulder at him, "You don't have to do that." My heart flutters when his hand brushes the mark on my neck. He holds my shoulder.

"I want to. Tip your head back." I do as he says.

I haven't had anyone help me bathe in years. He pours the warm water over my hair. The warmth spreads through my body as the water saturates my hair and cascades down my back.

"Your hair is stunning. I have never seen such a color on a young woman before." I smile and he works the soap into my hair. He scratches and massages my scalp.

My lips part, and a small appreciative moan escapes. His hands still for a moment, and then he continues. He rinses my hair slowly, making sure all the soap is out. As the water runs over it, he moves his fingers through the strands. A shudder runs through my body at the feeling of the slight tugs, and my chest explodes with appreciation. A little more of that veil of hatred begins to lift.

I remember his fingers on the guitar strings and how expertly they moved. I find myself wondering what they would feel like on my breasts, between my thighs. He clears his throat, and I open one eye to look at him. I feel my cheeks reddening. He smiles at me and moves a stray hair that falls into my face. He gently moves his fingers over my cheek and around my jaw.

"You are beautiful, Nye." He says, his eyes bouncing from my eyes to my mouth.

My lips part slightly, and my heart races. My breath quickens as I anticipate what comes next. He leans closer, "I am going to kiss you for real this time, Nyathera."

I nod breathlessly. "Okay." He smiles and puts his lips to mine.

This time he moves slowly. No rushed movements like before. He is exploring my lips with his like he is marking every crevice in them. His tongue prods my lips, and I open for him. His tongue glides over mine in hot circles that take my breath away. He moves his hand to the back of my neck and tilts my head up slightly to deepen the kiss. My soul explodes.

I reach up and run my hands on his jaw, the stubble there scratching my fingers. He stands and looks down at me. Peering up at him through my lashes, a rumbles sounds in his chest. I nod at him and move forward more. He quickly undresses. I let my eyes wander over his body, the cords of muscle in his pecs and biceps, and every dip of his abs. The bulge in his boxer briefs is impressive. I lick my lips, wanting to taste him, and he smiles.

"Like what you see?" He asks on a whisper with a smile that is so seductive I almost combust. He pulls his boxers down, and his erection springs to life. It is massive. I don't know if I can fit it all. I look at it and then at him. "You'll be okay, Nye. It doesn't bite." He lowers himself in the water behind me, "but I do."

He nips where my shoulder meets my neck. I let out a little yelp as his arms snake around my waist and up to my breasts. I lean my head to the side, and he kisses the mark. Every glide of his tongue against the mark sends electrical waves through my body. He rolls my nipples between his fingertips as he sucks on the sensitive spot right below my ear.

"Xavier." I sigh.

"Tell me what you need, little one." I let my legs fall apart and he chuckles.

"Use your words."

"I need you. Inside me. Now." I say, voice laced with arousal.

He slowly moves his hand down my abdomen to that little sensitive nub. But he doesn't move. "Please," I say, bucking my hips to meet his hand.

In an instant, he is standing and ripping me from the tub. "If we are going to do this, we will do it right." He says, throwing a towel around me and picking me up.

I wrap my legs around his waist as he slams his lips to mine again. A fervent type of kiss. Like I am the air he breathes. He carries us to the bed without so much as a slight separation in our lips. He lays me down on it, crawling over me, pushing his body between my legs. The feeling of his skin between my thighs has me rolling my hips. The slickness from the water chills the air, and my nipples tighten. His gaze drops to my breasts as he licks his lips. He peers back up at me and kisses me. Hot and fast. I wrap my arms around his neck, and his tongue darts into my mouth.

He kisses my neck and down my chest, stopping at each nipple to devour them. I could finish just with his mouth on me. His lips are like a match to the fire that is just beneath my skin. My back arches trying to get closer. I feel him smile against my skin as he kisses lower down my abdomen. He stops at my pubic bone and smiles up at me. A heart-breaking smile.

"You smell amazing, Nye," he says, pushing his nose into my skin.

And then his tongue is on me. Tracing my clit as if marking it to memory. I gasp, and my hips rock against his mouth. I lace my hands into his hair as my orgasm grows closer and closer. My core tightens, and the ecstasy creeps over my skin. He slides a finger inside of me, and I think I might explode. He adds another and moves them in the same rhythm as his tongue.

"Oh, my Gods, X." I moan breathlessly. He smiles. And continues. With one more flick of his tongue and pump of his fingers, I am falling over the edge. I moan his name, and he continues to move his fingers in and out of me as I ride out my orgasm.

He is watching me with so much lust in his eyes they have glazed over. When my orgasm settles, he crawls back over me. "That was one; let's see if we can get another."

I go to protest, and he kisses me. I taste myself and his mint toothpaste on my tongue. He moans into my mouth and stops.

"I took the serum months ago." He says. Looking at me with need.

"I did, too; we all had to when we saw the healers.." And with that, he pushes himself inside me inch by glorious inch. I whimper as he stretches me.

"You're doing such a good job. Almost there." He whispers.

His words sink into me like a caress. He looks between us where we meet. "Look how beautiful you look wrapped around me." I look down, and my eyes widen. He kisses me again and I relax into it. As soon as the tension leaves my body, he slowly moves in and out.

"You feel so good, Nye." He groans.

I can't even answer him. I am breathless. He continues to move in and out of me. I dig my nails into his shoulders, and he growls. Biting my neck with ferocity and then licking it to calm the pain. I moan in appreciation of how much he fills me. My core is tightening, and tingles start to spread up my spine.

We are both sweaty, moaning messes when I feel another orgasm. "Oh, my Gods, Xavier... Don't stop. Please," I moan.

He is grunting as he speeds up. Skin slapping against skin and moans are all that fill the room. Then I am falling. I scream his name as stars fill my vision. He keeps his rhythm as I ride out my orgasm, and then he follows me. His back stiffens, and he growls out my name. And it sounds beautiful on his lips like this. A few more hard pumps and he collapses on top of me. He lifts his head and kisses my nose and then my cheek. I turn my head to him and kiss him lazily.

"That was amazing," I whisper.

"I know." He states with a smug smile. I slap his arm, and he kisses me one more time before he gets up.

"Stay here," he instructs and heads into the bathroom. I can't say I don't admire his ass as he does. He comes back a minute later with a washcloth. "Spread your legs." He says.

I do as I am told and let my legs fall to the sides. He moves the rag up the insides of my thighs and then reaches my sensitive spot. I jump at the warmth of the rag as he cleans up our mess. He climbs up next to me, and I roll on my side to meet his gaze.

"I'm sorry." He says.

"For what?" I ask him.

"For not keeping you safe."

I kiss him again and stare into his eyes. Without saying a word, he nods in understanding. I kiss him again, harder this time, and he rolls me on top of me. I am naked, laying with my head on his chest as he draws lazy circles on my shoulder. My eyes drift close, and sleep pulls me into a wonderland.

Chapter

16

The children trembled, remembering the stories their parents had told them.

I wake to an empty bed and voices out in the living room. Throwing on a large shirt and wrapping my blanket around me, I head out my door and down the hall. I lean against the corner and watch everyone. Abbi is laughing with Kenzo and Fallon is dramatically telling Xavier about the hot springs. Dylan looks up and spots me first. His smile is wide, and his eyes dance with excitement. I smile back, not saying anything. He strides over and wraps me in a hug, spinning me around, "how are you feeling?" he asks.

"I feel better. How was the weekend away?!" I ask.

Xavier turns and smiles at me, Fallon follows his gaze, and her eyes meet mine. She instantly runs to me and hugs me. When she pulls back there are tears in her eyes.

She looks me up and down vigorously, "You're okay! Oh, my Gods! We didn't think that you would make it out of that alive, and if you did, we figured we'd come home to one of you dead." She laughs.

I smile at her. "We made a lot of progress over the last two days, believe it or not." I look to Xavier and smile.

She cocks her head, "oh? What kind of progress?" she says with a twinkle in her eye.

Before she can prod for more information Kenzo is sweeping me off my feet like he hasn't seen me in ages. "Nye! How you doing, darlin'?" He all but yells. The smile on his face lighting up the room.

I laugh as he puts me down, "I am ok. Really guys. You all did a great job nursing me back to health. I don't know how I am going to repay you."

"How about no more trying to die," Abbi says as she sweeps in for a hug of her own.

My chest clenches as I look at every single one of them. We have only known each other less than a year, but they are my family.

"I promise I won't try to die." I put my hand on my heart. "I am starving, though. What are we having for dinner?"

"How about beef stew?" Fallon asks as she and Abbi head towards the kitchen.

I watch them start to prepare. Kenzo puts a hand on my shoulder and smiles, "I really am happy you are okay, Nye. We were all terrified." He walks off, leaving Dylan and me. He smiles and turns.

"Dylan," I say softly. He turns around, "You are the best friend anyone could ask for. Seriously. If you weren't there that night…" I trail off and look at the ground. He lifts my chin with his finger, so I look him directly in the eye.

"You are the best person I have ever had to babysit." He smiles, "I will protect you with my life, Nyathera."

Those words make tears well in my eyes. I wrap my arms around his waist, and he hugs me resting his chin on my head. "Thank you for everything, Dylan."

"It's my pleasure." He lets go, and I walk towards the kitchen.

Stopping at Xavier, "Thank you for not killing me this weekend." His wicked grin says all I need to know.

"We aren't finished." He thumbs my cheek and smiles. He strides into the living room, where Kenzo and Dylan sit.

I look up and Fallon is staring into my soul. I walk over to her and pick up a knife to start cutting. "First of all, go sit over there and rest. We've got dinner tonight. Secondly…" she lowers her voice, dipping her head towards mine, "what is going on between you and X? That's not a look of pure hatred."

Abbi sweeps in on the other side of her, "They totally had sex."

I choke. "What?" They both giggle but then look at me pointedly.

I shake my head. "No!" I squeak out. "We just had time to speak to one another, that's all."

Fallon looks over to Abbi. "Mhmm."

"That's all," I repeat, popping a grape into my mouth so I can't answer. I guess I didn't realize how hungry I was, because I grab a handful more.

"Don't think we missed how he caressed your face." Abbi states.

"And the smiles they gave each other," Fallon adds looking at Abbi.

"I am not above asking him," Abbi says.

"Guys, seriously?" they nod. I sigh and look over my shoulder. Quietly, I say, "We might have had some other things to do while we were here. I won't go into detail because that's inappropriate, but it was a very nice weekend." I say with my cheeks reddening.

Abbi smiles, "I told you he would get you." I throw a grape at her, and we all laugh.

After dinner, we are all sitting on the couches. Something is off in the air like there is an electrical buzz surrounding me. "So, how was your weekend away?" I ask everyone. They all look at each other and back at me. "It's fine. I am sure we will have a weekend off, and we can get a day pass or something to go."

"We already got you a day pass," Fallon says with a smile. "We leave in a couple of days." I smile at her and take her hand.

"You did?" I ask, warmth filling my chest. I have never had a best friend, but I think this is how it feels. "You are amazing." I squeeze her hand a little.

And so began my life. Family I never had, a man I never thought I would find, and a purpose to life.

Present day

Xavier stares at me with a smile on his face, "You told them all of that?"

"And you're telling me you didn't talk to Dylan and Kenzo about it?" I laugh.

"Well of course I did, I won the most beautiful woman at the college." He says with a smirk. "I had to brag." He shrugs.

I slap his arm, rolling my eyes. "Come on, we have to get to the training arena, we have riding to do." I stand, adjusting my top and brushing off the dust from the trek up here. Xavier stands and takes my hand, interlacing our fingers. He gives it a squeeze. We walk down the familiar halls as the trainees file into the gathering hall. Some trembling and some beaming with excitement. There is a small woman standing alone in the back, I smile as I watch her, knowing she will do great things. The size of the person doesn't matter, but the determination does. She turns as I walk by and I wave to her. She gives me a weak smile in return. I pause, tugging on Xaviers hand. He follows my gaze to the young woman standing there.

"Go talk to her." He says with a grin.

"I think I will." I say, taking a step forward. Xavier follows behind me. When I reach the woman I hold out my hand. "Hello, I am Nyathera."

She stares at my hand and takes it in hers. "I'm Blaire, are you new too?" Her black hair cascades down her back and her bright blue eyes shine in the dim light of the gathering hall.

"This is the end of my second year."

She smiles, "Is it as bad as I have heard?"

"It is a little more difficult when you are our size, but you will make it to the end if you follow your heart." I say confidently. Xavier steps up next to me and the young woman's face lights up.

"Hello." He says smoothly. "How are you feeling about being here?"

Blaire stares at him in awe, "I..." she shifts on her feet, "um, I..." she shakes her head and looks at me, "I'm sorry."

I chuckle, "It happens a lot."

She looks back to Xavier, straightening her back, "I'm nervous and excited. After meeting Nyathera," She gestures her hand towards me, not breaking eye contact with Xavier, "I know I will be able to make it through this." She clears her throat, "being small isn't easy, and if she has made it, I know I can as well."

Xavier smiles widely, turning his eyes to me, "Yeah. She is kind of impressive." He turns his gaze back to Blaire, "you know, her brother is Bartholomew Nighting." He winks.

Blaire's mouth drops open as her eyes slowly slide to meet mine, "the all-savior?"

I glare at Xavier and turn my eyes back to Blaire, giving her a smile, "yup, that's my brother."

"Oh, my Gods!" she squeals, "I can't believe I get to meet you!" She clasps her hands in front of her face.

"There is nothing special about me, just that following in my brother's footsteps has given me more determination." I grab Xavier's hand, Blaire tracks the movement and shifts her weight again, "you will do amazing things here Blaire, I can already tell. Do not let anyone walk all over you."

She looks between us and nods, "I will do my best." She smiles as General Nortick starts to speak. "It was great meeting you two," she says quickly.

I smile and nod as she turns away to pay attention to what is being said. "Alright, now can we get to training?" I look at Xavier, warmth spreading across my body.

He chuckles, "let's go Miss Nighting." I slap his arm playfully as we walk out of the gathering hall.

"You know I don't like talking about my brother." I say quietly.

"You should be proud of where you come from, you may not see it, but you are just as good, if not better, than he is." Xavier squeezes my hand as we continue forward.

I stop him outside of the training doors, "It doesn't matter who my brother is or what people think. I am just me."

Xavier grabs my face in his hands, "You are whoever or whatever you want to be. No one can change that, but being proud of where you came from, and everything you have accomplished is okay." He runs a thumb over my cheek.

"I have always known what I am capable of, X, I don't want to be compared to Bartholomew." I search his eyes, trying to find his understanding.

His eyes change to something I can't read, and his body language turns ridged. "Are you okay?" I ask him, hoping what I have said didn't upset him. He nods and walks through the arena doors, leaving me behind. I huff, feeling a pit in my stomach and walk through the arena doors. I inhale as the familiar scent of exhaust and dust fills my nose. We have been here hundreds of times and every time I feel anxious.

Chapter

17

After training I kiss Xavier goodbye as he goes to meet with his father, and I walk towards the courtyard. Dylan and Fallon are already sitting at one of the outside tables as I walk out the doors. Fallon sees me first and smiles, giving me a wave. I wave back and walk towards them, "Hey guys!" I smile as I sit down.

Dylan reaches his hand out and I interlace our pinkies, initiating our handshake. Fallon shakes her head with a grin.

"Hey girl, how was riding?" Fallon asks as she takes a bite of a salad.

"Same as always. I do have some exciting news though." I say as I take a sip of my water I grabbed on the way out here.

"What's the news?" Dylan asks.

"Xavier and I saw the new trainees, and one of them is the same height as I am. I actually stopped and talked to her, and I am pretty sure she will do big things here." I smile at them.

"Since you have risen against all odds, I am sure she will as well." Dylan says, placing his hand on my forearm.

"I have a really good feeling about her." I say again.

Fallon smiles widely, "Then she will do great things."

I lift my face to the sun as the spring sun shines brightly in the sky. The forest of Mearin is in full bloom as spring makes an appearance. The breeze fills with the scent of new flowers and rain. I relish the warmth on my cheeks as we sit in easy silence.

"Well, I had a talk with General Nortick today." Fallon breaks the silence. I lower my head towards her. Waiting for her to elaborate. "I have officially applied to be a trainer here at the battle college." She smiles wide.

Pride washes over me, "I am so proud of you Fallon. You will make an amazing trainer." I take her hand in mine, and she smiles. Fallon is the strongest woman I know, not only is she beautiful and smart, but she is also the number one trainee of our training year.

"That is amazing Fallon, you've got this!" Dylan says with a smile. He glances at his watch, "We have to get back to the house." I glance down at my watch and notice that it is almost five.

We all stand and walk back towards the house. I bump my arm into Dylans, "Hey, you okay?" I whisper.

He gives me a tight-lipped smile, "yeah, just exhausted from training today. Professor Mary beat us into the ground on the mats."

I nod my head. And hurry towards Fallon who is ahead of us. I grab her hand, and she smiles. We return to the house and walk inside; it is quiet and dim. The lights turn on as we walk into the kitchen and prepare dinner. Everyone sits and eats together as we have done for the last two years. After dinner Abbi, Fallon, and myself clean up the kitchen.

"So, if you're going to be a trainer, are we not going to see each other again after graduation?" I ask Fallon, sadness of losing my best friend washing over me.

"I applied to be a trainer for two years and then I will be able to choose my base. So, you just have to make it for two years so we can see each other again." She smiles sadly. She takes my hand in hers, giving it a gentle squeeze, "it will be okay Nye, you'll have Dylan with you."

I pause, "Did Dylan choose the same base as I did?" I look over my shoulder to where Dylan sits on the couch with the guys. Xavier came back just before dinner in a pissy mood, so him and I haven't talked since he returned. "I wish you were all coming with me." I say quietly.

"We will still be able to visit each other." Abbi says matter of factly.

I smile at her and stand, ready to get to bed. "Let's promise to cause chaos wherever we go." Abbi and Fallon stand on each side of me, and we hug each other tightly. My world has changed drastically in these last two years, with so many different things thrown at me, and these two have been there for me every step of the way.

"Hey, Nye. Can we talk?" Xavier calls from the hall. I look at Fallon and Abbi, and they both smirk at me.

"I'll be right there, X," I say back. I drop my arms from Abbi and Fallon's waists, "I'll be right back."

"You'll be back, but not *right* back." Abbi laughs. I roll my eyes at her.

Dylan catches my arm when I walk by him, "Do you need anything, Nye?" I shake my head and smile. He looks to the hall and back to me, "Ok. I'll be right here if you need me." He forces a smile and lets go.

I place my hand on his shoulder, "thank you, Dylan, seriously." I smile at him, and he returns it.

Chapter

18

Panic set in as they realized they were trapped in a place where shadows ruled, and nightmares thrived. Nyathera, feeling a surge of bravery, turned to her friends. "We have to stick together!"

I walk away from Dylan and the others, towards the man who I didn't expect to fall for. The man who started my journey in Mearin with the feeling of defeat. Everyone has always seen me as Bartholomew's little sister, the one who doesn't accept that he is the all-savior because of jealousy. But Xavier, he sees me for me. I stop right in front of him. "Is everything okay?"

He smiles brightly, "Yeah. I just wanted to show you something."

I cock my head, "You just seem off."

He grabs my hand. "Come on!"

He walks us through the door, I found him singing behind. The air whooshes into our faces as soon as he opens it. The smell of dirt and mildew fills my nostrils. "Why are we going this way, X?"

"You'll see when we get there." He smiles at me. Not giving me anything.

We wind through the long stone pathway that leads to the cave mouth. The air is warmer once we exit the pathway and enter the cavern. The sky is starting to turn pink and purple with gradients of blue and orange in it. Still holding my hand, Xavier walks towards the opening of the cave mouth. "I... I don't think I want to go that close." I dig my heels in.

"I'll be right there with you." He squeezes my hand.

I nod, and we are moving again. My heart is racing, and my head starts to spin. I take a deep breath in, and X puts his hand on my lower back as we step towards the edge.

Looking out over the mountain range with the setting sun is breathtaking. The colors of the sunset mixing with the spring colors that are starting to brush the lands, makes it look like a painting. Mountain peaks topped with snow reflect the orange and pink of the sky. Far below us is a building made of stone, with tiny windows lining the roof. I inhale sharply at the beauty. Xavier comes up behind me and wraps his arms around my shoulders, resting his chin on my head. "It's beautiful," I say breathlessly.

"You are." He returns sweetly. I turn my head towards him, and he kisses me softly. "I wanted to share this with you. My sister used to take me out to watch the sunset when my parents would fight. And then when she died," He pauses, swallowing hard, "I would come to see the sunsets, and it would calm the screaming that was inside my head. I could talk to her like she was here with me." He inhales deeply and lets it out slowly.

I turn towards him in his arms. "Xavier, I am so sorry that your sister was killed because of my brother's actions." I cup his cheek, "But as you know I am not my brother and would never hurt you."

He smiles sweetly at me and kisses my forehead, "I know. You're so much better than he is."

He nods towards the sunset, and I turn around. The sun shines brighter as it dips behind the mountain tops. Like one last goodbye before it leaves for the night.

"Let's get you inside." He says, grabbing my hand. And we make our way back through the pathway and into the house. When we walk through the door, everyone turns to look at us.

"We were taking bets on who was going to get pushed off the cliff's edge!" Kenzo laughs.

I gawk at him and put my hand next to my mouth and whisper, "We know I would've won."

He laughs wholeheartedly and stands to give me a hug. "I'm hitting the hay y'all." He says with a yawn.

"Me too." Abbi stands and stretches.

"Looks like it's bedtime, guys. Nighty night." I say.

"Sleep tight." Kenzo says.

"Don't let the city of shadows and nightmares bite," Dylan calls. I laugh.

Fallon hugs me, "Thank you for supporting me, Nye." She hugs me tightly again, pushing me back to examine me. She looks between Xavier and me and then turns with a grin. "Be good, you two!" she calls over her shoulder, waving her hand at us.

I shake my head with a smile. I watch as Fallon walks down the hallway, wrapping a blanket around my shoulders. "I will only be as good as you let me." Xavier comes up behind me and speaks so only I can hear him.

The hairs on my neck stand on end and my breath catches in my throat. He kisses my neck once, "my room. Now." I don't move. "Get in my room now, Nyathera, or you will regret it." He bites the words out, in barely a whisper. His breath caresses the shell of my ear. I inhale deeply. His voice lowers into a growl. "Now. Little one." And he slaps my ass. I yelp and instantly feel warmth spreading to my core.

I slowly start walking to his room, dropping the blanket as I go. I turn slightly and see him watching me. I grab the bottom of the oversized shirt I had thrown on when we returned home and slowly pull it over my head as I walk away from him, dropping it to the floor, he has a full look at my bare back. "Nyathera." He growls low and quiet. I put my thumbs into the waistband of my shorts and tug gently. I hear his footsteps quickly coming up behind me, and I yelp. Taking off, I run past his door and toward the end of the hall. The dead-end hall. I turn and look at him coming up on me. My breathing increases, and my heart is ready to burst out of my chest. My back is against the wall, and I can't go any further. He doesn't slow down as he approaches. As quickly as I saw him at the end of the hall, he's on me, pinning my hands above my head with one hand and running the other down my side.

He clicks his tongue, "Naughty little one. Whatever shall I do with you?" His eyes are full of lust, and he grins, roaming his darkened gaze down my body. "What if one of the other guys came out and saw your tits on full display?" I don't say anything, "answer Nye."

"I…I don't know." He licks his lips and looks at my breasts, my nipples pebbling beneath his gaze.

He bends and sucks one into his mouth, biting down. I suck my lips into my mouth to silence a screech. He lets my nipple go with a pop.

"My room, now." He bites out and looks over my body again. "And take those shorts off when you get in there and close the door. I have to grab something."

"What do you…" He cuts me off.

"Now." His low voice brushing over my bare skin.

Laced with so much lust, I can feel it in the air. I do as I am told as I scurry to his door. Before I open it, I turn back to him. His hands are in his pockets, and the look on his face is devastatingly handsome. He waves his hand at me to go in. I look him up and down one last time and open the door; shutting it behind me, I lean against it and try to catch my breath. My body shakes with anticipation, and I can hear my heart pounding in my ears. Xavier returns, looking me up and down, devouring my body. Large strides bring him easily towards me and he crashes his lips to mine, my body melts and explodes in the same instance.

Chapter

19

Whispering words of encouragement to one another. They devised a plan. With a newfound determination, they began to run, dodging shadows and weaving through narrow alleys, desperately searching for a way out.

We wake up early and get ready for the day. Making our way out of the house, an eerie silence falls over Mearin. No trainees are laughing in the court, the battle arenas are empty, and there isn't a trainer or professor in sight. I look at Fallon, "Where is everyone?"

"I don't know. It's like everyone disappeared."

Just as she speaks, an announcement blares over the speakers. "Everyone, trainee, trainer, and professor, please report to the gathering hall. I repeat, all trainees, trainers, and professors to the gathering hall. This is not a drill."

A large blaring horn starts sounding off. I cover my ears and duck my head. Xavier comes up behind me and grabs my elbow, "We have to go. Come on!"

"What is going on?" I yell over the horn.

"My dad says something is happening. We have to go!"

I grab Fallon; Dylan and Kenzo come up behind us, and we all head to the gathering hall. My heart is racing as we walk inside, and everyone is crammed into the small space like sardines. Chattering erupts throughout the gathering hall. I hold Fallon's hand like it is my lifeline.

Abbi appears on my other side, dipping her head to my ear, "Someone said there is an incoming attack." I look at her wide-eyed.

My palms start to sweat, and my heart is about to explode out of my chest, "an attack on Mearin? That's never happened before." I state.

Abbi nods, "I am not sure if that is true or not." I look at Xavier, and he won't meet my gaze. He is standing with Dylan and Kenzo on the other side of the gathering hall. They are speaking with a trainer.

Dylan walks our way and stops right in front of us, "Nye, you will be with me for the next couple of days."

"What? Why? What is going on, Dylan?" I stare into his soul, fear flashes in his eyes.

He sighs, "They will tell us in a moment."

He looks down and walks around me, stopping right behind me as Xavier heads off with his father. I watch them walk to the back of the gathering hall, and Xavier follows him. Kenzo comes back to us tight-lipped and the anger radiating off him is palpable.

"Silence!" rings across the gathering hall as General Nortick speaks. He looks across the hall and stares straight at me, and I can't read the emotion in his eyes. He looks back at Xavier, who steps towards the door behind the stage, and then he looks back over to the entire crowd.

"We have been watching a fleet of Keltoids heading our way. We have reason to believe they are coming to attack." A collective gasp sounds across the gathering hall, whispering surrounds me as all the trainees try to figure out what he is saying. "I said SILENCE! With being in training for two years, you know what has to be done. We have four days to prepare you. Trainers will be with your house day and night to ensure you are ready. Be on high alert as we prepare. And may the power of the Gods be with you." He clears his throat and turns to Xavier catching his elbow.

He says something in his ear and then stomps off. Xavier's face has fallen. Fear resides in his beautiful eyes. He looks at me and then dips his head before leaving the gathering hall. The room has erupted into chaos. People are crying and yelling. Some have run out, and others are hooting and hollering with the excitement of battle. I can't move, blink, or breathe. It feels like Xavier just walked out of my life at such a crucial time. Is he coming back?

Fallon says something and I don't register. "Nye!" she says, shaking my shoulders. "Are you ok?"

I look at her with wide eyes. Just stare into her soul. "Yeah…" I trail off and look around.

Trainers are getting people into groups, and professors are walking around with the scribes; my best guess is that they are trying to form battle plans. Just as Fallon starts to speak, Beckham appears. He has a smug smile on his face as he approaches us. My breathing becomes erratic, and I search for Dylan's hand. He comes up and places his hand on my shoulder, moving me to the side. "Hello, house three, my name is Beckham. I will be training you in the art of killing for the next week." His gaze meets mine and I am sure I stop breathing.

"What are you doing here?" Dylan asks, malice lacing his voice.

Beckham smiles, "I am training you to ensure you stay alive." His eyes point to me, "At least some of you." He looks at everyone again and then back to me. "First, we have to section into groups. We will be one of the first houses on the training mats today. Xavier is occupied with the General, so I will be taking his sparring place with Nyathera." His smile turns reptilian.

My throat dries, but I hold my head high. "That works for me. I needed a break anyway."

He throws his head back, laughing, the kind of laugh that sends ice into my veins. "You really are a smart mouth." He turns on his heels and heads towards the fighting arena.

"Nye, are you okay? Why would they put him with us?" Fallon's voice is low.

I look at Fallon and sigh, "Because someone is trying to take me out. I don't know who, and I don't know why."

She steps back, "What? Why didn't you tell us."

"I didn't think there was an actual threat…" pleading with her to understand.

"I would want to know if my best friend was under attack, Nye. That is something you should've shared regardless of what you felt. It has been two years, and you didn't think to bring it up at all?" She takes another step back, "how can I trust you now? Is there anything else you've been hiding from me?"

I shake my head. Sadness bursts in my chest.

"I, I need time to process this." She shakes her head.

I reach towards her, "Please, Fallon."

"No! You could've gotten us all killed, Nye. You kept that secret from us, from me." She shakes her head, fear and tears filling her eyes.

"Please," I whisper.

She turns away from me and takes a deep breath, "I am going to ask to be transferred to another house. I wish you the best, Nyathera; I hope you survive. But it won't be because of me."

And she walks away. Leaving me to break as one of the only people who has ever cared about me walks away. Because of my own stupidity in wanting to keep it to myself. It was selfish and dangerous.

Dylan grabs my hand, and I pull it away. "She's right. I could have gotten her, and all of you killed! They could all end up dead because of me!"

He grabs my shoulders, "she will come around. No one wants to hear their best friend has a target on their back. Give her time." He says, practically shaking me, "I will not die because of you, I refuse to. If I die, it is because I was doing my job, whether for you or Mearin." He searches my face, but I give him nothing, "We have shit to do, and I need you to get it together because you have to fight hand-to-hand with the man that tried killing you. And I can't help you on the fighting mats." He sighs.

I look at his eyes, "Okay." Is all I manage to say. I shake my shoulders and roll my neck. Beckham stands across from me on the other side of the mat. His eyes shoot daggers into my soul. I push down the nausea and slow my breathing.

"You've got this, Nye," Dylan says with a gentle hand on my arm. I nod. I spent years and years fending for myself. I will not let this man take me down. I am strong, I am fierce, and I am going to kick this man's ass. The man that drugged me. The man that tried to kill me. I hype myself up, repeating my mantra. He. Will. Not. Win.

Chapter

20

As they raced through the city, they came upon a glowing door shimmering with a warm light.

The whistle is blown, and we move to the middle of the mat. Circling each other as we stare into one another's eyes. "Scared?" He asks.

I laugh, "the only thing scary..." I trail off

"Cat got your tongue?" He huffs.

"Nope, but there really isn't anything scary about you anymore."

His face contorts into a serpentine smile. My stomach rolls, but I don't show it. I will not show him a sliver of fear. I step closer and smile at him.

"Why are you smiling? Do you want to die, Nyathera?"

My smile grows, "Nope. Just thinking about kicking your ass."

He cocks his head. "You're really a slimy piece of shit."

Before I know it he is lunging at me. I roll to the side, my ribs cracking with the force of impact. I groan as I stand up fully. Fuck, I should have practiced that more.

"Got a weak spot, do we?" his voice a hiss.

I snarl at him and lunge, grabbing onto a leg. My broken rib stabs at my lung, making each breath a searing burn. I pull his knee sideways, and a scream tears out of his chest with the snapping of tendons. They sound like firecrackers as I continue yanking his knee sideways. He drops to the ground, and I climb on top of him. Using all my strength to keep a grip on any part of him I can. I wrap my legs around his arm and pull backward. He screams out, "You bitch!" and rolls backward, kicking outwards and catching me in the side of the face. I yell at the searing pain that starts to radiate outward from where his foot caught my cheekbone. My ears are ringing from the impact. Fucking asshole.

With pure hatred in his heart, he manages to climb onto his feet and, with gimping strides, grabs my throat, his long fingers wrapping around the entirety of it. Teeth bared, he spits as he speaks, "You are the reason we are in this war. Your brother just *had* to save Somania. Now, we take what he holds dear."

My vision starts to go black as he tightens his grip, slapping at his wrists he tightens his fingers, but I manage a laugh.

His hands loosen slightly. "Do you like the feeling of dying?"

"No." I croak, "I just find it amusing that you still believe he holds me dear." His eyes change for a split second, and he tightens his grip again.

My feet are now dangling above the floor, the tendons in my neck splintering, and the muscles start to tear at the seam. It feels like he is trying to rip my head clean off my body. He slams me back onto the ground, and the cracking of more ribs thunders through the arena. Searing pain shoots through my body and I cry out, but nothing except a gag can escape my lips. My head starts to spin, and my vision slowly blackens again. I will not die here. This is not the end for me. I am strong, I am fierce, and I will kick his ass.

I grab his wrists harder, digging my nails into the tender skin. I push my nails in as hard as I can as the last of my oxygen escapes. Heat radiates in the demon mark on my neck, igniting a strength from deep within. I rip skin and flesh off his arms, forcing an inhuman scream to escape his lips. He lets go of me, grabbing at the spot I just skinned. "What the actual fuck!" he squeals. Skin is stuck beneath my nails and blood runs down my arms.

My head spinning and vision blurry I charge him. Hitting him straight in the stomach with my shoulder. My body screams in pain but I will not give him the satisfaction of me tapping out.

Every time I have been called small or insignificant runs through my brain. I jump on top of him as he lays on the ground. Shrieking, I throw punch after punch into his face. His nose crunches under my fist. Blood sprays from his mouth and his eye starts to swell. He tries to stop me with his arms, but I dig my nails into his wrists again, pulling more flesh from his bones like ribbons, throwing the flesh to the side. Blood sprays my face and I lick it off my lips. His unswollen eye widens, watching me go completely feral. His screams fill the arena, and I can hear people shouting in the distance. White hot rage erupts coursing through my veins feeding my body as I continue my assault on his beautiful face.

"Fuck you Beckham! Fuck everyone against me because I am small! Fuck everyone who is trying to kill me! Fuck everyone who supports my brother!"

Over and over again I slam my hands into him. Even after he stops moving I continue slamming my fists into his face. Watching his face cave into nothing, brain matter spraying across the floor. My screams pierce through the air and the earth begins to shake. With every scream the shaking intensifies. I barely notice the trembling below me, dismissing it as Beckham crying.

Strong hands wrap around my waist and Dylan hoists me into his arms. I fight to break free of his firm grip, kicking and hitting at the arms wrapped around me. "Shhh…Nye. You're okay. He's gone." Dylan's voice washes over my body.

Slowly I stop struggling as my fight or flight calms down. I look at the mangled mess on the ground, my stomach turns, and I vomit. Repeatedly my stomach empties its contents onto the mat. Blood, skin, and vomit lay across the mat and my own body. Dylan gathers my hair in his hands as I finish vomiting. The pain in my ribs intensifies and the adrenaline and anger subside. I cry out in pain. Moaning as Dylan scoops me into his arms.

"I've got you Nye." I cry as the world goes in and out from pain.

"Where's Xavier?" I manage to croak out. My throat is burning from my screams and Beckham's gangly hands.

Dylan looks down at me quickly but doesn't answer.

"Dylan. Where is Xavier?" I ask with more fear in my voice.

"Nye." He whispers. I try to move in his arms, but pain radiates down my spine.

"Tell me." I snap.

"He is with his father. Who trained Beckham. And who instructed Beckham to take you out."

My blood runs cold. "Did Xavier know?"

Dylan nods slowly, "Xavier had orders to assassinate you, Nye." The world spins, and I roll myself from Dylan's grip. Hitting the ground. Sharp pain radiates through my body, and I vomit again. Dylan gathers my hair in his hands, and I recoil.

"Did you know?!" I shout through the pain. My body protests at the movement.

"No, I just learned from General Nortick's right-hand man." I glare at him. "I swear, Nye. You are so important to me. If I knew someone wanted to hurt you," His eyes well with tears, "If I knew he wanted to hurt you I wouldn't have let you fall in love with him, and I would've killed him myself."

I roll from his arms, hitting the ground with a thud…again, the shock making my stomach turn and pain radiate through my entire body. "There is no way Xavier was in on this, Dylan." I shout at him. I don't believe that the man I have loved for almost two years could betray me that way. Dylan scoops me into his arms again and we walk in silence. The pain in my body searing away any layer of strength I thought I had left.

Tears fall faster now, and Dylan glances my way, "I've got you, Nye. I will always have you."

I inhale on a stutter. My ribs cracking more as I do.

"You're the only friend I have now, Dylan." tears threaten to spill. "I just can't believe Xavier would do that to me."

Dylan sighs heavily, "then we believe him until he gives us a reason not to."

I lay my head on his chest, "It's just you and me now."

"Oh really? Here I was, thinking I was your best friend."

I jump at the sound of her voice. "Fallon?!"

"Listen, I overreacted. I'm sorry. Don't make me repeat it." She smiles, and I look up to Dylan. He has a sad smile on his lips as well.

"I love you guys," I whisper. Fallon grabs my hand and squeezes with a small smile. I look up to Dylan, who has a tear running down his cheek. I reach up and wipe it away/

"I love you too, little one." I give him the best smile I can.

I look behind him and notice a massive fissure up the side of the mountain. I don't remember that being there. As I watch the mountains, darkness invades my mind, and I pass out.

Chapter

21

They could hear the faint voices of their parents calling for them from the other side.

I slowly open my eyes and see people moving around me in beige cloaks. Screaming sounds in the distance, and my mouth vaguely tastes of onions. I groan as I roll to my left. A young woman in a cloak notices me first. "Oh! Careful, you took quite the beating" Her smile is sweet, and her round face comforts me. "I'm Meghan." She says.

"Hi, Meghan. Where am I?"

She smiles, "Your friends brought you to the healer's corner this morning. We gave you a potion to heal you up quicker."

She keeps staring at my neck.

"Where are my friends?" I ask her, ignoring the questions in her eyes.

"They are training." She says sadly.

I get off the cot and see my jacket lying on a chair. I put it on and notice I am in no pain. "Miss Nighting, we can't let you leave until you are cleared." Meghan says panicking.

I look at her blankly, "Are you the one going to battle? Are you the one who has to risk your life? Are you the one who endangered your friends without knowing it? No? then I will train with my friends to hopefully make it out of this war alive." I shove my feet into my boots and walk off.

I make my way to the riding arena. I no longer have a partner to ride with, so I must learn to do it myself.

"Miss Nighting, you will be training in daggers today." A professor I have never seen before says.

"Why?" I ask, crossing my arms across my chest.

"You no longer have a partner. After the announcement, Xavier Nortick disappeared with his father, General Nortick."

Of course, he did; what a slimy, scared little bitch. I nod and start to walk by him. He catches my elbow, the movement making my bones groan where his hand is.

"Nyathera, be careful. Some people are out for your head." My breath catches in my throat, and I shudder.

"But why?" I pull out of his grip. "Why are people after me?!" I yell.

"Because your brother stopped an important part of the war." He lets out a sigh. "When Somania was being attacked, General Graise, wanted to let the Keltoids take the land. He had visited with the Keltish leaders, and they had agreed to stop the war if they could have the golden land." He looks over my shoulder and back at me, "with Bartholomew stopping the Keltoids, it has dragged on the war and the Keltoids are not ready to negotiate again. They now want all of Mearin and its surrounding territory."

"That still doesn't explain what I have to do with this." I shift my weight from one side to the other, crossing my arms.

"Because Bartholomew is untouchable because of his fame, General Nortick has decided the next best person," he takes a deep breath, pinching the bridge of his nose, "the next best person to suffer for his supposed war crimes is you."

I stare at him for a moment. Not believing a word he says. My stomach turns and then I laugh. "This makes no sense to me."

He looks at me with annoyance, "just be careful Nyathera. Very bad people are coming for you. From Mearin and Keltia."

"And I will be ready." Anger roils through my body. He didn't answer a single question. He just spoke in circles.

For the next couple days we train, I have barely seen Dylan, Fallon, Abbi, or Kenzo. They've all been doing their partner riding lessons, and then when they are doing their weapons training, I am off learning some hand-to-hand bullshit, since I have been moved up in training classes after the escapade the other day. I walk into the house when someone wraps their arms around me, and my feet leave the floor.

"*Oh*, I have missed you!" Fallon says. I try to speak, but she's cutting off the oxygen to my lungs. She sets me down and I smile at her.

"How are you here at the same time as I am?!" I ask dramatically.

She giggles, "We all have the night off. The Keltoids are said to hit tomorrow" Her face drops a little.

My blood runs cold, "tomorrow? Already?" she nods.

Abbi shouts around the hallway corner. "Hey, Nye!" She hugs me when she gets close.

"Are you ready for tomorrow?" I ask her. She looks at Fallon and then back to me.

"No, I am being sent home."

I look at her, stunned, "What happened? Are you okay?" I ask her. Looking over her body.

"Yeah, but my wife has come down with the sickness. And it seems like it's not going to go well" Her face falls, and sadness replaces her once beautiful brown eyes.

"I am so sorry," I say, placing my hand on her forearm.

She gives me a sad smile. "You be careful now; do you hear me, Nye? You are smaller than most, but you are fierce. You are stronger than anyone initially thought, and I know you will make it through this battle." I hug her tightly, and she hugs Fallon again, "Keep each other safe, and may the power of the Gods be on your side." She gives us one last small smile before stepping out of the door and out of our lives.

Fallon takes my hand, and we walk towards the kitchen. "How has training been?" I ask her. She shrugs.

Dylan comes into the kitchen, talking to Kenzo. "Hey, ladies." Kenzo's bright smile fills the room.

"Kenzo has something he wants to tell us." Dylan's face is stoic. I freeze. Is another one of my friends going home?

"I have been appointed to the river brigade!" He beams with happiness.

My heart feels so much lighter. He was made to be there! They are a brigade of providers spreading the words of the Gods across the land.

I run and hug him, his large hands envelop me, lifting me off the ground and he whispers in my ear, "I will say a prayer for you every night." He kisses my cheek and sets me down. Tears prick my eyes as I watch another friend hug everyone and head on to their future. Their *safe* future.

Dylan, Fallon, and I are standing in the living room now. "So, now what?" I ask.

"Actually, Nye, I wanted to speak with you." Dylan says, rubbing his neck, "You know I…" the earth shakes, and the loudest mechanical roar I have ever heard resounds over the land, cutting his sentence short.

Chapter

22

"This way!" Nyathera shouted, and they all dashed toward the door, their hearts pounding.

I grab Fallon's arm, and we help each other stay upright as the earth continues to rumble. The siren rings through the training grounds. My teeth rattle as another roar sounds through the land silencing the siren. We run for the door. My fear switching off and pure adrenaline replacing it. Dylan runs ahead of us, looking around the corner at the end of the tunnel. He waves a hand, summoning us to his side. Fallon and I share a look and take off towards him.

We look with him as other trainees, trainers, and professors are all running around. Professors shout to the scribes and trainers are getting their trainees in formation. I follow Fallon and Dylan; we stop behind house two. "We've been put into house two as there are only three of us." I nod, understanding what Fallon said.

"Everyone will be placed on the walls!" a small woman yells ahead of us.

"Who's that?" I ask Fallon.

"That's trainer Sarah. She is our leader now." My mouth forms a perfect oh, and I stand in formation, listening, not questioning much as adrenaline courses through me.

"There are things you are going to see that have been thought to be a myth; please keep your composure and remember we are a team. We will make it out of this. The last two years have prepared you for an early battle." Her eyes meet mine, "you are strong." She looks away. "And may the power of the Gods be on your side." Everyone splits up.

Fallon grabs my hand, "Be careful, Nye."

"You too." I say shakily. We hug and she pairs up with a guy from house two.

Dylan comes up next to me. "Come, we are in the hand-to-hand shield." I look at him, fear gripping my stomach.

"Hand-to-hand?" I whisper. He throws me a smile. Another roar sounds—closer this time. The vibration rings throughout my body, rattling my bones. I cover my ears, and Dylan grabs my hand.

"We have to go!" He exudes confidence I haven't seen before. I nod. Fear now mixes with adrenaline. How can we defeat them with whatever they have brought?

I follow Dylan up the side of the mountain towards the walls. Smoke is billowing just beyond it, and the sounds of fighting fills my ears. A strong smell of sulfur is invading my nostrils, burning my sinuses. We stop at a vehicle and Dylan hands me twelve daggers and a bow with sixteen arrows. I grab them and start sheathing the daggers along my black leathers. Four on my left ribs, four on my right ribs, one on each thigh, one at each ankle. I throw a quiver over my back and the bow over my shoulder.

Dylan looks at me and I nod, "Let's kick some ass." I try to sound as confident as possible.

He smiles. "I love you, Nyathera." He hugs me, places a kiss to the top of my head, and stalks off ahead of me. My head is spinning. What did he just say?

I hurry to catch up with him. "I love you too, Dylan. You're the best guard dog anyone could ask for."

He laughs and grabs my hand. "Let's do this."

We continue our uphill climb to the wall. I stare at this massive stone wall covered in moss and dirt when we get to it. There are ladders every sixty feet. Dylan helps me onto the ladder's first wrung, and I make my way to the top. Breathing heavily, I see a hand reaching towards me. A man with a scar over his eye and dirty blonde hair is reaching for me. I grab it and he helps me over the edge of the wall. I look out over the land and my heart sinks. Bodies lay across the ground, unmoving. People are fighting, and screams are erupting through the air. My stomach rolls, and I have to fight down the nausea.

"What is happening?" I look to the guy who helped me.

"This is war Nighting! Better get ready because our wave is next." he replies.

My head spins, and my legs wobble. A shadow takes over the land. I look up and a massive, winged beast flies overhead. It looks like it is a…no, it can't be, they don't exist. My breath catches in my chest as Dylan comes to my side.

"What the fuck is that?!" I yell. "What the fuck *is* that?!" I yell again.

Dylan grabs my hand, and the guy beside us yells, "That is a dragon, dear. We haven't gotten to that part of training yet." His eyes swim with regret.

"Dragon?!" my vision blurs as fear and confusion grips me.

"Don't you think that would've been a good subject to bring up in classes?!" Dylan yells back.

"We didn't exactly have time to teach you everything you needed to know! Buck up buttercup" the man spits and turns back towards the carnage below.

They aren't real. They can't be real. Fire billows toward the ground and splitting screams assault my ears. In the wake of the dragon's fire is a path of soot. Dead fighters. Anxiety fills my mind as I watch in horror.

I step back, and Dylan grabs my arm before I step off the ledge. He grabs my face, "Nye! Get it together. We have to make sure we protect the new trainees! You will make it through this!" He searches my eyes, "*I* will make sure you make it through this." The dragon lets out a roar that rings through my head, dizzying my senses. I nod to Dylan.

A voice rings out from the other end of the wall. "Wave four! Get in formation!" We stand arm-to-arm with the others on top of the wall. "Attack!!!"

Everyone descends the ladders without hesitation. Descending into the battlegrounds one by one. I take a step forward and pause. Taking a deep breath, I drop my leg over the edge and place my foot on that first step. Descending into battle.

Chapter

23

Just as the Nightmares closed in, the children burst through the door and found themselves in the familiar woods, sunlight streaming down around them.

My boots hit the burned ground, sending soot into the air. I walk along the wall with my hand running along it, watching as dirt bikes and four-wheelers fly across the battlefield.

Dylan reaches me and grabs my hand—I jump at his touch. "Are you ready?" he asks.

I shake my head, "Nope. But what choice do we have?"

He nods and steps out into the battle. We move in formation with the others in our wave. A man with a scarred face charges at me as Dylan collides with another. Grunting and the sounds of punches fill my ears. I don't have time to say anything when the man collides with me, tossing me backward and sending a painful shock through my chest. I fight his arms as he grabs for my face. I scream as I fight against him, reaching for a dagger at my side. He pushes my face sideways and into the ground, grinding my teeth together, and I taste copper on my tongue. Soot and dirt invade my nostrils, and his fingers dig into the sensitive skin of my cheek.

My fingertips brush the hilt of one of the daggers on my thigh; I grab it and bring it up under his ribs. He squeals and pushes my face harder. The ripping of skin and the feel of blood rushing over my hand ignite my fight-or-flight instinct.

I pull the dagger out and shove it back in over and over until he falls on top of me. His weight grinding me further into the charred ground. I can't breathe as I try to fight him off me. I push on his body as hard as I can. "Fuck!" I scream as I move him a fraction of an inch. I'm bucking my hips and shoving him with all my strength. My arms slowly giving out. He is thrown off me when Dylan flips him. "Nye! Are you ok?" his words hurried.

I nod. "I'm fine," I grunt as I brush my pants off. I look down at the man I had just killed. Scowling, I spit my blood on him. "Fuck this, Dylan. Let's kick some Keltoid ass."

He stares at me, "Nye, your eyes…"

"Now is not the fucking time Dylan!"

"No. They're glowing!"

"What?" I feel a burn in my neck and realize it is the mark. The burning pain makes its way down my body like the skin is being peeled away. I cry in agony as the pain intensifies.

"Nye! What is going on?" Dylan's voice is laced with worry.

I double over, clutching at the different parts of my mark as the pain flows through my torso. I rip my shirt up and the dark red of the mark is glowing. "Dylan, please, make it stop!" I am screaming in agony; every sound being ripped from my soul.

"I don't know how Nye. What is that?!"

I watch as, inch by inch the mark glows intensely.

As fast as the searing pain began it subsides. I fall to my knees, huffing, and Dylan squats in front of me. "We have to get you back. We have to ask the healers."

"It's the demon magic Xavier used to heal me. I woke up with this mark." His lips form a tight line, and he shakes his head.

Wrapping his arm around my waist, he helps me stand. We dodge people fighting and fires as we head to the wall. My feet feel heavier and heavier as we get closer. He hoists me onto one of the ladders, and we climb to the top. Taking deep breaths, I climb down the other side. The war has penetrated the wall to the other side. Into the training grounds. Anxiety fills my soul, static lining my bones.

"We aren't safe, Dylan. I will be okay; we have to fight." Dylan looks at me with worry in his eyes. I touch his arm and nod. We will get through this. I look around, and men and women lay bleeding on the ground; both sides are losing far too many people.

Before I am able to speak, a voice yells from behind me, "Nyathera!"

I turn and Fallon is standing on top of the wall. Her blonde hair in a braid, loose strands blowing across her face. I look to Dylan, "Don't say anything to her, please." I plead. He looks at me, then Fallon and he nods. I look back up to where my friend is standing. She wears blue leathers. My heart flutters: she is a trainer. Pride winds through my body as I watch my best friend climb down the ladders. She runs to us and quickly hugs me.

"Oh, my gods! You're a trainer!" I yell over the sounds of battle. Forcing my attention on her and not the people dying around us.

She smiles wide, "Just happened before coming to the wall. I had no idea they needed one! So they asked me and I said yes!" She smiles wide and her attention is turned back to battle, "We have to move. You and Dylan go left. I'll take Grey with me and go right! We will meet in the middle." She lays her head against mine, "be safe. And may the power of the Gods be on your side."

I nod, and she does the same with Dylan. She looks at us one last time before nudging Grey, and they take off.

I look at Dylan, and he smiles, "Are you ready, Nye?"

I grab my daggers, "let's do this."

I have spent the last twenty-three months trying to survive, trying to prove I'm not like my brother. But this is no longer an option, I realize I am just like him as I step further into battle, throwing away every moral I thought I had. A body falls in front of us as we turn and run down the side of the wall. I look up, and the dragon has people held in his claws and is dropping them to the ground. It's black wings open, stretched across the sky have holes torn into them. Arrows stick out from the scales along its underbelly and its horns are pointed and bloody. My blood runs cold. I run to the woman that was dropped in front of us. Her body twisted in ways that aren't natural. Her eyes are vacant of any color. She's gone. I look over my shoulder to Dylan, and he lowers his eyes. I stand and look around us; Keltoids are coming down the ladders in hoards. One after another, men and women join the others in devastating brawls. Screams fill the air as both parties fight to the death.

Another man comes running towards us, Dylan steps in front of me, and my heart sinks. I grab a dagger and try to get a shot. Dylan and this man are face to face; punches sound as they fight. The man gets around Dylan and runs straight to me. He tries to grab me but stops dead in his tracks. Fear flashes in his eyes as he stares at me. "What the fuck are you?!" he yells.

As my fear and anger build, the earth begins to shutter. Sharp rocks protrude from the ground, and the earth splits. Static lines my bones and a surge of energy starts in my toes and coats my body. The man falls with a scream into one of the open holes in the ground. My heart stops as the man's screams grow quieter. I look up and see Dylan staring at me; he backs away from me, taking my heart with him.

"Dylan, please, we have to get away from here!"

He shakes his head, seeming to shake off his fear, and runs to me, grabbing my hand. We make our way to the end of the wall and circle back around like Fallon instructed. I throw my daggers at a man coming towards Dylan. The daggers puncture his skin with ease, hitting him directly in the throat. His gargled screams slow as I run up to his body. I reach down and pull my dagger from his throat and wipe it on my pants. Dylan has a sword in each hand, fighting with a woman. In one swift motion, he slices her head clean from her body. Blood sprays as her body falls to the ground with a thump. I inhale sharply but Dylan is by my side and encouraging me to run.

My body screams at me as we continue running. Each breath feeling more and more like flames in my lungs. I am drenched in sweat, and my braids have fallen out of my hair.

I stop, and Dylan grabs my arm, "You can't stop! You have to keep going!" The fear and sadness in his eyes hits me in my core.

"I just need a second." I have my hands on my knees as I try to catch my breath.

"We don't have a second Nyathera! We have to get going. Fallon is waiting for us." He pulls on my arm, and I just stare at him.

He starts moving away from me, sheer adrenaline taking over his body. A man rounds the corner, and Dylan stabs his sword through his abdomen and drags it out in one long stroke. I watch as he looks down at the man that has fallen to his knees and kicks him over with his boot. The man holds his hands in front of him, yelling in Keltish. Dylan smiles before bringing his sword down between his eyes, pinning the man to the ground. I flinch. Dylan removes the sword from the man's head and turns towards me.

Motion catches my eye, and an arrow flies through the air and lands in Dylan's chest. "NO!" I yell as shock fills my body.

Dylan looks at the arrow and back to me. The pain in his eyes rips into my soul. Another arrow hits his right shoulder as another lands in his abdomen. He falls to the ground in a slump. My body freezes. My stomach rolls as I watch my best friend fall on his side. The gentle giant. My protector. I force my legs to move and run to him as fast as I can.

I slide to a halt on my knees, dust and bloody earth rolling over me, and gather his head in my trembling hands. I still at how pale his face is. My stomach sinks, and my body shakes. The overwhelming sadness that strikes my chest is almost unbearable. I run my thumb over his cheek. "Dylan." I shake his body.

"Dylan, please say you're okay!" I say through tears, knowing he isn't.

My breathing is erratic, and my soul is slowly burning away. With his head in my lap, he places his hand on my wrist, giving me a small smile.

"Hey. It's going to be okay." He croaks out, blood bubbling in the back of his throat.

My tears roll down my cheeks and drop onto his shirt.

I cradle his head in my lap, placing my forehead to his, "Please, Dylan. War is easy to prepare for, but no one can prepare you for losing a part of your heart," I exhale on a sob, "this can't be the end. You can't leave me!" I grab onto his shirt like it's the last lifeline, pulling his chest closer to me. My soul breaks into pieces leaving holes where love used to be. "Please, Dylan, who will protect me?"

"You're stronger than you know, Nye." He reaches his hand up and brushes away a tear on my cheek with a weak smile.

I grab hold of him tighter, "Please just hold on. We are going to the healers." I say through body-wracking sobs.

"I have enjoyed babysitting you, Nyathera. I love you."

My traitorous heart skips a beat. He holds his hand up, and I interlace our pinkies, glancing at them quickly as the tears spill down my face. He places his palm flat to mine as the life dims from his face. I try to move his hand to continue our handshake, but his drops to the ground. I pick it up, holding it against my heart.

"Is that what you wanted to tell me?" he doesn't answer, and his eyes start to dim. His last breath escapes his lips, and my heart shatters. "No!" I scream. "No, no, no!" I shout over and over, pounding on his chest. "You are supposed to protect me! We were supposed to graduate together! There is too much that is left for you to do! Please!" my chest clenches, and my stomach turns. "You were supposed to be there." I inhale shakily.

I sit with him in my lap for what feels like a lifetime. Chaos erupts around me, men fighting next to me, a dragon flying overhead spreading fire within mere feet of me, and I ignore it all. He mended my shattered soul in such a short time, picking up each piece gently. His friendship was one of the few remaining sources of hope for me. When my tears no longer fall, the sadness is replaced with anger, guilt, and determination. I stand to my feet and yank the arrows from his bloodied body. I move behind him and lace my hands around his chest. With all my strength, I move him an inch. Digging my feet into the blood-soaked dirt, I move backward again and move another inch.

"We will get you to the pit; your soul will be free," I scream as heartbreak wrenches my body.

I slip in the mud created by earth and blood. Standing again I ignore the bile rising in my throat. Heaving breaths and aching arms. Inch by inch, I make my way to the pit. A woman runs straight towards me with death in her eyes and teeth bared. She throws a dagger. I barely dodge it; in a blink she's attacking me.

I drop Dylan as her fist collides with my mouth. I feel my lip split, and blood trickles down my chin. My ears ring, and my jaw aches as I right myself quickly. She goes for another punch, and I scream with fury. Thrusting a dagger into her stomach. I pull it out to attack again, and her dagger finds my arm, severing the muscle in my forearm. Searing pain mixes with my anger, and I smile.

Blood trickles down my neck from my lip, and my arm has a gaping hole in it as I stare with a wicked grin on my face. White hot fury runs through my veins, and my mark begins to burn again.

Her eyes widen for a moment, freezing her in place. I fist her hair in my hand and tilt her head to the side, sliding my blade across her throat. Blood sprays, and her gargled sounds are like a release of my fury. I toss her to the ground like the trash she is. I bend to pick up Dylan again. My hand doesn't close around his shirt as I grip him; the pain in my arm is too much.

I hook my other arm around his and drag on, screams leaving my body as I heave his large form towards the pit. I will get him to peace. Thirty feet is all that remains between me and the pit now. Eventually, I make it to that hole in the ground. I can't catch my breath, and my arm is in so much pain the edges of my vision start to fade. A copper blur catches my attention. Xavier is running towards us.

"Nye!" he shouts as he sprints in our direction.

Fear and relief washes over my body as I see him coming towards us.

He stops in front of me, looking down at Dylan lying on the ground. "What happened?" He reaches towards Dylan, and I swat at him.

"Don't you dare fucking touch him!" I spit out.

"What is wrong with you?" He asks, his face contorting.

"I know what the plan is, Xavier." I say through gritted teeth. "I wasn't as easy to kill as you thought I would be, am I?"

Xavier takes a step towards me, "Nyathera." He reaches a hand out and I back away.

"Don't touch me." I say, new tears welling in my eyes.

"The original plan was for me to take you out, but I didn't plan on falling in love with you. I didn't plan on my target being this amazing, beautiful, spunky woman that would capture my heart the way you did." He breathes heavily. His words penetrate my skull like a drug.

"You didn't think to tell me?" I yell.

"I told my father I would not be going along with his plan. If I told you, he would have killed you himself. He was training others. And then the battle came. You're safe now." He steps closer again. "And you will always be safe with me."

I look down at Dylan, "help me get him into the pit, he deserves to rest."

Xavier reaches down and sets Dylan on the side of the pit. I walk over to where they stand and I brush my thumb on his cheek one last time. Kissing his forehead softly I look at Xavier and we push him over the edge. I watch as his form descends into the murky blackness of the pit. My soul leaving my body as I watch my best friend leave this earth.

Xavier turns back to me and places his palm on my cheek and looks down at my arm, "we have to get you to the healers."

"I am okay," I back away from his touch. "We have to discuss this, but first we have to get through this battle."

Xavier grabs my arm, forcing me towards him and places his forehead against mine, "You are my everything, Nyathera. I defied my father's orders to be with you. I love you."

I sigh deeply, letting his words wash over me, feeling the love that radiates off of him. "I love you too, Xavier."

"You don't belong here…" He whispers.

I look up at him and he kisses my forehead, with quickness and stealth he turns my back towards the pit. "You belong somewhere else."

I cock my head as confusion grips my chest. "What…" before I am able to ask what he means, he shoves his hands hard into my shoulders, the movement jerking me backward as my thighs hit the edge of the pit. Xavier's face contorts into that of true evil. My chest constricts and my body stiffens. "Xavier!" I scream as my body flails into the mouth of the endless pit.

The last thing I see is Xavier's copper hair fluttering in the wind above. And I join Dylan on his descent.

Chapter

24

They were safe! "What just happened?" Nyathera asked. Her friends, wide eyed and trembling, shrugged.

The air leaves my lungs, and my heart lurches from my chest as I tumble backward. I scream and frantically try to find something to grab onto, the stone side biting into my fingernails, but all I find is endless darkness. I am falling to my death, and no one knows. Dylan's lifeless body slams into mine. Head over toes, I tumble into oblivion. Air whips past my face and whistles in my ears. My tears fall now, not only for Dylan and all the lives lost, but for me. I had just begun to enjoy life again and it is being ripped away from me, at the hands of a man I thought I had some sort of future with.

I sob and listen as the air around me whistles. My hair is blown into my face and sticks to my busted lip. My arm sears in pain, and all I can think about is the life I have lost. Selfishness fills me and heartbreak follows. After a few minutes, I no longer feel like I am falling but floating.

Floating somewhere, I can be at peace with my parents and my friend. A slight vibration fills the air and an odd calmness washes over my body. I inhale deeply and accept my fate.

My body slams into…water?! I am sinking deeper and deeper into dark murky water. I struggle to slow myself, flipping my feet over my head, trying to find the surface. My lungs strain to keep in the little bit of oxygen I have left. I see stars above me and swim with all my might. It feels like ages before I break the surface and suck in a massive breath of air. My lungs burn as I swim towards the bank. The water feels thick and velvety to the touch.

Ignoring the burning pain in my arm, I push forward. Paddling my way to the shore. My feet hit the earth, and I walk the rest of the way out. Flinging my body onto the dense earth, I breathe quickly, happy to be on land. I have to figure out where I am. I quickly rip a piece of my shirt and wrap it around my arm. Scanning my surroundings as I do so. The pain radiates to my shoulder, and I bite my tongue to suppress a scream.

The air smells of the ocean and forest after a storm. Trees line the landscape, and the sky is filled with stars. I just fell through the pit, I remind myself. Is this the afterlife? I breathe heavily as I continue to scan my surroundings.

There is the sound of branches breaking in the distance, and a wolf howls somewhere out of sight. I cringe as I try to stand. The world spins on its axis, and my stomach churns. I fall back to my knees and vomit. My gut wrenches with every heave. I wipe my mouth on the back of my hand and stand. I muster all my strength and head for the tree line; knowing I am at a disadvantage being in the open.

My senses are on high alert as I push through the brush. To my surprise, there is a clearing on the other side. I scan the large open area, trees line it on all sides, small white flowers are dotted throughout the tall green grass, and a slight breeze rushes through the forest surrounding it. The moons…*moons*? I shake my head and look again, there are for sure two moons in the sky. They illuminate the clearing with bright light, shadowing the forest. I find a large tree and sit against the base. My wet clothing does nothing to keep me warm, and my muscles quiver as a cool breeze glides over me.

I hold my arm against my chest and lay my head back against the tree's bark. The tears start to fall again. All the sadness and anger leaving my body with every salty tear trailing down my cheeks. The sobs wrack my body as I release adrenaline and sorrow. At some point, I must have fallen asleep because I am woken by something pressing into my leg.

I turn my head to look over my shoulder. As a small dragon nuzzles into my thigh. I jump abruptly, and it squawks. It looks at me and radiates gold around its green body. It can't be bigger than four feet tall and six feet long. It sniffs my leg again and curls up in a ball behind my knees. My heart is thudding loudly in my ears as I watch it. Its eyes flutter close, and its breathing slows. What the hell is happening? Dragons weren't real less than twenty-four hours ago, and now I have one cuddling my leg.

I inhale slowly, ignoring my fear, reaching a shaking hand down and stroking the back of its neck. The scales are cool and hard but feel as soft as silk. Running my fingers over the scales examining the way they change colors as the little one breathes.

Slightly larger than my hand, they shine with iridescence. The dragon seems to purr as I continue running my fingers over its scales. Vibration from the scales caresses my arm and my heartbeat slows. A sense of calmness washes over me. The dark is fading, and dawn is approaching. *I am so tired.*, and I wince when I switch positions, the pain radiating up along the bones in my arm. I look down at my forearm and realize that I am bleeding through the wrap. It hasn't stopped bleeding, and I know what that means.

Defeated, I move down and curl into a ball at the base of the tree. My heart lurches into my stomach, and my eyes fly open wide when the dragon moves towards me and wraps its body around mine, draping it tail over my legs. I relish the warmth its breath provides me, and I close my eyes again, relaxing into its scales.

What a strange world to be in. Dragons are real, I was pushed by my boyfriend into an endless pit that is obviously not endless, or I have died, and Dylan is dead. I stop. *Dylan is dead.* Guilt washes over me, and I start crying again. The dragon tightens its tail around me, and its scales vibrate faintly. I feel peaceful again. Slowly, the tears subside, and I lull back to sleep, listening to the sounds of the wind through the trees, and the strong heartbeat sounding from the dragon's chest.

"Hello," a small voice says. *"Are you dead?"* I startle awake and look around. *"Hi! You're alive!"* Her voice is full of happiness.

"Who said that?" The dragon's face is directly in front of mine now. I move back quickly and hit the tree.

"I am Runihura." It tilts its head. Its black eyes blink, and its nostrils flare.

"What the fuck is going on?"

"Excuse me. That isn't very polite. You're supposed to give me your name."

"How are you talking to me? You can't speak, you're an animal."

"Humans really aren't that bright, are they?" she tilts her head, *"I'm a dragon, not an animal."*

I huff. "What?"

"I mind-linked you. I chose you." My head spins.

This cannot be fucking real.

"Oh. But it is. Shall we try again? My name is Runihura, and you are?"

She has such a little voice. It's cute.

"One day, I will be a very large dragon. I wouldn't insult me." I stare at her.

"I'm. I'm Nyathera." I say with a shaky breath.

"What a beautiful name! I am so glad you are here. I have waited so long for you!" Her head snaps to the trees.

"Hide! Now!" And she scurries into the bushes.

Chapter

25

Slowly they stopped shaking with fear. Knowing that what they had just seen was no doubt a nightmare.

Staggering to my feet, I glance around the clearing with unclear vision. No doubt my blood loss and falling into an abyss has a lot to do with it. Only the sound of my heartbeat and each slow breath I take fills the air. I search for Runihura among the brush, but I'm only met with silence and moonlight. *I am alone.* I hear a twig break in the distance and back up slowly to the tree, keeping my back against it so nothing can come up behind me. Movement in the shadows across the clearing grabs my attention. I can't make out what it is, but it is large. Sweat beads on my neck, and terror seizes my body. The silence is deafening in the rapidly changing atmosphere, lowering my hand as I reach for my daggers. The shadow is moving closer to the clearing and then steps into the light.

A creature with the head of a bull and the body of a man stands on the other side. He is massive, and rage flashes in his black beady eyes. My breath hitches, and my heart rate increases. His nostrils flare before he takes large stomping strides toward me. He is in a full-on sprint. Backed into a tree, I can't move away as he descends on me. I hold my daggers ready to throw them when he lets out a roaring and reverberating sound then stops dead in his tracks.

He is staring over my shoulder, and I slowly turn to see what has caught his attention. A black wolf that stands at least six feet at the shoulders is stalking out of the bushes. Teeth bared and ears pinned to the side of its head. I hold my breath as it slowly walks by me and glances in my direction. Its brown and red flecked eyes flicker as it licks its chops. I can see my reflection in its eyes and feel a sense of possessiveness radiating off it, like he would eat me if there wasn't another threat. A heat washes over my face as I stare into the eyes of this enormous creature, *"mine"* fills my mind in the same way Runihura does.

The wolf bares its teeth and snarls, continuing towards the creature in a slow meaningful stride and lowers into a pouncing position. Extending its back legs, it takes off towards the creature, with supernatural force. The wolf rips into the creature before it makes it more than a foot.

Teeth curl around the creature's shoulder, and the animalistic noise that escapes the crying bull, man, *thing*, is deafening. The wolf shakes its head, and the sound of ripping tendons fills the clearing. Throwing the creature into the air and catching it by its head, the wolf growls. The sound reverberating off my spine. With a powerful crush of the wolf's jaws, silence descends on the forest. The creature goes limp in the wolf's jaws.

The wolf drops the creature, and its head snaps back, looking at me. Blood drips from its mouth, shining on its large fangs. Fear climbs up my spine, one paw in front of the other, it comes closer and closer. and I hold my breath, closing my eyes and turning my head as the wolf descends on me. His snout presses into my cheek, and he inhales slowly, a low, rumbling growl escapes from the beast. I hear a rustle in the bushes, my eyes fly open and Runihura comes into view. She looks bigger than before. Dragons can't grow that fast, can they? She stands up straight and puffs out her chest. She has definitely grown since last night. Her dark green scales changing color in the sun. Letting out a huff of steam she glares at the wolf, walking to my side as she does. The wolf whines, backing away and bows to her, and she bows back as if they are understanding each other. With one last glance at me, familiarity shining in his eyes, the wolf takes off into the brush.

As soon as the wolf is out of view I let out the breath I was holding. I place my hand on Runihura and sigh. "Thank you."

She turns to me, glaring, *"I told you to hide. And you stood there. Do you know what will happen to me if you die?! I will be weakened and most likely killed by my elders! You stupid human."* She flips her head holding it high again. My mouth drops open in disbelief.

"What?! You could've said that before you ran off! Also, how did you grow so fast?" I raise a brow at her, accusing me of being stupid, but she didn't tell me anything about dragons or the bond.

"Now that I am bonded, I will grow to my full size in a couple of months." She huffs steam and lowers her head to my height, *"Next time I say run or hide, listen."*

I nod because who in their right mind would fight with a dragon? A sassy one at that.

Chapter

26

*Without a second thought they hugged each other. Happy
to have come out of that nightmare alive.*

I stumble sideways as the earth shifts beneath my feet. Pain tears through my arm, and I bite my lip to muffle the scream I let out. I sit on the ground and slowly unwrap my arm. Warm tendrils of blood trail down my arm onto the grass as the clot peels away from the skin. The goopy mess that is my arm smells foul.

Runihura stands next to me. *"We have to get you to the healing pool. Get on."*

I stare at her for a moment, "What?" She huffs, and I swear I see her roll her eyes at me.

"You sure like that word. Get. On. My. Back. I'll take you to the healing pool. You can bathe in the water."

"Ummm…"

"Didn't we just discuss you listening to me? You die. I die. It is a mess I don't want to deal with."

I climb to my feet and place my hand on her shoulder. "You're a little tall for me to get on."

She huffs…again and lowers her belly to the ground creating a step with her front leg. Once on, she stands, and I struggle to stay on. I move my legs, so they are in front of…wings! *"Hold on to my scales right in front of you. It'll help you stay on."*

I do as I am told, and her scales are thick and as hard as steel. As soon as I get a grip with my one good arm, she bends her legs and springs into the air.

"OHHHHHHH MY GODS!" I yell as we head to the sky. My body surges backwards from the angle we ascend at.

Runihura giggles in my mind. *"Hold on tight!"* She says with what I can only assume is a laugh. She tilts her wings, and we turn in a circle before leveling out.

"This is amazing!" I yell with a giggle. Excitement numbing the pain in my arm, if only for a moment.

I look over the land, my breath catching in my chest at the beauty. Below us the forest spreads on forever, the lush green giving way to a large lake. The trees sway in a beautiful dance as the singing wind blows through their leaves.

The forest speaks in words of a language I do not recognize, coasting over my psyche in a spiraling embrace. Birds flutter from the treetops, dotting the sky with green and blue feathers. In the distance, fields of different crops cover the rolling hills. Lillies cover the ground with light pink and white, sprawling across the earth like fingers gripping on to the world.

In the distance there are dark mountains with lava falling over the edges in tendrils, pooling into a large lake at the base, mirroring the misty waterfalls that are on the opposite side of the lands. I squint to see better. A large palace comes into view as Runihura banks to the left, the sandy bricks illuminated by the sun in the sky are lined with ivy growing over their edges. The left side of the palace has a large greenhouse attached to it, and the greenery surrounding it outshines the greenery of the forest. People live here?! My heart races at the idea.

"That is where our king and his son live. And to the right of it, you'll see the City of Shadows and Nightmares." My heart stops.

"It's real?" I whisper. Run. My entire world is being reshaped in my mind. What was once thought to be a story our parents told us to make us behave, is coming to life before my eyes. It isn't supposed to be real. I must be dead. Or in a drug-induced sleep. Any moment I will wake up in the healer's tent, and it will all have been an elaborate dream.

"Ummm, I am very real Nyathera. This is a very real place, silly."

"I can't believe it is real!"

"Mhmm."

My pulse increases, and my breathing stutters. Add this to the list of things I never thought I'd ever experience. My entire life has been a lie.

"Lay your head down. We have a little bit before we are there. You will need your rest to heal."

"How can I rest with this scenery?" I ask her.

The land is beautiful, and the sky is clear and bright. The sun on my skin feels amazing. Runihura just snorts steam, and I listen. I lay my head on her cool scales, protecting my arm beneath me. The movement of flying lulls me into a deep sleep.

"Nyathera. We are here." Runihura's voice rings in my head.

When I open my eyes my vision is blurry, and I'm unnervingly tired. I notice blood cascading over her dark green scales, and my leathers are covered in it. I cry out as I try to lift my arm. The wound has turned black and is oozing with pus.

"I" my mouth feels dry. "I think my arm is infected." Runihura looks back at me slightly.

"Hold on tight. We are going down."

I grip the scales as best I can, with the slickness of my blood covering them, and lay my body against Runihura's neck to protect my face from the whipping wind. Runihura gently descends. I look down, and through tears in my eyes, I notice a pool of water. The different blues and greens sparkle in the sunlight. The greenery surrounding the pool almost shines with life. There are birds flying around as we make our way to the ground. With a light thud, Runihura lands, bowing down.

"Use my leg to help you slide down."

I do as she says and swing my left leg over to the right side. I slowly scoot my butt towards her shoulder and try to slide down. The scales are slippery against my leathers, and I lose control. Pummeling to the ground with a hard thud. My ears ring, and the wind is knocked from my chest. Pain shoots through my ribs and radiates through my abdomen like a lightning strike, and I scream out from the pain. Runihura puts her nose against me, and her scales gently vibrate. The pain lessens a little, and again, calmness washes over me.

"How." I clear my throat. "How do you do that?"

"It is part of my power as a dragon. Every dragon has a different one. Now get in the water. You're getting a fever."

I stagger to my feet one last time and start towards the most beautiful water I have ever seen. The smell of lilies and snapdragons fills my nose.

"You can't wear that into the water. You won't heal." Her voice full of annoyance.

I look down and realize she means my leathers. I look back at her and then slowly peel my daggers off me. "How can I protect myself without any weapons?"

She nods and looks at me with beautiful, deep, dark green eyes. So dark I thought they were black when we met. I give her a slight nod and lay my daggers on the ground. Unzipping my jacket, I shimmy my right arm out and peel the fabric off the other side. wincing with every movement. I unbutton my pants and pull them over my legs, stepping out of my boots at the same time.

With my body bare, the cool breeze sends goosebumps over my skin. Runihura has her head held high, surveying the land. Looking back at Runihura one last time, I take the first step towards the water. The grass is the softest I have ever felt. Like walking on little pillows of cotton. Grasshoppers jump as I wade through the waist-high foliage, and I stand at the edge of the water. The water sparkles like diamonds, and I dip a toe in. It is thick like the water I landed in when I got here. I take a full step in, and the sand cascades around my feet in an inviting dance. A vibration of energy surges through me as I step further into the water.

"Keep going. You must cover your entire body."

Taking a deep breath, I lay my body into the water and paddle with one arm out to the middle. The energy thrums through me, and the most beautiful music I have ever heard plays in my head. I take a deep breath and submerge myself under the water's surface. The water seems to be alive as it swirls around me in a sparkling dance. Wrapping around my arm like a cocoon as I watch as my wound starts to stitch together piece by piece with a tickling sensation. My lip feels tingly as the split closes. Serenity. Silence. Beauty. The water radiates all three. No chaos below the depths. My hair flows around my face, and I run a hand over my skin feeling the silky consistency that coats it.

I push towards the surface and take in a breath of the sweetest air. I lay on my back and float on the surface of the water. Closing my eyes, I sigh as the water heals my mind, body, and soul. A smile breaks my lips, and I call out, "Runihura! You should wash your scales. I bled on them."

She doesn't say anything, but I can feel her smile through the bond. I move my hand in front of my face admiring the thick drops that run over it. They radiate with shimmering rainbows.

The sun sets low in the sky, and I know it is time to get out of the water. I make my way back to shore, and when I step out, I notice my skin has the same glimmer as the pool. I see some clothing laid off to the side.

"Garden nymphs dropped off some clothes. Courtesy of the City of Shadows and Nightmares."

Of course there are garden nymphs here. Gratitude fills my chest as I pull the lovely tunic over my head. The silky fabric lays smoothly over my skin. I put on the cotton pants and replace the corset that holds my daggers. I pull my boots on and walk over to Runihura. She is lying in the tall grass when I reach her. I put my hand on the side of her nose and run my hand along it. "Thank you," I whisper. She nods her head. I scratch the scales behind her jaw as she purrs in a reptilian way.

I lay on the ground with my back against her side and listen to the birds and crickets as the sun begins to set.

The sky changes from blue to different shades of purple and pink, and clouds float by. I put my hand behind my head and admire the artistry of this forest. Every color of green that blends into the flowers and trees. The sweet smell of the air as it glides across my skin. This place isn't at all how my mother described it. This place is beautiful and calming. My eyes start to flutter shut, and I fight it. I want to watch the stars light up the night sky, but sleep wins as my body recovers from the last twenty-four hours of hell.

Chapter

27

Gasping for breath, they realized how foolish they had been to wander into the shadows without listening to their parents.

I wake up to a blanket of stars in the night sky. Each one twinkling with its own life. Runihura is still surveying the land as I sit up with a deep stretch to my back. "Did you sleep at all?" I ask, feeling guilt build in my heart.

"No, but I don't need as much sleep as you. I can go days without it if I am uninjured." Her sweet voice fills my head.

"Thank you. I know we just met, but I am so grateful for everything you've done."

She nods, *"I have waited twenty-one years to meet you."*

"What?" I ask her in surprise.

"There you go with that word again. Yes, I have waited twenty-one years to find the perfect bond. Someone who although small, is loving and fierce with a strong soul."

"And that's me?"

Her head perks up, and she looks into the brush. I hear the silence that falls over the forest and the air changes around me. I stand and walk to her side as she lays there watching the trees on the opposite side of the pool. Shadows move in the blackness, and my soul feels uneasy.

"We should go," I whisper, the unease washing over me like a cold shower. She nods and stands. She has grown another foot in the few hours I rested.

Bowing down she makes it easy for me to climb onto her leg and up her shoulder. She bends her knees and sends us soaring into the air. The wind whizzes by my head throwing my hair back. My stomach drops to my toes as we ascend into the night sky. I wish I could reach out and touch one of the millions of stars over our heads.

Looking down I still see those shadows moving, one steps into the clearing and it's just that, a shadow. A human made of smoky darkness. It vibrates like static, and it looks up at us, no face can be seen, but I can feel it's eyes boring into me.

"What is that?" I ask Runihura.

"They are the shadow people. They aren't usually aggressive, but since you are not from this world, they may be more inclined to be. Also, good use of our bond! It would have been hard to hear you over the wind."

I realize now I didn't say the words aloud, but she answered with ease. A small smile touches my lips at the thought. The dread I felt on the ground eases as Runihura levels out and we soar above the forest. Little specks of light surround me. They move in waves like the northern lights. Slight colors brush each speck like watercolors on an ocean painting. They brush against Runihura's scales and I reach my hand out to touch them. They are cold to the touch and hum with electricity.

"What is this?"

"Remnants of starlight. Every star that burns out joins the others and dances for all eternity. It powers the magic of the city."

I move my hand and fingers through it. Feeling the coolness against my skin. "It's beautiful."

I almost cry at the beauty before me. I continue this until we bank right and have to leave that ring of starlight. I grip Runihura's scales and prepare for our descent. The wind rips around me as I watch the ground come into view. The darkness sprawls across the world in an eerie mist that consumes everything around it. The only light is the stars and moons in the sky. The larger moon is a bright light blue, with darker specks shining throughout, encircled with a halo of the same light blue hue. The second, lower moon, a deep vermillion with darker maroon specks throughout. Not as bright but just as beautiful. The beauty of the night sky takes my breath away and is something only of dreams. The moons elongate shadows and create an ominous feel of eyes everywhere. I suck in a deep breath as I watch the ground get closer and closer.

"Runihura! Pull up! We are going to crash!" I yell out into the night.

Laughter comes through the bond, and I can feel my muscles clenching. I hold my breath and close my eyes waiting for the impact. A slight thud jostles me, and I open my eyes.

Chapter

28

They slowly take the path black towards their village.
None of them uttering a single word.

We are on the ground, and I slide down Runihura's leg and land on my feet. "I did it!" I say with a laugh. She puffs steam and starts walking away.

"Hey! Wait up!" I start to run towards her and realize she is heading towards a field full of…cows?

"What are you doing?"

"I need to eat. What did you think I was going to do?" She all but laughs at me through the bond.

"You're going to eat an entire cow?" as I speak my stomach growls.

"Maybe two. You should eat as well Nyathera. We have a long flight ahead of us."

"Where are we going?"

"Just eat and then I will tell you."

I roll my eyes at her and head towards the small lake I saw just passed the hedge. I push through the dense foliage and come out on the other side. The grass is just as green as it was around the healing pool and there is a baby deer just to my right. The moons reflect off the surface like spotlights. A sense of serenity forms around me as the breeze moves my hair. I walk to the lake and look in the water, its crystal clear. Looking around me, I strip off my clothing and step in. I swim out to the middle, pushing the water as I go. I tread water lightly as I look around me. I brought a dagger with me hoping to find something in the water that I could eat.

A fish swims by me, and I take a deep breath in. Submerging my head under the water I look around for the fish I just saw. Large rocks are covered in moss and the bottom of the lake is made of colorful rocks. This has to be the cleanest water I have ever seen. Although dark, the moons and a natural light that emanates from the rocks themselves allows me to see. Swimming towards the rocks I see a shadow shoot by me in my peripherals. I stop and turn but don't see anything. It zips behind me, and I turn quickly but there is nothing there. A buzz fills the water as fear creeps over my spine. I head to the surface to take a breath, looking around me in search of whatever that was.

Not seeing anything, in the water or on the bank, I inhale deeply, collecting my senses and pushing myself below the water's surface. Turning my face towards the bottom I dive again. Rounding the large rocks, I am met with a menacing face, my heart leaps into my throat and my lungs struggle not to gasp. Large black eyes lay on a fish-like face. Sharp teeth are formed into a sinister smile. This creature has long dark hair and reaches out large, webbed hands towards me. I start to swim backward as fast as I can. My heart beats unnaturally, and my lungs burn from the lack of oxygen. Fear grips me when the thing darts in front of me with its long-pointed tail disappearing behind a rock and emerging on the other side. The shining gray skin gives the creature a look of impending doom. Her torso is bare, and she has gills where her ribs should be. Her gray skin is stretched too tight over her bones, and she looks like she hasn't eaten in years. I turn towards the surface, straining my muscles to escape this creature, but she is grabbing at my legs and arms.

Fear engulfs my body as she grabs at me with razor-sharp claws. Her claws penetrate the soft skin behind my knee, slashing through the flesh. I scream out in pain, large bubbles obstructing my view, and I struggle in her grip. Her skin feels slimy, and her teeth snap at me. I thrash in her grip as she drags me lower and lower. I thrust my dagger towards her, and it slips from my hands. Slowly, it falls to the lake floor, and so does my heart. Holding my breath the deeper we go; it gets harder and harder. Her large jaws snap shut on my arm, and those sharp teeth sink into my skin; at the same time, she pulls out a small spear and stabs me in the side. Skin rips, and a burning pain erupts along my entire torso at the same time as a cloud of blood surrounds us. I scream out with the bit of air I have left, and the world starts to go fuzzy. I continue to fight against her to no avail.

Fading into the blackness, she abruptly lets go of me. I start sinking to the lake bottom. I think about everyone I lost and everyone I am about to join as the edges of my vision blurs more and more. I watch the water's surface, with its small waves and the starry sky above it. As I give up, a significant figure breaks the water's surface. The water fills with an electrical pulse as the figure gets closer, a tug in my chest erupts. My eyes slowly start to fall and I force them open as the figure heads straight towards me. They wrap their arms around my middle, dragging me upwards. My vision dims, and I fall into an abyss of blackness.

Chapter

29

Gasping for breath, they realized how foolish they had been to wander into the shadows without listening to their parents.

My eyelids flutter open, and sunlight assaults my eyes. Squinting, I roll onto my stomach and bury my face into the silky sheets. Taking a deep breath, I relax. My body stiffens, and I sit straight up. Rubbing my eyes to help them adjust to the light flowing into the room.

"Where am I?" I reach through the bond with Runihura. But I get nothing in return.

Humming comes from the open closet door. I look around for my daggers and don't see them. I notice heavy wooden lamp on the nightstand and grab it, flipping it over in my hands. Throwing my legs over the side of the bed and pushing the sheets off of me, I stand up. I slow my breathing to try and stay quiet. Tip-toeing towards the open door, I hold the lamp above my head. A plump lady with white hair and bright blue eyes comes out of the closet.

She jumps, "Oh deary, you scared me!" her sweet old voice washes over me like a blanket. "What are you doing out of bed? You need your rest."

She notices the lamp in my hands and shakes her head, walks up to me, and takes it out of my hands.

Confusion must read on my face, "You were pretty injured when the prince brought you here."

The attack flashes through my head, and I place my hand on my side, and I dig my fingertips into the flesh under the satin nightgown.

"Don't worry, we fixed you up. Though you do need to rest." She spins me by my shoulders and pushes me back towards the bed. I reluctantly climb back in, and she covers me up with a smile.

"The prince? Where am I?"

She steps back and looks at me, placing a hand on her heart. "Well, you're in the City of Shadows and Nightmares. The prince jumped into the water and saved you; he brought you back to the palace to get you healed up." She smiles and lifts the sheets so I can put my feet further under them, "He was really bent out of shape when he got you here. He paced outside your room as the healers worked on you all night." She smiles, and it meets her eyes with sincerity. She tucks the blanket around my shoulders, and I relish in the motherly care she provides to a stranger.

"Who is the prince? And why did he feel the need to save me?" Uncertainty grips at me. "My dragon! Runihura! Where is…"

"I'm here. You're okay, Nyathera."

"Where are you?"

"I am in the sheep yards." I don't dare to ask what she is doing.

I look back to the older woman standing next to me. "What do I owe the prince for saving me?"

Puzzlement crosses her face, "Why would you owe him anything? He did it on his own accord."

"There is always a debt," anxiety rises to the surface, I have nothing to my name that a prince could possibly want as payment.

She looks insulted momentarily, "Just lay down and get some more rest. I'll be back when it is time for dinner." She looks at my hair and then my face. "You will need to bathe, and something needs to be done with that hair of yours.”

I scrunch my nose at her, but the bed is comfortable, and I am exhausted. “Just a few hours. Please lock the door on your way out.”

She smiles and slowly nods her head towards me. “I’ll see you in a little bit.”

I sit up again, “Who are you? You’re the only human I have seen since getting here.”

“Oh, deary, I am not a human.” She giggles, “I’m a fairy.”

My mouth hinges open, “a real fairy?”

She pats her plump cheeks, belly, and hips, “I feel real.” I notice her perfectly pointed ears and a smirk forms on my lips as happiness fills my soul. “Get that rest. I’ll lock the door and be back in a few hours.”

I smile at her; she is the sweetest person I have ever met. Sorry, the loveliest and *only* fairy I have ever met. With a smile, she walks to the door with one last glance at me and locks the handle before closing it behind her.

Glancing around the enormous room I notice the lovely architecture that has gone into it. The ceiling is lined with beautiful oak wood, and the walls are dark blue, so dark that it could be mistaken for black. Floor-to-ceiling windows line the wall, and sheer curtains cover them, dimming the early morning sun just enough to keep it from blinding me as I admire the black framed windows. An antler chandelier hangs in the middle of the ceiling. A tree in a large pot sits in the corner. The four-poster bed is covered in blue silk sheets and a white down comforter. In defeat, I lay back on the fluffy pillows, pull the blankets around my neck, and close my eyes.

"Time to wake up, deary." A sweet voice fills my head, "Wake up. We have to get you ready for dinner." I feel a small hand on my shoulder shaking me.

Opening my eyes I see that sweet woman standing over me with her rosy cheeks and a smile on her lips.

"Rise and shine!" she says in a cheery voice. "I never got your name."

I yawn, "I'm Nyathera, but most people call me Nye."

"Oh, what a lovely name." she smiles and clasps her hands, "I'm Margie! Now, let's get you bathed!"

I look at her and cock my head, "like, you and I?"

"Yes, I have filled the tub with water already. Come, come." She says, and she starts humming as she walks to the bathroom. I get up and follow her to the ensuite.

The room's beauty flows into the bathroom, where a large soaker tub stands in the middle, full of steaming water and bubbles. I walk over to the sink, admiring the marble countertop and glance in the mirror. My hair is a rat's nest on my head, and deep bags lay under my eyes. Huffing I run my finger over them and sigh, apparently your best friend dying in front of you, falling into an endless pit, finding out dragons and fairies and the city of shadows and nightmares is real, your boyfriend betraying you, *and* being attacked by whatever those creatures were, is not suitable for the skin. Margie looks at my reflection and snaps her fingers; a fizzle fills the air, a tingle touches my skin, and the bags under my eyes vanish.

"There, sweet as a seeing berry!" she smiles.

I gawk at her and touch my under eyes again. "Where were you when I needed you all these years?" I say aloud.

"I have been in this kingdom for 350 years; before that, I was in the Fairy kingdom before it was burned to the ground..." she trails off as she catches a glimpse of me staring at her. "Oh." she says with a small wave of her hand. "Anyways, let's get you undressed and in the tub."

A few moments later, I step one foot into the wonderfully warm water and then the next. I slowly sink beneath the bubbles and sigh. With a smile on her face, Margie begins humming again.

"What is that song? I heard it when I went to the healing pool."

She stops, "It is the song of the city of shadows and nightmares."

"It is beautiful." I almost whisper.

She continues humming and comes to the tub, dumping a large bucket of water over my head. She starts scrubbing my scalp and combing over my hair and the loveliest scent of lavender I have ever smelled fills the air. Tingles envelope my head and a shiver instinctively shutters my spine. She dumps water over my head again, adds conditioner, repeating the process. Once she is done she hands me a sponge and instructs me to clean up. I do as I am told, running the lily-scented soap over my body. I splash the water over my skin to rinse it away and lean back against the tub.

Margie clicks her tongue, "You can relax after dinner. I'll draw you a new bath. We have to get you ready. You're already running behind."

Embarrassment washes over me, and I sigh, "I'm sorry, Margie." She smiles and helps me stand, wrapping a warm, fluffy white towel around my shoulders.

My chest tightens and a lightness floats through my soul. I haven't had motherly care in so long, I forgot how it feels. I smile at Margie and her warm eyes dance with her own true happiness.

I step out and dry off. Margie disappears momentarily and returns with a long-sleeved velvet dress— a deep red one. My breath hitches at the beauty, and she shoves it over my head, guiding the length of it to the floor.

Her smile beams as she looks at me, "You are such a lovely young woman, Nyathera."

I run my hands down the fabric and relish its soft feel. She walks me to the vanity and sets me on the stool. Picking up the brush laying on the marble vanity top she starts brushing my hair.

"I can do that, Margie."

"Oh, no need. This is what I am hired to do." She starts humming that lovely song again.

Taking strands into her hands, she braids around the crown of my head and down the lengths of my hair. Weaving each piece like a basket. She snaps her fingers, and bright white lilies appear. She weaves them together with other greenery and makes a small crown that lays on top of my head.

"You are amazing; this is beautiful," I say to her, a smile reaching my lips.

"It is all in a day's work, deary." She rests her hands on my shoulders briefly, smiling at me in the mirror, before disappearing again.

She returns a moment later with black silk shoes for me to slip on my feet and takes me to the floor-length mirror. I look at my reflection from head to toe. "Your magic does wonders." I turn to her.

"It is all you." She pats my arm. "Come on. The prince is waiting to meet you."

I inhale sharply. Panic catches me like a fish on a hook. "I..." I swallow hard, "I don't even know what I would say. He saved my life. The last person who tried to save my life…" my voice trails off as I think of Dylan.

"Just start with 'hi.'" She smiles and takes my hand. Her chubby little hand is warm in mine. She nods at me, and we walk out the door.

Chapter

30

Could what they have seen really lay at the bottom of the
pit? Or had they all had too much cake after lunch?

We walk into the large hallway. The ceilings are as tall as Mearin's mountains, and the walls are painted in a dark maroon. The hardwood flooring has a long dark blue antique carpet with swirling trees and stars that spreads from one end to the other. The floors squeak as we walk, and our footsteps echo off the large walls. The walls are lined with doors on each side and pictures hang between them. The only lights are those that hang on the wall, with a bluish flame. It is doom and beauty perfectly intertwined.

We walk for ages and come to a lavish staircase. The banister is carved into vines and leaves that spiral down the curve to the floor. The staircase opens to a large foyer with massive double oak doors. Runes are carved into the deep grain, and the handles are adorned in black crystals.

The landscape beyond is breathtaking. Fields open up and give way to the trees. The sky is turning pink with dusk as we walk through the grand room. Pushing open a heavy wooden door that reaches floor to ceiling, Margie gestures for me to enter. A table that is at least ten feet long sits in the middle with upholstered chairs surrounding it. At the head of the table is a high-back upholstered chair with a wolf carved into the wood, the eyes telling a story. Windows line one wall and the other hosts a large stone fireplace. I take a step in, and Margie closes the door. I turn around and I am alone.

Standing in front of the fireplace is a man in a black suit. His shoulders are impossibly wide, and his fringed black hair is slicked back perfectly on top of his head. He has one hand in his pocket, and another is holding a glass of dark liquid.

Keeping his back to me, he speaks, "I am glad to see that you are no longer a bloody mangled mess, Nyathera." He takes a sip of the liquid in his glass, "Sit, we have a lot to talk about."

My mouth dries at the sound of his voice. Low and grumbly but raspy and seductive. My name sounds like an expensive wine leaving his lips. I pull out the chair at the end of the table nearest the door and he walks towards the head chair. When he faces me, my breath catches in my throat. A tall handsome man looks down at me with the darkest brown eyes I have ever seen. His strong jaw is covered in light stubble and his eyebrows shadow his eyes. His suit is stretched against a large chest that is bare under his unbuttoned white shirt. Tattoos sprawl across his bare chest and up his neck. His tongue darts out and licks his full lips and I track the movement with my eyes. He clears his throat, and I snap my eyes back to his.

I choke a little as I speak, "Thank you so much for saving me." My words come out squeaky, I clear my throat, "I will repay you anyway I can. I don't have anything to my name besides a sassy dragon" I look to the side and back to him, "who I am sure would eat me, and then you, if I offered her. I can work, I know how to garden and fish. Or I can clean or do dishes. Whatever it takes to.."

He holds a hand up as he unbuttons his suit jacket and sits across from me. I can feel the weight of his eyes as he looks at me across the table.

The corners of his mouth tip up slightly before he speaks, "If you don't shut that pretty mouth I will shut it for you." His deep voice coasts over my skin, coating me in unprecedented arousal.

I snap my mouth shut and stare at him. My Gods he is beautiful. I have never seen a man with such otherworldly beauty before. A shiver runs down my spine as he stares into my soul.

He takes a deep breath through his nose, as if smelling the air, "There is no need for a repayment. I have a duty to protect those in my kingdom. Although you aren't from my kingdom, are you Nyathera?" His voice invades my senses and causes me to turn into mush.

I shake my head slowly, "I'm not. I fell into the pit, and I don't know how to get home."

His lips pull back in a small smile, exposing impossibly white teeth, and longer than normal canines, "there isn't a way home. But I can help you get started here if you would like."

I don't know what to say. I furrow my brows, a mixture of fear and excitement courses through me, "stay? I can't stay."

"Oh, but you must." He states simply, reaching for his glass again, "There is no way to get you back to the mortal world and I don't think Runihura would survive losing her bonded one."

I reach out to Runihura, *"are you okay?"* The sound of chomping comes through, and I know she is eating. A small smirk touches my lips, and I remember I am in the room with a very large, impossibly handsome man.

"I will do whatever is needed, your majesty."

He scowls, "Don't call me that. That is my father." He sets his glass down forcefully, "my name is Kai."

I swallow hard. The door behind me flings open wide and slams against the wall. Startling me. I turn around.

"Hey brother! You didn't tell me we had such a lovely guest!"

The tall man with red irises turns to me and grabs my hand. My heart stutters as the extremely handsome man with a square jaw and round straight nose coasts his eyes over me. His brown skin is marked in similar tattoos to Kai's. His hair in braids, decorated with gold rings and cuffs etched with runes cascades around his broad shoulders. Just as handsome, but more forward. I try to yank my hand away and he smirks before dipping his head and placing a gentle kiss to my knuckles.

"My name is Ezra; it is a pleasure to meet you." His smile is mischievous, and his gaze holds mine.

Kai clears his throat, and Ezra stands up straight releasing my hand. Instinctively I brush it on my thigh, and I hear a chuckle from the end of the table. One that is dark and sultry, making my skin tighten and goosebumps to erupt on my arms. Ezra stares at me menacingly and then smiles.

He too sniffs the air, "I see why you are keeping her." My stomach knots.

"We aren't keeping her." My stomach drops in fear, "She can stay as long as she needs to, to get on her own feet." Kai says.

"Ah man, Kai. Always ruining the fun." Ezra chuckles and takes a chair on the side of the table, propping his feet on the edge of it. His body facing mine, he slings his head to the side to speak to Kai, "Man, she is gorgeous, Kai. If you won't keep her, may I?" Kai just glares at him.

"I am not an object." I mumble under my breath.

Kai picks up his glass again. "No, you are not. Excuse Ezra for his lack of hospitality." Kai states from across the table.

"I would also appreciate you not speaking about me as if I am not in the room." I narrow my eyes on Ezra.

He throws me a beautiful smile and winks. "I can take you to another room."

I roll my eyes. "Does that work well for you?" All men are the same in every realm.

"Usually." He states blandly.

Kai chuckles, "Don't lie to our guest now, Ezra. And get your damn feet off my table." Ezra's feet drop to the floor as the table under his legs disappears and reappears within seconds.

Blinking quickly, I rub my eyes in disbelief. "What just happened?"

"Oh, the table disappearing and throwing my legs to the floor like a child?" he jerks his thumb towards Kai, "That was him, the old coot thinks he is cool with his party tricks."

Kai glares at him and I giggle. Kai smirks at me briefly and our plates are brought out. Mounds of beef and broccoli with potatoes and carrots.

"Please, dig in." He says. I pick up my utensils and cut a piece of the beef.

"Oh, my Gods this is fantastic." I mumble around my food.

Ezra is scarfing down his food like a child.

"Ezra! Use your fork. How many times do I have to remind you? You fucking barbarian." Kai's deep voice is full of amusement. Ezra stops mid chew and wipes his hands on his pants. Picking up a fork he glares holes into Kai. I laugh. A full belly laugh. Tears start to form in my eyes, and I can't stop.

I catch Kai staring at me and try to control my laughter. He has a smile on his face and a sparkle in his eyes. I cover my mouth and try my best to stop but I can't, soon Kai is joining me in laughter and Ezra looks between the two of us. Ezra's laughter is deep and fills the room. All three of us are laughing so hard that we didn't hear Margie knock.

She comes in and looks at us like we are crazy. "What are you hooligans doing to our guest?" she asks.

"I" I laugh some more. "I started it. But you should've seen…" I snort with laughter and Kai and Ezra laugh even harder. Soon Margie is joining in on it and the room fills with the sound of joyfulness. My stomach starts to cramp, I lean forward and smack my forehead on the table. The thud ringing through my ears as the sharp pain spreads across my brow. The room falls silent, I touch my forehead and look at it. With no sign of blood, I look up at Ezra, who again has his cheeks stuffed with food, and laughter bubbles up my chest again.

Chapter
31

I lean back in the chair and wipe the tears from my eyes. "I am so sorry. I forgot my manners as soon as he," I gesture to Ezra, "grabbed a fork like a toddler."

Kai beams, "There is endless laughter here. Never a dull moment with this one." I smile down at my plate. I have barely touched the food. I pick my fork up, showing it to Ezra and slowly move it towards the meat as I use my knife to cut it.

He watches every move. "Now. You try." I say with a smile.

"Haha. Funny. I know how to use a fork." He says defensively. I lift a brow at him. "I do, I just choose not to."

How do I feel so comfortable here? There has never been a place where comfort didn't feel forced, and I am happy for the change. But why does it feel as if I have been here all my life? Like some part of me belongs in this world.

He closes his eyes and puts his nose in the air. Opening one eye he glances at me before smiling. His red eyes gleam with humor.

I can feel Kai watching the interaction. His eyes flash with a familiar appearance. I smile at him, and we all dig in. "After breakfast tomorrow I can take you to Runihura if you would like? She's been grazing in the sheep fields for the last fifteen hours. She also seems to have grown a few feet."

I can't help the smile with the mention of Runihura, "She's been doing that. She was so little when I met her a couple of days ago."

"Dragons tend to grow quickly when they bond with someone. That growing tends to come with an insatiable hunger, more cows are coming tomorrow." He smirks at me, "The bond's a give and take of energy and power. Your bond gives her the energy and power to grow, and her power gives you the ability to enhance your own powers."

I stare at him. "What powers?" He lifts his brows.

"You didn't know?"

"Until a few days ago I didn't even know dragons existed. Or fairies. Or whatever those creatures were in the forest and lake. Or this city even. Or…" I swallow hard before continuing, "whatever you guys are."

Kai nods as if remembering I am not from here, "The bull was a minotaur, and they are keen on human flesh and the one in the lake was a lake siren, who," he flips his fork to the side, "also has a taste for humans." I just stare at him. "And we are demons." He smiles when I feel my jaw drop, those large canines flashing with the light from the fire. His tongue runs over his teeth as if showing them off and I have to squeeze my thighs together as I track the movement.

"I will teach you about our world if you would like?"

I freeze, he drops bombs on me and just goes on with the conversation like I am supposed to understand what he is saying? If I didn't just learn I'm sitting at the table with demons, I would give him a piece of my mind about how to interact with people when you tell them something so significant.

I mentally roll my eyes. "I don't want to be more of a bother than I already have been."

"Nonsense." Kai waves a hand at me, "It is no trouble at all. And it would do you good to learn so you can keep yourself and that dragon of yours safe."

I smile, "I think Runi would love that."

"Yes. Runi would love that very much." I roll my eyes.

Once we have had our fill of meats and pastries Kai stands and walks towards me. "Would you like to join me in the garden?"

"*OOOOO*" Ezra teases.

Kai shoots him a sharp look. Ezra holds up his hands and stands. "Until tomorrow, Nyathera."

He kisses the back of my hand again looking me straight in the eyes. What a beautifully weird creature. He strides out like he is walking on air. I look at Kai, and he shrugs. I giggle and Kai helps me push my chair back. I stand and look up at him. He smiles and holds out his elbow. I hesitantly place my hand around it. The warmth that radiates from him swirls around my hand and up my arm, my mark tingles. I drop my hand, my body going rigid. He stares down at me expectantly. When I don't replace my hand on his elbow he starts walking towards the door I entered the dining room through. He opens it, gesturing for me to exit. We walk through the foyer and into another room that looks like a library. I stop.

My heart swells at the thousands of books covering the walls. A large ladder on wheels leans against each of the shelved walls. I spin in a circle looking at the floor to ceiling shelves with the beautiful colors lining each spine of a book. The beauty is mesmerizing and my heart bursts. There are two oversized black chairs sitting in one corner with a small table and lamp between them and in front of the fireplace is an ornate couch. It is lovely with candles lit on the table that sits in the center.

"Do you like to read?" he asks, low and husky.

I nod with a small smile. "I never really had time after my parents," I swallow, "but I always enjoyed it before that."

His lips tighten into a smirk, "then you can come in here anytime you want to."

Excitement engulfs me, "Really?!" I clasp my hands in front of my face to hide the smile that crosses my lips.

"Really. As you can tell Ezra doesn't enjoy learning anything and Caine is more worried about the swords hanging on the walls than picking up a book. I come in here every Sunday afternoon to sit and read or do paperwork, if you would like to join me?"

I nod frantically, "I would love that." My cheeks hurt from smiling so hard. "Wait, who's Caine?"

"Caine is another demon that lives in this house. He is out today though; you'll meet him another day."

Another one? How many demons live here? He smiles with a quick chuckle and gestures for me to keep walking. Regrettably I do, looking back one more time before we exit through the French doors. We step out into an extravagant greenhouse. The humid air brushes my skin, sticking to my brow. I gawk at the allure of the greenhouse rows and rows of lilies and tulips as far as the eye can see. Hedges line the pathways through the middle that branches off in different directions. We walk down the stone pathway, my shoes tapping lightly as we do. Birds fly overhead chirping a lovely song and crickets sing in the distance.

"So, how did you end up in my world?" Kai asks gently.

I pause for a moment. "I am part of the soldier sectors. Everyone that is age twenty-one is collected on collection day. War came faster than we were trained for. Dylan, my best friend and bodyguard, was killed in battle."

I feel the tears pricking my eyes as I continue. "I dragged him to the pit, the one where we throw all our dead so that they can be at peace." Kai nods. Thinking about Dylan makes my chest ache. A tear slowly runs down my face.

Kai stops and gently grabs my elbow. I turn towards him, and he looks at me. Using the pad of his thumb he wipes the tear from my face. My eyes shut at his touch, igniting butterflies in my stomach. The warmth his thumb leaves behind numbs my skin.

"We don't have to talk about it. It's okay." He says softly.

I nod but continue. "Once I got him on the ledge he was just so heavy, and I was so tired," I pause, deciding if I should tell him about Xavier pushing me. "I fell with him."

He grunts disapprovingly, and we walk in silence. "I have been around a very long time. And I have never felt a human enter our world."

I look at him and lift a brow, "how long?" He doesn't look a day over twenty-five.

"A very long time." He states again.

I stop. "I am not going any further unless you tell me how old you are." I smirk at him. I am unsure where this confidence is coming from.

"You're welcome." Runihura sends me a chipper reply. I shake my head rolling my eyes.

He smiles, "I am three hundred and fifty years old."

My heart stutters and my mouth drops open, 350 years? "I need your skincare routine, because you look fabulous." He throws his head back and laughs. The sound is magnificent.

He looks at me, "I age differently than you. My father is over 600 years old. He has seen many battles in your world and ours."

I just stare. "Where is your father?"

"He is visiting with a neighboring continent to negotiate trade routes. He will be home in a little less than a year." I nod and we continue walking.

We come up to a stone fountain. In the middle is a statue of a sharp faced man wielding a sword. The statues face makes me feel uneasy, a tremble graces my muscles, "Is this your father?"

He nods his head again. It is getting darker, and a chilling breeze washes over me. "Come. I want to show you something."

With a slight bob of my head, we continue to walk the path that is surrounded by foliage. He steps through another set of glass doors. A large outdoor garden sits before me, even more beautiful than the one inside. Weeping willows scatter throughout, illuminated by fireflies, the green grass is short and lush, white lilies are dotted along the path as we continue walking. I can hear the babbling of a small brook in the near distance. We stop at a white gazebo adorned with vines and small yellow flowers wrapping around its wood.

Kai walks up the two steps and holds a hand towards me. I grab my dress, lifting slightly so I don't trip, and I take his hand and walk up the steps. He stops in the middle, and I am standing beside him. I admire the little flowers that seem to dance in the breeze.

"Look up." he whispers. I do and my chest clenches. The sky is filled with millions of light blue stars, like a blanket. "Every star is a soul Nyathera. So, rest assured, Dylan is always with you." He is gentle with the way he speaks.

Dylan said he would always have me. "It is beautiful." I say wiping a tear away, "thank you." He smiles. My heart squeezes as I stare at those stars, wondering which one would be Dylan.

We stand in the middle of the gazebo, in the middle of a massive garden, at the king's home, in the city of shadows and nightmares staring into the night sky.

"My mother is up there as well." he says, breaking the silence.

"I'm so sorry you lost her." I say back.

"It's okay. She was extremely ill, and we know she is no longer in pain."

I grab his arm and squeeze. The muscles under his suit twitch with my touch. He looks at me for a long moment. His eyes twinkling like the stars above. I am lost in his gaze when he finally clears his throat, "we should get you inside. It's getting chilly."

He unbuttons his suit jacket, and I watch every movement of his fingers. He shrugs his large arms out of the sleeves and wraps the jacket around my shoulders. I relish in the warmth it brings me. The scent of salted beechwood and embers fills my nose. He moves and I briefly admire him. His white shirt is taut across his chest and the sleeves bulge with every movement of his arms. If I was a savage I would be drooling. He smirks and turns back towards the way we came. I follow him and we walk in silence all the way back to the castle and to the room I slept in last night.

"Thank you" I say, taking his jacket off and handing it to him.

He grabs my hand and kisses my knuckles slowly. Staring into my very being as he does. "It was my pleasure Nyathera. I promise after breakfast we will go visit Runihura. I bet she is dying to see you."

I smile at him and walk through my door, closing it behind me. I lean against my door and close my eyes, letting my head fall back and sigh.

"He has that effect on most women in this world." I startle at the sound of Margie's voice.

She gives me a knowing smile, "come. I drew your bath that I promised."

Following her to the bathroom. "Thank you Margie."

She grabs my hand and squeezes it. "Anything to ensure your comfort here." With that, she leaves.

Chapter

32

*Nyathera and her friends vowed to heed their parents'
warnings from that day on. They understood that while
curiosity was important, so was listening to the wisdom of
those who loved them.*

I shimmy out of my dress and climb into the tub. The warm water envelopes my body like a hug and I sigh with relief. One by one my muscles relax allowing me to sink lower into the tub.

"I'll see you tomorrow Runi." I say through the bond.

"I am counting on it. Being away for long periods of time really has drained my power."

"I will get up bright and early. Stay safe." I don't receive a reply in words, but I can feel her. I smile and close my eyes, leaning my head back. I float in the tub for what seems like hours.

Stepping out and toweling off I walk into the room. There is a lilac satin nightgown laid on the bed. I walk over and pick it up. The fabric is smooth in my fingers, and I drop my towel, slipping the nightgown over my head. I hear voices arguing downstairs. Something crashes in the distance, and I jump. My heart landing in my stomach. Running to the door, I crack it open and peer out. There is no one in sight and this floor is ominously quiet. I take a step into the hall and carefully step on the wooden floors. Slowly and light-footed making my way to the banister, hoping to find out what is going on.

I get to the banister without making a sound. Patting myself on the back for being so quiet, I lean over to try to see what is going on. Shadows dance on the wall, and one looks to be in a dress or robe. Steadying my breath, trying not to alert anyone that I am here and lean over a little more. The banister creaks and I jump back, bumping into a little table that has a vase on it. The vase wobbles and I scramble to right it. My pulse races and my breathing increases. The voices downstairs halt. Holding my breath, I push myself against the wall in the shadows. A few moments later the voices continue in a hushed tone.

I brave going to the banister again and peek over to the floor below, being mindful to not put weight on the wood. Kai is walking into the foyer and turns to speak to someone who is still in the other room. Someone in a dress steps forward and I gasp. Throwing my hand over my mouth as if that will reverse the audible sound that came out of me. Both of their heads snap in my direction. The woman has the head of a bird! Green and blue feathers fan out over the top of her head and her beak is onyx black. Her beady eyes stare at me and Kai shakes his head pinching the bridge of his nose.

Stepping backwards towards the shadows, Kai calls to me. "Come on down here Nyathera. I'd like you to meet someone."

I step forward slowly. My heart rate increases. I take the first step and take a deep breath. I can do this. I hold my head high and place my hand on the railing. Trying to keep my stare away from the woman, I focus on the stairs one by one. I reach the last step and stand there. Once my eyes meet hers, she gives me a gentle nod and I return it.

"Nyathera, this is Aurora. She is one of my ambassadors."

I step off the last step and walk over to her, holding out my hand. "It is nice to meet you Aurora." She examines my hand and then places hers in mine.

"It is lovely to meet you as well Nyathera. I am sure we will see more of each other in the coming years." I throw a questioning look at Kai, and he simply dips his head.

"Yes, that would be lovely." I catch myself staring at her feathers.

"I am a harpy." she says gently.

I cock my head at her, "You're" I pause, wringing my hands together, "beautiful." The words catching in my throat.

She laughs, a bird's chirp, and I feel redness creeping up my neck and my cheeks. "Thank you. I don't hear that enough around here." She throws a pointed glance at Kai.

"You too, are stunning." She says.

I smile, "I think we are going to get along just fine."

At that she nods and heads towards the doors. "I will have more information in the coming days, Kai." He thanks her and opens the doors for her to exit.

When the doors close, his gaze turns from the floor to me. A burning furry resides behind them, and I step back. "What were you thinking, sneaking around here after dark?" his tone has changed, "Do you have any idea what can happen to you if the wrong creature walks through those doors? Not to mention eavesdropping on meetings that has absolutely nothing to do with you."

I look at him and scrunch up my nose. "I am in a world that I do not know. In a house that I do not know. With a man I do not know. When I heard something crash and bickering voices I needed to make sure I was safe."

I step forward. "And who are you to tell me what I can and cannot do? I survived for forty-eight hours on my own. I just so happened to be rescued by you." I look him up and down, "without my permission I might add."

He steps forward as well. "I am the prince of this world. What I say goes. And it would be in your best interest to remember that. You are not safe here and I will not be the reason you die! It is your duty as a *guest* in my home to remember who is in charge, Nyathera." His voice is raised and the authority behind it is daunting.

Pure rage bubbles in my stomach. "Where do you get off speaking to me like that? You are supposed to treat guests better!" I yell. "I don't care if you are the prince in this world, I am not from here!"

"If I didn't have a guest that couldn't protect herself from the creatures here and had the sense to listen to me so she could stay alive, I would be treating you better! Gods Nyathera, why can't you just stop and listen?!" He pinches the bridge of his nose again.

Now my blood is boiling. I let out an angry huff.

"I am going to bed. And I suggest you do the same before your stupidity gets you killed." He spits.

I gawk at him, the audacity of this man. He takes a step forward, and I let my annoyance win, sticking a foot out I feel my ankle connect with his and jerk it upward. His body lunges forward and the thud from his face hitting the ground vibrates through the floor. Satisfaction settles low in my stomach. He rolls over and looks up at me. His eyes blazing. My satisfaction is replaced with fear, but I stand there with my arms crossed.

"Did you just trip me?"

"I did."

He stands up brushing off his pants. "I haven't had someone trip me since I was a kid." He stares at me.

I take another step back. "Maybe more people should, to bring you down to their level. Since you think so high and mighty of yourself." I put my hands to my sides.

He laughs. The mother fucker laughs. I stomp my foot and start up the stairs.. What a fucking asshole. I still hear him laughing as I get to the top. "Goodnight Nyathera." He is still fucking laughing.

I turn my nose up and stomp off to my room. I am so full of anger and annoyance that when I reach my room, I slam the door. And when did anyone ever say this was my room? Rolling my eyes I flop onto my bed, burying my face in the pillow and let out a scream.

The frustration settles as I hear a door close down the hall. I roll over and stare at the wood ceiling. Maybe it won't be so bad having a dragon and living in the city. I have felt more comfort in the last three days than I have ever felt before. It is confusing as I am surrounded by demons and other creatures that were supposed to want me dead. But then again, everyone has wanted me dead since I was born. I sigh and flip onto my side, keeping an eye on the door. My lids flutter shut easily.

Chapter

33

As the forest opens up to their village the friends sigh in unison. They are safe.

Dylan's death fills my nightmares. The look on his face. That Keltoid asking me what I was. The pain that radiated through my mark, and Xavier shoving me into the pit. I wake up drenched in sweat. The satin nightgown clinging to my skin and my hair sticking to my forehead. My heart is beating at the speed of light, and my breathing is erratic. Taking calming breaths, I lean against the headboard. Movement in the shadows catches my attention, forcing me to sit up straighter. Kai steps into the moonlight and I jump, pulling the blankets up.

"What the fuck are you doing in here?!" I scream at him.

"You were screaming in your sleep. I wanted to make sure you're okay." The shadows dance across his face and, oh gods be, he's shirtless.

His chest is wide, and cascade into rippled abs. And that delicious v that disappears under his pants. I bring my gaze back up to his and our eyes lock. I have the same feeling wash over me as I did with the wolf. A small pinch on my sternum has me placing a hand to my chest.

"I am sorry I disturbed you. I am okay. Just a nightmare."

He cocks his head to the side and keeps his gaze on me. "Do you want to talk about it?" His sleepy voice is raspy.

I shake my head, "I'll be okay. Eventually."

"Well, if you change your mind, I'll be right down the hall." With that he turns on his heels and leaves.

I watch his back muscles ripple with every movement. The tattoo of a wolf and a dragon spread across his spine, comes to life as he moves.

He stops in the doorway, his hand on the knob. "I'll see you in the morning Nyathera." And he closes my door.

I huff out a sigh and lay my head back against the headboard with a thud. Flopping my hands on the sheets, I roll over, smushing my face into and then under the pillow.

Taking the sheets off I step onto the floor. I walk to the large windows and realize they are French doors that lead to a small balcony. I test the handle, and it opens. The cool night air brushes over my skin, sizzling out the burn that lies underneath, as I step into the darkness. The balcony overlooks the garden, and I walk to the railing. Placing my hands on the cool iron as I look out towards where the gazebo is.

Someone is sitting on their knees in the middle of it. My eyes adjust a little more when I focus on the shape. It is Kai. He is kneeling with his head turned towards the hole in the roof of the gazebo. The light from the moons enhance every dip and ridge of the muscles in his arms and his eyes are closed. I study him for a moment and a green hue starts to cast over my vision. Kais figure comes into focus clearer than before. I shake my head and the green is gone. I must be really tired if I am hallucinating. I turn around and walk back through the French doors and make my way to the bed. I leave the doors open a crack so that the breeze can cool my sizzling skin. Gods, it is hot in here. Letting out a sigh as I climb under the sheets and try again to get some rest. The rest of the night is spent in a fitful sleep.

Chapter

34

Glancing at each other they run off towards their parents.
Wrapping their arms around them tight.

When I wake, I hear the chirping of birds and the early sunlight shines through the windows. I stretch, rubbing my tired eyes and sit up. At the foot of my bed lies a green box with a golden bow atop it. I stare at it for a moment and then crawl to the end of the large bed and sit cross legged placing the box in my lap. I undo the bow and lift the top, in it lays brand new daggers with a ruby laid in the hilts. Intricate runes cover the wooden handles inked in gold, and the blade is made of a beautiful swirly steel. Picking one up, and flipping it over in my palm, I admire the craftsmanship that went into them. Under the daggers lies a brand-new leather corset with enough sheaths to hold each one. I pull it out and admire the faint lilies that are embroidered in the leather. The leather itself is smooth and soft, and the bones are perfectly curved in the bodice.

As I am examining the corset there is a small knock on my door. Laying the box and its contents to the side I stand up. My bare feet touch the cold wood floors, and I walk swiftly to the door, opening it a crack. Margie is standing there with a new silk tunic and leather pants. I look at her hands and then to her smiling face. "Good morning, deary." She says with a cheerful voice.

"Good morning Margie." I reply with a smile.

She pushes past me and walks into the room. "I see you found your gift from Kai."

"Another thing to thank him for."

She smiles and lays the clothing on the bed. "He knows you feel the need to protect yourself and wanted to gift you daggers that would be useful in this world." She turns and heads to the bathroom and the sound of the water in the tub turning on fills the room.

I follow her, "are you going to bathe me every morning?" I ask.

"That is my job. I can just come prepare everything for you and allow you time to yourself if you would like?" She looks at me and sadness flashes in her eyes.

"If this is what you want to do, I guess I can deal with it." She clasps her hands and smiles.

Once I'm done bathing and dressing in the beautiful clothing Margie brought me this morning; we head down to the dining room. The corset lays perfectly with my torso, with no pinching like my original one, and it accentuates my waist. We walk through the door to the dining room and Kai and Ezra are already sitting there. But across the table from Ezra is a very attractive man with blonde hair and ice blue eyes. His jaw is strong and squared and clean shaved. He turns his head to me and his cheekbones shine in the light. I gasp at the large scar from his chin down his throat that disappears under the collar of his shirt. His gaze rolls down my body and back to my face. Heat creeps up my neck and to my cheeks at the reminder of the fitted clothing I am wearing. I am surrounded by the most unearthly looking men I have ever seen in my life. I can feel my mouth has dropped open and I close it.

Kai clears his throat and my eyes land on his. "This is Caine. He heads my armies. Caine, this is Nyathera."

Caine nods his head towards me, "it is a pleasure to meet you Nyathera." His voice is deep and smooth.

Whiskey and bonfire scent fills my nose as he walks towards me to shake my hand.

"You can call me Nye." I say back, sheepishly. Kai stands and walks to the end of the table I am standing at. Pulling my chair out he gestures for me to sit. I sit and he helps me push my chair in. He walks back to his side of the table, Ezra and Caine watching him the entire time. Ezra and Caine share a look and then look back to me.

"Good morning, beautiful." Ezra drawls out in a lazy deep voice.

"Good morning Ezra." I nod.

"I see you found the corset and daggers." Kais eyes dip briefly to my clothing.

I look at them sitting smoothly against my body and back to Kai. "I did. Thank you so much. You didn't have to."

"It was my pleasure. You need weapons that will be useful in this world. Your old ones wouldn't work on the creatures here." I wait for him to explain but food comes before he answers.

"We have good news Kai." Caine says, breaking the silence. "The west borders no longer show any sign of kickback from the undead wizards that reside in Crandois."

Kai nods, "that is great news. Well done Caine."

Caine smiles like a kid who just received a piece of chocolate.

"Caine, how was Crandois?" Ezra asks.

"It was wonderful." He stops and glances up at Ezra, "and the women were *very* accommodating." Caine winks.

"I see you're using utensils this morning." I look at Ezra. His cheeks flash red for a brief moment.

He laughs, "I practiced all night to impress you Nye."

I smile and Kai chuckles. "Nye, after breakfast I have a meeting, but Ezra and Caine have offered to escort you to Runihura."

I smile widely. "I really appreciate that. I didn't realize how much I would feel the distance from her."

"It is the bond. Distance for too long can cause health problems for both you and Runihura. Like I said, you are one with your dragon now."

Caines head snaps to Kai and he chokes on his orange juice, "you didn't say Runihura was a dragon! I thought it was a dog or something."

I giggle and Caine's icy eyes snap to me. His gaze unnerving.

"And you thought I was an idiot." Ezra looks at Kai.

Caine throws a piece of sausage at Ezra who in turn throws a knife at Caine. Caine catches it with ease. I just stare at the two.

"Please excuse them. They have simple brains." Kai smirks.

They look at each other and then to Kai. Smiles spread across their faces as oatmeal whips towards Kai from both of them. The oatmeal stops inches in front of Kai and my stomach flips. Kai raises his hands and the oatmeal hurdles back towards Ezra and Caine smacking them both in the face. I cover my mouth as a laugh threatens to escape my lips.

"How did you do that?" I ask Kai.

"It is one of my powers, and I don't mean babysitting them." His eye bounce between them, "These two idiots have their own powers as well, but they forget how to use them daily." Caine and Ezra gawk at Kai for a moment and shake their heads before continuing to eat.

"Thank you, Kai. For everything. I don't want to be a burden for too long, so I would greatly appreciate going into town to find work."

Kai drops his fork, the sound making me jump, "you are not a burden, Nyathera. You don't have to work until you are ready and have learned to protect yourself."

I just stare at him, "I am capable of protecting myself. Dylan and Kenzo taught me how to fight hand-to-hand, and Fallon helped me learn better ways to use my daggers." I stop. I wonder how Fallon is, if she is alive.

"Your friend is alive Nye. I made sure to check,"

"How." I shake my head, "How did you know who my friends are?" I swallow hard.

This man didn't know me until a few days ago. There's no way that he could have known, I didn't tell him.

"Kai, there is a need for you in the study." A small man peaks around the edge of the door.

Kai nods, "We will talk later, Nye. Please. Finish breakfast, and then the boys will take you to your dragon." He throws a pointed look at Caine, and then Ezra, "And you two mind your manners."

They nod. "Of course, Kai. We will be perfect, gentlemen." Ezra gives him a mischievous smile.

My heart sinks at the sight of Kai leaving the dining room. I look at them both and they turn their heads quickly and examine their food.

"How did you get the demon mark on your neck?" I pause and look at Ezra. His cheeks are red, and he has a look of uncertainty on his face.

I clear my throat. "It actually wraps around my torso, but I was poisoned at the yearly battle training party. People are," I pause, "were, trying to kill me, and I don't know why. But the man I thought I was in love with." I pause and swallow the lump in my throat, "The man I thought I was in love with used demon magic to save me. When I woke up I had this mark."

Ezra and Caine share a look.

"What?" I ask anxiety creeping up my spine.

Caine sets his fork down. "No human has ever survived the use of demon magic before."

My stomach flips and the world spins. "What do you mean?" I whisper.

"It sounds like they were trying to finish you off," Caine says quietly. I guess Xavier was really in on it.

"Who was this man?" Ezra asks. His eyes flashing with anger. I hesitate to answer him. "Tell me, Nye, you are part of our world now and a human that tries to cause harm to one of us does not get to live to see another day. It is the law."

I look between both of them. "I can handle it."

Ezra slams his hands on the table and stands, "Who. Is. It. Nyathera." He bites out every word.

Fear starts to grip my throat. I feel my body shrink into the chair.

"We just want to make sure you are safe," Caine says softly.

I swallow down the fear. "If I tell you, do you promise not to kill him? I have questions."

Ezra looks at Caine. "We promise." Caine's gaze meets mine. "I will not let this fool kill him unless you give the go-ahead."

I take a deep breath, "His name is Xavier Nortick. The last time I saw him he shoved me into the pit." I pause as they stare at me, "My friend Dylan died in that battle. He was supposed to be fighting beside us, and he ran. And in return his friend died." Tears start to fill my eyes at the thought of Dylan.

"The man you were in love with tried to kill you?" Caine's eyes bore into me.

"I believed him when he said he fell in love with me and refused to carry out his father's plan," I sigh, realizing how blind I was, "but I was wrong. In return the man that Xavier told to keep an eye on me, to keep me safe, died."

"So, the man that tried to kill you, asked another man to watch you? Was this man in on it as well?" Ezra asks.

"No! Dylan was an honorable and amazing man. He protected me at all costs. Xavier was a piece of shit, and I should have seen that from the beginning." I look at each of them, "I should have killed him when he came to 'help' me with Dylan's body" I scrunch my nose as furry tugs at me. "Another man taken because their 'friend' was a pussy." Images of Xavier's copper hair blowing as I fell in the pit flash through my mind.

Ezra snorts, "Feisty, I like it. Let's go see your dragon." Ezra says softly, with a glance to Caine.

I nod and wipe an angry tear away. "Yes, let's." I say standing.

Chapter

35

Nyathera glances up at her mother, relishing in the safety of her embrace. Never wanting to experience that type of horror again.

We walk out the front doors and three black stallions stand in the driveway. I am flanked on either side by Ezra and Caine. "I have only seen horses in books. We don't have these in Mearin." Their beauty takes my breath away. These majestic beings have graced fantasy books in Mearin, and I am now looking at them.

I look at both of them and take that first step down the front stairs. I walk toward the horses and walk up to the one closest to us. I brush my hand over its nose and lean my forehead to his.

"This is Bruce, you must have a gentle soul. He doesn't usually take to anyone quickly" Ezra says, coming up to me. I lift my head and stroke his neck. He lets out an appreciative snort.

"He is gorgeous." His hair is silky and smooth. I run my hand down his strong side to the saddle. My foot doesn't reach the stirrup, and I feel large hands wrap around my waist before being hoisted onto the horse.

I grab the reins from Caine and wait for them to mount their horses. Caine leads the way, and we start down the long driveway. The horses hooves clack on the stones as we make our way out of the palace grounds. My body sways side to side as the horse walks solid and sturdy. Caine veers right and heads down a dirt path into a line of thick trees. I instruct Bruce to follow, and we continue on. The rustling of branches stops Bruce. His ears perk up and he looks straight forward, body stiff.

I rub his neck, "*Shhh*. What is it boy?" Bruce stomps his front hoof.

Ezra comes up to my side, "Do not dismount. Stay right where you are."

"What is it? I whisper.

Ezra holds his finger to his lips. My heart starts racing and my stomach sinks as a reptilian-looking creature steps around the bend of the path. It walks straight towards us, his forked tongue flicking out from its scaley mouth.

His raggedy cream shirt hangs over his scaly body, "What do we have here?" he hisses. Their presence makes me feel disgusted.

"Step back, we are on official business for the prince," Caine says in a stern and confident voice.

"*Oh*. The prince, huh?" He peers around Caine. "And who is the girl?" His beady eyes bore into my soul and makes me feel queasy.

"She is a special friend of the prince," Ezra says, moving his horse forward to block out the reptile's view of me.

The creature taps its chin with an inky black claw. "I will let you pass safely if you give me the girl. I could make some good money on her." My breath hitches at the thought.

"Either you let us all pass or we will ensure you cannot pirate anything, or *anyone* else, on these lands ever again." Caine's voice is laced with promise.

The reptile looks to contemplate it, the transparent eyelids sliding sideways over his yellow eyes as he tries to peer around at me one last time. "Of course." He says, waving his hand dramatically down the path and bowing.

We continue on, Ezra and Caine on either side of me. "Just remember girl, don't catch yourself out here alone." He hisses quietly as we pass.

I snort, "You better not catch yourself alone in my proximity." I say, catching the cock of his long neck and a smile spreading across his face.

We walk past him, and I look over my shoulder to find him staring at us. His forked tongue popping out of his mouth flicks in the air. Another steps out of the trees and stands next to him. They continue watching us and I stare right back until we round another curve, and they disappear out of sight. Taking a deep breath, I calm my nerves and look forward.

We get a reasonable distance away from the reptilians and Ezra grabs Bruce's reins. "You do not know what you just did. Almost every creature here respects the prince, but you are a guest here. Whatever they see fit to do to you while we are not around can end in catastrophe."

I look at him. Anger rolls through my soul. "I am capable of protecting myself. If I would have protected myself before I wouldn't have ended up here with ego-driven buffoons."

He rears his head back and lets out a laugh. "I see why Kai wants you to stay so bad." He says before falling behind me and watching my back. What does that mean? I shake my head as the trees open up to a large field full of sheep, and Runihura!

Chapter

36

*With newfound respect for her parents words, she starts
to talk about everything she had seen. Tears streaming
down her cheeks as her mother holds her hand.*

Warmth fills my body as happiness replaces every other emotion. Jumping off of Bruce, I run into the field. Bees buzz around me and puffs of dandelion fly through the air as I run to Runi. *"I have missed you!"* I shout down the bond.

"I have missed you too! I have become so tired." She lifts her head towards me, and I pause. She is massive. Her dark green scales reflect in the sunlight and the horns on top of her head come to a sharp point at the end.

"Oh, my Gods Runi! You're massive! And Beautiful!"

"I know!" She turns in a circle, showing off her beauty. The confidence and happiness barrels down the bond.

I reach her and hug her leg. "I can't believe how big you've gotten! I am so happy to see you." She lowers her nose to me and pushes me with her head. I almost fall over but right myself easily. She crouches down and I immediately climb up her leg and onto her back. Running my hands over her scales I admire the beautiful iridescence of them. She spreads her wings, and they must be twenty feet wide.

"Are you ready to fly?!" I say out loud. Runi bends her knees and springs up into the air.

The wind rips out the braid Margie carefully plaited this morning. My stomach lurching into my toes reminds me to hold on. Looking towards the ground, I see Ezra smiling at us. Caine is pale, almost grey. He really doesn't like dragons. I wave and they return it.

"WOOHOO!!!" I yell. Runi levels out and I put my hands out to the sides. The warmth of the sun kisses my cheeks, and I close my eyes, turning my face to the sky. Runi snorts in approval of flying as well.

"I think we should stay. Until I at least get some money saved up." I say to Runi.

"That can take a long time, Nye. Are you sure that is what you want?"

"Yes. The prince is very nice, and I feel comfortable here. I have never felt this comfortable before."

She is silent for a moment. The atmosphere changes as her body stiffens. *"Hold on,"* she says sternly.

"Why" she doesn't answer but dips her right wing and starts heading back towards the guys. We are only about seven feet from the ground and Caine and Ezra duck as we fly inches above their heads. A vibration starts in Runi's chest and travels up her neck. She opens her mouth, and fire erupts across the field. The two reptilians come into view and as they start their run towards Caine and Ezra they get hit with the billowing fire from Runi.

I gasp as the reptilians hiss. The weird smell of sulfur and burning flesh fills my senses as I hear their screams ring through my ears.

"What just happened?!" I yell.

Runi levels out, and with a strong voice says, *"If you want to stay here, we must earn our keep. I think saving those two was a good start."*

"But you killed them."

"If I didn't they would've killed your bodyguards." I rub her scales in appreciation.

"Fuck yeah!" I hear coming from behind us.

I look over my shoulder and see Ezra fist-pumping the air and jumping up and down. I chuckle, "The boys must have enjoyed the show. You're a boss bitch Runi." She snorts and I feel the satisfaction that courses through our bond.

"Now it is your turn to be a 'boss bitch'" She pauses. *"Nye?"*

"Yes?"

"What's a boss bitch?"

I giggle and rub the scales in front of me, *"It means you are amazing."*

"Duh."

I can't help the small laugh that escapes my chest.

We come back down to where the boys are. "That was awesome!" Ezra says. He high-fives me and touches Runihura's neck.

"Tell him to get his filthy fingers off me before I turn his arm into my mid-morning snack."

I giggle, "Runi says she would prefer you take your hands off her."

"That is NOT what I said."

I giggle again and reach up patting her neck.

"We have to get back to the palace, Nyathera. Kai will be waiting for us." Caine says, standing stoically like he hadn't just been cheering on the cremation of those two reptilian people.

I salute him, "yes sir!" the corners of his mouth tip upwards and satisfaction flows through me. I turn to Runi, who is eyeing the cows in a nearby field.

"Are you going to be alright?"

"I am fine. I won't keep you from your favorite demon any longer."

"He is not my favorite demon!"

"I can feel everything. I am going to have a snack. I'll see you soon." With that Runi takes off into the air leaving me questioning what she means.

Caine and Ezra have already mounted their horses by the time I get back across the field. "Are you ready?" I nod to Ezra, and he gets down to help me onto Bruce.

We take the same trail back to the palace, the atmosphere a little calmer now. When we ride through the opening of trees at the end of the path, I notice Kai standing on the front steps. The sheer beauty of this man takes the air from my lungs, I have never felt such power radiating off of someone before. He smiles when his gaze catches mine. We stop in front of the stairs, and he walks down them. Coming over to Bruce and me, "How was it seeing Runihura?" he asks.

"It was wonderful. You should've seen her!" I exclaim happily.

Caine walks up beside him, "I'll talk to you about it later. Nye is safe and Runihura took care of it."

Kai nods to Caine. Kai reaches his hand out to me, and I take it. Warmth spreads over my arm at his touch—a flicker of amusement flashes in his beautiful eyes. He helps me off Bruce and I pat Bruce's neck one more time before a young boy comes and grabs the reins of all three horses.

"This is Borris. He is one of the sons of the stable hands. He helps out when he isn't studying." Kai says softly.

I smile at the young boy, "It is very nice to meet you, Borris. My name is Nyathera, but you can call me Nye if it is easier."

"You are very pretty." He says with a small smile.

Kai pats his head, "Go on now. Your mother will be making dinner soon."

Borris smiles at me again before leading the horses back to the stables.

Kai places his hand on the small of my back sending goosebumps up my spine. That small tug in my chest erupts again. Like the tug of a string that is caught on something. I touch my chest as Kai pushes me forward slightly. He guides me up the stairs and through the large doors. Once inside he drops his hand and I almost whimper at the loss of it.

"Thank you for having them take me. I really missed her. And she has grown again! You should see her. She's so pretty!"

He shines a bright white smile. "I am glad. We can take you whenever you want to see her. If I can't, one of the boys can."

I nod. "I appreciate that."

"I am going to the library before dinner is served if you would like to join me?" He pauses, waiting, "I have some papers I need to go through." He looks at me expectantly.

"I would enjoy that." I say with a smile. We walk into the library, and I am in awe for the second time, at the number of books lining the shelves. Some look older than time. Fantasy, romance, history, biographies, and many more line the shelves in alphabetical order.

"Pick whatever you would like and make yourself comfortable," Kai says before sitting at the desk in front of the fireplace.

I walk over to the shelves reading the spines. Running my finger over each leather-bound book. I take my time inspecting each one and reading the back cover. I glance at Kai, admiring his features. When he glances up I quickly look away. I settle on a romance, full of heartache and turmoil. I walk over to the large black chairs and sit in one. Folding my feet under me I open the first page. After a while, I find it hard to keep my eyes open. I close the book and look over to where Kai is still going through papers. The sun is starting to set and bright oranges cascade across the sky. A slight hint of stars sparkle in the distance.

"When I was small my mother told me that the City of Shadows and Nightmares was a cold demonic place. That monsters would grab children in the night and drag them down here. I never imagined it would be a real place or that it would be so beautiful." I continue staring at the sky. "A lot has changed in the last few days. Things I never thought I would witness. Dragons were said to just be a nightmare. And now, I know that the bodies of the lost don't just fall into an endless pit but grace the sky with their souls." I sigh.

Kai is staring at me from across the room. I can feel his eyes boring into me before I even turn my head and meet his gaze. He stands and walks to the windows next to me, looking up. "From what I have heard, the city gets a bad reputation in the human world. We aren't monsters though, not all of us at least. We have just as many bad apples down here as in your world." He glances at me, "No place is without its flaws. Dragons have never existed in the human world without a demonic presence." He turns to look at me. "It is demonic here though." He winks and flashes his teeth, making me giggle..

"How did the Keltoids have a dragon?" I ask him.

He looks over my head for a moment and then meets my gaze again. "I am unsure. They must have someone, or something linked to our world helping them."

My stomach churns at the thought. "I have to find a way home. I have to help my friends."

Kai sighs, "I wish I could do that for you. I really do. But with you being a human, well…" He trails off.

I sit up on my knees anticipating what he has to say. He stays quiet for a moment, moving his gaze between my eyes.

"Well, what?" I ask.

"You are the only human I have ever heard of surviving the use of demon magic. And because of that it has made you half-demon. That is why you have the mark."

My heart stops. "Me? A demon?" I whisper.

"As Caine and Ezra explained, no human has ever survived the use of demon magic. So, we don't know much. But because of your altered DNA, you are part human and part demon." He says it as if he didn't just turn my entire world upside down. My heart races and I can feel the world spin. I look at him for a moment and then his eyes change. "Are you okay Nye?" He asks.

I just blink at him. Rage towards Xavier and my parents starts to bubble in my belly. I clench my fists and stand. I can feel something building inside me and the ground begins to shutter. Kai comes closer to me, reaching a hand outwards. My hands burn and my body shivers. "Nye. I need you to take a deep breath." His voice sounds distant as if he is in another room. "Nye. Listen to my voice."

The ground starts to shake, and books begin falling off the shelves. "How could he do that to me?" I ask.

Kai shakes his head. "I don't know. But we will figure it out."

He touches my shoulder and the burning in my hands starts to subside. The earth slowly stops shaking. I look at him and his face is etched with worry. "How long have you been able to cause earthquakes?" My breathing is heavy, and I cock my head to the side. He looks into my eyes and all I see is someone truly concerned for me, or himself.

Chapter

37

Nyathera's parents share a glance, turning back with a smile. "Nyathera, dear, those are just fairy tales." Her mother runs her hand over her hair, tightening the hug.

Margie pokes her head through the library door, "Is everyone okay in here? We haven't had an earthquake like that since the first war." Her eyes look like saucers, and she is pale.

"We are okay," Kai says back to her, not taking his eyes off me.

"Are you okay Margie?" I ask moving around him so I can go to her.

She gives me a small smile. I take her hands in mine, and she gasps, "Deary, you're burning up!"

Kai steps beside me and she looks at him. He simply nods and she meets my eyes again. "If you need anything, you know where to find me."

She smiles and walks out. Seconds later she is opening the door again, "I almost forgot. Dinner is just about ready sir."

Kai smiles, "We will be right in Margie." She exits the room again and Kai looks at me.

I simply nod, not wanting to talk. I follow Kai from the library and into the dining room.

"Hello there Nyathera." Ezra stands to greet me.

"Hello." I say before taking a seat and staring at the table.

Kai walks over to the bar cart in the corner and pours himself a glass of amber liquid before taking his seat at the head of the table.

"Nyathera, we need to talk about your powers. With Caine and Ezra here, we can put our heads together and try to understand them more." Kai takes a sip from his glass, and something bubbles in my stomach at him taking away my opportunity to let people know about my powers at my own pace.

"Powers, huh?" Ezra's red irises shine with excitement.

"It makes sense, since demon magic was used on her and the mark proves she is a demon." Caine chimes in.

"Part demon," I quietly correct him.

I can feel something starting in my chest, like a hive of bees vibrating through me. I do not want to discuss this with them, I want to learn what these powers are and how to control them before everyone 'figures them out' for me.

"I can take her to the fields and see what her powers can do tomorrow, maybe train her with the soldiers." Caine's voice sounds distant as the humming in my ears grows louder.

"I think I could figure out a way for her to learn to control them better," Ezra smirks.

"She will make her own decision, as for now we need to figure out what they are and where they came from before we can train her properly."

I can see them speaking, but I can no longer here them as whatever this feeling is grows inside me. I know they are speaking about me and what is best for me. Like the men in Mearin, they think they have the final decision. I can feel the anger mixing with the vibrations as they I continue watching them argue over which way is best.

My mark begins pulsating, in a rhythmic pattern as I hear Kai's voice break through, "She will do it my way or no way. That is the final…"

"ENOUGH!" I feel the vibration leave my fingers and flow through the table I slammed my hands on. The table rattles with a great force as I stand there, seething at these men who think they know what is best for me. "I have been here for four fucking days, four, and you assholes think you know what is best for me?" I holler at each of them. "You think you can control what I do with these powers that I didn't even ask for?! What gives you the right to decide what I do with them?" My breathing erratic as I try and calm the static that is escaping my body.

The table splits down the middle in a straight line, flowing directly towards Kai. I look around the room as the candle flames grow and lick the ceiling above them. "I am a woman, not an object for you to test out theories on."

"Nyathera, please sit down." Kai has risen to his feet and is slowly walking towards me. "We will figure this out together in whatever way you deem fit."

I can't control the anger that is coursing through my veins, "you sit the fuck down, Kai. I will make the call when I am ready." Kai backs towards his seat slowly.

I take some deep breaths and focus on my surroundings. A red chair, the smoke from the fireplace, breathing slowly.

Inhale, exhale.

Inhale, exhale.

My body starts to relax, as the vibrations and humming recedes.

Slow clapping comes from my right, and I look over to Ezra, who has a wide smile on his face, "the power that resides inside of you is definitely something we haven't seen before. Only in stories."

I look to Kai, who despite being yelled at has a smirk on his face. Caine is sipping his water and ignoring it all.

"Runi."

"Where are you?"

"At the house, can you get on the grounds?"

"I am already on my way." I stand and look at the men sitting at the table. Without saying a word, I walk out of the dining room and into the foyer. I take a deep breath when I hear Kai call after me. I open the door and Runi

lands in the driveway, dust blowing as her wings beat. I run towards her and up her leg, settling in front of her wings. Kai appears on the front steps, and I pause for a moment before gripping the scales in front of me, signaling Runi to fly.

"Do you want to talk about it."

"No."

"Oh, good."

My knuckles are white with force at which I am gripping her scales, I close my eyes just as tight and take calming breaths. Runi flies over the forest and towards the healing pool, but banks right as we head towards the falls of lava.

We land on the edge of the molten lake, where the lava has hardened into rocks. I walk towards the lake below the falls, mesmerized by the glow of the molten stone. The heat beats into my skin and I welcome it with ease. I stand right on the edge of the lake, feeling like I belong here. Welcoming the sizzle as I stand on the hot rocks.

"There is something you should know about your powers, Nyathera,"

"I can control fire."

Runihura's growl sounds like words.

"What is that supposed to mean?" I don't open my eyes as I stand on the rocks and absorbed the power that the lava provides.

"In your tongue, the best I can translate is 'you're a boss bitch'"

The corners of my mouth tip up. "I will not be controlled by men, Runihura." She doesn't say a word. "I have spent my entire life thinking I would have to provide children to some man that my parents deemed appropriate, spend my life alone raising those children because he was off in battle." I take a deep breath in, "and then men *collected* women for battle almost four years ago. Men have made every single decision in my life, and I refuse to allow that to happen here." I open my eyes and turn towards her, her beautiful scales reflect the lava, "this is like a new beginning for me. A new Nyathera."

"If you are worried about how a man will control your life, then don't allow them to. You are extremely powerful Nyathera."

"I think I will keep all my powers to myself for a while, just you and I will know."

"Seeing as how I cannot link anyone else, your secret is safe with me."

I walk towards her and lay my forehead to her nose, "I would be nowhere without you."

"I know."

Chapter

38

Runi lays off to the side while I relish in the power surging through me. I examine the rocks and follow the flow of ripples on each one, the massive lava falls create a horseshoe shape barren of any life besides a small lizard that scurries up to me.

The little creature has blue flames down its spine, large blue eyes, and transparent skin. I lay my hand on the ground, and it scurries into my palm, licking its eye with its long tongue. I giggle at its innocence. It tilts its head, as if trying to read me, "hello little guy." I speak in a soothing tone. The little lizard spins in circles and curls up in my palms. "I will call you spark." I walk towards Runi who sniffs the air.

"What do you have?"

"A lizard, I am naming him spark."

"Useless creature."

"Be nice." I throw her a warning glance.

"You have to put him back. He will die without the lava."

"I know, something tells me this is where he belongs." I look at Spark and envy his freedom. I nuzzle the flames on his back and set him back on the rocks. "Be free, Spark."

I climb up Runi's leg and we fly back to the house. When we land I lay my forehead to Runihura's, "thank you, again." She huffs in return before springing into the air, the hair on my head whips around as she does, and I watch her disappear over the forest.

"That's not fair!" I hear Ezra yell from the side of the house.

"It is so! You don't just get your way because you're the youngest!" Caine bickers back.

I walk around the side of the house, past the bushes. Peaking around the corner, Caine and Ezra are throwing punches and wrestling on the ground. Kai stands at the door with his arms crossed over his chest watching the two with a smile on his face. The second I walk around the corner; Kai's eyes find me. He gives me a nod and continues watching the boys fighting on the grass. Walking towards Kai I dodge Ezras foot as Caine pins him to the ground.

"What are they doing?" I walk up the stairs and stand next to Kai.

He turns his head towards me, "the beginning ritual to annual game night."

"Annual game night?"

"Because we work so hard to keep this City safe, we enjoy a game night every now and then." He looks at me and back to the boys, "but once a year we go hard, and the winner gets to be in charge for the next four months." He smiles, "They do this every year. And Ezra never wins."

I nod as if I understand and watch Caine sit on Ezra's chest, pinning his arms under his knees. "Give up?"

"Never." Ezra states through gritted teeth.

Caine slaps Ezra, igniting a flame in Ezra. His eyes shine bright like the lava falls and Caine is thrown off of him, straight into the air. Caine lands on his back, directly on the steps in front of us. He looks up at us, "Good to see you've calmed down, Nye." and he takes off towards Ezra. What an asshole.

"That's enough." Kai's deep voice rings out, "Ezra you lost, again."

Ezra looks at Kai and then me. "Nye. Tell them I won!"

I shake my head, "I just got here." I shrug.

Ezra's mouth drops open, and Caine throws his arm over his shoulder, walking into the door behind Kai and me.

"I was actually moved up in classes for hand-to-hand in Mearin, I weirdly miss it." I look at Kai.

"I will happily spar with you anytime." He smirks.

I pat his arm, "I like being alive." Walking away I can feel his smile.

I follow the boys through the door, it leads into the kitchen. I smile at the servants bustling around and walk into the dining room. Somehow the table has been fixed already. Ezra and Caine are setting up an overly large wooden game board. The little pieces in their hands look like all the creatures that reside in the forest. Small wooden buildings are laid out on a map that sits on the game board. "What's this?" I walk closer and examine it.

"City and Stones." Ezra chirps as he continues placing pieces on the board.

"Huh?" I look at Caine.

"It is a game of wits; you get to start as whatever creature you choose and you mentally 'battle' your way through the map."

As if that made any sense to me, I sit down. "Can I play?" Both Ezra and Caine pause, looking at me in confusion.

"Actually, usually only men…" Ezra is cut off when Kai stands next to him.

"She will be playing if she chooses to do so." Kai says simply.

Ezra and Caine share a look. Ezra hands me a small wooden piece, carved to look like a fairy. The wings are intricately carved into beautiful butterfly wings. I smile at her.

Kai sits in his normal seat, and they explain the game to me. I grab the dice, two ten sided blue rocks, numbered one through ten. I roll them, they show fifteen. I look to Kai, "Move your piece along the map fifteen spaces. You will then get a card with a quest on it."

I move my piece and Caine hands me a card, "for those who seek this magic place, guess it right and move a space." I scrunch my nose, "is this a riddle?"

Caine nods, "you won't get it."

I scowl at him, close my eyes and think, where is a magic space that would allow you magic? I look at all three of them, "the healing pool." Kai looks at the paper, and then back to me. His eyes dancing with amusement as Ezra and Caine stare at him.

"She's right." he chuckles.

Ezra throws his hands up, "what?!"

A smile brushes my lips as happiness pulses in my chest. "That was easy."

Caine rolls, moves, and picks up his card. "Don't stay long, or your future will burn, get this wrong and lose a turn." He thinks for a moment and looks to Ezra, who in return shrugs.

"I know." I giggle.

"Oh yeah?" Caine faces me crossing his arms, "Kai, I am going to let her have this one since she is so confident."

Kai sighs, "fine."

Grinning, "the lava falls."

Kai slaps the table with a laugh, "she's right again boys!"

Caine throws his head back, "well…"

"You lose a turn." Ezra laughs.

It is Kai's turn, "what are you doing?" I ask as Kai moves his chair over to the side of me.

He smiles at Ezra and Caine, "my card reads, 'pick a team for this shall not pass, those who lose will join the mass.' And it has an image of a dragon on it." His eyes sparkle as he smirks at the boys.

"What?!" Caine throws his hands in the air.

"Come on man," Ezra whines.

I look over to Kai, who's boyish grin makes his face light up.

We play the game as teams for the next three hours, ultimately kicking Caine and Ezra's asses. They leave Kai and I to clean up.

"Thank you for tonight. I had a great time."

Kai pauses, "you are welcome to join us anytime you feel like it."

"And I am sorry for my outburst earlier"

"You never have to apologize. I know that the human world keeps a thumb on the woman, I don't want the demon realm to be that way." He continues picking up, "at least not in my city."

I nod just as the door to the dining room opens and a scrawny man peeks in, "Sir, there is a prisoner that I think we will need your.." he clears his throat, "expertise for."

Kai places his pieces down in the box, "I'll be there in a moment."

The man nods and closes the door, "what prisoner?" I ask.

Kai's eyes meet mine, burning deep within me. "We had an issue earlier today and my men went to find the soldiers that escaped. Don't worry."

I cock my head, not understanding why I would worry, "and why should I worry?"

Kai walks to the door without another word, closing it behind him. I set my pieces down, fighting the urge to follow him. I count to ten before I decide that if I should have been worrying, I should know what I should be worried about.

Taking a deep breath in, I head for the door, pausing with my hand on the handle as I step into the foyer and out the front doors. The night breeze blows my hair across my face, deepening the weird dread that has coated my skin. Shaking off the feeling I walk down the front steps and into the driveway. The sound of voices off in the distance catches my attention and I follow them. The path into the woods, that I hadn't noticed before, is muddy and dark. A green hue graces my vision and lights the path. I shake my head, but the hue stays. I guess this is here to stay.

Following the path to a large round door in the side of a small grass hill in the middle of the forest. I can still hear the voices as I approach the door. Pushing it open, I am met with a dark tunnel twisting further into the ground. I run my hand along the muddy wall as I continue down the path into the earth. The cold musty air sits heavy on my shoulders as I get deeper and deeper into the unknown.

Light shines at the end of the tunnel, following it the voices get clearer. I pause at their words, "where the fuck is he?" Kai's deep voice glides through the area like water in a river. Wrapping around my senses as the anger in his tone is apparent.

A man familiar voice sounds, "I…" the sound of a punch invades my ears as I stand in silence, flinching as another sounds. "I don't know! I was just told to follow her!"

"So, you thought following her into a pit that you didn't know if it would end in death, was a good idea?"

"Fuck off, I was just doing what I was told to do." The voice is familiar, but I can't place it. Another punch sounds through the tunnel.

Gargling can be heard and laughter. I brave walking around the end into the light. Kai stands in front of the man from the battle in Mearin. The scar over his eye shimmers with blood. Water spews from his nose and mouth and his eyes are bulging.

"Kai! Stop!" I scream as I run towards the man.

When Kai turns around I freeze, his eyes are feral, and his canines have lengthened more. "Get out of here Nyathera!" He demands with a growl.

"No! I know him." I run to the man's side, "what are you doing here?" I kneel in front of him, reaching for the rope around his ankles.

The man eyes me with a grotesque smile. My brows furrow as I look at him, "I came to find you." When I try and answer he head butts me with such force my ears ring and spirals of color shine in my vision.

I look up at him, feeling the warmth of blood running down my face, "who sent you here?"

The man laughs and struggles in his restraints, "you'll see soon."

Irritation builds in my chest and a small smile spreads across my face. Holding my hands out the earth vibrates, "answer the question."

The man laughs manically, creating a burst of adrenaline coursing through my veins. Kai steps next to me and puts his hand on my shoulder, "let me deal with this, please."

I stop and turn my gaze to Kai. He nods once and I settle the vibrations. Wiping my brow, I look at my blood-soaked fingers, "I am staying. He is from my world." I wipe my hand on my pants, "and obviously deserves this."

Kai looks at me with furrowed brows, "are you sure you can handle this?"

I stare into his brown and red flecked eyes, "yes."

He gives me one more glance, before turning back to the man, shoving his hands into his pockets. Water starts pouring from the man's mouth again, excitement courses through me as I watch this man work his magic on the piece of shit before him.

I have never felt this way about torture or the anger that I am constantly feeling that bubbles in my gut. I am uneasy, and…aroused?

I can feel heat creeping up my neck when Kai turns to me and smirks, his eyes look down my body and back up slowly. Can he tell? The other men in the room advert their gaze when I look up at them. There is no way.

"Your scent has changed, Nyathera." Kai continues to work on the man, the screams filling the small space as

Kai strips pieces of flesh from his bones. I immediately feel uncomfortable, I don't even know what that means.

"It means we can scent the changes in your emotions, I advise you leave." Kai only side glances at me, and the urge to run takes over.

Running from the tunnel and into the night air I sprint towards the house. I don't stop until I am safely in my room. Leaning against the door and sliding to the floor. What is going on with me? I run my hands over my face and into my hair, gripping the strands and pulling.

"Come on deary, let's get you soaking in the tub." Margie's voice startles me. I look up and her friendly blue grey eyes shine in the dim light of the room. She reaches a plump hand to me, and I take it. We walk to the bathroom where the water is already on in the tub. I strip my clothing and sink into the tub, closing my eyes. I hear Margie walk out and close the door behind her.

Listening to the wind outside the windows, I can hear the screams from that man dying. I close my eyes tighter, ignoring them. When I can no longer drown them out I start singing the song my mother always sang to me. "Walk it slow, take your time. Life will show you what is meant to be. You are strong, you are loved, don't let fears hold you down."

Sighing I get out of the tub and look in the mirror. the gash on my forehead from that man headbutting me is almost completely healed. I no longer know how I feel. Scared? Angry? Confused? None of those, I almost feel…numb? I get dressed for the night, sliding under the covers I try and forget about everything I have seen and heard.

Chapter

39

I don't leave my room until dinner the next day. When I open the door to the dining room Kai sits there with Ezra and Caine. No one says anything. I sit in the chair and a plate is brought out for me.

Kai looks up from his plate. "Nyathera, there is something we need to tell you."

I set my fork down, and meet his gaze, "okay."

Ezra and Caine stand, "I am not going to be a part of this conversation." Ezra states seriously. I look over to him and then Kai, who nods at them as they disappear.

Kai takes a deep breath, "I am sorry about last night. There is a lot of things that are different in this world, you should not have had to deal with any of that…"

I hold up a hand cutting him off, "I do not care that you tortured that man, in fact, I want you to train me to do so."

He raises an eyebrow, "you want me to," he pauses, "you want me to teach you the ways of torture?"

"Yes."

"Don't you think that is a little much for a woman?"

Furry erupts again, "Woman are capable of doing anything a man can do, maybe even better." I look him dead in the eyes, "a woman can give you life, she can take it away," I lean over the table, "and she can destroy it from the inside out."

His eyes light with amusement. "And I would enjoy every second of it Nyathera." His gaze lingers on me as I sit in disbelief. "Did you expect me to argue with you?" he tilts his head.

I stare at him, "I didn't expect you to be on board so easily."

He sighs, "Nyathera, we all have a scent, and we can tell when it changes and what emotion is associated with that scent."

I can feel my cheeks heat, so he did smell what it did to me.

"And it is nothing to be embarrassed about, it happens a lot. Most people don't realize that they have a dark side." He picks up his glass and takes a sip, "especially someone who is learning how to be a demon." He smirks at me.

I stand, "I.." looking around the room I look for a reason to escape his gaze, "I think Runihura needs me." I start to move towards the door.

"Nyathera. Sit down." Kai's voice glides over my skin like a cold shower, sinking into my bones. I pause and turn to him, he is now standing at the end of the table and gesturing to my chair. Slowly I walk to it and sit, unsure of why I have this deep-seeded need to obey.

"There is something more we need to talk about." He starts, "we have come across some information I think you need to hear."

I look at him and lift a brow, "okay."

Tight lipped his gaze falls to his plate, "You have been half demon your entire life." He pauses, staring at me.

I stare at him in silence. Hoping he continues.

"A piece of your soul was given to the city of shadows and nightmares when you were born, ultimately altering your DNA." He pauses again, and sighs, "The demon magic used on you activated that side of you."

Laughter bubbles up and I can't control it from erupting. It echoes off the walls and ceiling, "Did you say a piece of my soul? And I have always been a demon?" Heaving laughter rattles my body, but when I meet his gaze again his face is stoic. "Are you fucking serious?"

His pinched brows indicate that he is in fact serious. I don't know how to feel. My body goes numb, and I stare at him.

"Your parents made a deal with my father to save you at birth. You were born too early, and your mother did what any mom would do."

"So, when they told me my white hair was due to a piece of my soul being here, they weren't lying?"

Kai shakes his head, "no, and…" he trails off.

"And what?" I demand, anxious to find out what he has to say. Not like my life has just been completely changed.

"My father gave it to the stars."

I freeze, "well. At least I got this awesome hair out of it. I don't blame you; I blame my parents for not informing me of the truth."

His face contorts into confusion, "are you not mad?"

I sigh, "Kai, I have no room for anymore anger, I feel…" I trail off looking for the right word, "numb to it all." I am sure later this will all hit, but at this moment, I really don't care. That ping in my sternum appears again and I rub at it. Static lines my bones as if something is trying to escape. I close my eyes and breathe in deeply, still rubbing my sternum.

"After dinner, let's go for a walk so we can talk."

I give him a weary smile. "Okay." My mind races with everything that happened the night before and what Kai has just told me. I am half demon. This is another thing to add to my 'reasons I think I am actually dead' list.

Kai chuckles, "Do you really have one of those?"

My eyes widen. "Did I say that out loud?"

He shakes his head, "let's talk about it after dinner." Kai continues eating.

"Can we talk now? No one is here."

He looks up from his food. "There are too many ears around here, we will talk after you eat."

Again, I nod. My hands are shaky with everything running through my mind. *"Did you know?"* I reach out to Runihura in hopes of getting some sort of answer to all my questions.

She doesn't respond. I sigh and glance at the food on my plate. Fish and greens are piled on my plate. My stomach growls and I see the corner of Kai's mouth turn upwards. We eat in silence. All the questions running through my head don't allow me to speak. When finished, I set my fork and knife on the plate and stand.

"Where are you going?" Kai asks with a tilt of his head.

"I am going to the garden. When you are ready I will go wherever you need to talk."

He stands, "I'll go with you now."

He walks over to me and holds out his elbow. I look at it and step away. He gestures for me to exit the dining room, and we walk through the palace and out to the garden. The fresh smell of roses fills my nose as we step onto the stone path. We walk to the middle and then Kai pulls me towards the wall of foliage.

"Where are you taking me?" I ask digging my heels in.

"Somewhere where we can talk in private." Reluctantly, I follow him through the bushes, and it opens up to a field with a lake in the middle.

Weeping willows line the water's edge and flowers are scattered through the lush grass. The sky is starting to turn to a burnt orange and the sun is laying low in the sky, shining off the lake. The mountains behind the lake have snow on top of their peaks and the forest on the other side provides a song as the wind rustles through the leaves.

I stand next to Kai and admire the beauty. All these years that I thought this place wasn't real, I was missing out on sunsets like this. I sigh at the calmness washing over my tired bones. Letting in all the emotions I have put to the side I wait as my heartbeat steadies and my breathing evens out. I work through the emotions silently as I watch the stars transparently appear in the evening sky. I catch Kai staring at me out of the corner of my eye.

I turn to face him, "What?"

He smiles, "I haven't seen you calm since you arrived."

I smirk. "If you knew what was in my head right now, you wouldn't think I was calm."

He smirks, "I know."

My heart flutters away carried by the butterflies that erupt in my stomach. That pull in my chest tugs again and I rub my sternum.

"Are you okay?" Kai asks, looking me over in question.

"Yeah, I have just had this tugging sensation in my chest for the last week." He smiles broadly.

"Good." I look at him in question. "It just means that everything is settling into place. Everything will be okay." I cock my head to him. Before I can ask him anything he is stripping his clothes off.

I turn around, "Oh my Gods, warn a girl next time."

He laughs behind me, and I hear him running. I turn and Kai is running towards the lake in nothing but his boxer briefs. Muscles pinch and curve as he does so. The tattoos on his back seem to come to life with the movement. "Come on!" he calls over his shoulder before diving in.

I shake my head and laugh, "I am okay." How is it that I feel so comfortable with this man? I have known him for all of a week now and I feel like I have known him my entire life.

He looks at me with just his eyes exposed in the water. The brown and red eyes sparkling like a crocodile watching its prey. That tug in my chest strengthens, and I try to rub it out again. I walk to the water's edge and notice Kai has disappeared.

I turn in a circle looking for him. My heart rate increases at the thought of another situation that I can't control. He springs out of the water with ease and comes right towards me. I scream and start running towards the bushes on the other side of the field.

"NO!" I yell with a laugh. He grabs me with both arms around the waist spinning me in a circle. Before I can react his hands are behind my knees hoisting me over his shoulder. "Kai stop!" I want to sound serious, but the laughter is uncontrollable. I slap at his back, but he laughs as he throws us both into the warm water.

The water hits my face with a smack, forcing water up my nose. As my feet tumble over my head and my hair sticks to my face, a large arm wraps around my middle again and pulls me towards the surface. I brush the hair out of my face and cough with a laugh. When I clear my face of hair and catch my breath, I am met with a beautiful smile. I look up, and Kai's eyes bore into my soul. My breath hitches as that tugging sensation starts in my chest again. I place my hand on my heart, and Kai covers my hand with his.

"Do you know what that tug you are feeling is?" His voice almost a whisper.

I shake my head, looking at him through my lashes.

"When do you feel it the most?"

I think about it momentarily while moving away from Kai's arms. I shudder at the loss of his touch, craving for him to touch me again. "When I am near you or you cross my mind," I say with the realization that he is the center of the tugging.

He smiles.

"Does that mean your magic was used to try and kill me?" My breathing is erratic now. The thought of this man being the weapon used against me shatters my heart.

He shakes his head slowly, "No." I wrack my brain trying to figure out what this could mean. "I don't know then."

He moves closer and reaches towards me. I don't move away. I let him wrap an arm around my middle. Because as much as I don't know this man, I crave his touch. To feel his warmth. His eyes make my soul feel like it is on fire. "Tell me, Kai." I look him in the eyes, pleading for an answer. Any answer. I haven't had any real answers in years.

He takes a deep breath. "Promise me you won't freak out when I tell you." My heart rate increases tenfold. He pulls me a little closer. "Promise me," His voice full of eagerness.

"I promise."

"I want to start by saying you aren't dead. You are very much alive. My kingdom is a real place, and you are half-demon. Runihura is a real dragon, and she chose you to bond with." He takes another slow breath, "the way you and Runihura are bonded, we are bonded. Two souls turned into one."

My head spins, "you chose me to bond with?"

He smiles, "No. I knew who you were when I felt your presence in Mearin. *What* you were. And who you would become. Nyathera," He pauses briefly, searching my eyes, "you're my mate. Put in this universe to be part of me—my twin flame. Part of my soul was missing until you came within proximity of my world. It is the reason I can hear your thoughts; the reason I knew where to find you when that siren hurt you."

I can't breathe. I can't think. The world spins and my vision blurs. "I was created for you?!"

He cradles my face in his hands, "No! *NO*, you weren't created for me. Our souls have found each other since the beginning of time. We are meant to be together. To make us stronger, smarter…happier." He finishes on a whisper.

My eyes whip back to his. "I, I need time to process this. I don't know if I am ready for a *mate*!" his eyes fall and his shoulders slump, sending shocking waves of sadness rushing to my core. I touch his arm, "That doesn't mean I will never be ready. But I am learning so much in such a short time and someone is, *was*, trying to kill me…" I trail off with a sigh, "Just give me time to process everything. I didn't grow up this way. We found love and we married it. We didn't have mates." He lifts his eyes to mine and his shoulders straighten.

His face taking on a stoic look, "that is all I can ask. The choice is yours." His voice is now that of a prince and not the fun-loving man I just saw. "But believe me when I say I will continue to keep you safe, and allowing me in, accepting the mating bond makes us so much stronger." His voice dropping to almost a whisper.

I sigh, "The last person who tried to keep me safe died. The man I was falling for was trying to kill me. And death follows me wherever I go. I was a mistake to be born, and I am now paying the consequences the Gods see fit."

His hands grip my shoulders, his fingers pinching the skin slightly. "You are not a mistake." The sincerity and determination in his voice shocks me. He leans forward and kisses my forehead. The simple gesture igniting a flame and creating a wild need in my soul. To never let him leave. I feel like I am whole.

I look up at him, "Please. Just a little time."

He nods, letting go of my shoulders and grabbing my hand. We walk back to the shore, and I drop his hand.

His expectant eyes bore into my soul and my brain swims with confusion. I give him a small smile and walk back towards the garden. We walk back in silence, Kai not more than ten feet behind me. Now and then I hear him sigh or say something to himself. I have a mate. I was created for someone.

"Not created for me," he says behind me, kicking at the rocks. He has his hands in his pockets and he's whistling.

I shake my head but can't help the smile that reaches my lips. Maybe my future will be full of love and happiness, but for right now I need to live in the heartache. I deserve to grieve and live for myself for once.

"You deserve the world." Kai's voice fills the silence and warmth spreads over my body.

Chapter

40

Nyathera's mind swirls at the idea of what she saw being a fairytale. "But, mother, my friends and I saw it. It was real."

When I get to my room Margie is standing there waiting for me. She gives me a small smile and walks into the bathroom. She helps me bathe and I appreciate the silence for once. I slip on the lilac silk pajama top and bottoms and climb into the fluffy bed, pulling the covers up around my neck.

Margie walks to the door and stops, looking over her shoulder, "You should give him a chance Nyathera, he has waited centuries for you."

And she walks out, the door clicking behind her. I roll onto my side and look at the windows, wondering if Dylan is actually up there. A tear runs down the side of my face as I close my eyes. Sleep evades me for hours. I toss and turn with no avail. I throw the covers off and sit up on the side of the bed. Stepping onto the cold wooden floor I pad across the room to the door. Opening it I notice the house is silent.

I slowly walk down the stairs to the first floor and scan left and right. Through the library door, I see the flickering of flames illuminating the walls. I walk to the door and peek in. Kai sits at the desk with papers scattered across the top and his face held in his hands. His shoulders are slumped, and he looks defeated. I clear my throat and his head snaps up, eyes meeting mine.

"I couldn't sleep." He nods and gestures to the chair across the desk from him. "Can I ask you a couple of questions?" I ask, my hands shaking.

"Of course. You can ask me anything and I will answer to the best of my abilities."

I squint at him, "But it will also be the truth right?"

He sighs, "I will tell you anything you want to know."

I sit across from him, and he stands up walking to the chairs in the far corner and grabs a blanket. He walks back to me in quick strides and places the blanket over my shoulders. I give him a small smile and wrap the blanket around me tighter.

"Ask away." He says leaning against the desk and crossing his long legs in front of him.

I shift in my seat. "Is Dylan really in the stars?"

He pauses, "He is. Every soul that comes through that pit, unless a nightmare, turns into a star."

I nod, my shoulders relaxing, "so he is at peace?" Kai nods. "I got him killed; he was so worried about me that he didn't focus on keeping himself safe. If I wasn't so weak I would be able to protect myself. If this damn mark didn't start burning we wouldn't have been going the way we were. I killed him." Tears well in my eyes and I blink them away.

Kai pushes off the desk and squats in front of me, placing a hand on my knee, "You are not weak. I know everything that happened in the human world. You were given a run of unfortunate events, but you handled them all with poise and you stayed strong. Even when Dylan was killed, you made sure he was at peace. Not worrying about your own life. That is strength, love, and friendship." He moves his hand, and my soul reaches out to grab it.

I take a deep breath, "Why does the earth shake when I am mad or scared? It happened on the battlefield and then it happened here."

Kai looks at the floor, "It is part of the magic you received when they used the demon magic on you." he trails off for a moment, wringing his hands together, "it activated a plethora of powers that you haven't yet come into. I noticed the flames when you had your moment in the dining room." He lets out a breath as if he has been holding it this entire time. "I am sure there are more that we don't know about."

I let his words roll over me, I don't need to think of that right now. "One last question." I say quietly.

"Anything," he says sincerely.

"I saw you the other night in the gazebo, clear as day through the dark. How and what were you doing?"

He stares at me for a moment, "That is part of my powers…"

My back stiffens, "Your powers?"

He nods, "I am the only demon who has ever been able to see in the dark as if it were day, except…" He pauses, his eyes flashing with sadness.

Anticipation grips at me, "except what?"

He clears his throat, his eyes filling with tears, "I am the only demon who can see in the dark, except for my mother, and Caine."

My breath hitches and I grip the blanket tighter. He stands in front of me and then sits in the chair next to me.

Our eyes meet and for a moment I feel like I can see directly into his soul. I reach out and take his hand in mine, his large, calloused fingers scratch against my palm. Flashes of a small boy being yelled at because he was out late, and a woman with the same ebony hair as Kai holding him while he cries. 'Let's go for a nighttime hide and seek, shall we?.' Her beautiful smile causes the room to brighten. She takes the boys hand, and they run to the front door, laughing the entire time. My heart swells at the images flashing through my mind.

"You just saw my memories, didn't you?"

I nod slowly, "I didn't mean to."

He smiles, "I am glad you did. I will share anything with you."

"Then tell me what you were doing in the gazebo that night."

He sits up, shifting towards me a little more, and puts his elbows on his knees. Glancing up at me, "I was telling my mother I found you. She was always there for me through everything, she told me when I was a young boy that I would always find my mate. That I just had to be patient."

I clear my throat, "I should try to sleep." I stand and Kai does as well.

He takes my face in his hands, "You are safe here Nyathera. I will give you as much time as you need to accept…or deny the mating bond. But you need to know that I am so happy that I have found you, that you have come into my life. I haven't been happy in over 200 years, since my mother died. And when I saw you facing that minotaur, I knew. I knew who you were and what you would become. Because in other lives I have found you, and I don't want to let you go."

"You saw me facing that minotaur and didn't intervene?" My voice higher than I wanted.

"I did, though." He says, dipping his chin.

"I didn't see…" I pause. "You were the wolf." My heart stutters.

He places a soft kiss on my forehead and rests his against mine for a brief second. Then he pulls away and holds his elbow out for me. Not giving me any answers, I sigh. Placing my hand on the crook of his elbow I look at his face, his eyes are like a vast desert with many secrets to unveil. I smile at him, and he smiles back.

When we get to my door he takes my hand and presses a light kiss to my knuckles, "Good night Nyathera."

"Good night Kai." I open the door and walk back into the room. My head is still spinning from all the information, but that can wait until another day. My soul feels at ease as I climb into the sheets and close my eyes. Tomorrow is another day, and I will go visit Runihura right after breakfast. And with any luck, Kai will come with me.

"I'd be delighted to go with you and meet her." Kai's voice rings through my head as if he is standing right next to me.

I snap up straight in bed like a current of electricity was shot through my body. I look around the room, studying the shadows, and there isn't a single soul in my room besides me.

Shaking my head I lay down and close my eyes.

"Is this a new thing? Like, when I speak with Runihura?" I speak in my mind with the hope that he hears me. An onyx wall appears in my mind. I admire the shiny exterior of it. A chuckle sounds in my mind, and I know that wall is there to stay.

As I drift to sleep, a husky, rich voice glides through my mind, *"Goodnight, crazy girl"*

Visions of that small boy from earlier dance through my head. A woman with a cheerful smile helping him cook, draw, chasing him through the garden. Pure happiness radiates through me. All night I have dreams of this little boy and the happiness his mother brought him. And I wake up wondering if I could bring that kind of joy to his life like she once had.

Chapter

41

With a smile her mother kissed the top of her head.
Nyathera stared at her, knowing that even though her
parents don't believe her, she would never adventure too
far from home.

Kai isn't at breakfast, something about a meeting with Aurora. Ezra and Caine kept me company in his absence. After breakfast I walk out those front doors and Bruce is already waiting out front in the driveway for me. He whinnies and shakes his head when he sees me and I smile, "Hi boy, do you want to go for a ride?" He stomps his front hoof in the gravel making stones and dust fly. "Okay, hold on."

Before I can get my foot in a stirrup two large warm hands wrap around my waist. The feeling washes a warmth over my body, and a tingle runs down my spine. A small chuckle vibrates the chest my back lays against as I am hoisted up onto the saddle.

Kai.

My nerves ignite with him in such a close proximity as he lays a hand on my thigh, "good morning Nyathera." he says with a deep sultry voice, his smile beaming.

I smile at him, "Good morning Kai. We missed you at breakfast this morning."

His smile fades some, "I had some…business to attend to."

"Anything I can help with?" He shakes his head, removing his hand from my thigh.

Cool air invades my leg where his hand was. I shiver as a cool breeze coasts across the palace grounds. Kai holds out his hand and a deep blue cloak appears in it. I tense.

He smiles, "Here. This should keep you warm."

"Let me guess, another power you possess?" He smiles wider and drapes the cloak over my shoulders, closing the front with a gold pin in the shape of a bird.

The cloak is soft and warm, lined with silk. His face is mere inches from mine as he reaches his arms on both sides of my head and raises the hood. I hold my breath as his hands remain on each side of my face. He smells delicious and warmth pools in my lower belly. I smile as Bruce stomps his foot again. "We should get going." He says giving me a wicked grin.

A midnight black horse appears beside me, Borris leading it by the reins. "Good morning, Borris." I smile down at the young boy.

"Good morning, Lady Nyathera." He dips his head slightly.

I chuckle. "You can just call me Nye."

The boy's eyes meet mine and he smiles with all his teeth. "Okay!" he says as Kai takes the reins from his hand.

Kai ruffles the boy's hair, "Where is your hat?"

Borris' face falls, "I couldn't find one this morning and Mother says we cannot afford a new one."

Kia's eyes fall to the boy and then up to me. "Nye, we need to make a stop before we head to see Runihura if that is okay." His eyes are filled with something I can't quite read but I nod.

Kai mounts his horse and turns him towards the west side of the palace. I follow behind him, admiring the sway of his hips with the horses movement as we make our way towards the small houses. Servants and their families watch as we walk by with smiles on their faces. Everyone says hello and dips their heads. I feel uneasy with the attention but ignore it. Kai is silent as we continue toward the small house at the very end of the line. He dismounts and reaches his hand out for me when we stop in front of the quaint house. I drop onto the muddy earth and follow him. The siding is baby blue with ivy growing up the sides. The paint is chipping, and the wood of the front steps is splintering.

The wooden front door cracks open and a lovely blonde-haired woman steps out. "Is everything ok sir?" She looks concerned as Kai steps towards her.

"Mildred," Kai says with a smile.

"Did Borris break something again? I will fix it. He is just a boy; I am sure he didn't mean…"

Kai holds up a hand before her ranting can continue. "Borris is just a boy and if anything is broken I will simply replace it. Don't worry about any of that." His voice is calm and sincere. She drops her gaze to the ground. "Mildred, I am not my father. I am not bringing anything to you with ill intent." Her sky-blue eyes meet his gaze again. "I wanted to come and let you know that we will be providing winter clothing for your family and all the families here, as well as increasing pay. I want you all taken care of during the winter and for the years coming." Mildred's eyes start to well with tears, "I would also like to introduce you to Nyathera, she will be staying with us for a while."

She meets my gaze and smiles, "It is very nice to meet you, Lady Nyathera." She dips her head in my direction.

My chest freezes and my gaze slides to Kai and then back to her, "You can call me Nye." I smile.

She nods with a look of confusion on her worn face. I look through the door over her shoulder and notice a bare home. No couches or tables, no kid's toys for Borris. Or for the little girl with the same blonde hair as Mildred who comes running up and tugs on her dress.

My mind flashes to when I was a little girl and tried to get my mother's attention. Mildred looks at the girl, "Just a minute Bee, mommy is talking to the prince and this nice lady."

I squat down in front of the girl. She sucks her thumb and hides half her face behind her mother's dress.

"Hello. I like your teddy bear." The girl smiles and holds it out towards me. "What is your bear's name?"

"Bear." She says her little voice is sweet and confident.

"I like that name. Do you have other toys?" The little girl's bottom lip quivers and I look to Mildred who shakes her head in defeat. "How about I bring you some?"

The girl's eyes light up and she shakes her head rapidly. "Yes, peas!" she shouts. I can't help the smile spreading across my face or the heartbreak I feel in my soul. I look up to Kai who is smiling down at me with happiness flashing in his eyes.

"Are there other kids in this little village?" I ask him, standing.

He nods, "There are about forty more kids and a baby on the way."

My stomach drops, "and do they all not have toys?"

He looks away, "my father isn't very loving towards his village of workers. He pays minimally to them."

I clear my throat and choke back the tears that threaten to leave my eyes. "Kai," I say. "I need you to take me to the city."

His eyes snap to mine. He stares into my eyes for a moment and then smiles. "Will Runihura mind?"

I stare off behind him and reach for Runi. *"Runi, I have something I need to do here. Will you be okay if I come visit tomorrow? I cannot let these children not have toys or clothing that fits properly."*

"That is why I chose you, Nyathera, you have a heart of gold. I will be fine with the cows."

I giggle, "she is fine with it." Kai looks at me and his face lights up with joy.

"I would like to purchase toys and clothing for the kids here. And some gifts for the new baby." I send into the onyx wall in my mind.

Kai's eyes widen. *"I think that is a wonderful idea. I will join you."*

I tell Bee and Mildred that I will be back and walk over to Bruce who has been grazing peacefully on the straw laid beside the house.

Kai walks up beside me and dips his head to my ear. "You let me in, again."

A shiver runs down my neck and I turn to smile at him. My nose grazes his and I jump back. He smiles wide. "This isn't right. They need to be treated better." I try to distract myself from the eruption happening in my stomach.

"I agree. And I believe I found a way for you to help me." He says around his smile.

I cock my head, "how?"

His smile widens and he grabs my hand, his fingers interlacing with mine and sparks ignite between our hands. "I would like you to be the liaison for our workers and the less fortunate in our kingdom. Help me make sure their lives are better, and they are being taken care of properly." He looks at our hands for a moment longer and then into my eyes.

My heart stammers under the weight of his gaze. A smile graces his lips, and he radiates happiness. I look around me, at all the kids playing on the road through this tiny village and the people walking around in old clothing. My heart breaks, this was me not long ago and I wish I had someone who would have spoken up for me.

I look back to his handsome face, "can we start by buying the toys and clothing? And then we will draw up a plan to improve their homes and the road."

Kai's smile widens even more. His canines shining. Gods, he is a beautiful man. That string in my chest tugs lightly and he hugs me. Crushing my cheek to his chest. I freeze. But relax into his body as his warmth wraps around me. I slowly lift my arms and wrap them around his torso. His body hard against my palms. "Thank you." He says. His chest heaving with every breath. "This will mean so much to them, to me."

I pull myself from his grasp and smile. "Come on, I need to see everything the city has to offer."

He helps me onto Bruce's saddle and mounts his horse. We walk side by side down the dirt road that leads to the city. Anxiety grips at me as more and more people come into view.

Some look like the harpy that was in the foyer a couple of nights ago, some have shiny blue scales, and others look like Kai and I. Creatures of all shapes and sizes roam the streets of the city. They stop and stare as we enter the city but continue what they were doing as soon as we pass. Children of all kinds run through the street laughing and markets line the dirt path. Buildings made of stones have wooden signs hanging in the front. Clothing stores, fish stores, jewelers, a toy store and many more. The awnings of the shops move in the breeze that grazes the city streets. Different aromas fill the land, aromas I have never smelled before. I sniff into the breeze and my mouth waters. The dust swirls around Bruce's hooves as we continue walking. The rustic look of the city is peaceful. I glance over and Kai is staring at me.

"Where do you want to start?" He asks.

I look around and decide that I need to focus on the promise I made. "The toy store first."

Kai grins, "you are a lovely person." He looks over at me, "inside and out."

I smile shyly. He dismounts and helps me off Bruce. We step through the entrance of the toy store. The smell of rubber and plastic fills my nose.

A round man with a bulbous nose and grey eyes greets us, "Prince Kai. What do I owe this pleasure?" Kai looks at me, "My lady would like to purchase all the toys in your store."

My heart pauses briefly. His lady. The man's dirty round face goes blank, and his eyes widen. "I am sorry sir, I don't understand."

I step forward, "I would like to purchase all the toys in your store. The kids are ages new baby to as old as your toys go."

He looks at me and back to Kai. The man smiles revealing broken and decayed teeth. He turns to the worker, and I see his ears. They are pointy, like Margie's. He's a fairy.

"Gorn, collect all the toys and have them loaded into the wagons. We have a delivery to make." He turns back to us, "We have not had any business in three months, it is getting hard here prince."

Kai looks to me with a grin and back to the man, "This is Nyathera, she has agreed to be the liaison for the people in these lands that are struggling. She is going to help me ensure your lives are better."

The man looks me up and down, and he whispers to Kai, "But she is a human sir." Shock at the realization fills his face.

Kai looks at me, "She is half demon, and she is here to stay. We will accept her as one of our own, and she will be treated as if she were part of the royal family." He turns his gaze back on the man.

The man's face pales a little and he dips his head, "Of course sir."

I step towards the man, "I am grateful that I will be able to help the people of this city. Near and far. I grew up without any help and I want the best for all, I hope we can do business closer to the holidays."

The man's face lights up with the possibility of making more money, "My name is Crylin, I am looking forward to doing business with you Nyathera." The man's eyes roll down my body, lingering on my hips. Kai clears his throat, and the man jumps.

"It is nice to meet you Crylin, please inform the other shops, that we need winter clothing for the kids and the adults. All sizes."

He nods and waddles to the register. I pause, how are we to pay for this.

"Charge it to the palace, Crylin." Kai smiles at the man and then looks back to me. My heart is racing, and Kai places a hand on my lower back, "I'm sorry." He says.

I shake my head, "no need to apologize. It is going to take everyone, myself included time to adjust to this change."

Kai nods and leans a little closer, "you, Nyathera, are perfect."

My breath hitches and my soul shutters. His eyes stare into my very being, as he studies my face. He gently pushes me towards the door, and we walk out the front. All the toys are being loaded onto wagons. I notice a small bear; it is white and has a red bow around its neck. I pick it up and smile at it, "I am going to hand deliver this one to Bee."

Kai smiles at me, "*We* are going to."

I smile, "you want to come with me?"

He nods, "I think you are going to be able to teach me many things, Nye. Generosity is one of them."

My soul sings as he looks at me. "Let's get these toys and clothing back to the people of the village."

His smile lights up the city and everyone around us fades away. His head dips closer to mine before I pull away. He clears his throat and stands up straighter.

We make our way down the dirt path back towards the worker's village. All the workers flock to the street and watch as we come up with four wagons behind us. Kai jumps off his horse and climbs on top of one of the covered wagons. Everyone looks up at him, including me. His black hair is a stark contrast to the light blue skies behind him. His brown and red eyes filled with happiness as he looks at me.

He speaks in a voice loud enough for everyone to hear. "Ladies and gentlemen, this lovely woman is Nyathera. She has accepted the position as the liaison for all of you. To ensure you have fair pay and everything you need." Everyone looks at me and I awkwardly wave. "She wants to ensure you are all taken care of starting with toys for all the children and clothing for everyone. And a feast right here tomorrow afternoon."

Everyone is silent until cheers erupt. No one questions anything. Kai hops down from the wagon with ease. And my heart lurches into my throat as I watch the muscles in his legs flex with the impact. Men and women bring their children to the wagons, and they surround it. Children's laughter fills the air as one by one they receive new toys to take back to their homes. People come up to us, shake our hands and thank us. I look around for Bee and Mildred and notice them walking back to their home.

I place a hand on Kai's arm, and he follows my gaze. "Please excuse us for a moment," he says to everyone and puts his hand on my back, guiding me through the crowd.

"Mildred!" I call out.

She stops and turns around, Bee's small hand in hers. I catch up to them, "I have something I think you will like, Bee." Her big blue eyes gaze up at me. I hand her the bear I saw at the toy shop, "I thought bear would like a friend." She reaches for the bear and turns it over in her hands. She looks back at me and flings herself onto my knees, wrapping her tiny arms around them.

"Thank you Princess Nyathera." I pause, my head spinning.

Kai looks at me and then squats in front of Bee. "Bee. She is not the princess, but she will be a friend to you all."

Bee looks at him and smiles, "She will be the princess. She loves you."

Kai's eyes widen at the same rate mine do. His slow smile forms a dimple on each cheek. "Does she now?" he glances up over his shoulder at me.

"Mhmm, she doesn't know it yet though. But she does." Bee smiles and skips off with a bear in each hand.

"I am sorry." Mildred says hurriedly.

Kai stops her, "Do not apologize Mildred. There is nothing that has been done wrong." Mildred smiles and hurries after Bee.

Kai turns to me, smiling wickedly, "You love me, huh?" I shift on my feet popping a hip out. He tracks the motion and looks back into my eyes. "Or you will." I roll my eyes and Kai chuckles. "Let's get back to the palace and prepare for tomorrows feast."

I look into his eyes, not wanting to look away. His gaze changes from that of playfulness to something deeper, possessive almost. I touch his arm and electricity thrums through my bones. He looks at my hand and places his over mine. "We will talk after the feast." I lick my lips and my mouth goes dry.

I nod, because I can't form any words. This man, this prince, just rearranged my brain in a week, and I don't know how to feel about it. My body craves to feel his; to feel his connection, my heart yearns for him, and my soul is reaching out to his soul. But my brain can't comprehend everything my body is trying to tell me.

The string in my chest pulls again. I look over at Kai as he rides his horse, admiring the forest that is going by. His black hair and tawny skin shines in the afternoon light. And I can't help but stare at his full lips as he smiles into the sky. He looks over and his chocolate eyes meet mine. I bite my lower lip, and it catches his gaze.

He slowly raises his gaze to mine, "Nye," he takes a breath and looks away.

"I feel it." His head snaps towards me. "I feel the tugging and my soul calling out for yours. I just don't know how to allow it." He stops his horse and grabs Bruce's reins forcing him to stop as well.

He jumps off his horse and reaches up, grabbing my waist and tugging me off. He wraps his arms around me, placing a hand on the back of my head as he pulls my body closer to him. "Nyathera. I don't know how to help you with that. I want nothing more than for you to accept the mating bond, for you to let me love you the way that no one ever has. To let me spoil you in this world and have you as my equal." His chest rises and falls.

I wrap my arms around his waist and grab his shirt at the back. Holding onto him with need. "I don't know. I can feel something building under my skin. Like static lining my bones. And the only time the tugging and the static subsides is when I am close to you."

He places his lips on the top of my head, holding me tighter. "Please, let me try and love you the way you deserve to be loved." I look up at him and his eyes are swimming with need.

I release his shirt and step back from him. "I don't want to risk your life by being by your side."

He looks at me with fire in his eyes. He steps towards me, and I step back. His hand reaches out to me with a speed I have never seen. He grabs the back of my neck with one hand and grips my hip with the other. My mind swims as he pulls me against him. In one breath he crashes his lips to mine. My heart stops and stars invade my vision. My soul feels like a puzzle that is being put together and I sigh. I run my hands up his back, digging my fingers into him and pulling myself closer.

He withdraws his lips slowly, searching my eyes as if an answer resides there that I don't know the question to. I smile and press my lips to his again. Slowly exploring every dip of muscle in his back. He prods my lips with his tongue, and I open for him. Allowing him to explore my mouth with his and deepen the kiss. He growls and tightens the grip on my neck, forcing me closer to him and running his other hand to my waist.

Pulling away my breathing is erratic, and my heart is pounding in my ears. "That." I swallow. "That was…"

"Intense?"

I nod. "Did that feel like…"

"My soul was set on fire, and holes were filled with the missing piece?" He finishes my sentences with ease. I put my hands on his chest as he loosens his grip on me. Not wanting to separate from him.

"We have to get back to the palace."

I sigh as he steps away from me, but he grabs my hand and walks us over to his horse.

"This is calypso. She has been my horse since I was a little boy."

I run my hand along her neck, and she snorts in response. Kai climbs onto her saddle and I feel a sense of loss. I turn to get on Bruce when Kai reaches his hand down to me. I take it and he lifts me with ease onto the back of the saddle.

Chapter

42

That night, Nyathera laid in bed, listening to the wind in the trees. A voice whispered on the breeze, "come play with us." She covered her head and closed her eyes tightly.

Once back at the house Kai leaps off of Calypso and helps me down. He stares at me for a moment before placing his hand on the same spot on my lower back. His hand warm in contrast to my cool tunic. He opens the door to the house and Caine and Ezra are standing in the foyer, arms crossed and staring at us like disappointed parents. "Wanna tell us where you were?" Ezra says.

"We were expecting you hours ago." Caine chimes in.

Kai looks at them and then back to me, "can you guys give us a moment?" Kai says, not taking his eyes off me.

"I don't think you understand we were supposed to…" Kai's gaze snaps back to them and they look at us.

Bouncing their gaze between Kai and I. "oh!" Caine says and starts to walk off. Ezra just looks at us with a wide grin. Caine appears beside him in a second and slaps the back of his head. "Come on you buffoon!"

Ezra waggles his eyebrows at us and disappears into thin air. Caine waves his hand and does the same.

"Where did they just go?" I say snapping my mouth shut.

"Another power you will have to learn about, but right now I think we need to talk."

I just stare at him, "Talk? About what?" he reaches for my hand. "Kai. I felt every emotion you felt. But I still stand by giving myself time. The kiss." I swallow the forming lump in my throat. "That kiss was magical. The universe righted itself. But I have to protect you and the others from me. If I accept, I will end up getting someone killed."

Kai shakes his head, "My mother warned me that my mate will be just as stubborn as I am. But she never said that my mate would be so stubborn that she makes dumb decisions. You don't have to protect us; we are the most powerful demons in this world. We have fought wars for centuries and you're too scared to let yourself be happy. Sorry, your parents broke you into a pathetic excuse of a human."

My stomach drops. That word rears its ugly head again, pathetic.

"Oh, and I can choose to deny the bond as well. It will cause a tremendous amount of pain for both of us. Like being skinned alive or having your beating heart ripped from your chest. And now I am thinking that will be the easier road. You kissed me. And you kissed me like that." He waves his arm to the side, gesturing in the direction we came. "Just to tell me you *don't* want me. Sorry, Nyathera. I will not be attending your feast tomorrow."

I step towards him. "Kai,"

"No! I am the prince of this city, of this world. I am a very powerful demon. And now, now I will let you see just how fucked up I am. Fuck you Nyathera."

I slap him across the face. The force behind it whips his head to the side. A red handprint blooms on his stubbled cheek. I immediately regret it, but who does he think he is to speak to me in that tone, to call me pathetic?

I step towards him, "I survived on my own for years, I survived being drugged, and then drugged again with demon magic, I survived battle in the human world, I survived the fall into the pit, I survived the creatures here. And you wouldn't let me die because you're so wrapped up in having a mate that you don't see the bigger picture." I shove his chest, "*You* don't see what *I* have been through, you have only seen what you want me to be!" Tears well up in my eyes and my heart starts to shatter. My fingers burn and flames begin flickering up my arms, "You are the one with a god complex. What you can provide me outside of what I need in here," I tap my chest, "has nothing to do with the mating bond, *that* is you waving your wealth and your power around like it is a flag to be flown over every city."

I look at my hands and notice a long trail of flames in each one, flames lick at my tunic searing it off my skin. I hold up my hand and examine the flames. Whips, I have whips of flames coming from my bare hands. Flames travel up to my shoulder and all I feel is warmth and rage and sadness. I flick my wrist, and the flame whips lash out. Tilting my head back, I allow the burning of the mark to cascade through my body, surging energy to my soul. Kai stands in front of me with a grin on his face.

I flick my wrist towards him, and a wall of water appears in front of him, blocking my flames. I scream and do it again, catching the curtains in the window on fire. The ground begins shaking as I let the anger roll over me. "Why do you think you can treat me this way? Force me into this mating bond?" My voice doesn't sound like my own, it is feminine and powerful. "I have worked too hard at protecting myself and those I love to let you keep me here like a pet. I will not be created *for* someone." I let the whips snap on the floor. Two ropes of water encircle me, pinning my arms to my sides. I fight against them, and they don't release. The more I fight the tighter they get. I dig my boots into the wooden floor and the house shifts. "Let. Me. Go." I bite out.

"Not until you calm down. I had a feeling you had more fire power than increasing candles, but I wasn't sure. I had to piss you off to know." My bones start to ache from the ropes of water encircling my body. "I needed you to release your demon."

"You fucking asshole!" I scream, and a massive earthquake strikes the house, vases fall from tables, and chandeliers swing side to side.

"Nyathera," Kai says my name again, but his voice is a far-off sound.

I scream and fire erupts around me, but the water doesn't let loose. Steam fills the foyer as the water and fire collide. I feel the terror creeping into my skin, "Please Kai, I can't be tied up again!" The water remains in place. My breathing becomes erratic, and my heart feels like it is about to burst. "Let me go!" my voice now echoing through the palace.

****

"No! No! I won't do it again!" I am back in that basement, tied by my hands and ankles as the man who owned the restaurant walks around me. The smell of the mold invades my nostrils, and I feel the mud on my body, my bare body. "I just needed to feed myself. I haven't eaten in three days; it was just a couple of rotten apples!" I feel the crack of the whip, the splitting of skin, I gnash my teeth together to suppress the scream bubbling in my chest.

"Ten lashes for each apple you stole. And then I will decide what I am going to do with you." He licks his lips and continues walking around me. "You sure are pretty." His eyes gaze down my naked body. I can feel the bile rising in my throat.

"Maybe I will make you my pet, force you to marry me." I vomit on his boots. He slaps me across the face, blood filling my mouth, and I sob. CRACK the sting of the whip tearing the skin on my back sends radiating pain through my body. I scream out in agony. He yanks on the restraints on my arms, dislocating my shoulder. I grit my teeth and suppress the scream.

"Please! I will work it off." The man's decaying smile and rotten breath hovers in my face, "Oh. You sure will, girl."

****

Waves crash through the basement; a dark form stands in front of an onyx wall. "Nyathera, you're safe. I'm here." A warm hand caresses my cheeks, and I feel my eyes roll back to their original state. Kai's worried eyes are the first thing I see and then I feel his warm hand on my cheek and the other wrapped around my back. I shove him away and push myself backward until my back is against the wall. I place my hand on my chest as I try to calm my breathing. Kai walks toward me, "Who was that?"

I hold a hand up to him, "Stop."

"Nyathera, I didn't know that happened to you. I will find that bastard."

"I said, stop." I spit through gritted teeth.

"Tell me who that vile human being is, I will send the soldiers."

"I said stop Kai!" The earth rumbles as fire fills the room, swirling around us.

"I'm sorry, I didn't know what you have been through." His eyes fill with sincerity and pity. *Great.*

"Don't worry about it, I took care of him." I choke out.

Kai's eyes are full of questions. "I'm sorry. I don't know how to deal with the emotions I feel for you." He takes another step closer.

I look at him and the tears fall. "Did you see all of that?"

He looks at the ground, "I did." His eyes meet mine and worry flashes across them. "He deserves nothing more than death." He says.

I grin, insanity finally gripping hold. "I cut off his dick and shoved it down his throat." Kai's eyes widen. I laugh quietly, the dread of that day is like a fresh wound that won't heal, "I was seventeen. *Seventeen*, Kai. I was trying to take care of myself after my parents died and Bartholomew never returned because of his fame. I took three rotten apples from his garbage."

I'm sobbing at this point, not for me, but for the girl I was back then. The weak girl who had no one. "That's why I don't know if I can accept the mating bond. Because how can I love you the way you deserve when I can't even love myself?!" My body wracks with my sobs and before I can take another breath Kai is scooping me into his arms. I don't fight.

"You didn't deserve that. You don't deserve anything you are going through now, but why deal with everything alone? I am here, I can help you train and learn to use your powers. Be stronger than you have ever been. And you are strong Nyathera. You're the strongest woman I have ever met. You are also the most beautiful being I have ever seen. I want to help you. Not cage you up like an animal. Not force anything on you. I want you to be my partner, my equal, my love." His eyes find mine as he carries me up the stairs. My stomach turns into a knot and my soul is screaming for him.

I reach my hand up and touch his face, steam rises from his skin where my fingers touch his cheek. "I have fire whips," I say.

He chuckles, "And a wall of fire."

My mind is swimming. "Can we figure out what else I can do?"

He smiles but his gaze doesn't meet mine, he continues walking up the stairs. "Another day, you have a feast to plan, and you need to see the other parts of the city."

I hold my breath as he takes the top step onto the landing, "Will you go with me?" I ask in a whisper.

He sets me down, "do you want me to?"

I nod my head, "I need you to."

He grabs my hand, "Then I will be there with you, in every step of life. No matter how long you take to decide I will wait. And I will never let you go through anything alone again."

My heart explodes and I can't help but stand on my toes and kiss his cheek. I have been alone my entire life, and the people I can count on are either dead or in the human world, possibly dead as well.

A tear runs down my cheek and he thumbs it away, "Don't cry Nyathera." His large hands encompass my face, and he presses a kiss to my forehead and then my cheeks and finally the tip of my nose.

I giggle and grab his wrists.

"That's better." He smiles at me. "Go get ready, Margie is waiting for you. I nod and give him a small smile. He drops his hands and walk down the hallway.

Chapter

43

Her dreams were filled with monsters never seen before.
A green dragon at her side as she faced a beast with the
head of a bull and the body of a man.

I plop onto my bed, examining the sleeves of my tunic. The singed edges stop at my shoulders, but my skin isn't burned. I sit up and try to make those whips appear again. I am focusing on a little wooden table sitting by the bathroom door. "Come on, come ON!" I try, but the most I get is a little flame that appears on my pinky finger and disappears as quickly as it ignites. In frustration I flop backwards onto the bed, staring at the beautiful wooden ceiling.

"No ma'am." I shoot up straight. Margie is standing in the bathroom doorway with her arms crossed. "You don't get throw a tantrum because you can't do something. Instead, you will practice and perfect it." Her voice is stern but caring.

"Margie, I have all these powers and no idea how to control them. I almost burned the palace down for Gods sakes."

She rolls her eyes, "I believe the prince offered to help you learn to use them." She raises a gray eyebrow at me.

I sigh. "Is he always so flip-floppy? I mean, one minute he is sweet and the next we are fighting."

She smiles and walks over to the edge of the bed, sitting down with a groan. "That is what mates do. They are destined for each other but bicker and annoy each other to no end. My Henry and I would fight for days, so many stools were broken during that time, but the love we had for each other was stronger and our souls always pointed us in the right direction." She places her warm palm on my cheek, "you and the prince have found each other in every lifetime, from the beginning of the universe. And he may not say it, but he has loved you from the moment he knew he had a mate. Try to look past his outbursts, or at least understand them, he is just a man trying to navigate in a world where he has to appear tough. He is a very good, caring, handsome man." She winks.

I smile at her, and she stands. I hop off the bed, "Margie."

She stops and turns to me with a smile, "yes, deary."

I clear my throat, "can I give you a hug?" She looks at me without saying a word, "I mean, I never had a mother who spoke with me about anything, and when she did she spoke as if I was the bane of her existence. And I just need…" She wraps me in a tight embrace. I set my chin on her plump shoulder, and she runs her hand up and down my back. Tears start to roll down my cheeks and I sniffle.

"You never have to ask for a hug, I will give you one anytime you feel like you want one. Your mother may have never shown it, but children are our entire world, she loved you."

I rest my cheek on her shoulder, "Thank you, Margie. You have no idea how badly I needed this."

She pats my back twice and I step back. She runs her hand over her pale blue dress, "Well. Let's get you in the tub, shall we?"

Margie helps me bathe and curls my hair, adding pearls and baby's breath throughout the waves. She picked out a pale lavender gown with a V-neck that dips just below my breasts. The back is open with a sheer lace of lilies woven in. The gown has long sleeves that billow out to fight the cool air that autumn brought with it. I walk to the floor-length mirror and run my hands over the silk material. "It is lovely." I look at Margie.

"The prince picked it out, he said the lavender would look lovely against your tan skin." She smiles and my heart warms. I turn side to side watching the long skirt flow on an imaginary wind.

I walk over to Margie and kiss her cheek, "thank you." I whisper.

She smiles, making her chubby cheeks bunch around her eyes. I place my hand on her shoulder and smile back. I turn and walk to the stairs and Kai is in the foyer waiting. He is dressed in a black suit with a lavender dress shirt underneath. His thick black hair is styled perfectly on top of his head. His eyes meet mine as I start the descent down the stairway. His mouth drops open slightly and I get closer to him and stop. His eyes roam over me from my hair down to the matching lavender slippers I paired with the dress.

"You look stunning Nyathera." A grin on his lips.

I smile and look down at the dress, "whoever picked this was an idiot, it doesn't match my skin tone what-so-ever."

He grabs my hand, "Margie told you I picked it didn't she?"

I smirk, "she did."

He shakes his head smiling, and spins me in a circle, "You Nyathera are going to keep me on my toes for years to come."

I giggle, "you look very handsome." I smirk, reaching up to move a lock of hair that has fallen onto his forehead, and we walk hand in hand out the front door. A white and gold carriage drawn by Calypso and Bruce sits in the driveway. I look at the carriage in disbelief. The intricate curves of the gold on the sides swirl in magical waves.

"It is beautiful," I say without looking away.

Kai's lips are next to my ear, "I made it for you. So, you can go to and from the villages and cities whenever you choose to do so."

I look at him, eyes wide, "for me? Kai, you can't do that."

He shushes me, "I can, and I did."

I look back to the carriage, "Thank you." Appreciation courses through my veins as I stare at the carriage even longer.

We climb into the luxurious carriage, the seats made of red velvet, and a mural of the night sky lines the ceiling and walls. I run my hands over the paintings, relishing the finery of the hand painted stars. Kai climbs in next to me, his large form taking up the small seat across from me. I admire his large legs and sharp features as he struggles to sit without smacking his knees on the doors. I cover my mouth to stifle a giggle.

His eyes meet mine, and I lose it. I can't hold the laughter back as he smacks his head. "I should have accounted for our size difference when building this." He laughs, rubbing his head. He shifts his body down so his knees are on either side of my legs, and his shoulder blades rest against the back of the seat.

The carriage starts to move, and I watch out the little window. "I want you to meet more of my people, introduce you to them. Not everyone in the city is poor, but they definitely need help in making sure they are treated fairly. My father never cared but I want to have a good relationship with the people of the city. I want you to help me."

I smile, "I would love nothing more than to help you."

"You will be heavily compensated for your time as well, no freebies in my city."

"Absolutely not, I don't need a paycheck, Kai. I am content on helping these people at no cost to you, or them."

"Too bad, an account with the palace has already been set up in your name. Save it or spend it, either is fine." He smiles, his eyes gleaming.

He looks out the window before speaking, "I don't want to be like my father. He is cruel and careless. I want to be something more, to give my future children a father they are happy to claim."

My heart clenches, "You want children?"

He swallows hard, "well, someday maybe."

We sit in silence for a long moment, "Kai, the fact that you are so worried about being like your father and you are taking steps to not be like him, proves that you are nothing like him." He smiles, but it doesn't meet his eyes. "Plus, do you really think Caine and Ezra would allow you to be like your father?"

He chuckles, "probably not."

I throw him a grin, "you are a good man, Kai."

I watch the trees go by as we continue our venture to the city. The trees stop and a large lake with mountains in the distance comes into view. I sit up straighter watching the seagulls dive towards the water and the kids playing on the water's edge. I can feel Kai staring at me, so I turn to look at him, "what?"

He shakes his head, "nothing."

I smile, knowing there is something he is thinking, but I am too fixated on the view. The sky is a tangerine color as we continue past the lake and vast vineyards come into view. My head is almost hanging out of the window as we pass by. There are workers of all different types working in the vineyard. They have massive hats on their heads, no doubt to shade them from the sun, and there are dogs running through the rows.

"There are dogs here?!" I screech with excitement.

Kai chuckles, "There are."

I look at him, emotion falling over me, "I need one."

He full-on laughs. "Maybe one day I will get you a dog."

I stick my bottom lip out and give him the deepest puppy face I can.

He laughs again, "Okay. We can go during the next breeding season and get one for the house."

I clap and bounce excitedly. "Maybe two or three."

"One will suffice." His smile beaming.

"Or two or three" I whisper.

Raising a brow, Kai shakes his head, and then I see it in the distance—the city of Shadows and Nightmares.

I look at the large buildings coming into view, "Is this a different part of the city?"

He nods, "we are going to the upper-class side of the city first. There are people we need to see to ensure you are named the liaison of the people."

I nod, "But can we go visit the other side again?"

He smiles widely. "Of course."

I turn my head back to the buildings coming into view. The large city is a bustling labyrinth of narrow cobblestone streets lined with towering stone buildings that have stood for centuries. Different species weave through the crowded streets, their laughter filling the air with a lively energy. Merchants peddle their wares from colorful market stalls, while street performers entertain with music. The aromas of sizzling street food and exotic spices waft through the air, creating a tantalizing atmosphere. As we ride through the ancient city, I can't help but marvel at the rich tapestry of history and culture that permeates every corner.

A small boy runs up to the carriage, his mother yelling for him to stop. "Stop the carriage!" I yell to the coachman. The carriage stops and I open the door. I look at Kai and then back to the little boy.

"Hello. What is your name?" I ask the boy.

He smiles at me, "I'm Dylan."

My heart stops for a moment and my body seizes. I swallow hard as Kai's hand lands on my shoulder. "Hello, Dylan, my best friend's name was Dylan as well." I choke out, "I am Nyathera."

The little boy touches the carriage, his big wholly black eyes staring into my own, "Hi, Natherine."

I giggle at the little boy trying to pronounce my name, "You can call me Nye."

"Hi Nye! Can I be your best friend?" he asks excitedly.

I smile, "Of course you can."

He turns back to the gold detailing, "I like your carriage."

I look down at him, his black eyes admiring the gold on the carriage. His dusty brown hair blows in the wind. "Would you like a ride in it?"

His eyes light up, "Yes, please!"

I look over to his mother, who smiles and nods as she sees Kai sitting next to me. Reaching down, I pull the small boy into my lap. "Let's go around the fountain a few times." I say to the coachman. "Does that sound okay?" I ask Dylan.

He nods enthusiastically. I can't stop staring at the little boy in my lap, watching out the window, waving to his mother as we pass by her. My heart breaks and expands simultaneously. We circle the lovely fountain three times and stop right in front of his mother. I open the door and help the boy climb down, and he runs to his mother.

"Mommy! Did you see me?! Did you see me in the carriage?!"

Her smile is bright when she looks down to the perfect little boy she created. "I did!"

She walks to the carriage, "Thank you," she says, "What was your name?"

Kai jumps in, "This is Nyathera, the liaison to the people in the city of shadows and nightmares."

She smiles at me, "It is wonderful to meet you; my name is Nicole."

She grabs Dylan's hand, and they walk away. Kai squeezes by me and jumps out of the carriage, holding his hand up for me to take. Taking his large calloused hand in mine, he helps me out of the carriage. The sight of the city takes my breath away. Statues sit in front of the large buildings, and ivy trails up the sides. People have started to gather, and music plays softly in the distance.

Kai stands on the edge of the fountain and holds his arms out. His godlike features shine in the evening sun, "Hello, everyone! I have someone very important to introduce to you. Please be respectful as she learns her new role as the liaison for the people of the city!" He holds out his hand again and I take it. He pulls me onto the edge of the fountain. "This is Nyathera, she will be helping me ensure the people of this city are treated equally!" people clap, and I feel my cheeks heating. "Say something," Kai says just for me to hear.

"Hello everyone! I am excited to work with you all and get to know each and every one of you!" Kai wraps his arm around my waist and pulls me into him as the music gets closer.

He looks deep into my eyes as everyone around us claps. I pull away shyly and step down. He jumps off the edge, "Dance with me."

Glancing around me, I notice that the people are starting to dance as well. All different species of demons and creatures coming together. He grabs my waist again and spins me, swaying to the music that has gotten even closer. I look over to where five men are playing instruments, walking over the cobblestone hill opposite the fountain. The sounds reverberate off the stucco buildings and fairy lights illuminate overhead. Children dance around us, and laughter fills the air. Kai holds me at arm's length and steps back as women line up on each side of me and men stand in front of us. They start moving, and I follow along, a rhythmic dance that everyone seems to know, except me, that is.

I try my best to follow along as Kai holds one hand behind his back and the other up bent at the elbow. I place my hand on his like the other women are with their partners. He smiles as we move in a circle, and he steps away. The women grab their skirts and sway them back and forth before twirling and curtseying. The men stomp once, twice, and then shuffle towards us and then away. Kai jumps onto the edge of the fountain and sways his hips, arms over his head as the music picks up. I cover my mouth and giggle as people cheer. He holds his hand towards me, and I sway my hips towards him. He grabs my waist and hoists me onto the fountain where we dance and dance.

A lifetime later, when the sky is lit up by those souls in the sky and the travelling stardust, we head towards a small building with a sign in the front. 'Drink now, ask questions later.' I smile at the sign and people bustle around the entrance. The sun has started to set as we make our way through the crowd. The smell of ale fills my nose as we zig-zag through the crowd to the bar. Caine and Ezra are standing there, and Ezra throws his arms out as we get closer!

"Hey you two!" Ezra shouts loudly, clearly already having multiple drinks.

I smile at them, "I should've brought a change of clothes." I whisper to Kai.

He looks me up and down, snapping his fingers. My clothing changes into dark leather pants and a long-sleeved black shirt. I look down at the clothing and back to him, "This is what you chose?" I admire the silk slippers, and he snaps his fingers again, laced black boot with a heel appear on my feet. I wobble at the change in my center of gravity.

His smile is wicked as he bounces his eyebrows. I slap his arm, and Ezra grabs my hand, "Come dance with me, Nye!"

He drags me to the dance floor into the center of all the people. The music is upbeat and fast. I throw my hands in the air, and we dance. Women of all kinds grind on Ezra, and I laugh along with him as he turns them down. I glance over to the bar where Kai is leaning on both elbows on the edge watching me like a hawk. I give him a come-hither curl of my finger and he laughs but saunters my way.

Before he can reach us a woman with bright red hair stops him, running her hand up his chest. He grabs her arm and whispers something in her ear. She tips her head back and laughs but his gaze turns deadly. She rips her hand free and stomps away, and Kai strides towards me. Scooping me into his arms and kissing my forehead.

"Who was that?" I yell over the music.

"Her name is Yolanda. My father wanted her to be my bride, and I declined."

My heart sinks as I stare over at the woman who had her hands on him. Kai grabs my hand and pulls me to the bar, dragging Ezra with us. He smirks and jumps onto the bar. Every woman in the bar starts screaming as he unbuttons the top three buttons on his shirt and rolls up the sleeves. His muscular forearms flex with the movement. I am staring up to him when the barkeep hands him a bottle of something that smells like rubbing alcohol.

He smiles at me as he screws the top off, and Ezra is there, head back and mouth open. Kai squats in front of him and pours a large shot straight into Ezra's mouth and the crowd erupts into screams. I look around as the women fan themselves. Ezra shakes his head and throws his arms into the air. Ezra makes his way into a group of women on the other side of the dance floor. Kai looks at me, mischief in his eyes. I shake my head and put my hands up, but he stands and walks the four steps to me.

Yolanda appears out of nowhere and shoves me out of the way, opening her mouth wide for Kai. Annoyance bubbles in the back of my chest. I grab her shoulder and use her to get onto the stool in front of Kai, standing below him, I give him a wicked grin. I turn my gaze back to Yolanda and wink. Her mouth drops and annoyance creeps across her too pretty face. Kai smiles wide and grabs the hair at the base of my neck and tugs my head back. I inhale sharply at the tingle that spreads down my spine. I open my mouth and stick my tongue out and he growls at the movement.

Dipping his head to my ear, he whispers, brushing his lips on the shell of it, "I want to see more of that."

I try to speak, and his grip tightens on my hair, women in the bar start screaming as he licks up my neck, goosebumps following in the wake of his warm tongue. All eyes are on us, and I have learned, that is just the way he likes it. He stares into my eyes and pours the alcohol into my mouth. I immediately feel warm and fuzzy, the alcohol seeping into my bloodstream. Before I can swallow it all, he loosens his grip and crashes his lips to mine, sharing the shot with me. The entire bar cheers and I can feel my cheeks heating, but Kai's lips on mine are the only thing I want to focus on. He spins me to the other side of him and holds the bottle above his head, "next round on us!" He yells across the bar. More hoots and screams erupt.

I notice Caine sitting at the end of the bar, staring at us with a smile on his face. I smile at Kai and grab the bottle from his hands. "He won't drink anything that compromises his senses. He is a party pooper.' I smile at him and saunter down the bar towards Caine.

"Hey Caine. Take a shot with me." I squat in front of him and bat my lashes.

"As pretty as you are Nyathera, I will not be partaking. Thank you though" As always, he wants to be the perfect soldier. I sit on my ass, a leg on each side of him.

"Come on big guy, one shot and I will leave you alone." I place a finger on his chin and push, trying to tilt his head back. He fights against me, "Please." I give him the best puppy dog eyes I have ever given.

He smiles and shakes his head, tilting his head back and opening that perfect mouth of his. "Good boy." I purr as I pour a hefty shot into his mouth.

The crowd erupts again and Kai walks down the bar to stand with me. He helps me to my feet and pours another shot in my mouth. I smile up at him and then I see a pale hand with red nails sliding up Kai's thigh out of my peripherals.

I look to the person attached to that arm, Yolanda. I jump down next to her and fist my hand in her hair, tugging her head back, knowing she wishes it was Kai, allowing my eyes to glow a little and look directly into her overly blue eyes. "If you want to keep that hand I suggest you remove it from my mates leg."

Kai jumps down next to me, placing his hand on my lower back, "I would listen to her, she feeds men their own dicks." Yolanda's eyes widen and she scurries away. "There is no competition, but I plan to reward that confidence later, crazy mate. And you called me your mate." His eyes are fixed on me. My stomach soaring as he stares at me.

I wring my hands together, not knowing what to say. "Um, I hoped it would get her to stop touching you." I say looking away.

He puts his pointer finger under my chin, lifting gently, "I know." He smiles widely.

I smile, and back away swaying my hips to the beat. Ezra comes up from my left and dances with me, his large hands sprawling across my abdomen. Kai's low growl can be heard through the entire room. He moves towards me like a predator ready to pounce.

He glares at Ezra, I chuckle, "Hey now, there's no competition here. Put the claws away." I repeat his words with a wink.

He chuckles, "you will be the death of me Nyathera."

I laugh as Kai spins me in a circle again.

And we dance the night away.

Kai grabs my hand and drags me out of the pub. The world is wobbly as we weave in and out of the crowd. "Come on! You have to see this!" He wraps his arms around me, and then air and stars surround us, swirling like they are dancing.

My feet leave the earth and inhale sharply, "Kai!" I scream until the earth is beneath my feet in a quick moment. When the stars and night sky vanish, we stand on a cliff overlooking the lake. I turn, taking in the sprawling fields and the dark blue lake, griping his hand with brutal force. "Oh, my Gods, Kai. It is beautiful." He stops me, spinning me towards the mountains. The sun is starting to peak above the mountain tops, casting pinks and purples across the land, taking the breath from my lungs. Kai wraps his arms around my waist, pressing my back to his chest.

"This is the second most beautiful thing in this entire universe."

My pulse quickens, "What is the first?"

He inhales the scent of my hair, "You Nyathera."

My knees almost give out at the sound of my name on his lips. I lean my head back, the liquor coursing through my veins. I can hear the thumping of his heart against the nape of my neck. The tugging in my chest intensifies and I want nothing more than to turn and kiss him again.

"Do it." His deep husky voice rings through my mind.

"It's the liquor talking. Not me."

He chuckles and we watch the sunrise.

****

The carriage stops outside the front steps of the palace. I must have fallen asleep because Kai shakes my shoulder lightly. I wipe the drool off my face, embarrassment soaking my skin. He smiles and helps me out of the carriage. And we walk to the house.

"Thank you for last night. I really need to immerse myself in the city in order to help the people more." He smiles, grabs my hand, and starts up the steps, but I don't move.

"Nyathera?" Kai's voice sounds

****

Dust clouds form around me and children run screaming through the village. Women fight as winged beasts grab them and take off into the air, only to drop them from hundreds of feet. Men are scrambling around with pitchforks and hammers, trying to fight off these creatures and save their families. My heart sinks as I watch a small blonde girl run up to me. Tears and dirt stain her face. "Help us!" she yells, her little voice so full of fear. I look back to the village, flames engulfing most of the houses and bodies littering the earth.

****

"The village," I say. Kai is standing in front of me, both of my hands in his.

"What about it?"

I run into the house and up the stairs, Kai right on my heels.

"Nyathera, what is happening?" I swing open my bedroom door and then the armoire in the corner. I throw different tunics out until I find the silky one Kai had gifted me.

I drop my dress and Kai stutters behind me, "Um. I'm sorry."

I look over my shoulder and he is hiding his eyes behind his hands, "We don't have time for this Kai. We have to get to the village…Now."

He looks at me as I drag the leather pants up my thighs. "What do you mean?"

"I had a," I search my brain for a moment while doing up my pants, "a vision," I say and try to lace up the corset.

He walks over and helps me do so, his fingers running over my spine with every string he tightens. "What about?"

I put each dagger in its sheath, one by one, "I don't know if it is going to happen tonight, or another day, but we have to get there now."

"Nye, calm down. A vision of what?"

I throw another glance over my shoulder. "The village." My words come out rushed and high pitched.

He nods and disappears into thin air, returning a moment later dressed in fighting leathers. The outfit formed perfectly to each muscle in his body. Gods save me, this man is stunning. I shove my feet into my boots and start towards the door.

He places a hand on my shoulder, "Let me have Caine and Ezra check it out first, and if they find something I will transport us there."

My mind is frantic with the image of that little girl's eyes, begging me to help them. I know that is the right way to do it, so we don't scare anyone if nothing is wrong, but gods I need to save her. I nod and Kai stares into the distance for a moment.

"They are on their way now." He looks into my eyes, questioning what is going on. I sit on the side of the bed and bounce my leg.

"Tell me what you saw." He sits down next to me, the bed dipping, and rests his hand on my knee, stopping me from bouncing it.

And so, I do. I tell him every detail, right down to the feeling of fear and guilt that clutches at my heart. He wraps a strong arm around my shoulders and pulls me close. His scent wrapping around my senses.

He places a kiss on the top of my head and freezes. "There is no sign of danger to the village, but they told the people of the village that you need to rest and will be there tomorrow."

I let out a slow breath, relief washing over me, "What did I see then?"

"I will have guards in the village every day and night to ensure they are safe. I believe you did have a vision, but it was of the future." He sighs.

He wraps his arm around me and holds me for what feels like an eternity. "There has to be a way they were able to sacrifice a piece of your soul." He says it slowly, as if in thought.

"What do you mean?"

He looks at me gently, "witches are the only species that I know of being able to have visions. Somewhere, somehow, you have received that ability."

"What does that have to do with sacrificing a piece of my soul?" I bite my lip as the anxiety kicks in.

"It means," he pauses, "it mean that someone used a witch, or was a witch in your family. They used that magic to separate a piece of your soul."

I don't even want to think about it, I want to forget it all, I allow my soul to reach for him, if only for a moment. Eventually my worry fades, and my mind goes blank.

Chapter

44

A small boy with ebony hair and brown eyes appeared in her dream. He fought alongside her, protecting her from the monsters of the city.

The liquor still courses through my veins and my heart thuds in my chest. Kai smells of salted beechwood and embers and he is so warm. My soul is begging me to let him in more, for me to combine our souls into one. I need to take my mind off everything that has gone on in the last couple of weeks. In the words of Fallon, 'You never know when you will get to fuck someone again.' And I have this perfectly handsome man sitting right next to me, with his god-like features and the back and forth that has happened between us. I know he wants this as much as I need this. Confidence overtakes me and I stand facing him.

He looks up to me and I step between his legs. His lips part slightly as I step even closer. He places his hands on my thighs, electricity thrumming through my body at his touch. His hands move up my legs and to my waist.

Straddling his legs, I push my chest into his, "please help me take my mind off everything." I whisper.

He doesn't say a word but grips the hair at the base of my head and pulls my head back. His lips gently brush against my neck and a moan escapes my lips. I lower my ass onto his legs, and he trails kisses up my throat and across my jaw.

He lets go of my hair. My eyes meeting his, "There is no going back after this Nyathera, I will never be able to stop wanting you."

I look deep into his brown and red flecked eyes and press a gentle kiss to his lips. When I pull back his eyes are wild, animalistic. He shoves his mouth over mine, capturing my lips in his. He kisses me with a passion that the universe could never compare to.

The world flips and rights itself in that moment, stars align, and the Gods sing a praise. I open my lips for him and his tongue grazes across mine in feverish licks. A groan escapes his lips and a second later he is flipping me onto the bed. Placing his large body over mine and pressing against every inch of me. His hand grips my hip, digging his fingers in with bruising force. I whimper and he nips at my jaw. I open my eyes, and he is staring into my soul.

Taking in my very being. He leans up on one arm and uses the other to shred my corset and tunic from my torso, leaving me in a thin bralette. My nipples peak under his gaze and he looks at my bare skin. "You are exquisite." He traces a finger down my sternum between my breasts, goosebumps trail the movement.

He watches as my back arches to meet him. A low growl escapes his chest as his eyes meet mine. The glow of ferocity in his eyes is that of a predator ready to devour its prey. He kisses me again, taking the air from my lungs. The tugging in my chest strengthens the more his hands roam over my skin. I twirl my fingers in the hair at the back of his head. "Kai, please. I need this."

That is all it takes for him to sit back on his knees and pull his jacket and shirt over his head. His abs ripple with the movement and need pools in my core. I unhook the clasp in the front of my bra and his eyes follow every movement. He slips the straps over one shoulder and places a kiss to the top of my breast and then does the same on the other side. I slide my hands down his back soaking in the feeling of his skin under my fingers. Smooth tight muscles pinch as my fingers run over them. He trails kisses down to my nipple and sucks one into his mouth. My back arches at the contact of his warm tongue flicking over the hardened bud. He worships my breast like it is the last thing he will ever do, pulling a breathy moan from my lips. A knot starts to form in my lower belly as pleasure builds. As if he can sense it he kisses back up my neck. "I am going to make this last."

I shove his shoulders, and he flies off me and onto his back. His eyes widen and then set into a seductive glare. I smile and kiss him, hard. Our tongues tangle as he grips my hips and pushes his body up to mine. He feels massive straining against his pants, and I sit up straddling him. I run my hands down his torso and a breath leaves his lips. My fingers find the button of his pants and I pop it open, tugging it down slightly. His sizable swollen head pokes out from the waistband, a drop of precum coating the tip. I lean down and kiss him again, but before he can deepen it I kiss his jaw and then his ear, nipping his skin from the base of his ear down his neck. He growls, the sound reverberating through my body. I continue my descent down his body, kissing every rippled ab as I go. His skin is sweet and smooth and perfect. I kiss the perfect v above the waistband of his pants, nipping at the sensitive skin. He lets out a groan as I tug on his pants sliding to the floor and sitting up on my knees.

His large erection springs to life and my eyes widen. Blue and purple veins trail up the bottom of it all the way to the head. It bounces slightly when I meet his gaze. He has a smoldering look and a smile on his lips.

"I don't know if I can handle that." I whisper.

His smile grows as he sits up, reaching out and gripping my chin. "You're capable of anything you put your mind to."

He kisses me again, gripping my chin harder. I sink into the kiss, relishing in the taste of his tongue. He pulls back and reclines onto his elbows, his eyes holding my gaze.

I slide my gaze over to his cock and lick my lips, "you can do this Nyathera." His words urging me to do what he wants, what I want.

I grip him at the base, his skin smooth like silk in my palm. I stick out my tongue and glide it from base to tip, not breaking eye contact as I swirl my tongue around the head. The sweetness of his skin mixes with the saltiness of his precum and I moan, sucking the velvety tip into my mouth. His head falls back and his chest rumbles with a beastly sound. I push my head down as far as I can, opening my throat and letting him invade it. I work the base with my hand as I slowly move back up to the tip and again flick my tongue over the top. He lulls his head back towards me and I meet his eyes, they are glossy and full of the same need I feel between my legs.

I continue to devour him. Soaking up every drop of precum with my tongue.

"You're doing such a good job." His words roll over me, pushing me to go faster and deeper.

I drop my other hand to my swollen clit, creating small circles as I lower my mouth over his length again.

He catches what I am doing, smirking, "do you like this Nyathera?"

I nod and hum over his cock. "If you keep that up I am going to come before I get the chance to pleasure you."

I drop his dick with a pop and his hands are under my arms throwing me onto the bed, one hand gripping my wrists and holding them above my head, the other sliding down my body and between my legs.

He kisses me with brute force and pulls his head back, "what do you need?" His voice husky. I lift my hips towards his hand, needing to feel some sort of pressure. "Use your words." His eyes burning with lust.

"Touch me" I whisper in a raspy voice.

"I can't hear you." He smiles wickedly.

"Touch me, Kai, please." He palms my center and warmth spreads across my body, he kisses my neck and slides his fingers to my clit. Creating small tight circles on the swollen bundle of nerves. My back arches and a small cry escapes my lips.

"That's a good girl Nye."

As the words leave his lips, arousal builds tightly in my core. He shoves a finger into my center, curving just enough to hit the perfect spot. I moan louder and he presses his mouth to mine to quiet me. He pulls his finger out and puts two back in, using his thumb to press on my clit. "Kai!" I moan out as the pressure builds and builds.

"I love the sound of my name on your lips," he says, picking up speed with his fingers.

My hips raise to meet his hand, creating the pressure I desperately need. Before I can get my release he retracts his hand staring into my eyes and sticking his fingers between his lips.

"You taste delightful Nye," he hums, licking each finger clean.

My mouth drops open slightly at the sight of him. He positions himself between my thighs, tightening his grip on my wrists. A small amount of fear builds at the sight of how monstrous he is. His eyes meet mine and he kisses my nose before placing himself at my entrance.

"Say it Nye." His eyes begging, "Say you need me to fill you up and help you take your mind off everything right now." My brows furrow. "You have to say it, or I cannot fuck you. Please, before I combust."

A small smile spreads across my face, "I don't know. Maybe there is someone else that can do that for me."

His gaze burns into my soul, "No one can fuck you the way I can Nyathera, now say it so I can prove it to you."

Licking my lips I whisper, "fuck me Kai."

With a groan, he slides into me one glorious inch at a time. My head falls back at the sensation of him stretching me, "Oh my Gods." I say breathlessly.

He pauses, "Look at yourself wrapped around me. You take my cock so well." I glance down between us and the need starts to twist in my stomach again.

He moves his hips back sliding out of me before slamming back to the hilt. I scream out at the tremendous amount of pressure building in my core. He smiles at me and repeats the action:

Again,

Again.

And again.

His forehead falls to mine as he picks up the pace, "Oh my Gods!" I moan, "Oh my Gods!"

"The Gods can't help you here, Nyathera." His deep voice washes over me and pressure builds as our bodies slap together.

The sound of skin on skin, wetness, and our breathless moans fill the room. He pulls out and flips me onto my stomach, tracing kisses down my spine, "put your hands out in front of you," his breath right in my ear.

"What?" I say on a breath.

He pulls my hands out in front of me, forcing my spine to stretch forward, "grip the sheets." He says demandingly. And a deep seeded primal need to obey washes over me. I grip onto the sheets in front of me. He grips my hips, forcing my ass into the air, exposing all of me to him. "You are beautiful," he mumbles, running his hands over my ass cheeks, smacking one.

The sting mixes with my pleasure, and I moan.

"Do you like that, Nyathera?" I look over my shoulder and he's smiling at me.

I nod. He raises on his knees and slams into me without warning. I grip the sheets tighter, so he doesn't throw me forward into the headboard the with force of his thrusts. He slams into me over and over again, gripping my ass cheeks in both hands. I know I will have bruises there, but the pinching pain pushes me closer and closer to climax. I moan out again, louder than the last time. He picks up speed and I rip the sheets with my grip. He growls and falls forward.

His front covers my back. "Come for me Nyathera."

He keeps his pace, hitting the right spot. When he reaches his hand around my hip and glides his fingers over my clit, white-hot ecstasy blurs my vision. My core tightens, and he sends me over the edge with a few more strokes.

I scream out in pleasure, and he growls, "say my name."

He doesn't stop his thrusting as my orgasm rips through me. The earth begins to shake as another climax hits me. "That's it, baby. Shake my world." Shattering glass echoes in from the hallway and the chandelier clatters above us. He sits up again and picks up his pace, "Say my name Nyathera." He demands.

"Kai," I say through shuttering moans. The earth rumbles as my release grows stronger, the bed frame cracking beneath us. "Louder." He commands.

"Kai!" I scream as another orgasm tears through my soul.

His hips stutter as he joins me, "fuck." He grinds out. He slowly thrusts in and out as we ride out our orgasms. The earth slowly stops shaking as the last of my climax rolls through me.

I look over my shoulder at him and he smiles, "You are perfect." He says slipping out of me and running his hand over my swollen center.

I jump at the sensation and roll onto my back. He smiles down at me leaning over me and placing a small kiss to my lips.

I place my hand on the back of his neck and kiss him. "Thank you." I whisper with a smile.

He pulls me into him and wraps his arms around me. He's sweaty and smells divine. I kiss his chest, and he sucks in a breath. He holds me for a minute before moving away. My body and soul crying from the loss of his warmth.

He turns, his eyes roaming over my body, "I will be right back." He walks to the bathroom, and I watch his perfectly round ass as he disappears. I hear the water in the tub turn on and then the smell of peonies wafts into the room. He returns a moment later and scoops me into his arms, "let's get you cleaned up."

I wrap my arms around his neck and smile. No one has ever taken care of me this well, sure giving me a washcloth works fine, but this is pampering I have never experienced.

The room is full of flickering candlelight. The flames dance off his golden skin and his eyes shine. I run my hand over his cheek and force him to look at me. He smiles sweetly when his eyes meet mine and he sets me down.

"Get in the water." He says smoothly. I don't want to move, my heart needing the contact. "I will join you once you're in."

Reluctantly I let go of him and step into the hot water. My body shivers as I place my other foot in. I lower myself into the bubbles and a slight sting settles between my legs. I gasp, and he smiles, brushing my hair from my face.

"You did so well, baby." My heart flutters when he speaks. He places a foot behind me and climbs in. Sinking his body into the water and pulling my back to him. I lay my head on his chest, and he places his mouth on the top of my head. He splashes water over my shoulders and runs his hands up and down my arms. Bringing his hands out of the tub he holds his palms up; ropes of water appear and dance in front of me. Twisting his wrists they move in a smooth swirling pattern. The flames of the candles shine through the water, creating a beautiful rainbow. I look over to the candles sitting beside the tub.

"Focus on the flame." He whispers.

I inhale deeply and focus with all my strength on the flickering light. Kai takes one of my hands and lifts it out of the water, "command it with your mind to be in your palm." His mouth is right next to my ear and my body shutters. He chuckles, "Focus on the flames, not me."

I turn to him, "I don't want to focus on anything else."

He gives me a look and jerks my arm gently to remind me that I am doing something. I lift my hand a little higher focusing back on the flames. I repeat a cadence in my mind as I stare at them. *"Come to me, we can be power and light, and goodness."* With a flash the flames jump into my hand, licking at my skin in the same dance that Kai's water ropes are.

I look at him and laugh. "I did it."

He smiles widely. I reach my hands out and whips of fire appear before us, tangling with the cords of water. Steam fills the room as they collide. I move my wrists in a circular motion, the same way as Kai. He chuckles, "I knew you could do it."

I close my hands into fists and the flame disappears. I turn to him and straddle his legs, "Thank you." I run my hands over his strong shoulders. "For everything."

He glances at me and wraps his arms around my waist. Pulling me closer and kissing my swollen lips. Leaning into him I wrap my arms around his head, running my fingers through his silky. Holding his mouth to mine.

A knock at the door makes me jump, "Nyathera? Is everything okay?" Margie's voice glides through the bathroom.

My eyes wide, I look at Kai and back to the door. I freeze, not able to form words.

"We will be out in a minute Margie," Kai calls out in his best impression of my voice, and I slap my hand over his mouth. He snorts under my palm. Margie laughs and her retreating hums fill the bathroom.

"You did not have to say anything. I was going to!" I push his shoulders.

"You weren't though, and she would've come in instead of just talking through the door if you didn't answer." I shove his shoulders again and kiss his lips quickly before climbing out of the tub, water sloshing over the sides. After I wrap a towel around myself, I open the door and survey the room. Kai is getting out of the tub and wrapping a towel around his waist. I look back to him and take in his muscular form, soaking wet and glistening. I sigh at the sight.

I silently wave my hand to him.

"Nye. I own this house; I am allowed to be in here. You don't have to sneak me out." He stands next to me, adjusting the towel around his waist and we both jump at the sight of Margie standing in my doorway.

Kai's eyes are wide, no doubt mirroring my own. "Well, you've got this covered." He says, kissing my cheek quickly, before disappearing into nothing.

I scoff at the space where he was standing, now completely alone with Margie. "Um, hi." I say sheepishly and smile.

Her grin beams as she shakes her head, "you two had fun I see." She looks towards the bed frame, now cracked.

I follow her gaze and wince, "I will replace that."

"No need." She snaps her fingers, and the bed is as good as new.

"I'm sorry." I say, heat creeping up my chest and dusting my cheeks.

"No need deary. I was young once; I am just glad you have accepted the bond."

A shudder wracks my spine, "I haven't." I say quietly.

Her gray blue eyes snap to me, "what do you mean, you haven't?"

I walk over to the bed and sit on the edge of it, she waddles over and sits next to me. Taking a deep breath in, I lay my whole heart out for her. From my first memory all the way up to the vision, "that is why I can't accept the bond." I let out a breath, relieved to have told someone. She smiles sweetly at me and grabs my hands out of my lap.

Holding both hands in hers, "you worry so much for such a young, beautiful woman. Having a mate will make you extremely powerful, just being in such close proximity to Kai has already shown just how powerful you two can be together. You created an earthquake during your..." she clears her throat, "time, together. You Nyathera are strong and so is Kai, you're destined for one another. And the universe will have its way. It is whether you decide to accept that and allow love into your life for the first time. I won't judge you either way, but I can see the way he looks at you, and Nyathera." She breathes deeply, "that boy has been in love with you for so long that it has been painful to watch." She pats my hands and stands. "Now come on. We have to get you ready for dinner. The servants are cleaning up the mess in the house." She turns away, "allow him to at least train you so we don't have to patch cracks in the walls and pick up all the glassware the next time you two are together." She chuckles and walks into the closet.

I flop back onto the mattress and sigh. "Margie?"

She peeks her head around the doorframe, "Yes deary?"

I sit up onto my elbows, "was it wrong for me to..." I stop.

"No, not in the slightest. As long as he asked for your consent."

A small smile crosses my lips as I remember what we just did, "he did."

She nods and goes back into the closet.

Chapter

45

Warmth and happiness surrounded the young boy. And she knew that they would be good friends, had this not been a dream.

Margie picks turquoise blue satin pants that billow around my legs and paired them with a white shirt that crops just above the waistband. The long sleeves provide some warmth against the cool air flowing through my windows. I walk over and close them, shivering slightly. I slip on the black fur lined slippers that Margie left by my bed and look in the mirror one last time. My white hair flows around my shoulders in loose curls and there is a light dusting of pink blush on my cheeks. I notice my eyes glow with an emotion I haven't felt in so long, or ever, and I stare into my reflection. Since getting to Mearin and now here, having three full meals a day, I am no longer a scraggly girl, but a woman with curved hips and a stomach that is no longer skin and weak muscle. I admire my figure for another moment before walking to the door and hurrying to the stairs.

I stand at the top of the staircase and look down into the foyer. Kai opens the door and a beautiful woman with long straight black hair and dark almond eyes stands there. She jumps into his arms and kisses each cheek.

Kai spins her in a circle, "I have missed you!" She says with so much enthusiasm that I feel nauseous. Kai sets her feet back to the ground and kisses her forehead. My heart drops to my feet. Does he have a girlfriend? I turn to leave and the floorboards creak. I freeze, I immediately feel Kai's gaze on me. I turn back around with a grimace. "Nyathera, this is Alessandra. Alessandra, this is Nyathera."

Alessandra crosses her arms and scowls at me. "You didn't tell me we were taking" she glances over me, "guests."

Kai nudges her with his elbow, "be nice. She is my guest, and you will treat her with respect."

She looks at me from head to toe, again, and rolls her eyes. Grabbing her bag that she dropped in the doorway, she stomps into the dining room.

I turn to leave, "Nye. It is time for dinner."

I keep my back to him, so he doesn't see the tears threatening to fall. I shouldn't even be crying; it was just sex. Just sex that set my soul on fire and brought me true happiness.

I shake my head, "I'm not hungry." I choke out, keeping my voice neutral. I walk back to my room and shut the door, leaning my forehead against it and letting out a deep breath. A breath I didn't even realize I was holding. A knock on the door makes me jump, "who is it?" I call through the thick wood.

"It's me. Are you okay?"

I roll my eyes. "I am fine, Kai. I don't want to eat."

It is silent for a breath, "Are you lying to me?"

I sniffle quietly, gathering my emotions and shoving them down. "No, I am fine." My voice cracks, Gods damn it. I huff.

"Okay." he says quietly. I hear the floorboards creak as he walks away. Another tear escapes and falls down my cheek. I turn towards the bed and slam straight into a wall of muscle. Kai is standing between me and the soft mattress of my bed. I look at him, and his eyes are full of perturbation.

I try to move around him, but he grabs my shoulders. "You lied." he says firmly, wiping a tear from my cheek. Leaning into his palm on my cheek, I look down not wanting to meet his gaze. He dips his head and catches my eyes, forcing me to hold eye contact. Gods, he is hot. No, no, he has a girlfriend. "Tell me what is wrong?" His voice firm.

I hold his stare and feel the annoyance creeping under my skin, "you have a girlfriend, and you were what?" I throw my arms out wide. "Hoping I would have left before she found out. You lied to me, Kai." My eyes burn as more tears form. I drop my gaze to the floor, so he doesn't get the satisfaction of seeing what he has done to me. He laughs. With his entire body, he laughs loudly. My eyes snap back to his face. His white teeth are shining in the dim room. Static lines my bones as a sizzling burn creeps over my body.

"Alessandra?" he questions, tears filling his eyes as he tries to catch his breath.

I fold my arms across my chest, popping my hip out and cocking my head to the side, "So? Were you going to tell me at all? Because I would have appreciated it if you told me before you *fucked* me!" I yell.

He wipes a tear and controls his laughter. I can feel the rage building in my core again. The earth tremors lightly as the anger builds.

"Alessandra is my baby sister."

My mouth drops open, and I snap it shut. I can feel the red creeping across my cheeks, and my mouth dries with embarrassment. "Sister?"

Kai laughs again but controls it much faster. I look at the ground, and he grips my throat. He tilts my head up and looks directly into my very being, "Yes. She has been on a trip across the sea trying to settle disputes with the Ganglioans." His eyes drop to my parted lips, "if you wanted a challenge, all you had to do was ask, crazy girl." His thumb trails across my throat, creating a wave of arousal.

I can't focus on anything but his grip on my throat—electricity tingles where his skin meets mine. Need begins to pool between my legs, and I fight the urge to push into him. He glances at my lips for a heartbeat and then back to my eyes, inhaling the air deeply. "The only one for me is the beautiful woman standing before me getting excited about my hand around her throat," He smirks. I back away from his grip, and he shoves his hands in his pockets. I roll my eyes at him and turn towards my door. He whispers in my ear, "If you play nice with my sister, we can explore…" his breath caresses my earlobe, "the very thing that just made the room fill with that lovely lavender scent of yours."

My breath hitches, and he chuckles and winks before opening the door for me. He places his hand on the small of my back and leads me down the stairs and into the dining room. His sister sits in the chair to his right, next to Caine. She has her hand on Caine's bicep and is batting her lashes without embarrassment. Caine happily ignoring her as he drinks his wine.

Ezra sees us first and smiles, "I heard you caused an earthquake." His tone is light and teasing. I put my hand over my face to hide the embarrassment.

"I told you I was better than both of you," Kai says with amusement in his voice. I smack his arm lightly.

"He only thinks he is, come to my bed, and I'll help you create an explosion." He winks teasingly, and Kai stiffens. I can feel the vexation radiating off of him.

"No thanks, I like a man with at least one brain cell." I wink at Ezra, whose mouth forms a tight line, and then he laughs. I giggle right along with him.

Alessandra clears her throat, "are you two done? I want to speak with my brother." Her tone sharp. "But with strange ears in the house, I don't think that will be possible, will it, Kai?" she glares at Kai, her eyes like daggers.

Kai looks at me, and his grip tightens and loosens on my back, "anything that you have to say to me can be said in front of her."

She scoffs, "You trust her that much?" sounding offended.

Kai nods, "She is my mate, Alli." His voice pure and powerful.

Alessandra's mouth drops open, eyes wide. "This," she gestures towards me, "is your mate?"

Kai growls quietly. "Alessandra." He warns.

"What? I just figured your mate would've been…. different." my stomach turns when her eyes meet mine, "No offense." She forms a tight line with her mouth, scrunching her nose.

I smirk, not allowing the offensive words bother me, or at least show on my face, "None taken; with how Kai looks, I figured his sister would be..." I look her up and down, "different."

She places her hand on her chest with fake offense. But then she grins, "I like you."

I genuinely smile. Kai pulls out the chair across from Alessandra, next to Ezra, and I sit. I smile up at him as he places a kiss to the top of my head.

"Nyathera! I need you!" Runihura's voice echoes through my mind. I bolt up and slapping my hands on the table.

"What's wrong?" I send down the mind link but get nothing in return.

I turn to Kai, who is staring at me with confusion. "Runihura," I breathe out. I take off out the front door and down the front steps.

"Nyathera! Wait!" Kai is on my heels, running after me as I sprint to the stables.

I run with as much speed as I can muster. Speed I didn't even know I was able to reach. Ice fills my veins as I try again to get a response from Runihura. I get to the stables and burst through the doors. Bruce is bucking and snorting in his stall, undoubtedly feeding off the adrenaline coursing through my veins. I try to reach out for Runihura again and receive nothing in return. Fear creeps over my skin. Kai runs through the stable doors just as I am saddling Bruce.

"Get on Calypso. Runihura said she needs me, but I can't get an answer from her."

Without question, Kai jumps on Calypso, and we take off towards the cow fields, down the path, and into the opening. I don't see Runihura. Panic grips my chest as I jump off Bruce and run through the opening. As I am scanning the area I run into something, like an invisible shield. I place my hand before my face and feel the hard surface. Dark green appears in a ripple of light, spreading around my hand, and then up, up, and the sun is blocked out as if someone had built a wall. Runihura appears in all her glorious beauty.

"Oh, my Gods!" I wrap my arms around her leg, "You." I look up towards the sky, "You are massive, Runihura!"

She snorts, *"I told you I will be a big dragon one day."* Her sweet voice washes over me and calms the nerves in my body.

"What is wrong? Are you okay? I came as fast as I could."

My breathing slows down as she lies in front of me, nose to nose, *"I am out of cows..."* she tilts her head, *"and sheep."*

I stare at her for a moment. Throwing my hands up, I step back, "Are you fucking kidding me?!" I shout, "I thought you were in danger!" she blows steam my way, a warning, no doubt.

"I haven't seen you in a few days, and now that I am the size I am, I need more cows or sheep or some sort of game to keep me fed."

I stare blankly at her, "you missed me."

"And I am hungry." she nods.

I place my hand on her snout and then my forehead, "I missed you too." Her head snaps up, and she growls. I turn to where her eyes are fixed. "Oh. This is Kai."

"So, you brought me a snack?"

I roll my eyes, "No. He's…" Runihura stands at her full height. She is so massive I barely come up to her ankle.

Kai freezes, "Hello, Runihura." He says gently. "I have been waiting to meet you." Runi blows steam in his direction.

"Be nice, Runihura. He's my mate." Runihura pauses. I can hear her strong heartbeat through her scales. She turns away from me and walks towards the other side of the clearing, like an orange cat who didn't get their way. "Oh, come on, Runi."

I run towards her. "Runi! Stop."

She freezes and turns towards me, *"I told you I am starving, and you bring your mate, that I can't eat…"* Her voice is mocking.

"He is the one that can get you more cows," I say, crossing my arms.

She looks over to him, *"Then he may be of use."* Runi spreads her large wings and launches into the sky, breaking the sound barrier with her speed. I watch as her retreating form blocks the sun circling above us; she goes higher and higher until she looks no bigger than a toy dragon. Tucking her wings, she dives straight towards the ground and towards Kai.

"Runihura!" I yell, with no response. My heart rate increases as panic sets in.

Closer and closer to Kai, who is just standing there, arms crossed. She looks like a blur as she picks up speed; within feet of Kai, she opens her wings and angles back toward the sky. The hair on the top of Kai's head blows as she whizzes past him, but he doesn't flinch, his face remains stoic and unamused. I let out the breath I have been holding. I run to Kai, gripping his arm in both hands, and he smiles, "I like her." He says. I roll my eyes and pat his arm, calming my own nerves.

Runi lands in the middle of the field and walks to us in a few steps. *I guess we can keep him.* Runihura says.

"I haven't decided if I want to keep him." Her eyes snap towards me, and she blows steam again.

"Everyone that I let into my life dies. I can't subject him to that kind of life. Always looking over his shoulder wondering if he is next." I place my forehead on her snout.

"What does he say?" Her voice is sweet and sincere, mothering.

I take a deep breath before telling her everything he has said. She bows down and puts her leg out for me. *"Get on, bring the mate; let's see if he is worthy of YOU."*

I look back to Kai, who hasn't moved since I started my conversation with Runi. He smiles, "Come on. She wants to take you for a ride."

His eyes widen, "I am not sure that is a good idea."

I cock my head, "Why? Are you scared of dragons as well?"

A slow smile spreads across his full lips, his eyes looking towards the sky as the sun is blocked and darkness falls across the field. I follow his gaze and an enormous black dragon circles above us. Kai's eyes meet mine, "because Erebus may get jealous."

My mouth drops open at the sight of his dragon. I have never seen anything so big. His black scales shine in the light, and orange and red line each scale, creating the illusion of lava running between them.

I look to Runi, whose head is turned towards the sky, tracking Erebus's every movement. *"Erebus would prefer we do not take his rider. He thinks I won't be strong enough to carry you both because I chose a half-breed."*

I scoff, "Tell Erebus that Runihura can carry us both." I look to Kai.

He smirks, "Erebus disagrees. And I don't think we should fight that." The earth rumbles as Erebus lands next to Runihura. He towers over her. My breath catches in my throat as Erebus turns his head towards Runi and me. "Don't be a bitter old man, Erebus. This is Nyathera and her dragon, Runihura." Kai chuckles.

"He knows who I am and thinks Runihura is weak."

Kai laughs, "Well, let's find out." Kai sprints towards Erebus, efficiently running up his left leg and settling on his back. He gestures towards Runihura, "let's go."

"Are you ready to kick some male ass?" She nods and lays down so I can climb up her leg.

Once settled, Kai looks over, "We should find an easier way for you to get on her; you're kind of small for a dragon that size." I flip him off, and smirk, and with a bend of her knees, Runihura springs us into the air.

Wind whistles as we take off into the sky. My heart rate accelerates, and the feeling of my stomach dropping increases my adrenaline. Runihura levels out, and I scan the sky for Kai and Erebus. I look to the ground, and they are nowhere in sight. A blur whizzes by us, and Runihura tips slightly to the right. I look and see Erebus and Kai circling back around.

I laugh and squeeze my legs, "Let's show them what a girl can do." Without hesitation, Runi tucks her wings, and we start to freefall. I grip the scales on her neck and hold on with all my strength. My ass leaves her scales as we dive at an accelerated speed. I yell out with a laugh, "Yes!"

She levels above the forest canopy, and I snap back into place. She flies along the tops of the trees, and I see Erebus and Kai right in line with us to my right. Kai smiles, and they speed up in front of us.

I lay my body against Runi's scales, "Come on, Runi!" She speeds up, and we pass the boys before shooting into the sky with graceful ease. Runi spins as we ascend into the clouds. Leveling out, I sit up and stretch my arms to the side. The cool air stings my cheeks as we slow slightly. I tip my head to the sun, allowing happiness to fill my heart. I rub her scales right before me, "You are amazing, Runihura."

Darkness covers us both, and I look up to Erebus flying right above us. I hear a light thump and turn to look behind me. With a wicked grin, Kai walks between the spikes down Runi's back towards me.

"Hold on, Nyathera. I am going to teach Erebus something."

"What do you mean?" She doesn't answer but starts tipping to the right. I grab the scales and hold on with all my strength. Kai tips, and he falls toward the ground as we roll over. Erebus makes a giant U-turn, but Runihura spins and descends without issue. We are under Kai, and he slams into the scales before me. His hair whipping around over his forehead with the force of the wind ripping around us. I laugh, and Runi snorts. Erebus finally catches up to us, and Kai sits before me.

"That wasn't funny!" Kai yells over the roaring of the wind.

"It kind of was." I can't control the laughter at this point.

Kai moves closer, and I hurry back so he is in control. He holds Runi's scales with one hand and grips my knee with the other. Electricity shoots up my legs and straight to my heart. I wrap my arms around his torso, admiring the feeling of tight muscles under my hands.

"Erebus is not happy." He says.

"Is he ever?" I smile and place my chin on his shoulder, "He will have to get over it."

We effortlessly glide over the trees with Erebus behind us and Runihura in the lead. Another field is ahead of us, and Runihura lands in it; Erebus lands behind us. Kai slips off Runi's shoulder and stands by her claws. He is a brave man, for sure, and he holds his hand out for me. I slide down, and he wraps an arm around my waist when I slam into him. Kai takes my hand and walks across the lush green field to the weeping willows in the distance. I look back to Runihura, lying next to Erebus, and smile.

"Do you think they will get along eventually?"

Kai smiles, "I think they will get along just fine. Can you feel the extra electricity surrounding us?"

I stop and realize the hairs on my neck and arms are on end. I look up into Kai's eyes, "Yes." I breathe out. Mesmerized by the look in his gaze.

"They are mates, Nyathera." My heart stops for a moment.

I swallow hard, "Do they know?"

"Erebus can feel it, but Runihura is young; she will eventually figure it out."

My mouth dries, "She should know Kai. It isn't fair to randomly drop that information on someone."

His face falls, "I will talk to Erebus later. Right now, I want to show you something."

I follow him through the branches of a weeping willow, and when the lake comes entirely into view, my heart stops. Beautiful waterfalls flow in a horseshoe shape, cascading into the lake; lilies grow on the rocks surrounding the waterfalls. The deep blue water shines like diamonds as if someone had collected the night sky in a pool. Deer and rabbits scurry around in the soft green grass as butterflies float into the sky. The trees block out the cool air from autumn and create a springtime environment in the bowl.

I glance over to Kai, who is smiling and staring at me. Looking back at the landscape, my body relaxes. "It is beautiful." I whisper.

Kai moves his arm around my waist, "You're beautiful."

My breath hitches, and my stomach clenches. I look back to Kai as he removes his arm. He pulls his shirt over his head, his back muscles on full display. He turns back to me, stretching his arms to the side.

"What do you say, Nye? Care to take a dip with the demon prince?"

My mouth goes dry. I scan his handsome face with his sharp nose and strong jaw. I think of those full lips on my skin and the feeling of his chest against mine. I stare as my gaze roams over his perfectly sculpted abs and to the v right above his waistband. He smiles wide, white teeth gleaming in the sun. I shake my head and smile.

I reach for the hem of the white top; Kai's eyes track my movement as I slowly drag the shirt over my head. He licks his lips. I opted not to wear a bra today; apparently, he likes it. A slow grin spreads across his beautiful lips as I hook the waistband of the satin pants.

"Like what you see?" I say with a smile.

He doesn't say a thing as I drag the pants over my hips. I am standing there in nothing but my skin. Taking a deep breath, I walk towards him, his eyes roaming over my body as he bites his bottom lip.

"You are stunning." He whispers as I get closer.

I stand on my tip toes and kiss his lips lightly, but before he can grab me, I take off running towards the water. I can hear his huff as I jump in. The water is surprisingly warm and velvety. I come to the surface, and he is pulling his pants over his feet, tripping over them as he tries to get out as fast as he can. I giggle as he runs towards the water and flops into it.

He doesn't surface, and I feel calloused hands wrap around my waist and pull me under. I thrash until Kai's face comes into view, and he smiles. He touches my cheek, pulling my waist closer to him. His warmth spreads across my body as our skin touches. Electricity fills the water, and I notice that the water is forming a tiny whirlpool around us. I look towards the spinning water and back to Kai, who has a wicked grin. He lets go of me and swims away. I follow him as he keeps the whirlpool around us. He is heading straight toward the large rocks at the waterfall's base. The water is tumbling with rapid speeds from the force of the waterfalls surrounding us. He holds out his hand, and the whirlpool calms the water enough for me to see a cave in the rocks. Kai turns and smiles at me before entering the dark hole.

I brace myself as I enter the cold blackness, so dark I can't even see my hand before me. A moment later, the night vision kicks in. A tunnel of slippery rocks pushes us forward. I continue swimming straight, the air in my lungs now burning. I need to breathe, and I fight my diaphragm with every passing second. I swim faster through the inky black, trying to find the surface, but it doesn't come. Suddenly, I see a green light coming through the water's surface. I race towards it, and as my head tears through the water, I inhale. Sweet air fills my lungs, and I cough with so much force my head hurts. I take in a few more dizzying breaths and open my eyes. My world stops for a moment.

Chapter

46

Nyathera awoke in the bright morning light. Still imagining the creatures of the City of Shadows and Nightmares.

The water's surface and the dark cavern is filled with an illuminating substance. The green glow looks like constellations floating through the darkness. I spin in a circle, treading water, my body calming. Kai is on the sand lining the outer sides of the cavern. He holds out a hand, and I swim towards him. He pulls me onto the bank, and I stand next to him. Both of us wholly bare and covered in the shiny substance. I reach a finger towards his chest and draw a line in the glow. He shutters as he watches my finger trace circles and lines.

He smiles when my eyes meet his. "I came here as a child to escape my life," he says quietly. "My mother showed it to me when I was five, and it became the only place I felt safe." He swallows hard, "After she passed away, I would come here every so often to feel like I was closer to her." He looks down at me and kisses me on my forehead. When he steps back, his lips are covered in the green glow, and I can't help but giggle. He walks over to the water and steps in, "are you ready to go back?"

I admire the surrounding rocks, running my hands through the glowing substance, "Can we stay just a little longer?"

He smiles and walks back to me. He pulls me into his chest, staring deep into my eyes, "I can't imagine a world without you, Nyathera. I would go to the ends of the universe to protect you."

He kisses me gently, lowering me onto a boulder against the wall. He lowers his hard body over mine, and I wrap my legs around him, pulling him closer. He kisses me with a force that I feel throughout my body; as my arousal increases, so does the tugging in my chest. The tugging keeps pulling me to him, the man who is a beast to the mortal world but a gentle man with me. Something in my heart twinges at the thought of not accepting the bond, but I must ensure it is best for us both. If I don't accept, he will stay safe. But if I do accept, we can both be so powerful that we can conquer anything that comes our way.

"Stop thinking." He whispers, his lips brushing against the sensitive skin right below my ear. I let my mind go blank, only focusing on where our bodies are connected. He kisses down my neck and across my chest, taking his time on each breast. "I love these." He nuzzles his face between my breasts, "Gods, do I love these."

I giggle as he pulls a nipple into his mouth and nips at it. I let out a breathy moan, and he does the same to the other side. He kisses my ribs and then my navel, peering up at me as he nips at my lower abdomen. He holds my gaze, and he kisses each thigh. Nipping and licking the skin slowly. My back arches instinctively as he nuzzles his nose on my pubic bone.

He inhales deeply, "you smell absolutely delectable."

My heart beats rapidly as his tongue darts out and connects with the sensitive bundle at the apex of my thighs. I cry out and lace my fingers into his hair. He makes tight circles with his tongue, building that tight knot in my lower belly. "Oh, my Gods Kai."

I can feel him smile as he continues his assault on my clit. Licking and nipping at the sensitive bud. He slows and drags his tongue up my slit and circles it around my clit again. My breathing is fast and short as I moan out his name.

"Say my name again, baby."

I tighten my grip on his hair, "Kai." I breathe out on a moan.

He slips a finger into my wetness, and that is all it takes for the earth to start shuttering. He works his fingers in and out with the same rhythm as his tongue. My climax grows closer and closer as he continues. I scream his name as the earth shakes as ferociously as my release. He pumps his fingers slower as I ride out my orgasm; he looks up and smiles as he licks his fingers clean. Crawling over me, he looks deep into my eyes, "I was right; you are delicious." I can feel the redness creeping across my chest and cheeks.

I bite my lip and smile, reaching up and wrapping my arms around his head. He kisses me, my release on his tongue intertwining with his taste. I moan quietly, which results in a deep growl from him.

He places his forehead on mine, "I will never get enough of you. Never." His lips are on mine again, my tongue gliding across his teeth. My soul cries out for this man, begging me to be his. I run my hands over his back, digging my nails into the skin. In one swift motion, he is inside me. "Fuck." He growls, "I could stay here forever."

I start to giggle until he begins to pull out and slam back into me slowly. Every incredible inch igniting all the nerves in my body. My back arches to get more contact with him.

"Don't be gentle," I whisper.

He stiffens but doesn't stop. The sound of slapping skin and moans fills the cavern, echoing off the walls. I dig my nails into his back again, and he increases his speed, drawing out a scream as he brings me closer and closer to the edge. "Let go for me, crazy one," he growls in my ear.

And that is all it takes for my body to obey. The earth rattles, and I scream his name at the same time as he stiffens and growls his release. He lays on top of me and chuckles.

"Fuck, you are perfect." He raises onto his elbow and looks into my eyes, moving a stray hair from my face.

I smile at him, "That was amazing."

My breathing quick and my heart rate fast, I kiss him. He smiles at me and looks down, "Let's get back before Alessandra throws a fit." He stands, his muscular body covered in green glow and sweat. He glistens in the light. I lick my lips, and his eyes immediately snap to my mouth. I stand, walking over to him as his eyes roam over my body again.

"Why do I feel the need to have you inside me all the time?" I ask quietly. Sliding a hand up his abdomen.

He smiles, lowering his voice, "our souls being bonded creates that need. Most mates don't make it out of their houses for a year. It's a primal need to create new life. Like animals breeding."

I freeze, "will it stop?"

He chuckles, "we can learn to control it, if that's what you want."

I smile and saunter away from him, "I'll keep this feeling for now," I dive into the dark water.

Chapter

47

The friends met up and discussed their adventure the day before. Not wanting anyone else to hear.

Once on land, we dress quickly. Taking my hand Kai leads me through the weeping willows and back into the field. Runihura and Erebus are nowhere in sight.

"Where are they?" I look at Kai, his eyes glazed over as he stares into the distance.

He chuckles, "Runihura felt the bond. They are, ummm, off somewhere."

I cringe, "Oh, gross."

He chuckles again, "come on. We are walking back to the horses."

I roll my eyes and follow him as he takes off towards the forest. The ground is damp, and the cool air rustles the leaves. The sound of birds chirping in the trees creates a calm environment. The forest is dense in this area.

Kai is knocking down bushes and creating paths for us to walk through. I see raspberries ahead and run to them.

"I wouldn't eat those." Kai says amusement dancing across his face.

"Why? They are just raspberries." I pop one in my mouth and swallow.

"Those aren't raspberries Nye" I stare at him waiting for an explanation, popping a few more in my mouth. The sweet juice coating my tongue.

"They are psychedelics; we call them seeing berries." He laughs. "You're about to be on a good trip."

"What the fuck?" panic tingles up my spine, "why didn't you tell me sooner.?!"

He laughs, "because everyone has to try them once in their life."

"I would have liked that to be on my terms!"

He places a hand on my forearm, "I'll be right here with you." He grabs a handful and pops them in his mouth. My jaw hinges open as he swallows them.

"*Oh*, my Gods Kai. Who will make sure we don't die?"

He chuckles, "We will be fine. Don't worry. I won't let anything happen to you."

As we continue through the forest, I wait for whatever is going to happen to set in. The colors in the trees become more vibrant, the smell of the earth invades my tongue. I flick my tongue in and out of my mouth, trying to get the dirt off of it. A cartoon sparrow in a blue vest and fedora sits on a low branch.

"Hello. I like your pants." The bird says in a sing-song voice.

"Thank you! I wasn't sure about the color." I say looking at my pants and back to the silly little bird.

The bird looks over its shoulder and back to me, it spreads its wings and lands on my shoulder, whispering in my ear, "You Nyathera, are a very powerful demon. You will save the world."

My stomach tightens. "What?" I ask the little sparrow; Kai is staring at me with a smirk. I cock a brow at him.

His smile grows wider, "You're talking to a leaf." He chuckles, the sound reverberating around me, creating ripples in the air.

I roll my eyes, "the bird…" I trail off as I turn and notice that there isn't anything there besides leaves. "It was there!" I protest.

Kai's smile turns into a painting. His body is all sharp edges and shapes. Like abstract art, he stands before me. "Come on, the field is right over there."

His voice fades off as he speaks. I look to where he is pointing, and the trees swirl into watercolors. I reach my hand in front of me; the wind is slow around my palm, and my skin is melting into pools of starlight. Panic rises in my belly. Beauty and fear all rolled into one, gripping at my soul as the world around me changes. Kai comes up beside me and twists my hair in his fingers, "You're hair looks like snowflakes."

I snort, "I haven't heard that one."

The birds chirping is getting louder as we slowly reach the field. Spots of color flash along the ground and up the trees. We burst through the trees into the field, laughing at the leaves doing a dance. Kai flops to the ground and lays on his back, the grass moving like water after a stone is thrown in. I do the same while laying my head on his stomach. He lifts his hand into the air, twisting and twirling it. I place my hand up next to his; the sight of our flittering hands melding into one takes my breath away; the color of the sky mixing with our skin and rainbows is beautiful. The air tastes sweet, like cotton candy at a springtime fair.

Kai laces his fingers with mine, the feeling of his calloused fingers more intense than before. I release some power, letting flames lick over our skin. I smile as they wrap around our arms. Kai creates waves of water, and it wraps around my flames, the steam rising from our hands turning into people dancing, their little faces appearing in the flames.

"We should eat these before sex," I say. Snapping my mouth shut as I realize I said that out loud.

Kai laughs, "I will try anything with you." He taps the end of my nose, and I laugh. I close my hands and the flames disappear. Laying my hands across my stomach I open my eyes and stare into the sky.

I don't know how long we lay there watching the clouds turn into funny little animals, but Ezra's voice breaks the colors. Splitting them down the middle as if he is splitting the earth. "There you two are!"

I look over to him; his light brown skin glows in the sunlight, and his arm movements look like they trace the sky. The funny little sailor's outfit fits funny on his large muscular frame.

I giggle, "Helloooo, sailor."

He stops and cocks his head. "Okay?"

Kai looks over to him, "Hey man! Watch out!"

Ezra runs sideways, his scent wafting towards us, "mmmm. You smell amazing."

He laughs, "What did you two get into?"

Kai flops back down, and I flop my head back onto his stomach. He plays with my hair while we lay there, "seeing berries." Kai tugs lightly on my hair, ripples of pleasure roaming over my skin. "Want some?" Kai asks Ezra.

Ezra laughs again, "hell yeah I do!" Kai grabs some berries from his pocket and hands them to Ezra, who doesn't hesitate before throwing them into his mouth. Ezra stands above us, watching the tree line, "You guys have been out here for a couple of hours."

I snort again, nothing funny, but I can't contain it.

"We ate handfuls; Nyathera here thought they were raspberries." Kai laughs.

"Bro, the ground is like water!" Ezra yells and flops beside us, placing his head on my stomach. His head is warm and looks vaguely like a cheeseburger.

I twirl his dark braids between my fingers, watching them cascade off my fingertips. "I want to do this again."

Ezra and Kai laugh, "Our girl has a thing for the finer things, huh, Kai?"

Kai snorts, "She sure does." He strokes my cheek with his finger, and my breath hitches. Ezra is playing with the side of my pant leg, rubbing the silk between his fingers, but brushes a hand down my thigh.

"You know, we could both make you feel amazing, Nyathera," Ezra says quietly.

Kai growls, the sound filling the field, "Or not, but can I watch?" I laugh, but Kai stiffens, "Oh, come on! It isn't like I haven't watched you before Kai."

My heart freezes and my spine tingles. Kai's dark eyes look down at me, *"Do you like the sound of that?"*

It has to be the berries, but I nod.

Kai smiles and thumbs my lower lip. "I'll ask when you aren't tripping balls."

I laugh at that. We lay here for what feels like an eternity. Kai is under me, and Ezra's head is on my lap. All playing with each other's hair. It feels like someone took water, gave it a furry texture, and slapped it onto our heads.

Chapter

48

The friends never spoke of it again. Even as they grew older and heard the story being passed down to the younger children.

I don't know when we fall asleep, but I wake up with Kai wrapped around me and Ezra piled on top of us. I stretch and shove Ezra off. He flops to the side with a groan. Kai doesn't stir. I stand and walk a few feet away, sitting down in the soft grass and wrapping my arms around my knees. I look at the sky, which is now freckled with stars.

"It's beautiful, isn't it?" I look over and Ezra is staring up at the sky with me.

A cool breeze rolls through the field. I shiver, and a large arm lays over my shoulders. I look at it and then at Ezra, "I am pretty sure if I let you freeze to death Kai will kill me."

I smile and lean my head on his shoulder. I soak up his body heat and continue staring. "My best friend is up there," I say in a whisper.

Ezra looks down at me and back to the night sky. "The one who was killed in the battle with you?"

I nod, a tear falling down my cheek.

Ezra wipes it away, "He is always with you, Nyathera. And now you have us to protect you. Kai would destroy this entire world to ensure you were safe."

I give him a small smile, "I know. But I have yet to see the demon in him."

"You haven't seen the extent of his work yet," Ezra says.

"I would like to." I say quietly.

Ezra's eyes snap to mine, "He isn't the same person with anyone else. He is cruel and brutal. Especially when it comes to protecting those he cares about."

I take a deep breath in, "Aren't we all? I mean, I slit a woman's throat without a second thought when I was trying to get Dylan to the pit." Ezra's eyes widen, "and I also fed a man his own dick when I was seventeen." I shrug.

Ezra's eyes widen, "you what?! I didn't know you're that crazy!" his voice raising a few octaves. "I like it." His voice lowering.

I look at him slowly, "You are literally a demon…" I say mockingly.

He laughs, a cynical laugh, and Kai stirs behind us. I look over my shoulder, past Ezra's arm, and notice Kai smiling at us; he crawls over to us and sits on my other side. Ezra's arm falls away and I snuggle into Kai's side. "Our girl here is a fighter, Kai."

Kai burrows holes into Ezra with his glare, "you know what I mean."

I look between these two men, one my fated mate and the other willing to sacrifice his own life for a woman he just met.

"We would both give our lives for you; all of us would. You are my world, and they will protect you at any cost. We love you, Nyathera." My mouth dries as Kai speaks into my mind. *"you're one of us now."*

I slide a finger down the wall in his mind, watching it ripple the entirety of its never-ending span. He visibly shudders.

"you're playing a dangerous game, Nye."

I smile and do it again, Kai's eyes flash with amusement in the starlight. Ezra watches Kai's hand making circles on my thigh.

Kai looks over my shoulder to Ezra and smiles, "What do you need, crazy one?"

My head spins, and I bite my lip. I can smell Ezra's scent behind me, like amber and wood, but Kai's scent pulls me in. My body says both, and my soul says Kai. "I don't want things to be weird."

Ezra laughs behind me, "I could have another woman in my bed within an hour afterward. I am simply making my friend's mate happy, so if you want me to go, I will. No one is pressuring you." Kai's eyes are warm as they stare into mine.

"I don't know," I say quietly.

Kai looks at Ezra over my shoulder and nods. "If you do anything out of line, Ezra, I will rip you limb from limb."

Ezra chuckles before he places a kiss on the back of my neck. Kai's eyes light up at the sight, my body tenses when Kai grips my hip, and Ezra's hand snakes around my waist. My breathing turns erratic as Kai's lips crash onto mine. My eyes close, and a small moan rumbles in my throat.

"You can have both of us or none of us; we need you to tell us what *you* need." Kai's voice is gentle. *"It will help with the burning need of the bond"* Kai's lust filled voice rings through my mind.

I slowly let out a breath. Ezra moves my hair over my right shoulder, grazing his teeth over the sensitive skin below my ear. My head instinctively rolls to the side, giving him more access. Kai bites his lip as he watches his friend bite and lick at my skin. A low rumble emerges from Kai's chest as he reaches for my hand interlacing our fingers. I sigh when he laces his other hand in my hair, tugging gently.

They both shift onto their knees, and I follow their movement, "Nyathera. You have to give us permission."

I look into Kai's eyes, full of lust and need. I nod slowly, and Kai smiles before gripping both sides of my head and crushing my lips with his. I open my mouth a little more, and his tongue invades mine. Ezra's hands trail over my hips and thighs, massaging them lightly, and he pulls me back into him. He is hard against my ass, and it makes my insides tighten. I look down at Kai's body and notice he is as well, and my mouth waters at the idea of tasting him again.

"Taste another day; this is for you." Kai's husky voice fills my mind.

I lick my lips, and Kai smiles, tugging his shirt over his head. His muscular body ripples with the movements. Ezra pushes me gently into Kai's arms, and Kai spins me to face Ezra. Ezra's eyes scan over my body as he rips his shirt over his head. His body looks like it is made of marble. His chest is broad, and his abs are solid.

"Do you like the way he looks, Nye?" Kai's breath grazes the shell of my ear, and I lay into him more.

I nod, my nerves on fire as Kai traces kisses down my neck and across my shoulder. Ezra watches every move he makes.

Kai hooks his fingers under the hem of my shirt and tugs, "Are you sure this is what you need right now?"

I take a deep breath in and nod. Kai pulls my shirt over my head and throws it to the side.

Ezra's eyes immediately land on my breasts, "you were right Kai, they're perfect."

I giggle, heat covering my cheeks, "you told him about my boobs?"

Kai chuckles behind me, the sound vibrating through my body. His hands roam up my stomach, and he grips each breast in his large hands. "I can't help it, they are perfect."

A calloused thumb grazes over each nipple and my breath hitches. A knot begins to form in my lower belly as he pinches each in his fingers. A small moan escapes my lips and Ezra moves closer, looking at Kai again to ensure he is allowed to touch me. My chest tightens with the thought. The tugging in my chest increases as Kai kisses my neck with the same rhythm as his fingers assaulting my swollen breasts. Ezra kisses me. Gently at first, testing the waters. I stiffen at the feel of his lips on mine. Not sure how to feel about it. Kai bites my shoulder, and I lean into Ezra's mouth.

"This is so hot. I've never had people worship me before." I send down the bond with Kai.

"There is only so far I can let him go. You're mine. I am only doing this for you."

"You don't find this fucking amazing?"

A chuckle invades my mind, *"Oh, Nyathera, this is the hottest fucking thing ever. My mate and my best friend?"*

He audibly growls. Ezra bites my lower lip, and I sigh, following his retreating mouth—Kai's hand slips into the top of my pants, Ezra's gaze following the movement. I loop my arm behind me and around Kai's neck, trying to push him lower.

"Greedy girl." Kai groans out.

"Please." I beg.

Ezra's body stiffens when I speak, "We should give the woman what she needs."

Kai's eyes snap to Ezra, "Be careful what you do, Ezra." He nods.

Ezra's fingers hook into the waistband of my pants, and he tugs them slowly. "Stand up," he commands.

Kai stands, dragging me up with his arm around my waist. Ezra stays on his knees and pulls my pants to my ankles, helping me step out of them. Ezra looks up to me and back to where Kai's hand lays on my pubic bone.

"Kai…" he says slowly.

"Make my mate feel good, Ezra."

Ezra's hands slide up my legs and he grips my thighs. Colors explode around me as Ezra doesn't even hesitate to place his tongue on my swollen clit, dragging my legs over his shoulders. I cry out at the pleasure, and Kai pinches both nipples lightly again. My hips instinctually rock on Ezra's face, and they both groan. "Fuck Nye," Kai growls behind me.

He grabs my chin and turns my head to kiss me. Swallowing the moans, his best friend is pulling from my body. Pressure builds and tightens in my stomach. Ezra pulls his head back right before I fall over the edge, and I groan. He licks his lips and stands, putting both hands on my hips and spinning me towards Kai. Kai kisses me, his tongue invading my mouth, teeth clashing together. The force pushes me back into Ezra's hard chest. My soul erupts with arousal, and my need for Kai to fuck me takes over.

I watch as Kai takes a nipple into his mouth, and I moan with pleasure. "Kai," I whisper with a moan.

Kai's growl erupts something in me, and I reach behind me, gripping Ezra through his pants. His breath hitches, and Kai looks up at me and follows my arm to where my hand is. His eyes burn at the sight of me palming his friend's erection. I slowly move my hand over Ezra's impressive length straining against his pants, pulling a low grumble from him. Kai drops to his knees and runs his hands up my thighs. My body arches at his touch, electricity following around his fingertips. His nose nuzzles my navel, and he places a kiss right above my flaming clit. I rock my hips forward silently begging for more.

"Lay her down, Ezra." Kai demands. Without a thought, Ezra sits on the ground, sitting me between his legs.

"Spread your legs for him, Nye." Ezra's gravelly voice gliding over my skin. My legs fall apart wide, resting my knees on the ground. Ezra grabs my breasts as Kai crawls over me. He trails a finger over the swollen nub between my legs, and my back arches into the touch. He trails that same finger from my center and over my clit again.

"Gods, you are so wet." He licks his finger, and I track his full lips, sucking my arousal off it.

My chest heaving with need. He reaches down again and slips one finger in. Stars erupt in my eyes at the much-needed pressure. Pumping his finger in and out slowly, building up my climax. My head falls back onto Ezra's shoulder. I moan as I get closer and closer, "more."

"What was that?" Ezra whispers in my ear, still rolling my nipples between his fingers.

I moan louder as my climax builds, "more!" I say louder.

Kai's eyes meet mine, and he picks up speed. My breathing is rapid as Kai's fingers pump in and out of me. I grip onto Ezra's thighs, and he bites my neck. My moans and wetness the only sounds surrounding us.

I am right on the edge when Kai stops, my body sagging against Ezra. Kai stands, and my eyes trail up his body. He looks like a God standing in front of me. Frustration twirls in my chest. Kai unbuttons his pants and drags them down his legs, his massive erection springing to life. My eyes snap to its red and purple head and the precum seeping from it. Ezra helps me stand, and Kai wraps his arms around me, holding me to his body. He kisses me slow and deep. I push into Kai and tilt my head to deepen the kiss. Kia slides his hands down my back and over my ass, hooking the back of my thighs with his palms and lifting me so I can wrap my legs around him. He breaks the kiss to watch himself enter me. I throw my head backward as Kai stretches me around him and I let out a moan. Kai walks forward until my back slams against Ezra's hard chest. My body is on fire between them, their skin brushing against mine. I feel Ezra's hands on my sides, lifting me.

Kai pulls back and slowly moves back inside me. "Fuck." His voice is laced with arousal, and it sets my soul ablaze.

"Do it again, Kai." Ezra says breathlessly.

Kai pulls back again, pushing every inch back inside me a moment later. I lean my head back against Ezra's shoulder, and he kisses my jaw. Ezra's hand moves around my abdomen, his fingers finding my clit. My hips buck at the pressure. Kai growls as he pulls out again, slamming back into me with brute force. My eyes roll, and stars fill my vision again. *"Come for us, Nye."* Kai's voice fills my head as the sound of slapping skin fills the air.

The tightness in my belly coils tighter as my climax nears. My moans become louder and louder the closer I get to falling over the edge. Kai moves faster inside me, and Ezra's fingers keep time with him. I scream as I fall over the edge. White fills my vision, and the earth rumbles.

"Fuck that is hot," Ezra whispers.

My hips buck to meet Kai with every movement. I roll my hips as Kai slows, not wanting him to stop. Ezra pushes me over to Kai, who doesn't pull out of me. I feel Ezra's body leave mine, and Kai drops to his knees, pulling out of me and rolling me to my stomach. He trails kisses down my spine, my skin tingling where his lips touch. I haven't even come down from my orgasm before Kai is over me and entering me from behind. I gasp at the new angle, my head tipping back, and my eyes meet Ezra's. He has his giant cock in his hand, rubbing a thumb over the tip.

"Do you want to watch him come while I fuck you, Nye?" Kai whispers in my ear.

I answer on a moan as he rocks in and out of me. His front sliding against my back. His hand wraps around my throat, and he gently squeezes. My air is cut off and blackness forms in my peripherals. The mixture of fear and Kai's movements sends euphoric vibrations through my entire body. My eyes don't leave Ezra's hand as he pumps it up and down in time with Kai's thrusts. The tightness building in my core again. "Kai." I moan.

He growls, "Say my name again."

"Kai," I whisper.

"Louder so he can hear you." His command sends pleasure throughout my body. He slaps against my ass as he increases his thrusting.

"Fuck! Kai!" I scream out as he shifts off of my back.

"Look at him, Nyathera. Look at how hard we make him." His words, mixed with his thrusts and the sight of Ezra stroking himself feverishly, set my skin on fire. Flames flicker at my fingertips, scorching the grass and the earth rattles. Ezra's eyes widen and then set into a seductive glare.

The tugging in my chest increases when Kai whispers in my ear again, "I love you, Nye," he nips my ear lobe, and I find my release—screaming his name repeatedly.

Kai stutters and growls as he fills me with his own, and Ezra shoots streams of come as he groans. Kai lies over my back again and kisses my cheek, *"that was probably one of the hottest things I have ever done."*

My chest tightens a little, *"what was the hottest thing you have done then?"*

He smiles against my neck, *"you."*

I gasp as he pulls out from me, hating the emptiness I feel. Ezra is already pulling his pants over his hips with a smile on his face.

He squats before me, "That was hot, Nyathera." I give him a lazy smile, and he chuckles and stands.

He slaps Kai's shoulder and walks back towards the forest. Kai helps me stand and get dressed. I stand in his arms momentarily, staring into his brown eyes.

"Nothing is going to be weird between us now, right?" I say lazily.

Kai grins, "nothing has changed."

I smile. "Thank you for today. It was one of the best days of my life."

He raises a brow, "What was the best day of your life then?" asking the same question I did minutes before.

"Meeting you." His smile shines brightly, and he kisses me again before taking my hands and walking me through the forest.

Chapter

49

*But whenever they saw shadows dance in the fading light,
they remembered the City of Shadows and Nightmares, a
place they would never risk returning to.*

We enter the driveway to the house; Kai grips my hand in his and smiles at me. Butterflies erupt in my stomach, and I can't help the grin that spreads across my face. I look up at the beautiful palace before me. The tan bricks have been standing for centuries and the ivy growing on the sides tells a story. Each one weaving together like the men that live in this house. Caine runs out the front door. Kai stands straighter, "what's wrong?"

"We have Ganglioan forces spotted on the east coast."

Kai's grip tightens on my hand. "Where is Alessandra." Kai's gaze is deadly.

"I tried telling you earlier, but you had to follow her to play in the forest." She steps onto the top step next to

Caine. "If you had listened to me for a moment, I would have told you they chased me out of their territory because they didn't want to negotiate. The king said, 'I will see you soon, pretty. Don't worry, we will have what we need.' I didn't think much of it because they have a small army. But apparently, they have human allies."

My heart sinks, and my stomach whirls. "Who?" I say, looking at her; she rolls her eyes at me.

"Kai, we have to leave." Alessandra urges. Kai glares at her, his teeth bared.

"You could have told me as soon as we came to the dining room instead of insulting my mate." He takes a step forward, but I grab his arm. He stops, and I look into his eyes.

I step forward, and he nods, "who are the humans they made their allies."

"I am not speaking to you." She crosses her arms.

Anger starts to build in my chest, "who are they, Alessandra!" the earth rattles on command as I walk closer, and flames begin to climb my arm.

Alessandra's eyes widen, "I don't know. Something called the Keltoids." Her voice shaky.

My heart stops. I turn slowly to Kai, who is now walking towards me. A look of pure rage flashing in his eyes.

"Are you friends with them or something?"

My gaze snaps back to hers, "No. They killed my friend." Fire engulfs my body.

Alessandra squeals, "Control your pet, Kai."

Kai stands beside me, reaches through the fire, and grabs my hand. I will the fire to not burn him, to let him in.

"My mate! Not my pet!" Kai growls.

Alessandra steps back as the fire dies out, and I step past her, "you are the reason they are here!" she shrieks; I turn towards her, dropping Kai's hand.

I am less than a foot from her, and she glares at me, "He is only using you for his pleasure, Nyathera; someone like you could never be worthy of most powerful demon."

I slap her across the face. The sound reverberating off the walls of the foyer. Her eyes snap back to mine, and a red handprint welts on her cheek, "I am a survivor, a warrior, and I am pretty damn powerful. Watch how you speak to me." I bare my teeth. She scowls, tears welling in her eyes. I turn from her and head into the dining room where Ezra is waiting.

Ezra stands as I walk into the room, "Nyathera, it's the Keltoids helping the Ganglioans."

"I know," I state without blinking an eye. "And I know someone on their side."

Kai looks at me, "who?" Caine and Alessandra have come into the dining room as well. I look at Caine and Ezra, squeezing Kai's hand.

"Xavier." His name leaving a bitter taste in my mouth.

"The fucker who tried to kill you?!" Ezra says, placing his hands on the table.

I nod, "He left when the Keltoids attacked Mearin. And he found me easily when I was trying to get Dylan into the pit. Then he told me he was instructed to kill me but couldn't because he fell in love with me." I close my eyes tightly and open them again. "He took my desperation for granted and faked a relationship for two years. Randomly visiting with his father, disappearing at odd times. He even told me I would die by his hand, and his hand only." I take a deep breath, "but I didn't think he meant it literally." I sigh and look at Kai, whose eyes are set in a dark scowl., "But I didn't think they would come here!" My body shakes with adrenaline. "I have an idea." They all look at me with blank expressions.

"How could you know anything? You don't know our world." Alessandra's voice is laced with venom.

"I don't know *our* world yet, but I know how humans fight. You might be stronger, faster, and have powers on your side. But humans plan attacks and battles. They study their enemies for months, sometimes years before they actually attack."

Alessandra huffs and plops into the chair across from me. Kai's eyes find mine, worry tracing his brow. *"I'm fine. I promise."*

He runs his thumb over my cheek, "I know," he whispers and places his forehead on mine. "Tell us everything you know about the Keltoids."

I sit and gesture for everyone to do so as well. "The Keltoids have been at war with us for over 500 years, killing many. That is why Mearin was turned into a training camp. Men and women alike are collected the year of their twenty-first birthday. We train for two years and are thrown into battle." I place my hands in my lap, taking a breath, "The Keltoids attacked Mearin about a month ago, which is how I ended up here. I don't know how, but they have a dragon, an enormous one. And these mechanical machines that wipe out buildings like they are building blocks. They are okay with hand-to-hand combat but aren't very good with swords. Their archery team is impressive," I swallow and think of the arrows that had killed Dylan. Kai places a hand over mine. "I can write down everything I can remember. That way, everyone has a copy, and they can memorize it. How long do we have before they attack?"

Caine looks to Kai, who nods, "Ten days."

I swallow the lump in my throat. I stand, and everyone watches me. "I need to see Runihura and ensure she is ready for battle."

"I am ready Nyathera." Her sweet voice filling my mind and calmness washing over my body.

"You are not going to fight." Kai stands and pins me with his gaze.

"I'm sorry?" Kai reaches for my hand, and I pull it away, "I have more powers than you all have; I know their fighting style. I am going to battle with you. I will not let you all die."

Kai sighs, "Nyathera, I just found you. I cannot let you go."

I look to Ezra, who adverts his stare to the floor, kicking at something that isn't there. "Caine?"

Caine sighs, "I have to follow orders, so if the order is you don't leave, I can't let you leave."

I look around the room at the boys and then Alessandra, who is examining her nails, "Let her go. We will see if she is worthy of Kai." At that moment, I almost feel respect for her, "plus, if she dies, then someone better can come along," and that respect is gone.

I turn my gaze back to Kai, "Please, Kai, we are stronger together."

He grabs my hands and sighs, "You don't leave my side."

I squeeze his hand, "thank you."

Kai sits and pulls me into his lap, "tell us everything you know about their fighting style."

So, I do. We spend the next five hours going over what I know about the Keltoids, and they tell me about the Ganglioans, how they are made up of primarily undead wizards. I tell them I know how to mix potions and am ready to train more in hand-to-hand combat that is effective in this world, so I understand their fighting style.

Alessandra looks at me the entire time like she doesn't believe a word I am saying. "How do we know she isn't one of them?" her voice slices through the room.

I slowly lift my head from the map we are going over and meet her glare. "Alessandra, instead of focusing on the fact that I threaten you, maybe you should focus on what we are saying so you don't end up dead."

Her mouth drops open. Snapping it shut, she growls at me. "You would be the one to get us killed."

I stand from Kai's lap and walk around the table to her. Her shoulders round slightly like a kid who got caught stealing. I reach my hands out and pull her into my embrace. I hug her.

Squeezing her as she fights, I whisper, "I am not your enemy; I love your brother and your friends. If anything, I am the one who can save you all; I am a bomb in human form."

She stiffens, "Now hug me back, and don't tell anyone what I just told you. I just pieced it together while going over the battle plans; help me get into the middle of the battle and get them all out."

She nods almost instinctively. "I don't like you, but if you are going to kill yourself to save my people." She trails off and wraps her arms around my waist.

I hold her out at arm's length, someone so beautiful and powerful, the same height as me. I can feel the power soaking the air around us. She nods, and I let go of her. I turn, and all eyes are on us.

Kai opens his mouth to speak, but Alli holds a thin hand up, "Don't say anything." He snaps his mouth shut. Watching me as I walk around the table and take my place on the wooden arm of his chair.

"We have to warn the city," Caine says quietly.

"We need more intel before we say anything; Ezra, take Alli and your squad to do some recon for us. Caine, you take Nyathera and train her in our fighting style."

"Where are you going?" I look at Kai.

He swallows hard. "I am going to contact my father." His features are tight, and his body language tells me this isn't something that will be easy for him.

Chapter

50

*The friends would play along, knowing all too well what
kind of place the City of Shadows and Nightmares was.*

Tonight, I sleep in Kai's bed. I don't want to be alone, because tomorrow we separate until the Keltoids and Ganglioans attack. I lay in his large bed, watching the stars out of the floor-to-ceiling windows. I can feel Kai's deep breathing behind me, his warmth radiating off his body in waves. "I wish you were here, Dylan," I whisper.

Kai's hand grips my side, "He is always with you, Nyathera. In spirit. Call on him to help you, and you will always find his star in the sky."

I roll over, facing Kai in the dark room, "I thought you were asleep."

"I can't sleep knowing that we are going to be separated, not knowing if you will be safe."

I reach out and find his face, brushing his ebony hair from his forehead. "I have Caine to keep me safe; plus, I am pretty sure I can handle myself."

I can feel his smile coming through our bond, "You're strong, Nyathera. Remember that when you are training."

I run my hand over his stubbled cheek. I wave my hand in the air, and the candles light in the room. Kai lifts his head and looks around to each one, "impressive." He states with a wicked grin. He leans down and kisses me softly. I pull away and roll onto my back, a tear slipping down my cheek.

Kai places his finger on my chin, forcing me to look at him, "It will be alright. I promise."

I give him a small smile, but inside, my mind is in turmoil.

"I can hear your thoughts, Nyathera." he says, looking into my eyes.

"I'm sorry," I say and force a mental shield of fire into place.

He pauses, "Don't shut me out, please."

I open a door in the fire, allowing his darkness to collide with my light. He smiles and kisses me again. We spend the rest of the night wrapped in each other's arms. Him kissing every inch of me and I running my hands over every inch of his skin. Memorizing each dip and ripple of muscle, his scent. The sun starts to rise through the windows, and his eyes meet mine again; he kisses me slowly before rolling on top of me and making love to me.

When it is time to meet with the others, I take his hand, and we walk down the stairs. Aurora is standing by the front door, waiting for Kai. I look at her, and she bows her head subtly. I give her a sad smile as we reach the bottom of the stairs.

"It is nice to see you again, Nyathera." She grabs my hands and places her forehead on mine; her feathers smell of the sky and breeze and are soft against my brow.

She pulls back and looks to Kai, "Are you ready?"

Kai nods and she opens the front door, walking out to the carriage waiting for them. Kai turns to me, my hand in his, "Be safe, my crazy one." He whispers.

I smirk. "Don't do anything stupid," I reply.

He kisses my forehead and then my nose. I wrap my arms around his waist and kiss him, leaning into his firm body. "I love you," he says wholeheartedly.

I smile back at him, "I know."

He smiles and walks out the front door, dropping my hand as he steps over the threshold. I smile at him when he turns around before climbing into the carriage. My stomach twists in loss when the carriage door closes. Ezra and Caine come to stand beside me.

Ezra throws an arm over my shoulder. I lean my head against him, "he will be back when the battle starts." He says gently.

I inhale deeply, urging the tears not to fall. "I know," I whisper.

Caine grips my shoulder, "We have work to do."

Ezra drops his arm and wraps me in a tight hug, "I will see you soon! You'll have to tell me how badly you kicked his ass when I get home."

"You know I will."

"Come on, we have to go." Alessandra's voice breaks through the foyer. She stops in front of me and nods,

"You better know what you are doing." I smile, and she hugs me, "I won't say a word to anyone." She whispers. My body stiffens at the realization that I will no longer be alone in my plan.

I nod and hug her as well, "I will protect you as well, Alessandra."

She stiffens but drops her arms to her sides and turns away. Ezra and Alessandra get into a carriage of their own and take off.

Caine and I stand in the doorway until their carriages are out of sight. "Well, let's get on with it then." He says, turning to walk away.

I grab his arm, and he turns to me, "Thank you." I say shyly. "I know we don't know each other well, but it means a lot to me that you are willing to train me."

He stands to his full height, towering over me, "I have orders."

I laugh, "do you do everything you are told?"

He slumps his shoulders, "No." Sadness flashes across his eyes.

"Do you need to talk about it?" I ask gently.

He straightens again, "No, come on. We are going to the garden to train."

I spend the day doing push-ups, pull-ups, and sprints and dodging rocks that Caine throws at me. I am sprinting up and down the garden path.

"Stop. That's enough." He barks.

I place my hands on my knees, my chest heaving as I try to take in oxygen. "How. Does. This. Do. Anything?" My words come out staggered as I try and catch my breath.

Caine smiles, "endurance is crucial to hand-to-hand combat."

His smug smile pisses me off. He turns to walk past me, and I hook my leg around his. He stumbles but doesn't fall.

"Okay, then. Let's go Nye." He gets into a sparing position, and I copy.

We circle each other and I look for weaknesses. I see none, of course. I swing a fist towards him, and he slaps it, "No."

Did he speak to me like a dog? I throw another fist, and he slaps that one as well. He reaches towards me at an unnatural speed and taps my cheek. I gawk at him, and he does it again. I take a deep breath and summon fire. My hands blaze as I bring them back to blocking my face. His eyes widen before they turn to slits.

"Can you do that all the time?" he asks as we continue circling each other.

I grin, flicking my wrist towards the ground. A fire whip appears, and Caine freezes. His eyes trail over the whip and back to my own. He smiles before throwing a punch. I raise my hand and flick my wrist, wrapping the whip around his forearm and yanking on it. He flips and lands on the solid path with a thud. I release the whip and stand over him with my boot on his chest. He smiles and grabs my ankle.

Flipping my feet from under and pinning me to the ground, "Do not let your guard down. Not for a second." Electricity thrums in the air, like before a lightning strike. The hairs on my neck stand on end as I glare at him. He gets up and holds his hand out for me to take.

I grab it and shake the earth for a breath, just enough to knock him off his footing. I pull his arm towards me and dig my shoulder into his hip, flipping him over my back and onto the ground. Quickly, I straddle his chest and hold a dagger to his throat. He stares at me, and I get within inches of his face, "Do not let your guard down. Not for a second." I snarl and stand. Stomping back to the house.

I hear him laugh behind me, "Kai will be pleased to know you are doing well." He yells with a chuckle. I roll my eyes and slam the door behind me.

Chapter

51

They'd glance at each other as the elders spoke. A silent remembrance that only they knew of.

Dinner tonight is strange. I keep looking at Kai's empty seat at dinner, feeling the emptiness across the entire house. Caine sits across from me, looking up at me every so often. Servants bustle around the house, cleaning and packing bags for everyone.

I finally stand and find Margie, "will you please join us at the table?" She looks at the other two women she is sitting with. "They can come too. I can't stand the silence." She smiles and stands. I walk back in with Margie on my heels and the two other women, who I now know were Carmen and Ophelia. Caine looks up from his food and gives us a small smile.

He stands as they circle the table and motions for them to sit. "Hello, Margie." He says in a deep voice, his beautiful features lighting up as she sits.

"Hello, Caine. Thank you for allowing us to eat with you."

He smiles, "It was all her idea, and I think it is wonderful." His eyes shine like a kid.

I sit down next to Margie, and she squeezes my knee, catching me staring at Kai's seat, "he will be okay, deary." She smiles and piles food onto her plate.

The rest of dinner is full of laughter and stories from Margie. She had a lovely mate who crafted the world around her. As she tells us the story about how her mate passed, tears fill my eyes. The thought of losing Kai breaks me into pieces and shatters strings in my heart. I haven't even accepted the bond, and I can't imagine life without him.

"Are you okay?" I wait for a response.

"I am fine. I love you."

I run a finger down his mental shield, and a shudder comes back.

"We will be home in a couple days, stay safe and kick Caine's ass for me."

I smile, *"already on it."*

I am met with laughter, *"that's my crazy girl."*

I smile and send him a mental picture of the table, the smiles and laughter, *"I wish you were here."*

His sad smile fills my mind, *"I am with you always."*

My heart clenches. *"I'll see you soon."*

He sends back a mental image of him making a kissy face.

I laugh again. Margie grabs my hand, "I am glad you are happy this way. But please accept the bond so I can keep you."

I laugh, "I will think about it."

She kisses my cheek and stands to start clearing the dishes from the table. I rise and help, carrying armfuls of dishes back into the kitchen. The look of shock on the servant's faces makes me giggle.

"Hello," I say with a smile.

I place the dishes in the sink and turn the water on. I scrub each dish until I can see my reflection in them and set them on the drying rack. I towel off my hands and head back into the dining room. I am met with utter silence, not a sound in the house. I look through the different rooms to no avail.

I go to the garden and find Caine sitting in the gazebo, staring up at the stars. That wave of stardust floats through the air, and the moons are full. I walk towards him as the night breeze blows the strands of hair from my bun into my face. He looks at me as I step into the gazebo, moving over on the bench so I can sit with him.

"When I was younger, after my mother's death, my father would take me to the cliffs to watch the stardust dance across the sky. He would tell me, *'Your mother would be so proud of the man you are becoming.'*" I stare at him, waiting for him to continue. He inhales deeply and lets the breath out slowly before continuing. "And now they are both up there, and I hope they are both proud of my accomplishments."

I lay a hand on his forearm, and his eyes meet mine. Giving him a small smile, "My parents didn't even want me to be born, so I can't relate, but from everything I have seen and know, I am sure your parents are up there smiling down on you. Because you, Caine, are an incredible man."

He smiles and faces the stars again. We sit in silence for a while, but the night air is starting to get colder, and I notice the mountains in the distance now have snow on the top.

A shiver washes over me, "I am going to bed. I will see you in the morning." I stand.

"Eight am sharp, no later." His tone serious.

Turning with a chuckle, "I'll see you whenever I wake up." I walk through the garden and into the library.

I walk to the shelves filled with books and peruse the spines. Settling on a book about a young girl who finds her dragon, I curl up in one of the chairs in the corner and cover my legs with the heavy emerald, green blanket. Page after page I get immersed in the story. This beautiful young girl goes through these trials and, at the end of them, has to choose between her dragon or her brother. I fall asleep reading, a tear still on my cheek. A gentle hand lands on my shoulder, and I startle awake.

I look up into Margie's kind eyes, "Come on, deary. Let's get you to bed."

Stretching I give her a sleepy smile. She takes my hand and walks me through the house and to my door, "Sweet dreams, deary."

"Goodnight, Margie." She smiles and walks down the stairs. Opening the door to my room, I change into a nightgown made of lilac satin—it hits me mid-thigh and has a slit lined with lace on each side. Taking a mental picture in the mirror I send it to Kai. The wait is endless with no reply. Deciding he must've fallen asleep I crawl under the covers of the large bed. I pull the covers to my chin and lull into a deep sleep.

My dreams are filled with images of boots walking through pools of blood. A familiar laugh fills the room and the sounds of a whip cracks through the air. Kai lets out a growl and then I hear it. The voice I haven't heard in years…Bartholemew.

"So much for being a demon prince." He says mockingly.

The boots walk in front of me again; Bartholemew squats, jerking my chin up so I am staring him in the eye.

"Where is she?" he asks.

I tear my chin away from him and spit on his boots.

"Again," he orders. The sound of the whip cracks through the air again and Kai cries out.

I sit straight up in bed, drenched in sweat and tears. My breathing is heavy, and I climb out of bed and walk into the bathroom. I look into the mirror, and my hair is a mess. I haven't had a nightmare in weeks. But something felt off about this one. I shake my head and splash cold water on my face. Walking back into the bedroom, I notice the sun coming up over the lake.

Chapter

52

As they grew into teens, they remembered it as an overactive imagination. Blaming the loads of sweets they would sneak every day.

Rolling my shoulders out as Margie dumps water over my head I recount the dream from the night before. Maybe receiving all this information so quickly is messing with my mind, "it was the most realistic dream I have ever had."

Her face was stone as I recounted the nightmare I had last night. "It was just a dream," she says without a smile. She wasn't her naturally bubbly self.

"Margie."

"Hm?" is all she responds with.

"Are you okay?"

She sighs. "Of course I am, deary. I am just worried about the upcoming war. I worry about you kids." She bumps my chin with a finger, her smile not reaching her eyes.

I simply nod. She isn't telling me something. Margie leaves me to get dressed, a pair of brown pants and a brown leather jacket for training today. Slipping on my boots, I run down the stairs. I round the corner into the dining room, and Alessandra and Ezra stand at the table.

I run to Ezra and hug him, "Hello." He says his voice calming.

"Have you heard from Kai?" I look into Ezra's eyes; they are blank as I wait for an answer.

He rubs his neck, "Ah, he's just busy. He should be here in a couple of days."

He turns away from me, and Alessandra rolls her eyes. "Don't you have chores to do or something?" her voice full of disgust.

I glare at her, "I am not a servant, asshole."

She smirks and continues what she is doing.

"What are we doing today?" I ask, rounding the end of the table to see the book they are reading. It is large and bound in an oily fabric, the pages yellow with age. Alessandra snaps it shut.

"What the fuck?" My voice squeaks.

Alessandra stares at me. "It is a family book; Kai will show it to you when he is ready."

I roll my eyes and walk out of the dining room. First, she insinuates I am the staff, and then she hides a book that is *clearly* not a family book. My breathing becomes heavy, and my mind wanders. Something is off, and no one is telling me anything. I am insignificant in their eyes. Anger bubbles in my belly, but I don't allow the earth to shake or the fire to consume me. Instead, I run, I run with a speed that I could only dream of having a little bit ago. Through the forest and past the lake.

I stop at a graveyard, bending with my hands on my knees, sucking in air at a rapid pace and trying to slow my racing heart. Standing straight and putting my hands on my hips, I look to the sky, screaming into it. I let the anger escape my lips on the animalistic scream that erupts from my body, wracking my spine on its way up from the depths of my soul.

"Nyathera, where are you?" Runihura's voice bounces off the walls of my skull.

I ignore her and scream again, letting the animosity leave my body.

"Where are you, damnit." Her sweet voice demanding.

I look around me and notice the gravestones lining the paths, *"a graveyard."* She doesn't answer, but within minutes, a dark shadow is cast across the land. I look up and Runihura is circling above me, swooping down to the ground. When she lands, I sprint towards her, running up her leg and taking my seat right above her wings.

"Fly," I demand. She springs into the sky, air whipping my hair into my face and mouth. She doesn't say a thing—kshe just lets me stew in my anger. I am thankful she knows what I need without me having to tell her. I lay - flat on her back, and we fly. Over the city and forest. I don't even bother looking around me as the first tear slips from my eyes. A couple of hours later, we land in front of the house; Ezra and Caine run out to greet us, Caine stopping at the bottom of the steps.

I slide down Runihura's leg, and Ezra sweeps me into a hug, "We thought you left us."

I roll my eyes, stepping out of his embrace. I walk to Runihura and lay my forehead on hers, "thank you," I whisper. She nods.

"Don't forget that we are one. Even with mates. I am always here, always going to protect you physically and mentally." I smile. *"Plus, I don't need my rider to be a nutcase because she bottles up her emotions."*

I playfully smack her snout, and she blows steam and takes off into the sky. I watch her retreat out of sight and turn to see Alessandra in the doorway, her mouth hinged open and eyes wide. I smile, "she's impressive, isn't she?" Ali doesn't respond.

Ezra drapes his arm over my shoulders, and we walk up to a pale-faced Caine, "What's wrong? Scared of a little dragon?" Caine shoots daggers at Ezra.

I laugh, "Come on. We have training." Caine turns and walks towards the garden, "I'll see you at dinner, Ezra."

He squeezes my shoulder gently, "are you alright?" I nod. "If you need anything, I'm here."

I give him the best smile I can, "thank you." And follow Caine into the gardens. When I get there, the garden is empty. I look around and call for Caine, but I don't see him anywhere, not even a bee buzzes by. It is eerily silent, and I can feel eyes on me. I start down the path, and right before I get to the fountain, a strong arm wraps around my arms, and a calloused hand is pressed over my mouth. I struggle, kicking my feet and wiggling my body. I try to scream, but my mouth is clamped shut by the large figure holding me tight.

"Hook your leg around my knee and pull towards the other one." Caine's voice booms from behind me.

I try and fail.

"Again." He says, not loosening his grip. I do and fail another time.

His front presses to my back and excitement courses through me as a vibration wraps around my spine. My body briefly sinking into his on instinct. Needing human contact has never been as strong as it is right now. Shaking my head to knock this feeling away, I try again—*and fail*.

Over and over, I try to release myself from his grip. My cheeks sting where his fingers dig into them and my heart races with anger. I twist my hand slightly, and a rock rises from the earth directly in front of me; I put my boots solidly on it and shove myself backward. Caine falls flat on his back, knocking the air from my lungs. His grip loosens, and I squirm away, getting to my feet and facing him. He stands, and I jab.

One, two.

One, two.

One, two.

I punch his hands he is holding up.

"Good," he says as my punches get stronger. He squats to the ground kicking out a leg and sweeping my feet from under me. I hit the ground with a thump, my shoulder shifting from the hit. I let out a groan and stand. Using my other arm to call my fire whips to light.

He holds out his hands and steps back, "Stop. Are you okay?"

I don't stop. I walk toward him, tracing his receding steps.

"Nyathera. Stop!" He orders.

I crack the whip right next to his left foot and draw it back. The fire whip evaporates, and he smiles. "Good job today, Nyathera." His eyes drop to my sagging shoulder, "your shoulder is dislocated."

I look at it and grab my bicep; sucking my lips in, I shove my shoulder back into place, the snap echoing in the garden.

Caine's face contorts into disgust, "Um, okaaay. Let's get inside for dinner."

I follow him back into the house and into the dining room. Dinner was the same as last night, Margie brings in two new servants, whose names I can't remember. I push the food around on my plate but don't have an appetite. I take the plates into the kitchen and clean them and then head up to my room.

"Are you okay?" I reach through the mental bond, looking for his mental shield, a whisper, anything to tell me he is okay.

Nothing.

I toss and turn in bed for hours. And when I fall asleep, nightmares like the night before fill my mind. I am tied to a wooden board and water is being poured over my face. Bartholemew bellows, "Where is she?!" but there is no answer, so more water is poured over my face. I try to take in oxygen but only inhale freezing water. My lungs burn, and my heart hurts. I sit up straight in bed, run to the bathroom, and splash water on my face. When I enter my bedroom again the sun is coming up, just like yesterday.

"Today we mark you with protection runes to ensure you are safe from dark magic." Caine says nonchalant.

"What do you mean 'mark me'?" I ask timidly.

"The tattoos we bare are runes of protection, our spirit animals, and battle tattoos. Each one has a specific job." He pulls the hem of his shirt up, exposes his tight muscles beneath. The intricate runes and tattoos scrawled across his skin enhance every dip of the strength that is hidden. My mouth dries as my eyes peruse every dip and curve.

Clearing his throat, Caine drops his shirt, "Decide where you want them, and I will fetch the protection witch." He walks away without a second glance back.

I really need to get my shit together. I'm unsure about tattoos, but then again, maybe they will enhance the demon mark. Caine comes back within a few minutes with an elderly woman. Her face is rubbery and wrinkled and her eyes are cloudy. She dips her head in my direction.

"I am Minerva." Her voice floats through the air, not here nor there. Both feminine and masculine, young and old. She doesn't speak out loud, but in our minds.

"Hello, I am Nyathera." I walk towards her, and Caine puts a hand on my shoulder stopping me.

"We do not approach the witch. She is deadly." His voice is stern.

I nod, "I am ready Minerva." I say shakily.

"Let's begin. Where shall we place your runes child." Her voice makes me uneasy, but I take off my tunic, leaving me in just a bra. Caine turns around, staring at the door. I shake my head at him but look at Minerva.

I gesture to my left arm. "Will this be enough space?"

Minerva walks over to me, floating on air. She grabs my arm with a spindly hand covered in runes and wrinkles. *"This shall be fine."* She hisses as she turns my arm over. "*This will not be pleasant child.*" Her eyes look like cloudy orbs set into her head.

"Caine." I say softly.

He doesn't turn around, "yes?" he asks coldly.

"Can you hold my hand?" I stare at the back of his head, "please."

He turns around and meets my eyes. "Okay. But no fire." He smiles.

He sits next to me on the edge of the bed and takes my hand delicately in his.

"*Let's begin.*" Minerva says.

She waves a hand over my arm, twisting her fingers in a rhythmic dance. She utters words I cannot understand, and the pain begins. Like being burned from the inside out and having my muscles ripped apart fiber by bloody fiber. She touches her fingers to my skin, and the pain intensifies. I squeeze Caine's hand, and he bends slightly. My skin rips apart and red-light shines above my arm. Little by little Minerva moves up my arm. As she continues the pain intensifies, and I can't control the scream that rips through my soul.

When she is finished I am sweaty and my arm throbs. I look down and intricate runes and lilies cover my forearm and up to my shoulder. A panther's face lies on my bicep and the space between the lilies, panther and runes are filled with delicate stars. The tattoo itself is black and shines like the star dust.

"It is beautiful Minerva." I almost whisper.

She nods, *"I figured you would want something that represents who you are. The panther is your spirit animal; it courses through your soul. The lilies were an image sent from a woman who has passed, delicate and hardy, and the stars represent your new life here in the city of shadows and nightmares. The runes are for protection and strength. Remember the panther when you feel weak, the lilies when you feel like you can't control your powers, and the stars when you need a reminder of where you are meant to be."* With that she is gone. Tears prick my eyes.

"It has been a long few hours, let's skip the rest of training today and just eat ice cream." Caine smiles at me and I follow him downstairs and into the kitchen.

Sitting on the kitchen counter with ice cream in my hand, I watch Caine. He stares out the small window, not saying a word. "Is everything okay?"

He turns towards me, his eyes full of something I can't quite read, a look that should never cross a soldier's face. He sighs, "we have to take you to the Machimoi camp, Camp Khayma."

I scrunch my nose at him, "What is Machimoi?"

"The training camp in the mountains to the south. It is where we all learned how to fight." he says quietly.

I set my ice cream down, "why do I need to go?" I jump off the counter.

He sighs, "when a prince is missing, and the king is nowhere to be found, the mate takes over control of the city and soldiers. With Kai not answering and his father MIA, the responsibility falls to you."

I choke, "can you repeat that?"

His icy blue eyes meet mine, "Until Kai returns," he kneels and bows his head, "you are the Lady of this realm."

I stare down at his blonde hair, not saying a word. I touch his shoulder, "I cannot take on this responsibility." I look around the kitchen, "I haven't even accepted the bond. I am not fully his mate."

He looks up at me, "You have to." He rises to his feet, "he has claimed you as his mate, meaning the responsibility is yours."

"What about Allessandra?" My words catching in my throat.

Caine stands, "If Kai hadn't found you, she would be the one to take over. But because he did, the rules of the City state that you are to become Lady."

The room spins and my knees grow weak. I stumble sideways and Caine grabs me before I am able to collapse. "I," I swallow hard, "I am Lady of the City of Shadows and Nightmares?"

Caine nods, "yes."

"Where does it say this?" I snap.

"The book of rules, it is centuries old."

I look at him and then the small window over his shoulder, shaking my head.

"Fuck."

Chapter

53

Nyathera listened to everything her parents had told her through the years. And eventually the City of Shadows and Nightmares became a fairytale again.

We step out the front doors, no horses or carriage waiting. I look at Caine and he holds out his arm, no words, just a slight nod. He places his arm around my waist, "How are we getting there?"

A smile creeps across his face, "hold on." He straightens his back and large ebony wings appear behind him. My breath hitches at the sheer strength and beauty and he smiles. I examine the wings before he tucks them in and springs into the air. I wrap my arms around his neck and squeeze, lacing my fingers together. The wind rushes through my hair and a scream erupts from deep in my chest.

We fly above the palace and the world spins. We break through the clouds above and Caine slows. He adjusts his grip around my waist. And I screech. "I told you to hold on." The smile on his face is foreign. I haven't seen so much happiness from him. I am glad my fear makes him happy—I roll my eyes. I look up at him and admire the true beauty that is Caine. His blonde hair blows in the wind, and his strong feathered wings span wide. Gently I reach my fingers towards the delicate feathers. Stroking my finger along the length of the blackness. Caine shutters and his gaze snaps to mine.

Pulling my hand back quickly, my eyes catch his. For a brief moment something swims in those icy blue orbs and something jumps inside my chest, "sorry."

With a grunt his attention turns back to the sky before us. I look down and the city is below us, the bustling streets full of different types of demons and creatures. Blissfully unaware of the shit that is going down in the palace.

I tighten my grip as we enter the mountains. The cold air whips around me, stinging my cheeks. The smell of frozen rocks wafts through the air. My breath creates clouds as I let out a breath. The sharp points of mountain tops skim along the backside of my thigh and I tighten my legs around Caine. He chuckles. "We are almost there."

When we land we are standing in the middle of a valley between the mountains. The mud squelches beneath my boots as we walk towards the lines of tents set up on either side. Fires are set up every ten feet, I stop at one and warm my hands. "Where is everyone?" I watch Caine as he rubs his palms together. The callouses scratching.

"They are training today, just beyond that mountain." He points towards the end of the line of tents.

"Are we waiting for them?" I blow a breath into my hands.

"No. Warm your hands and then we will introduce you."

We walk through the rows of tents and stop where the path ends on a cliff. Below rows and rows of men stand in formation, working on drills. I watch as they move in unison.

"Huah!" sounds out in unison as thousands of men repeat a combination over and over. A man stands before them, his pale skin inked in runes much like ours. His long brown hair is perfectly pulled into a bun. The beard on his face is perfectly tailored.

"Who is that?" I point to the man.

"That is general Isaac, he helps me with training of the soldiers."

I nod and continue watching. All soldiers are perfectly crafted into death itself. Caine places a hand on my shoulder; I look up at him. "Come on, it's time."

We walk down the path; I slip in the mud and Caine grabs my arm. I chuckle at myself, and we continue forward. The unit comes into view, and general Isaac turns towards us.

He grabs Caine's hand and slaps his shoulder, "Caine. The men have been working hard over the last few days. They are shaping up well."

"That is wonderful to hear, keep at it Isaac."

I step around Caine and Isaacs eyes fall to me. He bows, "Lady Nyathera. It is a pleasure to meet you."

I laugh and Caine shoots me a look, I clear my throat, "As it is to meet you general Issac." I nod.

"Second unit, your full attention!" Caine bellows. Every soldier stops and stands at attention. Their eyes not looking at me at all. "This is Lady Nyathera, she will be head of the armies and the city in Kai's absence. Whatever she says will be deemed as an order and anyone who fails to follow her command will be executed on site."

My blood stops cold, "We will kill them?" I whisper to Caine.

He dips his head towards me, "that is the way of the Machimoi." I simply stare at him, because if words came out of my mouth I would certainly offend someone. "Now, say something to the men."

I clear my throat and wrack my brain, what would a lady say to an army? I face the men, and their eyes fall to me, some chuckle and that makes my blood boil.

"She's kind of small!" a man's voice sounds at the back of the unit.

I hold my hands to the sides, curling my fingers. The mountain begins to shutter, and the men all brace themselves. A rock forms beneath the man who insulted me and brings him to the front of the unit. I slowly let the rock down, so he is standing before me. His eyes wide, he looks around and back to me. "Did you have something to say, soldier?" Lowering my head I flick my wrists out and watch my fire whips appear. I look back at the scrawny man in front of me, smiling slowly at him.

"No…" He swallows hard as I saunter towards him, "No, ma'am." He stutters.

"I can't quite hear you." My whips drag behind me as I walk towards him, drying the mud laid on the ground, he backs up a step. I look at Caine who is standing there stoically, general Isaac wears a smirk. I look back to the man standing before me. "What is your name?"

"George." He says, eyes still wide.

"George, I think you will find it in your best interest to not insult me, or anyone else. I may be small, George, but I will turn your body inside out with the flick of my wrist. Is that understood?"

George nods frantically. I send fire shooting into the sky, "I said, is that understood?" that feminine, powerful voice erupts from my chest again.

He drops to a knee, "Yes, Lady Nyathera!" he squeaks. The entire unit behind him drops to their knees and bows their heads. I close my fists tight, and the fire disappears, and Caine steps beside me.

"That wasn't quite what I had in mind, but I think you got the point across." A small smile spreads across his face.

"I don't think that is what I had in mind either." I chuckle. "Stand." I command and every soldier rises to their feet. "We all know what is going on, and we all now know that Kai is absent at the moment." I pace before the men, as general Isaac had earlier. "As Lady of this realm, I am implementing a state of emergency, you will all train day in and day out, until you have perfected your drills." I pause briefly, "Anyone who is not up to the highest standards will stay behind and help those of the city. Anyone who does not follow this order will end up at the bottom of the lake, by my own hands. Understood?"

The unit stomps their left foot in unison, "Yes, ma'am!" My heart stutters and I look back to Caine, unable to hide the smile.

Caine nods, "let's get back to the palace and let them train." I nod, he wraps an arm around my waist, heat washing over me with his touch. Jumping into his embrace and wrapping my arms around his neck, we spring into the sky.

Chapter

54

And so, dear readers, always remember: the shadows may seem inviting, but they hold secrets that can lead you astray.

Day in and day out for the next eight days, I fly with Runihura, train with Caine, have dinner with everyone, go to bed, and have nightmares. Over and over again. My body and mind are tired. I reach out every morning and every night waiting for an answer from Kai, and don't receive one. I feel defeated; maybe Alessandra was right. The tugging in my chest is weakening, but I ignore it. It has to be the distance is too great to feel it fully. I sigh as I climb into bed; the Keltoids and Ganglioans are to be here tomorrow if the intel is correct. They had been spotted in our lands. Caine and I went to the city and evacuated everyone, and the threat became real at that moment. The fear in their eyes as they got on ships and walked through caves to leave for somewhere safe burned holes in my heart. But the rich helped the poor, societal ranking didn't matter in those moments. The only thing that mattered was ensuring lives were saved, and for that, I am grateful.

"Please answer me!" I shout down the bond.

But utter silence is all I am met with. The tugging in my chest is weakening, and my heart is slowly dying. The pain in the center of my sternum is a dull ache. Where is he? He said he would be home soon. I sigh, lying in bed, watching the waves of stardust dance across the night sky. A tear rolls down my face.

"Please come home to us." I didn't expect an answer this time, and I close my eyes.

And for once. All I see is darkness.

I am woken by Caine shaking my shoulder. I open one eye at him, the sun barely rising, "what?" I croak out.

"Come on. We have to go."

I sit up, stretching, "why?"

He looks out the window and back to me, "They are less than an hour from the mountains."

My heart stops, "already?"

He nods slowly, "Come on! Margie put your fighting leathers on the bed—there are new daggers with runes of protection on the hilts and a new corset to hold all of them. There is also a bow and some arrows downstairs with your name on it."

I look around, my head spinning from lack of sleep and knowing I am about to go into battle. "Have you heard from Kai?"

His face falls slightly, but he shakes his head, "No. I am sure he is with his father."

Caine leaves my room, and I stand, dressing in the fur-lined leathers and placing the corset on. I examine the hilts of each dagger, the carvings beautiful and intricate.

I reach out to Kai, *"They're here."* Sadness grips at my chest, where is he?

I wait for only a moment before shoving my boots on and meeting everyone in the foyer.

Ezra looks at me with sadness in his eyes, "are you sure you're ready to join us? I couldn't live with myself if something happened to you."

I let some of my fire brush my hands and rumble the earth just under his feet. He smiles, "Let's go kick some ass."

He shoves a metal helmet on, the sides peaked in eagle wings, and only his eyes and mouth are visible. Caine places a similar one on his head and leads me to the front. Runihura is waiting for me; Caine stops in his tracks. "She won't hurt you, Caine." I say gently.

"I would, but you seem to care about these ones." Even with the fear I am feeling, I let the giggle bubble.

"Come on, you can ride with me." I grab Caine's arm, but he is immovable. I look up into his eyes, "Caine, we have to go. I flew with you, now you fly with me!" He snaps out of it and follows me to Runihura.

He pauses at her leg. As I run up to her shoulder, I wave for him to coax him along, impatience now filling my body. He runs up her leg with ease and takes a deep breath as he sits behind me. "Hold on!" Runi shoots into the sky, forcing Caine to grab my waist with brute force. He knocks the wind from my chest, and I grab his hand, pulling on it so he loosens his grip. Runi levels out and I see Ezra and Alessandra on horses below us.

"Stay at their speed," I tell Runihura.

She snorts, *"Slow beings, horses are."*

"Be nice; we all have to work as one. Are you ready?"

"I was born ready. But are you?" I inhale deeply, trying to figure out if I am ready or not. The tugging in my chest lessens, like a small prick on my sternum.

I sigh, *"I have no choice but to be. The people of this city need me."* I inhale deeply, *"our home needs me."*

I feel her worry down the mental bond with Runi and I rub the scales in front of me.

"Has Erebus said anything about Kai?" He has to know something.

"He has been quiet when I have asked." She answers gently.

Anxiety grips me and the world spins. But we bank left and head towards the mountains. Not time for worry. The sun is just starting to peak above them as we make our descent. The mountains are still in the distance, but we are close enough to see the passageways. We land in the large field on the side of the lake closest to the mountain range. I slide off Runihura's back.

Caine follows. "Nyathera. That was amazing."

I slap his bicep, "When this is over, we will go for rides daily if you want."

He jerks his fist, "Yes!"

I laugh as Ezra and Alessandra appear on their horses. I walk over to Alessandra and put my hand on her shoulder, "have you heard from your brother?" she shakes her head slowly, worry etched on her brow.

I look to the ground, pain and fear roiling in my chest.

She grabs my wrist, "he will be okay, Nye."

I snap my eyes back to hers. "I know." I drop my arm, "remember what we talked about?" she nods. I give her a tight smile and walk over to Ezra, who holds his arms out for me.

I wrap my arms around his waist and squeeze, "we will all be okay." He says into my hair. Tears threaten to well in my eyes, but I hold them back.

"You better be." I smirk at him. The thought of losing another friend, of people I love with my whole heart rises to the surface and I have to fight the tears that threaten to escape.

We walk to the top of the hill, Runihura standing behind us. A shadow casts over us, and I look up to see Erebus circling above us. Hope flutters in my stomach that Kai will be with him. He lands right next to Runi, but Kai isn't on his back.

"Where are you?!" I shout down the bond, fear that something has happened to him sinking deep in my soul.

He doesn't answer and that all too familiar sound of a mechanical roaring fills the air. My heart clenches, the tugging in my chest barely there.

I look over as Alessandra joins me on the hill, "let's do this." she says, as she holds her hands in front of her and a clear light blue shield appears before us. She looks at me and a wicked grin consumes her face, "I control air." she winks as I gawk at her.

"Awesome," I say in disbelief.

She smiles widely.

Ezra appears on my right, a sword in each hand. He straightens, and large black feathered wings appear from his back.

The beautiful ebony shining in the sun, "What?! You too?!"

He winks, "I am a demon."

Caine comes up beside Alessandra, the same wings appearing behind him. He winks and grabs a bow from his back.

"Where are you? Where are you? Where are you?" I shout down the bond as that tug is a small brush on my sternum.

My heart aches as if I have lost someone else. *"Kai, please! Where are you?!"* I scream down the bond, looking for any minute glimpse of that wall in my mind.

The image of bloody boots flashes through my mind, weak and blurry. A tear runs down my face as I grab my daggers. The soldiers before us are lined up and waiting for the enemy to round the mountain tops. Thousands of men put their lives on the line to save their city.

Alessandra notices the tear falling down my cheek, "Nyathera. What is wrong?"

I look at her quickly, not wanting my eyes off the mountain tops for too long, "I can't feel him."

She gasps, fear shadowing her eyes.

"Where are you?! Kai, please! Where are you?!" I beg down our mental bond.

I feel a tight ping in my sternum, like someone poked me with a needle. When before it was tugging like a string stuck. Pain radiates across my heart, accelerating my heart rate. I clutch at my chest, *"Where are you? We need you. It hurts, please come back!"*

I think about everything that we have done together, every word that has been said to me, how he is the only man who has seen that I am a survivor and that I am strong. I take a deep breath and let it out slowly. The Keltoids and Ganglioans have made it to the top of the mountains. Thousands and thousands of soldiers line the mountain range. Their red uniforms stand out harshly against the clear blue sky behind them. I bottle up the fear and let pure white-hot rage fill my veins. No one will be hurting a single person in this city. Not when I know I can end this war as soon as their soldiers are all on this field. I feel my eyes glow and summon a fire whip in my left hand and let the fire consume the dagger in my right.

"Kai, if you can feel me, if you can hear me, I accept the bond! I want to spend this eternal life with you! Please be okay! Come back to us! We need you! I need my mate!"

The tugging that was once there fizzles out and is replaced with searing pain. Claws dig deep into my heart and rip it from my chest, the skin on my bones melts into nothing. The pain, the fear, the sadness, all turn into a metaphorical beast. Collapsing to my knees, I let out a scream of rage. The earth shaking around me and Ezra sliding to a stop in front of me. I look into his red eyes and frown. His pinched brow tells me he knows exactly what is happening. He bellows with his own rage and signals for Caine.

With the power of determination, I stand and watch the battle before me. Unknowing of what the next few hours will bring. With Ezra, Caine and Alessandra at my side, I sob. Runihura comes up behind me, her nose nuzzling my spine, but the pain of the broken bond is too much for her powers to dull. Placing a hand in Ezra's, I watch the mountains and the soldiers that are descending the steep slopes.

I drop his hand, bending my head down and let the pain mingle with my rage. The flames lick over my body and the earth below me rises, I throw my head to the sky and an eruption of fire soars into the clear blue of the atmosphere above me.

Lowering my eyes I can feel the power surging through me. Every twist and turn of my mark erupts with a light of red, pulling at my soul to continue forward.

With a much newer power, I whisper into the oncoming slaughter.

"May the power of the Gods be on your side."

Very special Thanks

A very special thank you to my husband, who has supported me through every twist and turn. To the friends who have helped me along the way, I thank you as well. Not only for supporting me, but for pushing me to continue. To Tocororo art and Jennifer DeHart for the beautiful artwork you see in this edition. And to all my readers, thank you. I wouldn't be able to do this without all of you!